THE MAN WHO SOUGHT ETERNITY
A Tale of Gilgamesh, First of Heroes

I0615701

Jeffrey Peter Clarke

THE MAN WHO SOUGHT ETERNITY
A Tale of Gilgamesh, First of Heroes

FICTION4ALL

PROLOGUE

Their coach swayed along a desert grit road, its garish livery muted by fine dust, the rattle of the air conditioning contesting the engine's growl. It described a wide circle, rocking from side to side, whilst the exhaust spluttered alien chemistry into wide earth and open sky.

The girl thumbed her study notes and read words that stirred with promise. As the bus slowed she pushed the notebook into her shoulder bag and peered bright-eyed through the dirt-streaked window at a scarred and abandoned landscape. Raised by the wheels, dust plumes drifted by in the heat of the day; departing spectres of those who once lived, laughed and toiled here - or so she imagined.

For some this was an excuse to pop another cola can, feign interest in the glossy itinerary replete with superlatives or raise a camera and snap what lay beyond the window to prove they had been to that famous somewhere-or-other named in the brochure. They had seen too many ruins these last few days. Were they expected to leave the coach again to suffer this infernal heat?

'Where are we?' asked an aged man, chicken-claw fingers clutching a wide-brimmed straw hat that boasted the tour operator's logo.

'Some place called Warka,' replied his dressed-for-the-shopping-mall, wife. 'That's what it says for Thursday afternoon, see – Warka. What's supposed to be at Warka, for God's sake?'

'Heaps of dried mud,' he mumbled, narrowing his eyes close to the window. 'Why they suggested we come out here, I don't know. D'you have that damned guide book?'

A sharp tap. A piercing electronic squeak. At the front of the coach their tour guide had switched on his microphone.

'Okay,' announced the stubbled face and mirrored sunglasses, 'the modern name for this site is Warka.' Another squeak assailed their ears as he moved the microphone away from the console. 'If you have been reading your brochure you will know that this was once a great city - yes, a very famous city. Its ancient name was Uruk.' Perhaps in hesitating he expected a question or two. There were no questions, though the girl and her two male companions eyed him steadily.

'Like most sites in the Tigris-Euphrates area,' he continued, 'known to the ancient Greeks as Mesopotamia, this is very old. It was at least as ancient to the Classical Greeks as the Greeks of those days are to ourselves - okay? The site was occupied for over five thousand years - right to the third century of the Christian era - a very long time - yes? And no matter how it looks today, this place is very special.'

Fingers rummaged noisily inside a plastic bag. Others stabbed and poked at smart phones. Most of the passengers settled back in their seats as if to say, 'Fine, but I'd rather be down by the hotel pool.'

The girl smiled at their guide and nodded encouragement.

'You see these ruins now,' he continued above the drone of the engine whilst prodding the sunglasses a little higher against his nose, 'and maybe you would not think this was once the

6

biggest and most important city in the land of Sumer. There are no stone temples, no marble sculptures - nothing like that. They used mostly bricks of mud that were dried in the sun or baked in kilns. Here in the alluvial plains of southern Iraq finding stone was not so easy and there was little timber for building. Such things had to be brought from far away and used sparingly. So, they made good use of what they had - clay.'

'We saw plenty of trees some way back,' croaked one of the elderly passengers. Here was a point to be made.

'Okay, yes, as the gentleman says, there are trees - but these are date palms that have always grown here. The ancients made use of the fibres, leaves and fruit, as people do in our own time, but the wood is not strong enough to cross large spaces. So, the people of those days built mainly in mud-brick and reeds - materials that do not last as long as stone.'

The coach engine roared as an angry beast. They shuddered to a halt and the guide gestured beyond the window. 'Now, as you can see, it is dry here because the Euphrates river has shifted far away. But long ago that river flowed close to Uruk so the land was irrigated and fertile. Here was once a city of maybe fifty thousand. As I explained earlier today, those people, the Sumerians, are a mystery to us. No one knows where they came from. Their language was unique. We know of no connection to any other. But they were the most resourceful and inventive people in the ancient world - okay? And right here in Uruk were discovered the world's first written records.'

7

'You mean these guys invented writing?' drawled a woman with white-creamed nose and floppy blue hat.

'Ah yes, they were the first people we know of to use it,' enthused the guide at this modest show of interest, 'and that was around five and a half thousand years ago - okay? The people of these lands were also the first to use the wheel for transport but remember, in those days they had no horses - only the ass and the ox to pull their carts.'

'How about that,' someone drawled wearily, 'ah got me a cart but I got no hoss.'

'It must have taken a hell of a time to go any place,' observed another.

'That is so,' replied the courier. 'But maybe they were not in so much of a hurry.'

The engine slowed to a murmur and he leaned aside to speak a few words in Arabic to the driver. Returning his attention to the party, his face broadened into a wide smile. 'Okay, here we can get out and see the ruins close up.'

'How long do we have to stay?' asked one in pink satin dress and high heels, mustering enough enthusiasm to stifle a yawn.

'Looks like those pictures they send back from Mars,' remarked her blue-rinsed companion.

'How long?' answered the courier, 'Well, we have allowed up to one hour and I will explain what you see as we go around.'

'An hour - is that all?' came the girl's voice from the rear of the coach. The courier perceived a blaze of light in the lowering dusk of indifference and smiled, 'Ah, one of our student friends. Yes, I'm afraid that is all the time we have. The afternoon is very hot. I think an hour will be enough.'

'Perhaps we'll hang about here for now,' nodded the blue-rinse. 'My shoes will be ruined.' Others muttered agreement. More smart phones appeared. Some hovered momentarily against the windows.

'As you wish,' replied the courier, though a few began to struggle from their seats.

A serpent hiss, a stamping-hoof clatter and the door at the front of the coach quivered open. Most eager of the eight who clambered out to tread ancient earth were the three students in T-shirts and jeans. They grinned at each other as someone hung stooping from the hand rail in the coach doorway to gasp, 'Christ, how could anyone live out here - it's a goddamned furnace!'

'It would have been more pleasant when the river flowed close by and the city was surrounded by green fields and palm trees,' responded the courier. 'The houses of the city dwellers were built around shaded courtyards for comfort. They could use their rooftops to avoid the humidity and maybe grow bushes and flowers. I think then it was a good place to live.'

'You must know a lot about Sumerian history,' said the girl as they moved away from the coach, wisps of straw-blond hair shifting across her face in the hot breeze.

The man adjusted his sunglasses again and her face was mirrored in them like a tiny votive doll as he replied, 'I am a university lecturer in Baghdad but doing this I make a little more money. Things are not easy in this country as you know. There has been much violence and still there is uncertainty.'

At that point he stopped and turned to face his diminished audience. 'Okay, people, where we now stand would have been some way inside the city wall. That wall was once nearly ten kilometres around and within its circuit lay temples, workshops, houses and gardens. Most of the excavations have been carried out around the great temples that occupied the centre of the city. Little of what we see belongs to the earliest phase because successive generations destroyed or built on top of what was there before. And so, the city grew upon its own ruins. The remains closest to us,' he gestured across the rubble-strewn ground to where lay a soft edged, irregular geometry of low walls and foundations, 'are belonging to the last period of the city when it was occupied by descendants of Alexander the Great – those we know as the Selucids. Afterwards, from Iran, came the Parthians.

Rising up behind, you see what remains of the great temple of Uruk's patron goddess, Inanna. She was goddess of love, fertility and war. Most ancient civilisations seem to have had such a deity. Maybe you know of her by her Babylonian name, Ishtar. The Greeks had their Aphrodite. To the Romans she was Venus.' Glancing up at the ruined temple he continued, 'As you will have read in your guidebook, we call this kind of structure a ziggurat. To the people of these flat lands the ziggurat was a mountain – perhaps a stairway to the gods.' He produced a limp handkerchief and with it dabbed his brow. 'Okay, we will walk around the ziggurat and there you can still see reed matting they laid between the courses of brick.'

'How old is the ziggurat?' asked one of the male students.

'Older than most of what you now see,' he replied. 'It dates back more than four thousand years and was rebuilt by those who ruled from the city of Ur when they conquered all of Sumer.'

As they walked on, he answered questions, dispensed more okay's and described what lay about in greater detail. Two of the party, oppressed by the heat, retreated to the cooler interior of the coach. But the girl's hazel eyes saw much as she studied the great ruin. Against the harsh sky it arose - a layered mound of facets and recesses licked almost smooth by the tongue of time; its once pristine form and measured features long vanished beyond human memory.

'By around four thousand years ago,' continued the guide, 'Sumerian culture and language were being replaced by that of Babylon to the north. For a time, the land fell under Assyrian rule, and then Persian - until Alexander, who you call, "The Great," came. We have to thank the scribes of Assyria and Babylonia for our recovery of Sumerian literature. They preserved and translated into their own language the writing of earlier days - okay? Much of what has been recovered came from the royal library at the Assyrian capital of Nineveh, far to the north. That city was burned by the Babylonians and Persians, six hundred and twelve years before the Christian era. But, and here is truly a miracle, the flames that destroyed Nineveh also baked and preserved thousands of clay tablets that otherwise would have crumbled to dust. Amongst those tablets were discovered many religious, historical and literary texts, including the oldest recorded tale in human history.'

'The Epic of Gilgamesh,' put in the girl with an enthusiastic smile.

'That is so,' he replied, 'the Epic of Gilgamesh. Gilgamesh - the man who sought eternal life. You know of him? You have read this?'

'Oh, sure, we covered it at college. It's why we grabbed those spare seats on the coach - just so we could see where he lived.'

'Okay - and this is the very place, but the Epic as we know it was put together over the many centuries after Gilgamesh lived and belongs more to myth than to history. Much like your King Arthur, I think. I have read about him, also.'

'But Gilgamesh did live,' responded the girl. 'We know that for sure, don't we? For people to have kept his name alive over all that time, he must have been more than an ordinary man - more than just another petty king.'

One of the party glanced at his watch and, with two others, drifted away to smoke cigarettes and talk amongst themselves on their way back to the coach, stopping only to pose idly for photographs with the ruins of Uruk a convenient backdrop.

'Ah,' replied the guide, seemingly unconcerned that his party consisted now of only the three students, 'who can know what kind of a man this Gilgamesh was. Legend says he conquered his enemies, rebuilt the walls of Uruk and glorified the temple of Inanna but legend is legend and there is little more anyone can say.'

'They had so many gods and goddesses in those days,' said the girl. 'Religion must have been pretty complicated.'

'But perhaps more tolerant,' replied the guide. 'Now we have Islam, a religion of one god, but it can be very intolerant the way Christianity was in your middle ages. This I say to you because soon you will be gone from this country with your memories. But if you can imagine – if only you can imagine what this city was like in her days of power and glory.'

The other students began to put questions of their own but the girl turned aside and sat down on a low, mud-brick wall whilst the voices of her companions and that of the guide, drifted away. Her gaze wandered across the sun-scorched monotony of rubble, trenches and toothless-jaw ruins. She regarded the sad and all but featureless heap that once had soared in grandeur as the pride and spirit of once great Uruk, a city returning to the formless earth from which it had long ago been wrested.

'Hey, Angie!' called one of the students.

'I'll catch up with you!' she replied with a wave of her hand.

They were gone. All lay still and silent beneath an empty sky. The girl drifted into fanciful thought, all but oblivious to the desolation. Oblivious to the heat. Oblivious to time itself.

A step away from the wall upon which she sat lay the softened edges of a rectangular pit. It was lined with part-tumbled bricks of baked clay. She wondered if perhaps it had been a burial – the final resting place of someone important, because it stood not far from the ancient temple mound. In the sand by her foot, small coloured fragments caught her eye and she reached down, scooping up several of them to place on the palm of her hand where she examined them closely. What were they? Fragments of painted shell or bone? Ivory, perhaps? One was a rich, deep blue that shimmered in the light as if trying to impart to her a memory of its past. Were these discarded little remnants once a part of something of great value - something wonderful?

'But they did remember you,' she whispered. The fragments slipped as passing time through her fingers and she spoke his name. 'They remembered you, Gilgamesh, king of Uruk. Through all the centuries they remembered and you became a legend. Gilgamesh - are your bones hidden beneath these ruins? If people have a soul, does yours still wander this lonely place? I sit beneath the same sky and breathe the same air as you once did. Oh yes, I do. If only -'

A movement. Her attention was drawn to the desert haze and she became aware of a figure some distance away - a young man dressed in white, long black hair cascaded about his shoulders. Arms half raised, he seemed transfixed at the sight of the ruins but she could make out nothing more. Thinking it odd that he should wander the desert alone she looked about to see if there were others nearby, companions perhaps, who might be waiting for him. There were none so she wondered if he might be a nomad. Did she hear the man cry out or was it her imagination? When she returned her gaze to the desert the figure had vanished.

A breeze sprang up. Invisible spirals gathered about, hovered for a while then scurried away with her thoughts.

In those brief moments the city was whole again amidst green fields. Close by the great river glinted sunlight. Boats swayed colourful upon the water. Inanna's temple soared white against a smiling sky, a sacred jewel in Earth's crown. Her voice carried his name as a soaring eagle across the land. 'Gilgamesh!'

CHAPTER 1
GILGAMESH THE KING

Sangasu was a rough man of the country, a hunter and trapper, his hands often stained with blood, his clothes smelling of the animals he snared and skinned and of the earth that often served as his bed.

Afternoon sun still blazed fierce when he raised a hand to shade his eyes. Beholding Uruk at last in the hazed distance, he urged the ass onward with a gruff cry and a swish of his stick. At one side of his toiling mount hung a leather bag to contain his sustenance of bread, cheese and dried figs. To the other, a pair of leather-capped flagons to contain rough beer. All were now were empty.

Much wearied from travelling, the image of the city rekindled his hope and strength. Three days had passed since Sangasu had set out at first light from his humble home in the wild lands, attired in deerskin cap, cape and loincloth of stitched animal skins. By day he had detoured to where he hoped there would be water. At night he had rested under the stars, mindful of lion and wolf but had encountered neither. His night-time company had been the beast that carried him and the fearful image that haunted his thoughts day and night, the image that urged him so desperately on. In the day, buzzards and vultures had circled against a searing sky in anticipation of their next meal - the man they saw alone in a sea of desert. Having forded the great river where it was wide and shallow he eventually reached one of the tracks used by traders who came and went from marshland and desert. Some way ahead he would need to cross the sluggish waters of canal and irrigation ditch, then finally a narrow branch of the river that snaked in close to the city wall where stood Uruk's busy quay. Here were moored boats that came and went to places he would never know. Worlds of dreaming.

The land no longer stretched away as desert but had become green pasture. In time Sangasu found himself riding through the barley fields where Uruk's people toiled naked in the heat, wielding wooden scythes with keen, flint-edged blades. Across this patchwork land the crops had ripened full and plentiful and the main harvest of the year was almost done. Passing by, he watched them gather the barley, bundle and bind it in readiness for ox and cart. Already the aroma of the orchards laying closer to the city had livened his senses.

A short way from the floating bridge, he dismounted, tethered the ass to a bush close by the water then sat down against the trunk of a date palm where the shade from surrounding trees offered modest relief. Important as his journey might be, there was still time to rest his aching bones before crossing the river. Time as well to feast his eyes upon the glorious sight that was his destination. Sangasu clasped hands about his knees and breathed in deeply. Here was a splendid view of the city and her great wall. A strong wall of burned brick, clad with dazzling white gypsum. A wall fit to resist the guile and battering of the enemy. Always there had been an enemy. Bright in golden afternoon light with the long shadows of palm trees cast across its

17

seamless face, the wall curved about Uruk as a protecting arm.

Some way behind this rampart arose another, higher wall that defined the temple platform within the holy precinct called Eanna. Its cornice, sheathed in burnished copper, blazed sunlight. Rising in majesty above this was the portal of earth and heaven, gateway to the gods, the white-plastered, recess-walled temple of Inanna. Inanna – she who the people of Uruk revered as Queen of Heaven. Before it her brightly coloured banners swayed lazily from cedarwood masts. Sangasu wondered if the hand of man might ever again enrich Sumer with wonders to equal Uruk and her temples.

As with all dwellers in this land, Sangasu possessed some knowledge of the city and its affairs. It was common knowledge that Uruk's king had brought low the ruthless Agga, ambitious ruler of mighty Kish, Uruk's old rival far to the north. Since those bloody days Gilgamesh had enlarged the city wall, had enhanced and beautified the shrine of Inanna with coloured mosaics of precious glass and stone - all aided by the spoils of war.

It was commonly believed that Gilgamesh was fifth in line of the deified ones who had ruled over Uruk since the time of the Great Flood. Born of Ninsun the Wise, herself a minor goddess according to many, Gilgamesh was champion of the people, his rule sanctioned by the city elders and by the priesthood of both Inanna and of remote and mystical Anu, father of the gods and ruler of the heavens. As for the king's father - the trapper knew nothing beyond the rumour that he was a priest from the precinct of the Kullab district where Anu's temple stood. Others declared his father to be a divine hero but Ninsun's private life was shrouded in mystery and so speculation remained no more than that. Sangasu had heard, recited by the city's children, how the deeds of Gilgamesh were a beacon by which every red-blooded male might set the course of his own life when he reached manhood. And when conflict came.

Would Kish rise again? Would another town seek glory by aggression? Always the star of fortune must rise for one as it descended for another. Passing traders talked of intrigues and changing alliances and the nomads might also carry news of value. There were disputes over water, over territory and over livestock though the priests taught that such things were in the hands of the eternal gods and not of frail mortals. The gods made themselves known in wind, in tempest, and in the fortunes of mankind. Much of this Sangasu understood, though in his unending days of toil it counted for little.

But what had driven him in desperation to Uruk with no skins to trade, with nothing to exchange for even a morsel of food or a cup of beer? He hoped someone, perhaps the priests of Inanna, would be feeling generous. Perhaps they would offer him beer and bread to ease the thirst and emptiness he felt within. Perhaps also a place to rest for the night where he might think over his plans for the following day.

Sangasu the hunter and trapper could never have guessed the nature of events taking place in Uruk. Events in which he, a man of so little importance in the great wide world, was destined to play a brief yet vital role. But for now he had found unexpected comfort. Sangasu closed his eyes and lost touch with the day. When he awoke the sun had gone and in descending darkness a figure stood watching him.

***

The sky was brightening when the drum rattle echoed through narrow, shadowed streets. People moved aside to wait and watch as the party approached. 'Make way for the king!' cried the herald. 'Make way!'

The sun had not cut the horizon as they passed by on their progress to the Southern Gate. Uruk's people were familiar with the chime of gilded harness that adorned the king's spirited asses. Familiar with the ornate but cumbersome chariots whose wooden wheels furrowed the ground. Their king often took this route, accompanied by the royal companions, each attired in white tunic, each boasting a finely crafted spear tipped by polished bronze.

'Keep aside!' ordered the herald, passing on ahead with the sound of his drum giving way to the snort of asses and rumble of wheels. Then they were gone and people continued about their business.

The day was one of peace within Uruk because the market stalls were closed. All but the very youngest and the very oldest, or almost all, laboured in the field and orchard below whilst their chatter drifted across to the temple on still, humid air.

***

Later that morning, below the white facade of Inanna's temple, three shaven-headed priests relaxed upon a low mud-brick bench, cushioned by the softness of lambswool rugs. They were shaded in part from the sun by a stepped recess of the wall, in part by an awning of woven rushes suspended above their shaven and oiled bodies. About the limestone floor beneath three pairs of splayed feet was spread rush matting. Upon the matting rested sandals, dishes of dates, dried figs, fresh fruits and, casting a shadow across these, a terra-cotta jug, round-bellied as the owners of the three copper drinking tubes that had been placed upon the rushes next to it. The beer jug, alas, was drained almost to its sediment-laden bottom.

One of the three began to snore. Another glanced at him disapprovingly, adjusted the folds beneath his woollen kilt for greater comfort, leaned back against his cushion and closed his eyes. His companion to the other side did likewise.

'Pardon, holy ones!'

Two pairs of eyes sprang open. Oblivious to the intrusion, the portliest of the trio, continued to snore, each exhalation of air ending in a lip-quivering splutter.

'Ah,' exclaimed the first priest, eyeing the lean, deep-tanned form of a fuzzy-haired slave of the temple, as the boy knelt out of respect before them, 'I take it you have brought fresh beer - though I see no sign of it.'

'He hasn't brought any beer,' remarked the second priest, wafting his face with a fan of woven reeds. 'We'd see the jar standing in front of us if he had.'

The third priest snorted, stirred, passed wind loudly from his rear and at last opened his eyes. 'What! Is it the beer?'

'He hasn't brought any beer,' repeated the second priest.

'Holy ones,' nodded the boy with exaggerated anxiousness before three well-fleshed, questioning faces, 'there are men from the town of Larsa wanting to speak with you.'

'Men from Larsa!' exclaimed the first priest. 'What are men from Larsa doing here at harvest time and *what* do they want with us?'

'They didn't say, holy one,' answered the boy, rising to his feet before permission to do so had been given, 'but they are impatient and demand to be heard. They sent me because they could find no one else to bring their message.'

'Oh, very well,' grumbled the first priest, glancing at the other two for signs of agreement, 'show them up here and *then* go for the beer.'

'No problem, holy ones!' With a cheeky grin, the boy scurried off bare-foot down stone steps to the precinct, to reappear several priestly yawns and grumblings later with two men striding close behind. One of the pair, the priests observed, was tall and fine-featured with well-groomed hair and plaited beard. A patterned headband kept sweat from his eyes, a fringed white gown of embroidered linen swayed about his slender body and on his feet were leather sandals set above the toe with semi-precious stones, their glitter muted at present with a coating of dust. In one hand was clutched an ivory-handled flywhisk.

With leather bag clutched to his chest, his bald-headed companion, almost as portly and as sparingly dressed as the three priests, was evidently a slave. In recognising the status of the taller man,

22

the three priests arose awkwardly from their seats as he halted before them.

'Holy ones,' he began, showing his left hand where was fixed the bronze ring that proclaimed him an official attached to the royal household of Larsa. 'I regret interrupting your well-earned period of contemplation but no representative of your king seems available today. I went to the House of Assembly but was told the elders of your city are absorbed in council with townsmen and must not be disturbed. I waited in the heat with no offer of refreshment and nowhere to stable our asses. It seems I was not expected, though a messenger had arrived here shortly after dawn to announce my visit.'

'You must excuse our apparent laxity,' offered the first priest, 'but the king and his retainers left Uruk at first light for their sport and we ourselves were given no notice of your arrival. What the elders are about today I really can't imagine.' Turning to the lithe figure leaning casually against the wall a short distance away, he barked, 'Boy - why are you idling there? Fetch the beer!'

'Ah, that won't be necessary,' said the envoy, thinking the request had been made on his behalf, 'I found a beer-seller by the precinct gate before ascending to the temple. I will leave the document in your safekeeping and inform our lord that he may expect a response within a few days - at Lord Gilgamesh's convenience, of course.' He glanced impatiently at his mute companion who, reaching into the leather pouch, withdrew a clay tablet, larger than a man's hand, densely inscribed with clusters of wedge-shaped characters. 'I trust someone will read this to the king on his return.'

'Someone!' put in the second priest with an indignant cough. 'Our king will read it for himself. Does the Man of Larsa not read *his* own documents?'

'He has others to do that sort of thing for him,' replied the envoy with a hint of condescension. His slave handed the tablet to the first priest, who studied it intently for some moments before looking up at the envoy. 'Our lord won't be pleased with this, I know it.'

'What's in the message?' asked the second priest, straining to peer over his shoulder.

'It's about the canal running between our domains,' answered the holder of the tablet. 'It has overflowed and flooded fields belonging to Larsa.'

'We know all about that,' put in the second priest. 'The landslip that blocked the canal is on your side and so has to be cleared by your people.'

'So you say,' sniffed the envoy, 'but the canal was dug by your men for *your* benefit and *its* waters have caused the landslip. It is the duty of Uruk to maintain its waterways and dykes in good order and this has not been done for some time.'

'But -' began the first priest.

'No – I'll not remain here to argue,' interrupted the envoy with raised hand. 'The decision on such matters is not yours or mine to make; it is your king's. I have delivered the tablet to a priest of Inanna and you must make certain it is brought before lord Gilgamesh upon his return - whenever *that* might be.'

So saying he turned about and, his mute attendant trotting behind, proceeded to the steps leading down to the lower precinct and vanished from sight.

'Confounded impudence!' puffed the third priest, slumping back into his place on the bench and seizing a dried fig. He hesitated to regard the empty beer jug before uttering again, 'Confounded impudence!'

'Quite,' agreed the second priest, re-joining him in the shade. 'It does not bode well; yet Larsa is not strong enough to make demands on Uruk. Lord Gilgamesh will no doubt let them know it.'

'Ah,' said the first priest, setting the tablet down to one side of the bench, 'and he may well reply by his own hand. At least *he* can read and write, which is more than you can say for the Man of Larsa, or that scheming monster the Man of Kish.'

'So our king should,' remarked the second priest, 'our ancestors invented writing, after all.'

'They say we were amongst the first to ferment beer as well,' munched the third priest, eyeing the jug once more, 'though you'd hardly believe it now.'

Shading his eyes, the first priest turned his gaze to the legs and feet of the youth who sat part hidden within the next recess along the wall. He cleared his throat then called loudly, 'Damned layabout! Beer! Now!'

Roused from his daydreaming, the boy scrambled up and hastened away toward the stairs. The first priest returned to his place within the recess, squeezing back into the shade as the sun was now high overhead. The heat had grown in intensity.

'In my day,' mumbled the third priest, his mouth stuffed almost to capacity, 'he'd have been punished for his idleness. Hmmm - slaves are not what they used to be. Dear me, no.'

'Quite so,' breathed the first. 'And what is more I think this visit from Larsa's envoy may be more than just a complaint over waterways. There are rumours of envoys from Kish going there. Given half a chance they will conclude an alliance against us – you'll see.'

Time passed. With eyes closed, each of them imagined the boy struggling up from the cool, sunless depths of the temple stores down below, a well filled jug clutched in his arms, its contents slopping around to seep about the baked-clay stopper. He must now be out in the sun and ascending the stairs from the precinct, his feet burning on hot bricks and stone paving. Any moment now he would appear around the corner and -.

'Er, holy ones!' came the voice.

Three pairs of eyes sprang open to regard the youth then looked about for the welcome burden they expected to find placed on the matting before them.

'Well - where *is* it?' demanded the first priest, wiping sweat from his brow, his disbelieving gaze hard upon the boy. 'Where, yes, *where* is the beer you have been repeatedly told to fetch?'

'D'you wish to be scourged?' demanded the second priest, angrily.

'Pah,' blustered the third, 'he ought to be scourged - there's no question about it!'

'Please, holy ones,' responded the boy, glancing back along the wall, 'I was prevented from carrying out your wishes by -.' His wide-eyed attention fell once again upon the indignant priests. 'Holy ones, you have more visitors.'

'*More* visitors!' groaned the first priest. 'By Namtar and the demons of the abyss - is it another envoy? Is it someone else with nothing better to do than complain to us, priests of Inanna, about blocked canals, straying cattle or thieving peasants?'

'I don't think so, holy ones,' replied the boy, unable to suppress a white-toothed grin. 'It's a delegation of your own people - elders, merchants, artisans and wealthy persons. They insist on seeing you without delay. And, er, holy ones, some of them look pretty angry to me.'

'A delegation of *our* people,' groaned the third priest. 'Is there to be no rest. I thought they'd all be helping in the fields now the harvest is underway. It's only right and proper.'

'Apparently they aren't,' answered the first priest, peering around the edge of the recess to observe some ten individuals, each robed or kilted according to his status or occupation. 'And who do I see but Kuraka, elder and spokesman for Uruk's council of elders. Why him, I wonder. Why now.'

The group approached with determined step behind their leader, a tall but slender, slightly stooping figure with mid-length, greying hair, avian nose, braided beard, belted white robe and the pointed cap of a noble. The lashes and brows of his eyes were darkened with antimony both to emphasise his status and to deter the flies. Bowing slightly as he came to a halt then dismissing the boy with a wave of his arm, he raised and clasped both hands against his chest out of respect for the deity and her worthy representatives. The remainder of the party did not.

'Holy ones,' Kuraka began, 'as you are doubtless aware, I am owner of grazing land outside the city and of several workshops within. Because I am known to all, from farmers to tax collectors, I am elected to speak on behalf of the many.'

'Elected, you say?' frowned the first priest. 'What is so important that you should be elected and that you should descend upon us at this time of the day - and when the king is absent?'

'It's because our glorious king is absent,' replied Kuraka, 'that we have chosen this moment to present ourselves. We ask that you listen to our plea for it greatly concerns many of Uruk's people. Afterwards we will depart in peace for we wish to trouble no one.'

'Except,' added another of his party, gruffly 'that it's *our* troubles need to be addressed.'

'No man in Uruk should stand in fear of honest expression,' said the first priest. 'Say what is on your minds and we will give it due consideration.'

'You are most gracious,' replied Kuraka, glancing back at his small company before continuing. 'We have discussed this matter at great length. We have prayed and offered sacrifice in generous measure to the gods. We have presented ourselves as supplicants at the altar of distant Anu but he appears to have little time for human affairs.

We have brought many gifts here to the house of his daughter and protector of our city, the Lady Inanna, but our lives in this world are taken up with mundane affairs and we do not seem to be worthy of her attentions either.'

'Oh, get on with it!' called someone at his rear.

'I thought the citizens of Uruk had been unusually generous of late,' observed the second priest. The third priest glanced in desperation at the empty pot.

The noble looked about uneasily then continued, 'You have the ear of Lady Inanna and we ask you to plead for us in our time of misfortune.'

'Time of misfortune?' sighed the third priest. 'Things have never been better, even if we are dying of thirst up here.'

'*Some* things have never been better,' replied Kuraka, 'but alas, the fruits of good fortune handed down by the gods contain a thorn.'

Turning away from the priests, he looked out beyond the city wall to the ripe, well-watered fields and toward the low hills. There, beyond the reach of the canals and irrigation ditches, where the land was given over to grazing herds and wild beasts, arose a cloud of dust that drifted slowly in the blue haze.

'I trust you'll soon get to the point,' commented the first priest.

'For *all* our sakes,' breathed the second, glancing up at the sky.

'My point – *our* point,' replied Kuraka, returning his attention to the priests, 'is this. At present our city is strong. The Man of Kish sits with his tail between his legs and the corpses of his generals that our king had hung from our walls are long since devoured by worms. And for the time being the Man of Larsa does no more than grumble over petty issues.'

The priests adjusted their full kilts and settled back into their seats in anticipation of a long and tedious interview. Kuraka's followers were visibly restive and had begun to mutter amongst themselves.

'Our king,' continued Kuraka, 'is praised throughout Sumer for his exploits - except, that is, by the king of Kish. But now we have no enemy at our gates and no city for him to march against, he is unable to settle down in peace. His spirit of pride and aggression that served the people of Uruk in their time of need is now turned upon us. We do not say he is driven by malice, I hasten to add, but by the passions of youth. He must always prove himself to others and is only happy when there are conquests to be made.'

Raising an arm, Kuraka gestured out to the land beyond the fields where his attention had earlier fallen. 'Our noble leader presently expends his energies in sport outside the city wall. He has every war chariot together with the most able of our young men - not to test their skills for the well-being of our city - no, but in racing. Racing! For what! They are summoned before sunrise by the drums yet Uruk benefits not by a single ear of barley for all the effort they put into these pointless contests. The only ones to gain are the carpenters who are obliged to repair the chariots and have them ready for his next escapade – oh, yes, and the nomads of the hills who grow rich by selling asses to replace those that have died of exhaustion. Then there are the wrestling matches held in our market place. No man will stand up to face Lord Gilgamesh so he pits one against the other and has the crowd making foolish wagers. Where is the pride and dignity in that for him or our people?'

'Enough!' bellowed a voice from behind the nobleman. 'We're wasting time and words!' Another pushed Kuraka roughly aside; a hairy-chested, bear-like, wide-jawed man with generous beard framing a ruddy face, a thick, sweat-stained headband and a well-worn kilt of soot-blackened ox hide. They knew Sheshkalla, head of the guild of metalworkers, as one not given to idle conversation.

'There's the matter few dare speak of openly,' he declared, 'but you know full well what I'm on about! It effects the people far more than the time Gilgamesh wastes in harmless sport outside the city wall!'

'Our women!' called out another.

'Aye, that's exactly it,' resumed the metalworker. 'Our women; his sport within the city wall!'

'Yes, yes, yes,' cut in Kuraka, 'I was about to say - but this is a delicate matter.'

'Indelicate, don't you mean!' declared someone else from within the group.

'Exactly so!' stated the metalworker. 'But it matters little how it's put, when -.'

'Or where it's put as far as the king is concerned!' interrupted another.

Sheshkalla turned to him with a look that discouraged further comment then continued, 'The fact is no young woman, be she daughter, wife or

31

widow, peasant or noble, is safe from his attentions. Gilgamesh will make off with whoever takes his fancy whether she likes it or not - sometimes for days on end, and no man in Uruk dares bar his way. Big as I am, I doubt I'd survive a round with him.'

'Er, one did challenge him some time ago,' remarked Kuraka. 'The king merely brushed the man aside for his audacity. Another day he might have had him flogged. But I fear now for my own granddaughter - she is soon to be married but has no father to speak for her.'

'He took my daughter off the day before her wedding,' put in one man. 'She was obliged to comfort him mightily though to her credit she never saw fit to complain afterwards.'

His remark prompted sniggers from behind.

'Some people liken Gilgamesh to a mighty bull,' continued the metalworker, 'and maybe chastity was never top of *anyone's* agenda, but our women aren't penned-up cattle awaiting sacrifice to his lusts whenever the fancy takes him!'

'This matter causes vexation amongst the citizens,' added Kuraka. 'It is a burden harder to bear even than the tax collectors and -.'

'And the temple accountants, he's about to say!' cut in the metalworker, folding his arms to reinforce the statement.

'Quite so,' continued Kuraka, eyeing him uneasily. 'Word is about that the king is possessed by demons that have taken hold of his wits because his hands are idle. They beg the gods to drive out whatever so mischievously guides his actions.'

'We're well informed about this situation and you have our sympathy,' replied the first priest. 'We have prayed that Utu, the shining sun, would illuminate for him the path of reason. But it would seem this has yet to happen.'

'You must intercede for us,' declared the noble. 'Join with your brother priests of Anu. Make sacrifice. Pour wine on the altars. Raise your voices to heaven for the people of Uruk.'

'Blessed be the Lady Inanna!' chanted the second priest.

'Blessed be,' repeated some of the small congregation with scant enthusiasm.

After some moments in thought the first priest announced, 'I believe we ought to act upon what you have said. We should gather in one accord with the priests of Anu, place gifts from the people upon the altars. We should raise our voices so loudly that even if the gods are taken with higher affairs, they will hear us and perhaps take notice.'

'And what if Gilgamesh himself hears about it?' asked the third priest. 'He is supposed to be head of the priesthood.'

'So he is when it suits him,' responded the second. 'But he takes little enough interest in our affairs except on that annual and sacred occasion when there is a woman involved. I say we go ahead.'

'Yes, we will go ahead,' confirmed the first priest.'

'We can ask no more of you,' said Kuraka.

'On the other hand,' declared Sheshkalla, peering sternly at each priest in turn, 'if the gods prove uncaring we might be tempted to follow their example. We guildsmen might look hard at the donations *we* make towards *your* upkeep and, income from the lands you hold or no, you will certainly notice the difference.' He moved his face close to theirs with an ironic smile. 'I say it's time we saw some return for our investment.'

***

'A troublesome matter,' reflected the second priest when the delegation had gone. 'It needs much deliberation on our part.'

'Indeed it does,' agreed the first priest. 'Before evening libations we'd better consult with the priests of Anu. We have time this afternoon to decide how best to present our case.'

'We'd deliberate more meaningfully with the benefit of liquid refreshment,' munched the third priest. 'What is more, the sun is beginning to fall directly upon us and the heat will soon be intolerable. I say we take ourselves around to the other side of the building. It will clear our heads for constructive dialogue.'

'I think he's right,' added the second priest.

'Very well,' agreed the first, rising from his seat, glancing along the temple wall to once more observe the pair of dusty feet protruding from the adjacent recess.

'Boy!' he called, rolling up a section of the reed matting in which were gathered the drinking tubes. 'Boy!' he called again as the feet drew further in. 'Boy! Fetch beer and be quick about it or I'll have you flogged without mercy! Bring it to the east side where there is shade!'

'No problem, holy ones,' came the cheery reply.

'Indolent wretch should be beaten daily,' grumbled the third priest. 'Idleness, I always say, is a portal through which the demons gain easy passage.'

***

Their voices rose from the temple shrines. From amidst votive statues that stood with hands clasped to their chests in reverence and goggle-eyes that stared wide to infinity. From amidst offerings of grain, precious meat and vintage wine that surrounded the altars, voices drifted into the evening sky where the star of Inanna shone above the horizon. Through strange dimensions of time and space, as unseen tendrils in deep earth and dark sky, the messages wormed their hidden way until Anu lifted his head and asked, 'Who calls? Who distracts me from my thoughts?'

'Great Anu,' replied one of his kin from across the void, 'it is the people who regard you highest of all - those who sacrifice at your temple in Uruk. It is their voices you hear. They beg a favour from yourself and your daughter.'

'Do they really!' rolled back the voice. 'And what has any of it got to do with me? Their lives are tied to their labours, to the rise and fall of the rivers, to the passing seasons. Their kingdoms grow and wither in the blink of an eye. The universe expands and as it does, the affairs of humankind diminish and fade to nothing.'

'But Great Anu,' called another, 'though fragile and mortal, they are made in our likeness and follow our ways. They are a mirror of our own lives, however pale their image.'

The reply rolled as thunder. 'Perhaps they are but what am I supposed to do?'

'Please advise us, Lord Anu. The citizens of Uruk are sorely oppressed by their king, who no man dares confront. He is restless now his domains are at peace and inflicts mischief upon his people. Are we not to help them in some small way? You may recall, his mother is numbered amongst our kind, however distant she may be.'

Silence. Then, 'Oh, I suppose something ought to be done,' yawned the Lord of the Cosmos, 'but *I* can be of little use. I would appear as storm clouds above a nest of ants. The little sphere over which they crawl is just a grain of sand in the desert. You should ask Lady Inanna – no, better still - go to the one who moulded their feeble bodies in the first place. Consult with Lady Aruru; I doubt she has much to do nowadays.'

'Father,' chimed the clear voice of Inanna, 'what can the goddess do to help?'

'It's really quite simple,' rumbled distant Anu, 'have Lady Aruru create another in his image, A man who will gaze back at him as an equal. A man who will cast his shadow and know his thoughts. A man who is as determined to have his own way as does this so-called mighty king. Get on with it and trouble me no more; I have ages of contemplating still to do.'

***

Their voices crowded about Aruru, seated before an illuminated bronze mirror within the shadows of her temple. 'We have consulted with Anu,' they informed her. 'We wish you to create another man in the image of Gilgamesh. A physical equal who will find his way into Uruk and challenge

36

a king who oppresses them by the treatment of their women.'

'What' queried Aruru, passing a finely carved and gilded ivory comb through midnight hair that shimmered star crystals, 'another one like him to add to their troubles? Is that what you want?'

'Yes, a man to challenge Gilgamesh for the mastery he takes for granted. A man who will offer respite to the people of Uruk.'

'Dear me, I thought we'd finished with them ages ago.'

'Didn't we all,' replied one of the minor gods. 'But we think it's a good idea, so if you wouldn't mind - just once more. After all, they were your responsibility.'

'Oh, I suppose I could,' sighed Aruru, fluttering her long eyelashes close before the mirror. 'Yes, in the morning I will follow the great river toward the sea. I will walk amidst the shallows. I will take clay of the earth, the body of the goddess Ninhursag from which humans were made. I will mix it with the waters of Enki, her consort, to give it awareness and understanding. I will form its image from the same mould as that of Gilgamesh. I will set it down in the wild country, in the land of hunters and trappers beyond the fields and the canals of Uruk. There its life will begin. There this man of the earth will wander free and know himself as Enkidu. What happens after that must be left to others. I have enough to do.'

***

Sangasu had rested well after being offered refuge from the night in the humble home of a peasant who had pitied his situation and asked no

37

questions. Now, as the sky lightened, his troubled memories returned. With his hunger and thirst and that of his weary ass for the time being eased by what little the poor man was able give, he thanked his host and departed. He took the reins of his reluctant mount then continued on until he reached the crossing. Leading the beast, he trod the timbers of the floating bridge with caution as they swayed beneath. Relieved to be once more on firm ground he mounted and urged the ass on toward the Southern Gate that loomed a short distance from the quay of Uruk.

On reaching the gate, he hesitated before riding beneath the shadow of the great arch where chattering crowds came and went from the city. Here were traders. Here were artisans. Some with asses weighed down by vessels of clay, copper and bronze, some with ox carts bearing the produce of the fields. Some bore baskets of poultry, others fruit for the stalls in the market. Slaves hurried in silence, children darted noisily about, and always with glazed eye and fallen jaw were the foul, toothless beggars and wretched cripples, their shame ill-hidden by filthy rags and cast off hides. It was not the scent of orchards that pervaded here. Sharp-eyed dogs yapped, circling aimlessly, whilst pigs grunted and scavenged amidst the dust. The flesh of these latter was said to be held in contempt by the gods and was often scorned by the wealthy. Yet it was enjoyed readily enough by the common people who might otherwise taste no meat apart from fish bred in ponds or caught in the river.

Only on his occasional journeys to Uruk did Sangasu encounter more than a few souls at a time.

Only then did he hear so much noise, see so many colours and taste so many odours, not all of them, as now, to his liking. Such was the press of people that it was with difficulty he made his way through the gate and into the city.

Passing along the wide, processional street, Sangasu eventually found himself beneath the vaulted gateway leading onto the great square in which the city's main markets were held. On the far side of the square lay the walled precinct of Eanna. On approaching this, he had a fine view of the precinct with beyond it the upper platform from which the temple of Inanna rose. Arriving at the arched gateway to the precinct he tugged the ass to a halt. 'Should I go through?' he asked himself. 'Should I climb the stairs to the temple to ask for beer and bread? Should I state my business to the priests? Will the holy men even speak to me?'

A ceremony of offerings was taking place and many people, artisans, stallholders, merchants, women and children, stood or sat about to watch. Sangasu observed a man ascending the staircase to the temple platform as the rams' horns sounded. He recognised the figure of the high priest, attired in gilded robes and carrying his golden staff of office. Following behind in well-spaced single file were some twenty priests, their hairless bodies quite naked under the hot sun. The first of them held up the long tail of their leader's robe, keeping it clear of the dust. Was this Lord Gilgamesh himself, wondered Sangasu? He could not see the man's face.

Only once before had he seen the king. Then he had taken time from his labours and travelled to

Uruk to witness the New Year ceremony. The king, red-robed and wearing the false beard that adorned the ruler on such occasions, had headed the procession to Inanna's temple. At the top of the steps leading to the temple platform had waited the priestess in gilded robes and elaborate head-dress; she representing Inanna whilst the king played the role of her husband, Dumuzi, deity of crops and vegetation. Within the sanctuary, so people said, within a darkened room occupied only by a gilded bed, their physical union ensured the rebirth of life and new growth to the fields.

Today, most of the followers carried decorated pottery vessels of oil or wine, or woven baskets filled with fruit or grain. All lavish offerings for the goddess, Inanna. No, this was not the time to trouble them with his bizarre tale. Even without the distraction of the ceremony, they might still dismiss him out of hand. Except for the affairs of estates owned by the temples, he saw no reason for the priests to care about what went on in those lands far outside the boundary stones of Uruk where they had no interests at all. Sangasu decided the priests would not listen to him.

He continued on, skirting wide of the temple precinct wall, avoiding the busy market stalls. He did not care to be assailed by the shouts of fish and poultry sellers or tormented by the smell of cooking from the brick ovens now his hunger was returning in full.

The long, meandering street of gypsum-white houses through which he now passed was the only route he knew, though it seemed far from direct. But he eventually entered the palace square, a hardly less imposing area than that laid out before Inanna's precinct. To one side of this stood the palace of Gilgamesh. Assailed by rising doubt, he wondered if this was not after all a pointless errand. The king might be at the temple but even if he was in residence he would never hear of Sangasu's journey if the palace retainers dismissed him out of hand. But the horror arose again before his eyes. A horror that would be there in reality once he returned home.

Yet he could not leave Uruk without food and beer. He had to go on.

Glowing bright in the morning sun the palace rose from a low brick platform with recessed facade bearing cedar masts and coloured banners not unlike those of the temples. There was the portal, framed in limestone brought from other lands and set with ornate copper-sheathed doors of heavy timber, one of which stood ajar. Either side of the entrance stood a guard wearing burnished bronze battle-helmet and crimson cloak. Each man grasped a stout, bronze-tipped spear. A small crowd pressed noisily about the short flight of steps leading up to the palace entrance. Some waited to voice their grievances to the king, a few bore clay tablets with incised messages set hard to preserve that which, for Sangasu as for most people, was as mysterious and out of reach as the stars in the heavens. Others merely chattered or looked on idly.

As he approached, his heart quickened. On a low wall at the base of the steps sat two kilted officials. They attended to the nearest petitioners who vied with one another for attention. Each official held a wedge-shaped copper stylus in his

41

hand, poised above a hinged, timber-framed writing board containing damp clay. Directly behind each hovered a slave boy with woven reed umbrella to offer shade from the sun. Would the officials acknowledge the trapper's voice above the clamour or would he be ignored in favour of those of higher status? All men of the city except slaves and the outcasts by the gate enjoyed higher status than the likes of Sangasu. He waited, ears assailed by endless gossip, eyes fixed upon the officials whose faces were set in a mould of indifference.

One of the officials glanced up, distracted momentarily by the presence of the countryman who stared at them from astride his dusty mount. As though pricked by a thorn, Sangasu lurched forward and blurted out, 'Hear me! I have news for Lord Gilgamesh!'

The babble quietened. Faces turned.

'A demon stalks our land!' he cried. 'One of great stature, strength and cunning! Yes, one who lives amongst the beasts and protects them from the hunter! One more terrible than any man could face!'

The babble ceased altogether. More faces turned to Sangasu, some amused, some hostile, others merely puzzled. One of the officials raised up and said, 'Lord Gilgamesh knows the world better than any man. He would be aware of this if it were true. Many seek his attention with urgent matters. Take yourself off! Do not interrupt the business of -
.'

His words were stopped like a bird, pole-netted in mid-flight.

'Hold!' called a voice. It came from behind rush matting that covered a window directly above the palace door. 'Have that man dismount. Bring him to me!'

Those waiting for attention murmured angrily. Laying aside their tablets, the officials dismissed the petitioners, who in turn eyed the trapper darkly. One official turned to Sangasu and said, 'You had better follow us,' then regarding Sangasu's appearance added, 'but not too closely.'

Sangasu slipped from his mount and a slave boy hurried forward to take charge of it. From the dust and noise of the square he tottered. Past the guards at the door he pitter-pattered, clutching the bag that once held his food, eyes darting anxiously about. Through the portal into a narrow passage where half way on either side was an alcove. It alarmed him to see in each an armed man, ready to strike down any who managed to rush by those outside and attempt to enter uninvited.

Gaining the cool interior of a large hall, his rough sandals scuffed mosaics of coloured stone and brick. As his eyes adjusted to the dim interior he perceived precious ornaments and wall hangings on which were displayed spears and axes of polished bronze. On the air drifted an unfamiliar tang of incense and an equally unfamiliar sound - the gentle plucking of a harp. To Sangasu it was a strangeness that left him bewildered. They continued across the hall until reaching a flight of stairs at one side. At the base of the stairs they halted. One of the officials turned abruptly to demand, 'Your name! What is it?'

'Sss - Sangasu, the - the hunter and trapper,' he croaked, squeezing the bag against his chest.

'Sangasu,' muttered one, grinning at his companion then gesturing for Sangasu to follow.

At the top of the stairs hung a rich, ornate curtain that one of the officials lifted aside before announcing into the room beyond, 'Lord Gilgamesh, here is the man you ordered us to bring. He calls himself Sangasu, the hunter and trapper.'

'Have him enter then leave us to speak alone,' came the reply.

Never had Sangasu heard a voice of such calm authority. The first official held aside the hanging whilst the second gestured the new arrival forward. Sangasu hesitated, his legs unsteady as a new-born gazelle's. He gripped the leather bag as if it contained his salvation.

'Well go on you oaf!' growled the first official, 'and remember to kneel before your king and master or you'll be leaving head first by the window. And keep your distance so he doesn't get a whiff of you. He no more cares for foul-smelling yokels than he does for verminous beggars.'

Heart pounding, Sangasu advanced two steps into the royal chamber then halted. The air was heavy with incense. His gaze drifted from side to side. No one stood there to confront him. Fearful, bewildered, he continued to stare about. At the far side were windows covered by screens of rush matting to keep out the heat and dust. From one of these must have come the summons. Over the floor were spread patterned rugs and about the walls hung fabrics that glowed in the filtered light from outside and from oil lamps standing atop bronze posts either side of the room. There were two, low timber seats draped with dyed woollen cloth and positioned by

44

one window was an ornate couch of cedar, inlaid with ivory and supported by lion's feet of carved ebony. From the couch a figure arose.

'Mm - my lord,' mumbled the trapper, dropping with a thump to his knees. The figure stood silhouetted large against the reed blind. Sangasu, almost as terrified now as he had been by the cause of his setting off on his journey, pushed out his arms, sank lower and would have prostrated himself entirely had not the voice exclaimed, 'Oh, stand up! I'll not have you address your words to the floor!'

Sangasu, wretched in his begrimed attire, struggled awkwardly to his feet. Daring no more than a brief glance upward, he stood in abject silence, head bowed before Gilgamesh, the bag still clasped to his chest. But in that glance his sharp eye had observed much.

Before him loomed a man taller than most. A man of lithe and powerful build. A man little older than himself. Held in place by a crimson headband, raven hair fell about the man's broad shoulders to frame a determined, clean-shaven jaw and eyes of greyish-blue that fixed on him as if sizing up his prey. Perfumed oil endowed his muscular body with a subtle sheen and at wrist and arm he wore bronze bands of intricate artistry inlaid with gold, silver and lapis lazuli. On a slender chain at his throat gleamed a small silver amulet in the form of the sun. From the broad, ornate belt fixed by an engraved bronze clasp at his waist hung a kilt of soft leather. Sangasu dared not look up but kept his gaze firmly upon the floor.

'Sangasu the hunter and trapper,' said the king, 'you must have travelled far to deliver your message.'

'I - I have ridden from the wild lands, great lord, resting only at night. The journey has taken three days and - and there was little comfort for - for much of the way - other than the few water holes that decided my route.'

'You must take beer now,' said Gilgamesh. Sangasu raised his head far enough to see the king gesture to a small bench close by the entrance where stood a well-filled bronze goblet. The trapper suspected this had been placed there only moments before his entry into the royal presence. Dropping his bag to the floor, he reached for the goblet with trembling hands, fearing he might spill the contents. Though he usually quenched his thirst with water from the wells, Sangasu was familiar with the rough, barley beer brewed by his family and other homesteads in the area where he lived.

'When we have spoken,' continued Gilgamesh, 'I'll see to it you are given food and comfort within these walls.'

'P-please forgive me, Lord,' ventured Sangasu, clutching the precious goblet, 'but I am offered your kindness when more worthy men have waited since before I arrived.' The king's unexpectedly easy manner and the gloriously welcome beer did much to alleviate his fear. This was a beer unlike any he had known. A wonderful, light beer laced with honey and spices.

'Because,' replied Gilgamesh, 'you came bearing a message that may be of interest to me.

When you called from the street outside, I felt I had to hear more.'

'I - I do not understand, Lord,' breathed Sangasu, wondering now if this was perhaps a dream but at last daring to look Gilgamesh in the eye, albeit momentarily. In that glance he noted a scar that weaved down from beneath the king's headband to just below his cheekbone. Then another to the side of his left thigh.

'No,' replied Gilgamesh, lowering himself to the cedar couch, 'nor should you understand. But I'll explain as briefly as I can before you offer me your own account. You're not a man of the city so you'll not add your gossip to that of others in our streets, though I will speak to you now as a citizen familiar with our affairs.' He reached across to where a second goblet stood, pushed the small bench toward Sangasu with his foot and indicated that he move it further away still before sitting down.

'You doubtless know,' Gilgamesh continued, 'I conquered those who bore arms against me and I regret nothing. But I tell you, when peace came, I found myself pitted against an enemy no weapon could keep at bay. It had no form, it cast no shadow, yet it darkened my path even in the light of day. This was an enemy only I at first knew. An enemy that preyed upon me day and night. One against which my spear and my axe were of as little use as - .' he waved a hand dismissively in the air, 'as weapons of clay.' Gilgamesh shook his head and sighed, 'That enemy was boredom. Unimaginable, endless, boredom.'

Sangasu flinched when the king sprang up and turned to the window. 'It began to eat away at my days as birds picking at a carcass,' declared Gilgamesh. 'To counter this malaise I found pleasures and diversions within my own domains and now I hear the people complain I behave as a tyrant.' Gilgamesh turned again to face the room. 'Yes, a tyrant! As if they know the meaning of the word. Ha - it would serve them right if they did know it! But then I ask why, when I stood at the forefront in their battles and risked all to fill their tables with plenty - why should I not reap the benefits?' His gaze fell upon Sangasu, an ironic smile crossed his lips. 'Now you arrive, an uncouth yokel from the distant hills with this tale of yours. A demon you say - one greater and stronger than any man might face? Well I must say - that *does* sound interesting.'

'It's true, my Lord. I never before saw the likes of it – of him, until – until that day.'

'Then tell me all,' said Gilgamesh, sitting down once more, 'and when you have done you must bathe in the palace courtyard – yes, surely you must. Afterwards I'll have them bring you food and more beer to wash it down. And new clothes since those you wear must be consigned to the flames. But right now I'm impatient and I *will* hear your tale.'

Sangasu drained the goblet but held on to it as he began. 'I - I roam the hills far from Uruk, my Lord. I know the land well. I know the dried out watercourses and the lonely places. I know the routes taken by wild boar and gazelle and where the hare lies. Most of all I know the freshwater springs and the drinking pools where animals and birds gather. Th-there I see jackal and hyena, wolf and, and sometimes lion.' His expression became agitated as he continued. 'One m-morning I set out but – but I felt something was wrong in the land. I could sense no danger from lion or bear because these I know, as did my father and his father before him. I - I sensed a presence. A new creature had come into the world; one cunning and devious. It had thrown earth back in the ditches I had worked so hard to dig. It had destroyed my traps and torn apart the nets I'd placed days before. And – and most of those animals already snared had been set loose. My catch was meagre and what little I had concealed along my route to collect later was hardly enough for my family. It left me nothing to trade in Uruk's market.

I rushed back and forth all morning to discover why these things had happened. Later, I found myself with a thirst. There is a water hole close by, part hidden by bushes and reeds. Wild oxen and gazelle drink there. I saw them that day and I saw geese raise their wings in the sun. I saw no beast to be afraid of so I walked to the water hole and laid aside my traps and nets. There's an exposed rock jutting out from the bushes by that pool where I would often kneel to drink. It's where I now went. The beasts on the far side did no more than lift their heads because they had seen me often before and were not afraid.' Here Sangasu hesitated and said, 'Lord King, I fear my tale may try your patience.'

'Had I wished you to stop you would know it,' responded Gilgamesh.

Sangasu, swallowing nervously, croaked, 'P-pardon me, Sire,' then continued. 'I drank. I saw my own reflection shimmer against the sky. I would have drunk again, my lord, but – but,' his eyes widened and the empty goblet shook in his grasp, 'as I stooped, another reflection appeared close to mine. In my ear came a growl like an angry bear. I - I raised my head, and a dreadful coldness seized me. In the bushes not an arm's reach away, his gaze was upon me, his lips drawn back, his teeth bared! It was a beast in human form! A beast whose eyes burned! The birds and animals scattered from the pool at my cry of fear. I fled blindly, thinking he was close behind - thinking he was about to fasten on me! In my panic I felt his breath on my neck though now I think it was no more than the heat of the sun. When I knew he was not following, I laid low. I watched the pool until the sun was past its height but he was no longer to be seen. After a time, I returned to gather my traps and my nets only to find them torn apart. Mighty lord, I swear on my life this is true. It was a demon-man I saw!'

'And afterwards?' asked Gilgamesh.

'Afterwards, Lord, I ran back and told my family what had happened. Next day I hid on a hill some way from the pool and I saw him again. For three days I watched and he appeared each day. And - and on each of those days, after dark, most of my traps were destroyed. He drinks with the animals at the pool. He lives on roots and raw meat. He runs with the gazelles and roams the land at will, yet he looks like a grown man. A grown man of your strength and size, great lord, but wild and cunning as the wolves. The beasts have no fear of him nor he of them. It's as though he becomes whatever he wishes to be in their eyes. M-my father said he must

50

have come down from the mountains to the north or been cast out by the rogues who live there. But no one would claim that if they saw him. No - such a one would lack his stature and strength. Such a one would bare scars and signs of disease.'

Sangasu passed a hand across his face as if to erase the image from his vision.

'Great lord, what I saw was not a creature rejected by other men but one set on earth by the gods. My father hopes he will move on – hopes he will depart as suddenly as he came so we will be left in peace and I can once more go hunting. But I think he'll not go away. He will continue to destroy my traps, and those of other men who live as me. He will drive us from the land we know. We'll have too little for ourselves and nothing to trade in the towns of Sumer. If my father was sound of limb, which he is not, he would himself come to Uruk and ask for help. He said I must do it. He said to make myself known at the temple of Lady Inanna and beg to be brought before our lord the king. He said to tell of the man-beast and how the threat of him will affect not only us but other trappers who supply what the people of Uruk desire. He said to tell them the man-beast is more than any mortal could face. He said it will be an affront to Lord Gilgamesh and in his great goodness he will act to save us. Lord, I fear this being is sent to punish us though I cannot say why.'

'I think not,' replied the king. 'But now you will hear me. I had a dream not long ago - the very oddest of dreams. I will reveal this because in the light of what you have said there may be a connection. In this dream of mine a star fell from the sky, almost striking me as it came to rest on the path where I walked. Now a great rock, it attracted the people of Uruk and they gathered in admiration with not the least thought or concern for their king. As they stood watching I had to show them I was strong enough to move it out of the way. Only with the greatest of effort could I do that but it was a challenge I had to overcome. I dismissed the dream as nonsense but some nights later I had another, even odder. In this second dream, I walked a desert track. Everything about me appeared to recede, to become distant under an open sky - as though I walked upon a vast sphere. I found my path obstructed again, this time by a great axe. It seemed the only real thing in this odd world. I was wary of the axe because it appeared too big, too heavy for the hands of an ordinary mortal. I thought it had been placed there as a warning by some unknown foe. Then I came to understand that the axe would be mine if only I had the skill to use it. I took hold of the axe. I lifted it and when I did I - I felt I could take on a hundred men. I was loath to quit the dream and relinquish the axe because I knew how well it could serve me.

The priests and soothsayers I consulted could offer no better interpretation. Still, I remained puzzled until I spoke about those dreams to my mother, Lady Ninsun. She understands such matters. She saw in them a premonition. The great stone signified I really was to be confronted by a challenge - the axe was that same challenge in a different guise. But the answer remained vague until you arrived and announced yourself beneath my window whilst I listened to the endless complaints and petty bickering of others. Your words seem to have completed the circle.'

'Then, Lord, the – the coming of the man-beast was foretold.'

'It would appear so. He is evidently the challenge I am to overcome.'

'But, lord,' asked Sangasu, putting aside the goblet, 'what purpose can this have?'

'What purpose,' replied the king, turning aside to the window. 'Oh, there is a purpose. There has to be a purpose. But for the remainder of today I must think hard over your account.'

Gilgamesh raised his arm and with a clenched fist, struck a beaten bronze disk that hung by the couch. As it resonated loudly he said, 'You will accept my hospitality - all I promised you and more. You will stay here but you may not discuss what has passed between us or leave my palace until you are ready to depart the city.' For some time he was silent, then continued, 'I don't suppose you see many women out there – at least none a city man would care to lay hands on, yet I see you're young and fit enough to want to know what it's all about. Perhaps if you're kept suitably occupied for the evening, friend Sangasu, it will take your mind off our man-beast.'

As he finished speaking a young girl pushed through the curtains, slim and bare-breasted, her large eyes smouldering dark, her lips full and sensual. About her throat coiled an elaborate copper collar. On her limbs she wore ornate copper bangles. Gilgamesh said to her, 'Take this fellow and have the serving women scrub him thoroughly at the pool. See to it that his garments are burned. I imagine only the goats would relish his company as he is. Aye, and when he's clean have them massage him with oil then find him a linen robe. Lay out beer and food as you would for a favoured citizen and attend his table with your companions. Make sure his room and bed are comfortable and that he does not want for company in the night.'

Sangasu gaped open-mouthed as, with her gaze fixed on his, the girl beckoned him to get up and follow some way behind. Gilgamesh muttered under his breath, 'It'll make a change from having his pleasure with the sheep, I dare say,' then he summoned the captain of his palace guard. When the man appeared, sword at his side, hands clasped to his chest in deference, the king said, 'Tell the evening watch to keep an eye open for our rustic visitor. He is not to leave the palace until I authorise his departure from Uruk. Should he attempt escape by deception, then you're to slay him and burn his remains outside the city wall with the carcasses.'

**

Sunlight was yet to touch the white walls of Inanna's temple. Nor had it reached through shadowed date palms to feel its way across the patchwork fields and ripple silver on the waterways when the voice dispelled his contentment. 'Sangasu, you lazy boy! Time to get up! Lord Gilgamesh requires your presence as soon as you are bathed and have eaten. You should not keep him waiting.'

The space in the bed beside him was empty. It was a bed of divine warmth and comfort beyond anything he had known or imagined could ever be his. As for the girl who had just spoken, the one who had shared the bed with him, the perfumed goddess who had opened up the gates of pleasure and played his body with the deft-fingered skill of a harpist; she was dressed and on the point of leaving.

Sangasu wondered if he was still a prisoner of his own dreams as he slipped from the bed. He regarded the rare wooden furniture inlaid with ivory and gold, the fine fabrics and hangings. He moved with care, afraid to touch anything. He recalled the rude hovel of stone, mud and rushes from which he came and wished he could remain here forever.

***

The hunter and trapper, groomed almost beyond recognition, stood once more in his master's presence in a long kilt of white linen.

'You have a duty to perform,' announced Gilgamesh. 'I have summoned a woman from Inanna's temple. She is a servant of the goddess and therefore a child of pleasure. She will return with you to your own land. An ox and covered wagon are already prepared so she may travel in comfort as these girls must and not suffer daytime heat. When you arrive home you are to show her where this so-called man-beast drinks and have her wait beneath her shade. You must leave her to ensnare him in the manner she knows best. He may have filled your pits and torn apart your nets but if what my mother says is true, the trap this girl will lay for him won't seem a trap at all until it is too late. Should the gods permit, he will return with her to Uruk where I intend to have him offer me good sport. And once I have mastered him he can serve as I see fit. I'll depend on you for this, Sangasu. Do not let me down or disclose the purpose of your journey to anyone else or you will feel my anger. And take

55

care to moderate your description of this man-beast on the journey. The girl is no fool and has a will of her own. The fact that she was chosen by lot did not altogether please me. No, she's one I would prefer for my own bed.'

'I will do as you wish, Lord Gilgamesh,' replied the trapper. 'I'll keep her safe on the journey and I'll keep the true nature of the man-beast to myself.'

'Good. Now, Sangasu, I'll give you two gifts for your service. First, a decent cloak so when you next come to Uruk you may walk the streets looking like a citizen rather than a bumpkin. Second, a bronze spear with cedar shaft. A spear fit to bring down wolf, bear or lion. Use it to guard the girl - and guard her with your life.' The harsh eye of Gilgamesh recalled the gaze of the man-beast as he added, 'With your life, Sangasu! Keep those words uppermost at all times!'

***

Sunlight already spilled over the city wall when Sangasu left via the same gate by which he had entered. People had for some time been going about their business in the squares, the market and the narrow streets or taking to the paths and fields.

No longer perched astride the ass, Sangasu was for now a new man with an important role in life. He sat before a canvas covered wagon, gripping with ill-practised hands the reins of a sturdy ox. Tethered to the rear of the wagon trailed the ass. Amidst soft cushions within the wagon, shaded from prying eyes, the girl reclined.

Sangasu's departure had not been as early or as straightforward as he might have expected. He

56

recalled how he had waited and watched the morning sky brighten into full daylight before she emerged from a narrow, secluded side-gate in the Eanna precinct. As she climbed into the wagon he had appraised her alluring form caressed by a belted robe of finest white linen. Her eyes were dark as fathomless pools, her lips full and sensual. He had started the wagon forward only to hear her call for him to stop. Out from the gate had scampered two slave boys to hand up her polished bronze mirror and ivory combs. They had brought, too, a casket containing small ceramic bottles, golden pots and seashells that held pastes and colours for the adornment of her face and body. Next had come the jars of perfumed oil, hogshair brushes, bronze tweezers, razors and nail files, and the pumice stone to smooth her skin before she applied her oils and perfumes. They had carried out a basket of assorted garments exhaling clouds of perfume, then several pairs of sandals. Sangasu had looked on in disbelief as all her paraphernalia disappeared into the wagon.

And just when he thought the scurrying back and forth had ended, they had appeared one last time to hang panniers on the ass, containing not the hard-gotten fare of the countryman but a supply of dried meats, cheese, figs and dates, fruits from the orchards and two generous flagons of beer. The unfortunate creature's burden would be none the lighter for the absence of its master. The prospect of crossing the river on that swaying wooden bridge with an ox and loaded wagon had almost, but not quite, overwhelmed his fear of Gilgamesh.

***

'Tell me, Sangasu,' came the girl's voice once they had crossed the river, 'tell me more about this nameless man I am to meet. I gather he is rather wayward and not well accustomed to the manners of the city.'

'True enough, lady,' replied Sangasu. 'He's a man of the countryside and the open skies. Where he comes from I cannot say but surely the gods are in him. Not the strongest, not most cunning of crea – I mean men, would dare confront him.'

'Oh, I'm sure Lord Gilgamesh would,' she answered confidently from within her domain of comfort. 'He'll face any man and bring him down to size - believe me. I've seen our king when he gets his blood up. If I'm able to lure this rustic of yours back to Uruk, Gilgamesh will force him into service just to prove he can do it – unless he kills him first. The king likes to show off, you see. He likes to have his way. You'd soon know that if you lived in Uruk.'

'That may be,' said the trapper, 'but I say they're as close a match in strength and size as any two men could be and I'd not place silver on the outcome should they meet - if I had any silver to wager, that is.'

As he spoke, Sangasu was assailed by guilt over the part he was obliged to play in the king of Uruk's deception of this young woman. 'What has Gilgamesh told her?' he had asked himself. 'Does she have any idea what she's expected to confront? No, she does not.'

***

For much of that first day they talked, sometimes discussing the ways of the city, sometimes the ways of the country. Sangasu avoided the subject of the man-beast although he knew it must press as much upon her thoughts as it did on his own. Twice he asked the girl her name and twice she declined to give it but late in the day, when the heat was less intense, she climbed out to sit by him at the front of the wagon.

In the night, when she walked under the moon before retiring to sleep, and especially at sunrise when she bathed at the water hole and plied her body with perfumed oil, Sangasu felt desire stir in his loins. From a distance Sangasu watched her, fired also by memories the girl who had shared his bed at the palace. But those urges fled like a gazelle before a lion at the thought of Gilgamesh and the price that he would surely pay if temptation overcame forbearance.

What would the man-beast make of her?

CHAPTER 2
MAN OF THE EARTH

The sun was low when they reached the humble dwelling of Sangasu's family. Having reluctantly accepted an offer of food and goat's milk, the girl seated herself on the low bench with his mother and sister. But the odour of goats and pigs, not to mention that of Sangasu's unsightly family, were more than she cared to suffer. Especially when her flesh began to itch. She remained no longer than politeness required then returned for the night to the comfort of the wagon and the reassurance of her possessions.

At sunrise next day she still slept - the way of her kind, thought Sangasu as he called through the pale canvas cover of the wagon, 'Lady, we should go now!'

'What?' came her drowsy reply. 'It's barely daylight. I'll need fresh water then you'll have to wait until I'm ready.'

Sangasu had no choice but to provide what she wanted; cool, clear water in a crude pitcher of baked clay. Hoping it was enough for her needs and thinking it best to leave her alone for a time, he returned to the house and waited.

For a long time, Sangasu waited.

When at last she emerged from the wagon and called for him, her long hair was let down, the brows and lashes of her eyes blackened with fine charcoal and the lids tinted with antimony. About her was wrapped another gown of white linen, at her waist a belt of gilded copper links and on her feet sandals of gilded leather. Seeing the look in Sangasu's eye, she smiled with reddened lips, 'I hope my efforts will not be wasted on this ill-bred fellow, Sangasu, but it helps get me into the mood. Perhaps I'll need that out here.'

'Yes, lady, I dare say you will,' muttered Sangasu under his breath.

Throwing a woollen blanket over the ass and, with unaccustomed delicacy, helping the girl up to sit on it, he led her out to the low rise within sight of the water hole where the man-beast came to drink. The sun was well up by the time they were settled on the grass with Sangasu's new spear placed at his side by way of reassurance – his own as much as hers. Through the heat of the day and the unwelcome company of flies they faced one another in occasional, subdued conversation but only a few small creatures and birds approached the water hole. Nevertheless, with a girl of Uruk's famous temple as his charge, Sangasu's role was of such magnitude he imagined himself lord of this ill-defined realm.

The girl had with her an ornate, painted parchment fan with ebony handle which she employed from time to time when finding the heat oppressive. Other than by a restlessness to alleviate her obvious discomfort, the day was interrupted only by their need for food and drink and passed without incident.

On the morning of the second day, the girl said, 'I think I'll do without the make-up. Oil for my skin will be enough in this heat - and as for these damned flies -!'

Throughout that day they waited but still no one came to the water hole. Toward sunset, with little left to discuss between them, it was clear she was becoming restless.

On the third day she had Sangasu bring over the ox and wagon so she could take shelter from time to time amidst those comforts acquired from the temple. The ox was tethered by the pool where it had access to water and the long grass that flourished thereabout. Her beer almost finished that previous evening, they reclined in midday heat with a bowl of fruit and a flagon of brackish water from Sangasu's well set down between them. Sangasu reflected on how the girl had remained quiet throughout that morning, fluttering her fan impatiently, whilst he had paced about with growing apprehension. When at last she spoke, her words offered no encouragement.

'Sangasu, dear - much as I appreciate your company, I've sat on this damned hill far too long. Wandering off to relieve myself has become the high point of my day. My legs and my back ache, my face is burning and if something doesn't happen soon I swear I will die of boredom.'

'Please be patient, lady,' pleaded the trapper. 'He *will* return, I know it.'

'Patient!' responded the girl, 'I'll be patient *only* until sunset, but enough is enough. Tomorrow, I insist you return me to Uruk and darling Gilgamesh can say whatever he likes. Yes - if he feels strongly enough about it then he can come out here himself. He has precious little to keep him occupied around the city nowadays except racing chariots and behaving like a spoiled adolescent.'

The trapper sighed despair. He feared he would have to face the anger of Gilgamesh if he returned her to Uruk with their mission unfulfilled. When the sun was at its highest the girl retired to her wagon but reappeared mid-afternoon to find Sangasu dozing. Dust drifted on the air and a small number of wild cattle had gathered by the water hole. A few gazelles also approached and began to drink when something caught her attention. She sat watching intently, an apple raised to her mouth, the fan poised in her other hand. Prodding the trapper she said, 'Oh look, Sangasu, what's that odd looking creature down there with the other animals?'

Barely conscious until that moment, Sangasu yawned and propped himself up.

'I've never seen anything like that before,' she continued. 'If it comes this way, Sangasu, we might need your new spear.'

His countryman's eye was keener than hers and at once he knew. 'That's him!' Sangasu declared, scrambling to his feet and pointing hard. 'Lady, it's him! It's the - it *is* the one we've been waiting for.'

'What!' exclaimed the girl, the fan spiralling down from her hand. 'You mean I'm supposed to go and - and have - with -?' She turned to stare hard at Sangasu. 'No thank you!'

'Y-you must,' insisted Sangasu. 'Throw off your gown and go to him. Entice with your woman's ways. We'll both have to face Lord Gilgamesh if you don't!'

'Tut, tut,' she answered, regarding him sternly. 'It's *my* body we're talking about, not yours and nobody, you included, told me he looked like - like that!'

'The gods have a hand in this,' insisted Sangasu. 'I tell you, the gods are in him!'

'Which gods, I wonder,' responded the girl. She stared for a while at the new arrival then added, 'Very well, since we've waited all this time. Maybe I'll take a closer look – just out of interest, that's all. Since he hasn't done for you, he may not wish to harm me. Either way I intend to preserve a little decorum even in this fly-infested wilderness. I'll approach him in my own time and you, Sangasu, had better keep out of sight. Not so far away that you can't hear me shout for help, mind. And you'd better pray the gods preserve me from harm. If they don't, our dear Gilgamesh will take away more than your new cloak and spear!'

'I'll stay as low as you wish, lady,' said the trapper, backing some way along the path by which they had come, 'but just - just get on with it for both our sakes - please!'

Slipping off her sandals, the girl moved cautiously toward the water hole muttering, 'Get on with it. I like that. I should *not* be doing this. I'm being used – that's all. I must be possessed.'

And possessed she was, by an amalgam of fear and fascination as she stepped trembling behind a bush to observe the man-beast on his knees delving amongst the reeds with his head bowed to the water. Twice he raised up, looked about and sniffed the air as if sensing her perfumed presence. He behaved like an animal, yet there was something noble, something oddly familiar about him. So familiar that, after a time, curiosity overcame a fear that ought to have been greater than it presently was. Breathing deeply, clutching her apple, she stepped into the open and spoke, her voice drifting on the warm air like the beguiling notes of a flute. 'Er, good afternoon.'

The man-beast jerked his head up, twitched his nose and regarded her intently through a net of matted hair that imbued his face with a convincingly bestial appearance. From his lips emerged a low growl as, very slowly, he arose dripping from the water. The girl could see, in spite of his bedraggled condition, that he truly was a man. Utterly dishevelled, perhaps, yet wholesome and healthy. As they stared at one another she could sense no malice in him – no immediate threat, but instead perceived he was as wary of her as she was of him. She spoke again. 'Well, perhaps you would be a match for the king after all. You look as big and as powerful as Gilgamesh and,' her gaze fell to his loins, 'oh my, yes - as much a man in every sense of the word.'

Smiling, she took one step closer. The man-beast showed no sign of aggression but instead trod back a short way into the water.

'Do you know what I am, wild man? I'm a harlot from the temple of Inanna. I think you have never seen a woman like me before - is that it?'

The wild man made no sound but continued to gaze at her, his brown eyes glinting.

'Do you know of Inanna and her temple?' she continued. 'No, I'm sure you don't. I don't suppose you know anything about temples or cities. Perhaps nothing about real women from the look in your eye – a bit like poor Sangasu. Perhaps you don't understand what I'm saying.' The girl folded her arms lightly and smiled. 'Do you understand, wild man? Do you have a name?'

The wild man frowned then glanced aside to see the animals about the pool raise their heads and begin to move away.

'Well,' continued the girl, by now confident she was in no danger, 'we can't stand here all afternoon staring at each other. Tell me what you are called. If it will help I'll tell you who I am, though as one who offers the pleasures of Inanna, I usually avoid giving my name to anyone.' Still gripping the apple, she placed a hand over her breast, leaned toward him and said, 'I am called Shamkhat. That is my name - Shamkhat.'

His gaze remained on her as he prodded outstretched fingers against his chest. From his throat emerged, almost a growling, 'En-ki-du. I - En-ki-du.'

'Enkidu,' smiled the girl, tilting her head aside. 'Hmm - so that's your name is it - Enkidu.'

'Enkidu,' repeated the wild man, stepping clear of the water and lessening the distance between them to little more than an arm's length.

'Stay!' called the girl, raising her hand. 'Come no closer! Enkidu, I've been sent to offer you what men usually want and entice you to Uruk. But – but look at you. Your hair and beard are matted like trodden straw, your body and limbs fouled with mud and may the gods preserve us from what else. And your nails – they are like broken talons.'

The wild man remained silent, dripping wet in the warm breeze, a look of puzzlement on his begrimed face. The girl continued to regard him then added, 'You could be from the same mould as the king, I see that. I also see the same light in your eye but you are as odious to look at as he is pristine

66

and shining.' Still there was no response as she continued, 'I hope you haven't understood everything I said, Enkidu, dear, but I am doing my best. As for what I've been sent out here to do – sorry to be fussy but that's really out of the question for the time being. Now watch me. Note my words so each of us can earn the trust of the other. First, I will take a bite from this apple - see.'

The girl bit into her apple then held it out to him, red and well-rounded on the palm of her hand. 'Now, go on, you take a bite.'

The wild man dismissed her offer with a wave of his hand and a low grunt.

'Enkidu,' she said, coyly, sensing him even more wary of her than he had been only moments before. 'I think you still don't trust me. You're a little afraid of me, aren't you, Enkidu? Me – just a harmless girl. Well, I don't mind in the least. But this won't bite you - it's just an ordinary apple. Just an ordinary little apple. Quite as harmless as I am.'

The wild man shook his head, let out a muted growl and looked about to retreat.

'My,' said the girl, treading closer and reaching out until the apple glowed directly before his face, 'we're not afraid, are we, Enkidu? A great brute of a man like you - afraid of a woman and an apple?'

His gaze remained on her as, slowly, he reached out mud-stained fingers to touch the apple. He touched again, lifted it gently from her hand, scrutinised, sniffed it for a moment, took a tentative bite - then began to eat.

'There, Enkidu,' she smiled, 'now we can trust each other because we have shared the apple together. It came from the orchards of Uruk. See, it's your first taste of civilisation.'

About the pool, reeds swayed. The water shivered as though disturbed by an invisible hand.

A slight breeze brushed hair against her soft cheek. The wild man saw sunlight dance in her eyes. Saw her full lips slightly parted and the swell of her breasts beneath the gown. 'Woman,' breathed Enkidu.

'Yes, Enkidu - woman. I think we're beginning to understand each other. Now, get back into the pool. Wash away the dirt and the smell then come back here. Perhaps I'll be interested after all - perhaps I won't. Go on or I leave right now.'

Amused and greatly reassured by his docile behaviour, Shamkhat stood, arms folded, watching whilst he did as she asked, ducking then sluicing himself down in the middle of the pool where the water was clear. Once finished, once free of dirt, he hauled himself out by the overhanging rock to avoid poolside mud, then returned dripping wet to stand before her in the warm breeze.

'Oh, that *is* an improvement,' she smiled, seeing before her a man who, given the chance, might appear as presentable – almost – as many in Uruk. 'Now try to understand - in the wagon I have food and a little beer left from Uruk to share with you. I have perfumed oil to cleanse and soothe your skin and a bronze razor to get rid of that unsightly hair on your face. You're a challenge, Enkidu – I don't get that many. And provided you behave as I ask, I will attend to you well.'

She walked away from him then turned around, casually loosening her gown enough to expose her firm breasts. When she continued on the wild man followed, glancing from side to side, well aware of the hunter concealed nearby.

In the confined space of her wagon she attended to him as she had promised – as she would a noble of Uruk newly returned from the hunt and needing the soft, caring touch of a woman. To her surprise she found him meek and trusting - even when she took the bronze razor to his cheek.

'Well now,' Shamkhat smiled as he knelt before her, his arousal becoming obvious, 'I see I have a real man and not one looking quite so wild.'

She let the gown slip away completely to reveal to him for the first time the allure of a naked woman. Enkidu seized the gown and held it to his face. He breathed deeply the perfume of the one who led him so irresistibly on. At first it perplexed. Then it fascinated. Then it intoxicated. Enkidu experienced urges that further excited yet confused him. When he raised his head to stare at her Shamkhat was reclining on her cushions, the smile once more on slightly parted lips.

Through the remaining afternoon they lay together in the wagon then through the warm night beneath bright stars. Later, having returned to the wagon, there were voices and dreams. Drifting shadows. Dark birds that rose up in panic. Raging lions. When the sky lightened he awoke knowing there was another world beyond that which he knew.

'Oh, Enkidu,' she whispered in his ear, 'did my mind deceive me?' She ran fingers about his cheek, his shoulders then down his naked back. 'You cannot be the wild creature I recall meeting

69

yesterday. You are truly a man, handsome and wholesome. The gods surely *are* at work here.'

Sangasu returned, crouching low so as not to be observed. He watched them leave the wagon. Watched them walk together in the morning sun. Saw for himself the transformation of Enkidu. Returning later in the day, he watched them bathe at the pool but remained hidden as they sat down in the shade of the wagon to embrace in their nakedness. Then smitten with shame, touched with raw envy, he drew back and hurried away.

Enkidu shared what little remained of the beer with her, at first finding it distasteful. Occasionally he drank from the pool but little food passed his lips when he discovered his humanity in full. His desire for nourishment was held at bay by the fires of lust the girl had ignited.

It was after their return from walking in the hills the following day, during a time of relaxation, a time before passion consumed them once more that Shamkhat said, 'Enkidu, the beast has gone and the man has awakened. You talk to me. You understand much of what I say. I believe that knowledge must have been within you from the very beginning. And – Enkidu, dear,' she sighed, running fingers down his chest, 'what a gentle and satisfying lover you are. Why, I believe I have unlocked a casket of wonderful secrets. This has been all so unreal, but - but I'm so very glad.'

In Enkidu the girl had discovered a man trusting, untainted by greed or malice. One strange, yet so very familiar.

'Yes,' sighed Enkidu, as they sat close together at the rise where she had first spotted him, 'my

70

understanding was there all the time, though I cannot say how or why. I feel I have passed through a portal though it is one I never saw.'

'You must have memories of your childhood, whispered Shamkhat, 'and the place you came from. Surely you must.'

'Memories?' he answered, as a reddening sun touched the horizon and spectral gazelles traversed a distant haze. 'Yes, I have memories. Before I ran with the beasts my memories are through the eyes of others, as if I peer into deep waters. I remember where the rivers broaden, where they are shallow, where sands emerge to glisten in the sun. All I knew until you touched me were the herds, the grasslands and forests that went on seemingly forever. Yes, forests where a presence dwells that made me know the meaning of fear.'

'A presence?' she asked, feeling him stir with unease.

'I will not speak of it now. I prefer to think about the city and the things you described there as we walked the hills.'

'And soon, Enkidu, you will see the city, the rich fields and the canals. You will wonder at the great temples and the palaces. You'll be fascinated by the workshops where our people make wonderful things of gold and silver, of copper and ivory - and by the goods brought in by merchants from faraway lands. You will see the priests at their ceremonies, the colours and the young people in their fine clothes and perfumes. You have tasted pleasure with me, Enkidu - only tasted, I say, because in Uruk a feast awaits. You will draw the young women of the town like gazelles to the water hole, I know it. The girls of the temple will vie for your attention and you will forget about me.' She sighed and rested a cheek against his shoulder. 'There are people who say you can have too much of a good thing, dear Enkidu, but I confess I have never seen it that way. I won't be sorry to leave this wild place and return to civilisation.'

'I am not so sure,' breathed Enkidu. 'What you have told me glows like a star in my mind but it is a star that casts shadows of deceit and greed. The beasts have been my companions. They have hidden nothing. That's why I protected them from the hunter and trapper who brought you here; because I lived as they live. I cannot deny my wish to see Uruk but might not the city imprison me as surely as those traps set by him for those luckless creatures? In the morning I will run with the beasts again to savour the measure of my freedom. Perhaps then I will know what I must do.'

In the darkness Shamkhat smiled. Her fingers alighted upon him as fire-moths. The fires spread. The fires consumed. Soon, their cries of passion would take flight on the night air.

***

Morning sunlight had barely touched the hills when Enkidu left her side. At first feigning sleep, Shamkhat sat up to watch from her wagon as Enkidu made his way to the water hole where the gazelles already gathered. She saw, too, that as he moved closer they raised their heads and darted away. Startled as though a lion had appeared. In their wake sprinted Enkidu, trying to catch up but falling behind then stumbling to a halt. She pulled on her gown, slipped from the wagon and hurried to the water hole. There she watched him take up the chase again. Saw him zigzag from side to side then falter and throw up his arms before sprawling face down amidst sparse grass with the breath wrung from him. Enkidu struggled to his knees, clutched at the ground, tore up grass and earth with his hands before hurling it aside and turning his gaze to the water hole where Shamkhat waited.

'Enkidu!' she called. 'Enkidu!'

Enkidu started back, hesitating, stopping every few paces to glance over his shoulder. But the wild creatures were no longer to be seen. The manner of his progress told her how dispirited he must be. As he drew close she saw reproach in his eyes. When he stood before her she listened quietly as he sighed, 'They no longer know me. They no longer want me among them. Fear drove them away quicker than I could run. What has happened to me? What spell have you cast?'

His strength for the moment spent, Enkidu slumped to the ground at her feet and Shamkhat replied, 'I have cast no spell, Enkidu. Once you came to know me, you discovered what had been yours all along. You can never return to the beasts. Never. A greater claim is now yours.'

'How can that be when I have lost all I knew - all the trust, all the companionship I had?'

'No, dear Enkidu,' she replied, kneeling beside him on the grass to slip an arm over his shoulder, 'your eyes are opened. Now you are beginning to see what others take for granted. And the pleasures you have yet to find will be all the greater for it. You are stronger than any man except Lord Gilgamesh yet unlike him you are free of pride and boasting. Wisdom settles like a cloak about your broad shoulders as the days pass. There are many in Uruk who will gladly be your companion. There are many who will welcome your arrival.'

Enkidu stared at the ground a while before looking up at her.

'But what of this Gilgamesh?' he asked, taking her hand in his. 'You say he's lord of Uruk, you say he picks its fruits and sets its clay in whatever manner takes his fancy. That bodes ill, for though it seems I must accept the world you offer, I will never bow in servitude.'

'Lay such thoughts aside for now,' she answered, squeezing his hand. 'We must ready the ox and prepare ourselves to leave whilst the day is young. I will give you a linen cloth to wear then I must bid farewell to Sangasu and his family before we begin our journey home.'

'Home?' he breathed, glancing over his shoulder.

'Yes, and I hope by then, Enkidu, dear, you'll have stopped snoring in your sleep. Sometimes you sound like a big, contented cat – other times more like a vexed bull!'

***

With a veil to protect her face from the sun and a loose robe of fine, soft wool, the girl sat beside him as Enkidu turned the wagon about. For the last time he looked across to the water hole. There he observed a lion that had come down to drink. 'See - there is the new lord of these lands now I'm gone.'

'You will forget your life in the wild soon enough,' she smiled. 'But, Enkidu, we only have three days and two nights together and there is so much you need to learn. In the day I'll explain more about the manners and customs of Uruk. In the night our ecstasy will mingle with the stars. Our pleasures will be all the greater because they must soon end. Though – though their ending is not what I care to think about.'

Enkidu laughed, 'Yes, my lady of the city, if it was not for your company I think I might fly like a bird to this Uruk of yours just to be there all the sooner. Now my path has become clear I'm impatient to see everything!'

'You laughed,' said Shamkhat. 'It's the first time I've heard you do that.'

'Yes, I think so, too. The first time.'

Their wagon rumbled through the heat of the day. Shamkhat talked about Uruk and its people, the war with their old enemy, Kish, and the victory of Gilgamesh over its king, the contemptible Agga who claimed hegemony over all Sumer including the holy city of Nippur. Enkidu listened intently and when the sun was well past its zenith, when the land shimmered afternoon heat, he said, 'Tell me about the gods of Sumer. You have said more than once that such knowledge is given to everyone in the land - but it has never been mine.'

'Very well, I'll explain to you what every parent tells their child but don't expect too much of me. I may live within the temple precinct but affairs of the spirit were never my main concern. To tell the truth, I think our priests believe far less of what they preach than do the simple people who listen to them. Even so, this is what they say: First and above all is Anu, whose temple stands in Uruk. He is ruler of the gods and lord of the heavens. To him the gods and goddesses owe their domains in the land of Sumer. Partner of Anu is Ninhursag. Some say she is mother of all the gods. From her came the green fields, the crops and the fruit. Her greatest temple was built by the people of Kish. In the town of Ur the temple of Nanna rises above all others. He shines as sovereign of the night. There is the great lord, Enlil, whose temple stands in holy Nippur and is a place of pilgrimage for all the people of Sumer even though King Agga has armed men stationed there. Enlil is regent of Anu and holds power over earth, wind and sky. Ruler of the deep waters and father of wisdom, the arts and things that are created, is Enki. You would see his temple if you went to the ancient town of Eridu. Amongst the Seven who decree our fates is our own Inanna, Queen of Heaven, from whose temple I was sent out to find you. You have enjoyed her gifts with me, Enkidu, but you ought to know she is also goddess of war and is even more fickle and jealous than the rest. Utu, the shining sun, is bringer of justice. For his worship, Sippar and Larsa each have a temple.'

With the mention of each god or goddess Enkidu nodded, 'Oh, I see,' or, 'Yes, I'll try to remember.'

'Then,' Shamkhat continued, 'you should know about the dark one - Ereshkigal - she of the dread eye, who rules the underworld. There is Dumuzi, the cast off husband of Inanna, who is the growth and decay of the seasons and so passes back and forth between heaven and the place of grim silence where -'

'Stop!' laughed Enkidu. 'No more! My head is not large enough to hold them all and your account could take up the rest of our day. Why, I thought I knew many of them - the spirits that dwell with the creatures, those that move amongst the hills and the groves. And there is the beast that protects the great forest, but you have mentioned none of these.'

'No, Enkidu, the ones you speak of are minor beings that roam uncounted over the land. I tell you about the greatest - those who rule above all others. It's most confusing, I know. Even the priests cannot always agree if one is wife or daughter, or is the child or sister of another. I find it easier not to think of them at all - that way I avoid confusing myself.'

'Well, once we're in Uruk I'll listen to what others say about these matters until I'm wiser. If they laugh at my ignorance I shall remain silent. I have the strength that has always been mine and that will not be diminished.'

'In Uruk you will need that strength,' said Shamkhat. 'You said no man will be your master but no man will be master in Uruk except Gilgamesh. He fears nothing in this world except -.'

'Except?' queried Enkidu as she fell silent.

Her expression told him she regretted the remark even as it left her lips. For a while he thought she would remain silent but when she did reply, it was not an answer he expected.

'He fears the sick, the maimed and the aged. He avoids them whenever he can. It's – it's as if he fears their malaise. He acts as if their infirmity will reach out and taint him. When the mood takes him, our priests and the city elders may not approach closer than is necessary - not even at our ceremonies. I've heard people say he's incapable of pity though I think not. Well - not entirely. It surprised everyone who knew about it when he allowed poor Sangasu into his presence. He has never experienced real grief or suffering at close hand except for what he has inflicted on our enemies, and so he doesn't always appreciate what it can mean to others. It's in the company of the young and strong that Gilgamesh is most at ease and though of late he behaves as a tyrant he is not deep down an evil man – not like the Man of Kish. That you must understand.'

'And this Agga, this Man of Kish – you say he is a worse ruler than your Gilgamesh. How can that be?'

'Agga is a fiend,' she replied, with unease in her voice. 'He rules through his extended family. His brothers and his closer relatives all hold positions of power at Kish. They furnish his generals and the priesthood of his temples. No one would dare question his actions. No one would dare present their grievances at the temples of Kish as did the people of Uruk at my own. It is even forbidden to look him directly in the eye. Those who displease him suffer terribly. It is said even members of his own family are executed for disobedience. Others are blinded and maimed, then confined to crawl in the foul vaults beneath his palace. I doubt that Gilgamesh would ever condone that – in spite of his undoubted failings. And it is only Gilgamesh who could protect Uruk and bring Agga down.'

'Even so, should Gilgamesh not care for his people - more so those who suffer through old age and misfortune? Isn't that why he is lord of Uruk? It seems to me your king is a man who seeks glory for himself whatever the cost.'

'Many would agree, but no man would care to put that to him – except, perhaps, you.'

'Aye,' replied Enkidu, 'I'll tell him whether he wishes to hear it or not, then your mighty Gilgamesh will have to choose if he is to be my friend or my enemy. If he welcomes me as a friend and will hear what I say, then I'll have a comrade worthy of my strength. Should he bar my way then I'll bring him down to the dust. And if all you say is true, the people of Uruk will thank me for it.'

The girl smiled, kissed his rough cheek and retired from the heat of the day into the cooler shade of the wagon where she settled for a while. Closing her eyes, Shamkhat listened to the steady plod of the ox, to the rumble of heavy wooden wheels on sun-baked ground, to the creaking framework of the wagon. Her thoughts spilled out as a sigh. 'Ah, Enkidu, you are like a child whose life is only just unfolding. Your affections cannot begin and end with me though I have become more than a little fond of you. Too fond by far, I think.'

Soon, she was adrift on a calm-flowing river of sleep.

There was silence when she woke up. The wagon had stopped and through the fabric, she observed the sun well down on the horizon. Enkidu sat with a hand raised to shade his eyes and as she joined him he pointed into the distance. 'See, there are people over there, wagons, tents and animals. And there is smoke rising.'

'They are nomadic shepherds and hunters,' said the girl. 'They cross the wilder lands because they are forbidden to graze their animals on pastures owned by the temples or men of the cities who mistrust them. Enkidu, we should go to them and buy food. What I have left may not satisfy you and may not last out our journey. I can offer them payment for beer, bread and barley soup if that's what they have.'

***

They began to gather in their course-woven kilts and gowns. 'Who are these people?' asked the grizzled, grey-bearded elder shepherd, his watery eyes squinting from beneath a gnarled hand.

'It's a man and a woman,' replied one of the younger and sharper sighted among them. Others emerged from their tents of stitched hides to join them.

'That wagon belongs to one of the cities,' said another. 'It is not a merchant's wagon nor are they ordinary travellers.'

'They might be tax collectors!' exclaimed the elder shepherd. 'If that's what they are then we must look to our spears! They prey upon us as wolves wherever we pitch camp!'

'I don't reckon they're tax collectors,' replied the younger shepherd. 'No tax collector would travel out here with a woman – no, he'd have an armed guard. The man doesn't have that mean and grasping look about him, either. Looks to me like a nobleman though he's not wearing any finery.'

'He's as big and powerful a man as I ever saw,' remarked another, 'I say we let the spears lie and offer them hospitality - as long as that's all they're after.'

***

'They're gathering to meet us,' observed Shamkhat. 'I don't think they are hostile.'

Enkidu took the wagon on, approaching the small group and stopping no closer than the long shadows cast by them. The shepherds stood in silence as Enkidu swung from his seat to the ground, reached up and helped Shamkhat down to his side. No one could fail to note the stature and bearing of Enkidu. No one could ignore the alluring beauty of his companion.

'These are people of a noble house,' muttered one. 'Just catch a whiff of that wagon.'

'Then where's their retinue?' queried another. 'Nobles would have a retinue.'

But the elder shepherd had already decided and dropped awkwardly to one knee. Seeing the others follow his example, he declared, 'Lord, you have come upon poor but honest people with little to offer though we'll gladly share what we have with you.'

'I am Enkidu,' came the reply, 'and this woman is from the temple in Uruk. We ask only for enough to eat and drink to help us on our journey to the city.'

'We will pay in silver of Uruk for whatever we take,' added Shamkhat.

'Then you must eat with us,' insisted the elder shepherd. 'There is sweet water close by and you are welcome to a tent for the coming night should you wish it. Darkness is not far away.'

Enkidu accepted the offer with a simple, 'That is kind of you.'

Further discussion having settled the matter, he and Shamkhat were offered fermented milk in baked clay mugs then left for a time to watch the shepherds hurry about their business.

Shamkhat turned to Enkidu. 'I know something of these people. Their diet is simple but good and nourishing. What they cannot glean from the land they must trade for though they are not welcomed in the cities.'

'Not welcome - why?' asked Enkidu.

'Because what they cannot trade for they will sometimes steal. Often they will take sheep, so our livestock must be guarded. Yet to other travellers they are often generous. It is their way.'

Children ran here and there, some stopping to gaze in awe at the newcomers. Unseen babies cried. Dogs yapped. Goats and sheep bleated whilst captive wild birds squawked in wicker cages. An odour of cooking food drifted from small clay ovens smoking close to the main tent. Shamkhat estimated the camp must hold some twenty adult males plus their women and children.

She and Enkidu were ushered into the main tent and there invited to sit on woollen rugs, making up part of a packed circle with their hosts and their women around a smoking and not altogether pleasant-smelling fire. Much of the smoke, Enkidu noted, found its way out through a circular aperture in the top of the tent. Baked clay beakers were handed around then two of the shepherds ladled out rough beer from a jar carried between them. Young boys and girls pushed inside carrying beaten copper dishes bearing unleavened bread, goat's cheese, pieces of roasted wildfowl and sweet onions. One of these was set down before each adult. More drink in plain jugs was brought into the tent and set around the interior so as to be within everyone's reach.

Noting this, Shamkhat turned to Enkidu, saying, 'Enkidu, you must not drink too much beer. You are not used to it.'

Conversation quietened. Then ceased. Attention turned to the new guests. Shamkhat realised the shepherds were waiting out of politeness for she and Enkidu to begin their meal. Enkidu sensed it also and, clearly ill at ease, looked about the crowded tent to see what others would do. With the fire illuminating their faces and only the crack of flames breaking the silence, all eyes were on him. No one spoke. No one moved.

'Does the food not please our noble lord?' asked the elder shepherd at last.

'Please me?' answered Enkidu, glancing with consternation from the old man to Shamkhat. 'I am sure it will please me - I, er -'

'Enkidu,' she whispered, 'what is the matter? Take the food or you will offend these good people. They dine lavishly by their standards to honour us and can ill afford it.'

Enkidu leaned close and whispered, 'I have hunted with the beasts for my meat, dug roots from the earth and drunk at the water hole where you found me. How do I eat this food? It cannot be as I once did.'

'Enkidu,' she replied, coolly, 'stop fidgeting. You know by now how to eat with your fingers. Watch what I do, and then do likewise. Sit upright and remain calm.'

Enkidu sat awkwardly whilst, smiling at the shepherds, Shamkhat said, 'Please excuse us. We have a custom that requires we decline from eating first. Lord Enkidu did not wish to cause offence and so asked me to inform you of it before he begins.'

'The ways of city people are strange to us,' replied the elder shepherd, 'but this is a custom I never heard of. Be assured, we take no offence but would rather ourselves wait for your lord to begin out of our respect for him.'

'Ah,' insisted Shamkhat, 'our custom says that it is he who must wait for you. For us, the greater a man is, the more respect and humility he is obliged to show before his hosts. Lord Enkidu would consider himself ill-mannered - no, deeply shamed if he did not offer that respect to everyone gathered here. Please, begin eating and we will gratefully follow.'

'Pity there aren't a few more like him in the cities,' muttered one young man.

After some hesitation they began, much to the relief of Enkidu, who sighed and picked up his bowl, glad of the dim light within the tent that prevented their seeing how unnatural he found what the rest accomplished with unthinking ease.

'I should have explained about this during our journey,' said Shamkhat as general conversation revived, 'but I did not expect to meet anyone. Eat and drink slowly - a little at a time, especially the beer. A nobleman should never appear to hurry when taking his meal.'

'And that's how your mighty Gilgamesh eats?' he responded.

'He manages to behave like a gentleman on such occasions, if not on others,' responded

Shamkhat. 'If you intend to equal him you must do so in manner as well as deed.'

Pondering her words, Enkidu at last relaxed, glad to find himself no longer the focus of everyone's attention. And though the meal had begun quietly, the shepherds were soon chattering, laughing loudly and calling back and forth to one another across the tent.

As the evening wore on, she became aware of how much beer Enkidu had accounted for. Aware, too, that he smiled broadly and talked too readily, on occasion stumbling in mid-sentence, unable to finish what he had begun to say. More beer was brought in, the nomads' entire supply for which they must have traded goods and labour, thought Shamkhat. Meanwhile, Enkidu's grin had become a mask that had no wish to be removed. The voices of those around him rose and fell but their words had become meaningless babble - unlike the voice of Shamkhat when she leaned aside to hiss in his ear, 'Enkidu – drink no more beer. Please! They indulge themselves readily because we are here but *you* are not used to it.'

Enkidu looked about with hands pressed flat against the ground to steady himself. Surely the tent was moving. Surely they were on a broad river. Enkidu laughed and continued to talk without knowing quite what he said or why he said it. The elder shepherds, their own beakers laid aside, watched amused as the voice of Shamkhat scorched his ear. 'Enkidu, you've drunk so much. Your face is red as a pomegranate! Our hosts need their beds but will not depart until we do. We must give them our thanks and leave now. I say, now!'

'I have no - I have no wish to leave,' grinned Enkidu, attempting to focus on her.

'Enkidu,' she insisted, 'you will make me angry and if you do that I will leave and return to my wagon. Remain here and you'll become a fool in the eyes of these people. You may imagine yourself a strong bull but they will see a silly ass who is not even master of his own limbs and his own tongue! You hope to stand against Gilgamesh - remember? Why, if he walked in here now he'd trample you under his feet and everyone would laugh!'

Her remonstrations were enough. Enkidu knew humiliation. With Shamkhat's help, he rose unsteadily to his feet, his free arm swaying in the air to effect a gesture of farewell, though the words he mumbled were quite incoherent.

***

'There's a demon in my head,' groaned Enkidu, fingers splayed hard to his face. 'I feel it moving about - kicking its feet against my skull.'

Sunlight spilled into the tent. Shamkhat had already risen. Outside the tent people called to one another, children chased barking dogs and possessions were being gathered to load onto asses.

'It's the demon you invited in,' she replied, kneeling close by. 'It lives in jars of rough beer and springs into your mouth when you drink too much. Once you've eaten and walked in the fresh air it may creep away and hide or it may not. You have only yourself to blame if it doesn't.'

As they emerged from the tent, others were at work under a cool morning sky, gathering in sheep and goats. Across the camp drifted smoke from the cooking fires where the women sat, some heating

86

barley porridge in clay bowls, others pressing barley dough against the sides of heated pots to make course bread. The elder shepherd, waiting a short distance from the tent, saw them and walked over. 'Lord Enkidu! You are soon to go on your way and we, too, will move on. But you must not set out before taking your first meal of the day with us.'

'Why do you wish to leave this land so soon?' asked Enkidu as they joined others to squat about the fire. 'The pasture about here is good for many days and the wells provide sweet water.'

'Yes, the pasture is good,' answered the elder shepherd, 'but we must continue on for the safety of our flocks and ourselves. There are lions hereabouts - for several days they have followed us. We've seen our sheep and goats seized and devoured before our eyes. There is one, a ferocious brute - their leader. He comes close to our tents. All our young men who have spears are needed to keep him back. He's killed one of them already and now has a taste for human flesh. Since that time it is he who kills and not the females, as used to be. We fear some day he will take one of our women or children. There are too few of us to bear such losses.'

'The beasts of the wild must also eat to live,' breathed Enkidu.

Seated around the fire they discussed the land, also the wild creatures; subjects which no one understood better than Enkidu, though he avoided boasting of his knowledge. On the air drifted the bleat of sheep and goat, and the clatter of baked clay bells as the animals were herded together. Louder still carried the shouts of the young men and boys, and the constant yap of their scrawny dogs.

Another cry rose above the rest, urgent and distressed, as a boy burst in panic from amongst the milling livestock, arms waving wildly above his head. In the midst of the camp he stopped to yell out, 'The lions! The lions are coming!'

The three scrambled to their feet and were quickly joined by others. Enkidu, taller by a head than the rest, saw at once - one male and two female lions. The two females remained some distance away whilst the male approached, crouching close to the ground, part hidden by bushes and stands of tall grass. Enkidu gazed with a keen eye as the big male moved closer. The sheep, having sensed danger, jostled and bleated primal fear. Very soon the lion would be close enough to spring among them and seize his victim.

Three mop-haired young men pushed through, each brandishing a wooden, flint-tipped spear hardly greater in length than himself. The shepherds murmured anxious approval - from the women arose a babble of anguish.

'They carry all the good spears we have left,' said the elder shepherd. 'The others were broken in defence of our flocks when our man was slain.'

Enkidu watched the three move away, watched them spread apart and level their spears. Sensing the youths' approach, the lion raised a thick-maned head. Eyeing them, it let out a growl that boomed thunder over the small camp. Up it raised then circled about until positioned within striking distance. The three youths were now to be its prey instead of the sheep. Exposed on open ground, they hesitated, standing to face the lion as it moved closer. In a moment it would choose which of them to take and then would charge. One of the youths, fearing what was about to happen, raised an arm, cried out and hurled his spear. It flashed through the air but the lion pranced aside to avoid the weapon.

'Oh, he should not have done that,' groaned the elder shepherd. 'He should have kept a grip on that spear for when the beast was closer.'

The three young men huddled together intent upon retreat but the lion trotted with casual gait to take up position between them and the camp. A cry arose from shepherds as the lion crouched low, judged its distance, flexed its muscles and twitched its tail. It was about to leap forward. About to seize his victim. One of them it would drag away, torn and bleeding, to fill the bellies of itself and its kind.

The shepherds were distraught. Some prayed loudly to their gods, others averted their eyes or fell to the ground, too horrified to watch. The women wept in despair.

Enkidu stepped forward. Enkidu strode out from the crowd.

'No!' yelled Shamkhat pushing through. 'No, Enkidu! No-no-no!'

But Enkidu ignored her. Defiance shone in his eyes. He let out a growl of bestial aggression and sprinted toward the lion. His cry grew until it possessed him mind and body. Once more he was the man-beast. The lion raised up and spun about. It knew Enkidu. Enkidu knew the lion.

'The brute will tear him apart!' shouted someone, but Enkidu bounded on as the lion growled annihilation, tensed and sprang at this foolhardy creature whose newfound humanity betokened his death. Enkidu avoided the deadly leap. Avoided outspread claws and glaring teeth. Spun about then with a yell hurled himself onto the creature's back. Grasping the mane he bestrode the beast, gripped it hard with his legs, clawed forward to seize the jaws with powerful hands, seize and wrench them wide apart. The lion reared in a tumult-hail of grit, his fury shivering the air. The two flailed in whirlwind struggle but Enkidu would not release his hold. Enkidu would not be torn free. 'Now!' cried Enkidu, 'Now!'

Seizing their chance, the two young men with spears darted forward and, seeing the jaws open and the throat bared they struck hard. The first plunged his spear into the lion's neck, the other drove his blade deep into the hissing-cauldron mouth. They struck again and again. Mortal blows they dealt as the beast raged, red-jawed and venting blood. The lion would have broken off, would have fled back to its own, but Enkidu held on grimly as with yells of triumph the two struck deeper. The creature weakened until with a snarl of anguish it sank to the ground, gasping its life into dust-swirling air.

Only now did Shamkhat lift hands from her eyes.

Enkidu, naked, blood-stained and dishevelled, raised himself from the creature's visibly quivering body. He stepped away without a backward look. The three young men followed at a distance as, glancing at bloodied hands, Enkidu walked slowly back to the camp with the eyes of the shepherds fixed upon him in awed silence.

'This is no ordinary mortal!' rang out the voice of the elder shepherd as Enkidu passed by. 'The very gods are in this man!'

Men, women and children fell to their knees, chanting aloud their gratitude as if addressing the immortals themselves. From their midst hurried Shamkhat, hands outstretched to take his arm, her face wet with tears. 'Oh, Enkidu, I thought you were lost! You have saved these people and their precious sons. Are you much hurt?'

'I take no pride in it,' retorted Enkidu, ignoring her question. 'The creature I brought to his death was once a companion. Now I have betrayed him.'

'But you have saved the lives of others. You have won the gratitude of these people. And that lion - he would have killed you as surely as he would have killed their sons.'

Enkidu remained silent. Shamkhat gazed into his eyes, saying, 'Come with me to the well. Let me wash away the blood and dirt. Let me tend your skin with oil so you can appear before the shepherds as their saviour because that is what you are.'

***

'He is resting a while,' informed Shamkhat as, later that morning, the shepherds gathered with their elder about the tent.

'We must offer him the best we are able to give,' said the elder shepherd. 'We are all agreed that, poor as we may be, whatever he asks of us shall be his.'

'He will take nothing from you, I know it,' replied Shamkhat. 'It is not in his heart to expect a reward. But there's something I wish for him on my own behalf.'

'Then tell us your wish,' responded the elder.

'You considered him a noble, and a noble man indeed he is, but his nobility lies within and not through his possessions. He has no worldly goods and never did have. I ask you to make clothes for him from the hides you have ready to trade. Clothes worthy of his stature and his dignity. A kilt, a tunic and sandals - stout sandals that will last him well. I'll pay you in silver – more than the hides would have gained you in the marketplace.'

'We'll accept nothing from you,' answered the elder shepherd. 'Payment beyond counting is made by the saving of our young men's lives. Our camp will remain here as long as needs be now the beast that afflicted us is dead. I will bring our women together. We will make for this good man of yours a suit of clothes fit for a warrior. When he steps through the gate of Uruk they will know him for the hero he truly is.'

***

At the tent where the women toiled, Shamkhat oversaw the making of Enkidu's clothes. She watched them cut the hides with their flint blades and marvelled at their skills with copper awl, bone needle and leather thong as the kilt and cape took form. The skin of the slain lion was also being prepared for Enkidu to use as he pleased, though only in the city could the odious process be completed.

Three days would pass before the work was finished. Three days before their thoughts would return to Uruk and to Gilgamesh.

CHAPTER 3
CLASH OF THE MIGHTY

The sky to the east was lightening when she was roused by voices close by. Shamkhat lay for a while, listening. Then Enkidu opened his eyes and asked, 'Who is outside our tent?'

'Strangers have arrived in the camp attracted by the sight of our wagon,' she replied. 'Now they are asking about it and about us. They are merchants on their way to Uruk and have to be there in time for a ceremony.'

'Going to Uruk,' remarked Enkidu. 'Then their presence gives us all the more reason to be on our way, though I have been content these past few days.'

'And I, dear Enkidu,' she sighed, kissing him. 'No greater contentment have I known – except when you dashed out to wrestle with that lion.'

'We ought to discover their business,' said Enkidu. 'You must ask what they're about as you understand the affairs of merchants and the city.'

'Yes, the nomads will tell the merchants who we are, then the merchants will tell them in Uruk and Gilgamesh will get to know. He will not have forgotten my errand and he won't be too pleased when he finds out how much time we've spent here. I'll go to the well then over to my wagon and I'll see what I can find out.'

From a gap in the tent, Enkidu watched her set off to the well dug by the shepherds. And as he watched he thought of what she had told him about Uruk. About its king, about its people and the girls

93

who she claimed would so readily seek his company. Shamkhat was the only woman he had known. It seemed to him there could never be another. Did she think the same about him? No, how could she when to her he must still possess the mind of a child. Several times Enkidu whispered her name.

He turned his attention now to the strangers with their string of five, well-laden asses. There was a hook-nosed older man in white linen gown and cap. His hair was braided, his eyes narrow, his skin the texture of crumpled leather. With him were the two younger men, short-haired and naked to the waist, and a third, dressed as they were but shaven-headed, well-built and black-skinned.

Seeing her pass by, Enkidu next visited the well then returned to observe Shamkhat, fresh from her wagon and in conversation with the older man. The merchant noticed a shadow fall across the ground and turned as Enkidu said, 'I hear you are travelling to Uruk. We are also going there.'

'He has already told me about his business,' said Shamkhat. 'His asses carry herbs and spices for the banquet as well as resins and perfumes of Egypt for the guests.'

'That is so,' said the merchant. 'And I carry bales of finest Egyptian linen for the ladies of the court. I was sent to trade with the men of the west who cross the desert and set up market on the furthest borders of our lands. The granddaughter of Kuraka, a noble of Uruk is soon to be married. He is her guardian now because her father was killed in battle when Uruk and Kish were at war.'

'I know Kuraka and the girl,' frowned Shamkhat. 'He is an owner of land and property, and speaks for the elders in Uruk. His granddaughter is a trusting little innocent.'

'Why do you talk about them with sadness?' asked Enkidu.

'You may well ask, sir,' responded the merchant, before Shamkhat could reply. 'I was telling your lady how the other day we exchanged news with men travelling west from Sumer. They said a dark cloud already settles over the marriage because of -.' The merchant hesitated, gazed quizzically at Enkidu. 'Sir, you're a big man and appear not unlike the lord of Uruk. If I saw you going about the city I might assume you were one of the king's house. Are you, er –.'

'No I'm not,' laughed Enkidu, 'and if you wish to discuss his affairs you need have no fear on my account. From what I hear of him I doubt this Gilgamesh could ever be a friend of mine.'

'Many in Uruk would agree with you of late,' said the merchant, 'especially Kuraka who never much liked him anyway. It is the shadow of Gilgamesh that darkens the happy occasion. If no one steps forward to prevent him, he will take the girl to his bed before her wedding. He claims this as his right by custom, which of course it is, though by that same custom another may challenge that right. However, I doubt anyone will.'

'Is that so,' responded Enkidu.

'Indeed it is, sir,' exclaimed the merchant, raising his hands wide, 'because they dare not!'

'Oh, dare they not!' growled Enkidu. 'Well, the more I hear of this ill-behaved man, the more impatient I am to meet him!'

'Are you saying y*ou* intend to confront the king of Uruk?' asked the merchant in wide-eyed disbelief.

'That I may do. He imagines himself one of your gods. I think he is a man like other men. One having such power as his ought to behave with modesty.'

'Well, sir,' grinned the merchant, 'Lord Gilgamesh enjoys nothing more than a challenge, be it in love or war. He has to prove himself and when he triumphs he considers the challenge cannot have been great enough or that the outcome was contrived, so he has to prove himself yet again.'

'When will you be in Uruk?' asked Enkidu, his eye hard on the man.

'If we rest here a while to refresh ourselves and do not hurry, we will be at the south gate by the middle of tomorrow. That will give us ample time to deliver our goods, collect due payment then conduct further business at the market.'

'Then we must leave now and be in Uruk ahead of you,' declared Enkidu.

'We'll leave soon enough,' said Shamkhat. 'But, Enkidu, first there is a gift you must accept from the shepherds for the lives you saved.'

'A gift?' replied Enkidu. 'No, I have no need of a gift. They made us welcome in their camp. That is enough for me.'

'Enkidu,' she responded, sternly, 'these people will be deeply offended if you don't accept - and so will I! So please come along and don't argue. A hero should behave with dignity.'

'But not be ordered about by a woman,' he muttered. Though still he followed her.

A wry smile crossed the merchant's face as he watched Enkidu, meek as a lamb, walk behind the girl into the main tent. Turning to his companions he said, 'Now if anyone is to stand up to the Man of Uruk it could well be that fellow. If so, it's a spectacle I intend not to miss.'

***

'They feel strange on me,' smiled Enkidu, adjusting the kilt. 'They will deny me the cool breeze and the sun's warmth.'

'Sir,' replied the elder shepherd, 'all except the highest in the city will look upon the wearer of these garments with envy. Patterned finery may be good enough for those whose greatest labour is the exertion of their mouths or in raising their goblets but you are a man of great deeds and ought to dress as one!'

'Even I won't mind being seen at your side in the streets of Uruk now,' laughed Shamkhat. 'The fancy clothes some of them wear can be yours later if you prefer, I'm sure.'

'Finery - no, I think not, and I'm grateful to you for these clothes. I will wear them with pride as we enter Uruk. And it is to the city we must soon go.'

'Your ox is harnessed and waiting,' said the elder shepherd. 'Our people are gathered to bid you farewell. I think our merchant friends felt altogether ignored because they filled their flasks from the well then left in something of a hurry.'

'They are gone already?' responded Shamkhat.

'They are indeed,' replied the shepherd. 'Gone and out of sight for some time.'

'We will never catch up with them,' said Shamkhat. 'That means Uruk will expect us,'

'And Gilgamesh,' added Enkidu, 'he will also know we're on our way.'

***

The shepherds had bundled their tents and were ready to move on as Enkidu took the ox and wagon eastwards. For the rest of the day they travelled, meeting no one but seeing birds that Enkidu knew thrived in the land of the two rivers.

Next morning saw them enter pasturelands where the temple flocks were tended, then the newly harvested fields. Enkidu looked across the canals, lined with tall date palms and the irrigation ditches threading muddy water amongst the crops. He observed people going about their labours - more people by far than he had ever imagined. And in the distance there stood the city, bright beneath a blue sky. Shamkhat had several times described the white rampart that protected Uruk, the sun-blazed cornice of Eanna's upper precinct and the dazzling temple of Inanna that soared even higher above it. To Enkidu the city was a vision of wonder.

Once over the river, once amidst the noise and bustle outside the Southern Gate, Enkidu slowed the wagon to a halt. Outside the gate sat a number of white-robed scribes with reeds and clay tablets. These men were occupied in conducting their business with merchants and traders who wished their dealings, their goods and produce to be recorded. Enkidu gazed up at the great arch, at the

98

ponderous outer doors of copper-sheathed timber, at the bare earth rutted by wagons.

As they drew closer an odour assailed him – not just an odour of pigs and dogs but a vileness he had never before encountered. By the dark walls beneath the arch, between the inner and outer doors, he witnessed the maimed, the crippled and the blind. Discarded husks of humanity drifted together by the winds of misfortune, they huddled in wretched plight, begging alms from the passer-by. Gaunt with hunger. Ignored. Pitiful. The sight of them shocked Enkidu.

'Why the wretched condition of these people,' he asked. 'Why do they choose to gather at the city gate?'

'They wait in hope,' replied Shamkhat.

'In hope of what?'

'In hope of charity. In hope of there being another day, until the thought even of that becomes too much to bear. To them the gateway is a symbol. People pass to and from the city and that gives the dispossessed an illusion of freedom. A freedom that can never be theirs.'

'Then what use are your gods to them?' he asked, angrily. 'Why do they not gain comfort from the wealth of Uruk's temples? Why not from the power of Uruk's great lord?'

'The temples now and then hand out bread and beer,' she replied, 'but neither they nor the king can make up for what the gods have seen fit to deny.'

'Then such gods are not worth the name,' countered Enkidu, goading their ox onward through the gate. 'There's a foulness and corruption here I never expected to find in the cities of men.'

'The gods have their own tribulations,' responded Shamkhat. 'Immortal they may be but they are still afflicted with deceit, anger and suffering. We simply follow in their footsteps. I was always taught we should be grateful for what they have given us and not harbour resentment for what they have not.'

'Then what the gods withhold from those unfortunate creatures I have just witnessed should be offered instead by man,' replied Enkidu as they emerged from the shadow of the arch. 'It is surely within the lord of Uruk's power to do that.'

'You are as generous in heart as you are strong of limb, dear Enkidu. I think you'll find some of our people like-minded but others not so.'

They entered the great square with its complement of stallholders and merchants.

'Wait!' cut in Enkidu as they approached the Eanna precinct. 'Look - over there by that gateway. Those people are pointing at us and I see the merchant is with them.'

'Also Kuraka and others from the council of elders,' said Shamkhat. 'And there are three of our overfed priests coming down from the temple. They must have watched us approach the city.'

The group started toward them and quickly became a growing crowd as others joined their number. Passers-by, stallholders and artisans. Lowering their voices they began to converge about the wagon with eyes for only Enkidu. All except for one.

The bushy-haired slave boy of Inanna's temple, for a time trailing behind the three priests, slipped from their company unnoticed. Bare feet raising dust, he ran from the market square taking what he knew to be the quickest way, through narrow alleys, past the blank facades of houses where hidden courtyards offered green-shaded coolness. On he went in the heat, passing open-fronted workshops, startling pigs, dogs and geese where they scavenged for offal or languished in the shadows. On he scurried until entering the square opposite the king's palace. There he came to a panting halt.

Before the palace was the Lord of Uruk, returned from the morning's sport in his chariot of stout timber and gilded bronze. Milling about him in conversation, some in chariot, some on foot, were the chosen of Uruk's young men, each in hide kilt or the tunic of a warrior, each with servant in attendance to carry his bronze-tipped spear, his bow and his quiver of arrows. The boy wiped sweat from his forehead with the back of his hand, took a deep breath and headed toward them.

***

The wagon was almost surrounded and its two occupants at a loss for what to say when someone in the crowd declared, 'He looks like the king. It would be difficult to tell them apart at a distance.'

Those closest pushed back as Enkidu climbed down from the wagon. Murmuring began and another spoke out. 'He looks a bit shorter than the king but I'd say he was broader.'

'No,' put in a third. 'This man is taller by a hand's breadth - I'll wager on it!'

'Shorter, taller, broader!' exclaimed the newly arrived first priest, raising his staff of office to quieten them. 'What does it matter?' He turned to

101

Enkidu. 'Stranger, where are you from? What business have you in Uruk?'

'But I - I have already told you,' protested the merchant with palms raised.

'We must hear it from his own mouth!' interrupted the priest.

'I am from the wild lands,' replied Enkidu. 'I came here because I - because this girl brought me. I am to meet Gilgamesh.'

'Have you come here to challenge our king?' asked a voice from the crowd. They moved apart and a lean, white-robed figure in tall cap stepped forward. 'I am Kuraka – I speak for the elders of the city. We asked our gods to send us a champion of the people because no one in Uruk seemed worthy of the task. Are you that man?'

Enkidu peered across waiting faces and laughed, 'Am I? Perhaps I am! I scarce know what my purpose is. But if I do seek another man to test myself against I'm told your Gilgamesh might measure up! First though, I have to meet the man and hear what he has to say for himself. I'm told he's become an oppressor of late!'

'That he has!' called another voice, and forward stepped Sheshkalla the metalworker. 'He needs hammering down to size and you look the man to do it!'

'You *are* the man!' called out one and a babble of agreement followed.

'Wait!' exclaimed Enkidu. 'I am barely arrived in Uruk. I have yet to know where I might find him!'

'Oh, I'll tell you where to find him,' responded Sheshkalla. 'Our good king is outside his palace. He just got back from sporting with the young men of our town.'

'You mean the over-fed and under-worked hangers-on,' interjected someone.

'He is back early because there's to be a wedding,' said Kuraka. 'My own granddaughter's wedding, in fact. This afternoon she goes to the House of Marriage where her husband-to-be and the priests will be waiting. As is now his habit, our glorious lord will go there to claim his rights over her. He will take his pleasure with her first and thereby deny the husband his rightful consummation. I begged him not to insist upon this right at risk of demeaning my own office.'

'And his reply?' asked Enkidu.

'Before dismissing me his reply was, "A king's right is a king's right. It's always been so – not just in Uruk but throughout all Sumer." I could not argue with that but right is not necessity.'

'The women of the temple aren't enough to satisfy his appetites,' added Sheshkalla, glancing briefly at Shamkhat. 'He takes any women he fancies in the same way he takes what he wants from our beasts and orchards for his banquets. There's no denying he saved Uruk from a far worse fate at the hands of Kish a year or so back, but now things have gone too far. Enough is enough!'

'There's a good number hereabouts,' added another, 'who'd be willing to show him the quickest way out of the city, And for good!'

'That may be so,' continued Kuraka, eyeing the man uneasily before turning again to Enkidu. 'When he sets out, our king will cross the market square preceded by a drummer to proclaim his

103

arrival. He will be followed by his company of young men to ensure no one interferes. He will take her up to the temple of Inanna and will enter the shrine of the goddess. There he will enact the rite of fertility that once took place only with the priestess at the decreed time of the year.'

'Even our sacred rituals he uses for his own ends!' put in the second priest

'Then *I* will bar his way!' declared Enkidu. 'I'll persuade him to change his mind. I'll have him turn aside and let the woman and the people go about their business in peace!'

The crowd expressed its endorsement but the metalworker added, 'Uruk must have a strong king and I – most of us, that is, wish Gilgamesh no evil. But you'll have our backing in this matter - you'll see! If you succeed then the king must wave his claim to the girl. That's in our code of laws.'

Looking up to Shamkhat, Enkidu said, 'It seems my life is pre-ordained. You should return to the temple. Perhaps one of these people will lead your wagon.' A frown passed over his face. 'But say you will return to me. I'll find no contentment here if you do not.'

'I must go,' she answered, leaning down to kiss his forehead, much to the approval of the onlookers. 'Enkidu,' she whispered, 'I am the only woman you have known but you will meet many here and may find another more to your liking. But do not forget me. Do not forget our journey together in the wilderness. Know that my heart will always be open to you if you need me.'

'I will not forget,' replied Enkidu. 'I'll come back to you – that I promise.'

***

The temple boy dashed across the square toward the group of men gathered before the palace. Now as close as he could be to the king's chariot without attracting attention, he rushed suddenly forward, fell to the ground on both knees and with hands raised high cried out, 'Master – hear me!'

A red-cloaked guard stepped across to seize the boy's ear, hauling him painfully to his feet whilst growling close to his face, 'Clear off, brat or you'll get my foot up your arse!'

Feigning retreat, much to the amusement of Gilgamesh and his companions, the boy circled quickly about the guard who had neither the agility nor the quickness of mind to prevent him dashing back to the king's chariot. The asses snorted, quivering uneasily as he fell to the ground once again, arms raised in supplication. 'Have me beaten later, oh, Great One, but please hear me now!'

A second guard leapt forward to join the first, both grabbing the boy roughly by the arms then dragging him backwards in the dirt. 'Beaten!' yelled the first. 'You'll be chopped up and fed to the scavenging dogs!'

The spectacle gave rise to further laughter but Gilgamesh called out, 'Wait! Let him be for a moment!' As the boy struggled to his feet, as he brushed the dust from his limbs, Gilgamesh asked, 'What is it, boy? What's so important that you risk a damn good hiding? Out with it!'

'Your Mightiness!' exclaimed the boy, on his knees once more and shuffling up to the chariot. 'I have incredible news! A man has arrived in the city with a woman of the temple. I heard them say he

105

was here to give you a good – I, er, mean to - to offer you challenge.'

'Ah!' responded the king. 'It sounds as though the infamous man-beast has turned up at last! Tell me, boy, is he like a bear or a beggar? Is he tall or squat? Is he foul or groomed like a prize bull?'

'Er - well,' grinned the boy, glancing about.

The guards moved closer.

'Answer your lord at once!' ordered the first guard, raising his hand to strike.

'Well, Highness,' continued the boy, 'he looks like, er - like you.'

'Oh, like me!' laughed Gilgamesh, peering down from his chariot as the boy shuffled ever closer. 'I'm glad to hear he looks like me rather than I look like him. That can't be too bad. And where is this fellow hanging out?'

'Now, Magnificence - right now he is by the main gate of the temple precinct with a huge crowd about him.'

'So, my look-alike has acquired sudden popularity. Perhaps they really do think it's me.'

'I, er, don't think so, your Mightiness!' responded the boy. 'He isn't dressed the same.'

'Then we'll have to do something about it, won't we? No one in Uruk ought to be as popular as the king!'

'Shall I go back and find out more, master?' asked the boy, clasping hands over the solid front wheel of the chariot.

'I think not,' answered Gilgamesh. 'Our paths are bound to cross before long but I thank you for the information and your concern for your king.'

'No problem, great one,' grinned the boy. 'If a small reward could be arranged, I'll happily stay in your service forever!'

The guards appeared about to pounce as one of the king's followers called out, 'String the cheeky little sod up by his balls!'

'A reward!' exclaimed Gilgamesh. 'And just what did you have in mind? You are a slave of the temple, aren't you? Is it your freedom you'd have me give for something I would have found out soon enough anyway?'

'Oh, no, Highness!' responded the boy. 'I'm better off where I am than many who consider themselves free. I understand numbers, Lord. I can count and I can read a good few words - no problem. It's the rest - all those signs on the clay tablets. What I wish - what I really wish for, is to know them really well. As well as those who live by the art of writing.'

'Little bugger wants to become a scribe!' declared Gilgamesh, turning to his companions, whose mirth ignited spontaneously. The boy glanced furtively aside and appeared ready to bolt past the guards as both loomed in readiness to seize him. The king turned back to the boy, saying, 'You're an impudent scoundrel but you've caught me on a good day. What's your name?'

As quickly as it had begun, the laughter subsided and the boy replied, 'My name is Shannu, great king!'

Gilgamesh thought for some moments, looked hard at the boy then said, 'Well, I won't ask who has been teaching you but the scribe is a very important man. Few commoners are admitted to the

House of Tablets, let alone slaves. Still, I see no harm can come of it.' Gilgamesh displayed the bronze ring on his left hand before the boy. 'D'you know what this is?' he asked.

'Your Lordship's seal,' replied Shannu, ogling the ring.

'Yes, My Lordship's seal. At least the smaller of the two.' He leaned close to the boy, moving the ring back and forth, watching large brown eyes follow it. 'Believe it or not, I'm going to give you charge of it.' To the undisguised amazement of his companions he tugged the ring from his finger and offered it down to the boy. 'Take it, give it to the official in charge of the tablet house and tell him you are to be educated in the manner of a scribe and to be flogged if you do not properly attend to your lessons. Tell him he must return the ring to me before dusk tomorrow together with a true account of your message. And I do mean a *true* account!'

'Mighty One,' grinned the boy, clutching the ring to his chest, 'you have made real my greatest dream!'

'That may be,' answered Gilgamesh, eyeing the boy with an appropriate degree of sternness, 'but if you've been making this up and if that ring is not returned in time, your dream will become a nightmare. I'll have your head on a spike above the city gate for all to see. Now, off with you!'

The boy grinned widely but as he hurried back across the square one of the companions asked, 'Can you trust the brat, Lord Gilgamesh?'

'There's ample mischief about him but I think he'll repay my trust,' replied the king, stepping down from his chariot. 'And if he doesn't, he won't get far before he's caught. In any case I wouldn't mind an extra pair of eyes and ears about the city the way things are. But I hardly care right now since this afternoon I have other matters with which to occupy myself.'

His remark prompted a general round of discreet nudging, gestures and suggestive antics among the companions.

'We should rest now and meet again when my herald calls,' continued Gilgamesh. 'I intend to be back by sunset so we will meet again here. I'll lay my hands on a few flagons of the best wine, our meat will be roasted over charcoal by the riverbank and we'll enjoy the evening air free from the odours of the city. Something tells me a wagonload of women from Inanna's temple will join us after dark. I'm sure your appetites will not let you down.'

'And this crass fellow who thinks himself able to challenge you,' asked one of the companions, 'what of him?'

'Now I've had the rustic brought into Uruk,' grinned Gilgamesh, 'my first challenge, and his, will be to ignore him altogether. I'll let him think I'm not in the least concerned so he'll be obliged to find me. Then maybe we'll see what he's worth!'

***

The drum sounded with slow and steady beat from the roof of Inanna's temple and all throughout the city knew why. People gathered by the palace in early afternoon heat and about the market square where, to one side of the temple precinct the House of Marriage stood.

The sound of a different drum could be heard emerging from a side street. A smaller drum beaten to a lighter, quicker rhythm. Across the palace square, behind the drummer, walked the lord of Uruk in kilt of tooled ox hide and wide belt adorned with silver filigree. Striding haughtily behind him in tunics of white Egyptian linen and bearing ceremonial spears of gilded bronze, were some twelve of his young companions. Across the open space before the palace they passed with a babble of people streaming behind, then along the narrow streets leading to the market square. In the square, crowds had gathered but whereas before had been bustle and chatter, now there was almost silence. Their gaze remained on the king as he entered and crossed the square. Gilgamesh sensed how the people's mood had changed. Sensed all was not as it ought to be. In that otherwise subdued place, the drum clattered ominously, its voice shivering the oppressive air of this sultry day.

There was one whose dark eyes watched from a distance. The girl sat in shadow by a window on the upper floor of an inn at the far end of the square, a white shawl covering her lower face.

Another person was busy among the waiting crowd, one of smaller stature than most, one whose presence went unnoticed by the entourage. With a leather pouch slung over his shoulder, he dodged to and fro grasping in his hand a reed stylus and large, copper-hinged writing board borrowed from the temple stores. He stopped from time to time before a citizen of wealthy aspect to declare his purpose. 'Make your wager now, master. Place your silver. Who's going to win - the king or the wild man? Make your mark in the clay and watch me enter the amount of your silver.'

'Wretched boy!' exclaimed one. 'On whose authority -?'

Grinning widely, the boy held up his hand so that they could see the ring, several sizes too big, that tumbled about his finger. 'On the king's authority, master - see - no problem. Just place your wager with me and I'll record it before your very eyes!'

'What are the odds?' enquired another, eyeing the ring suspiciously before hesitating with small bronze pliers to clip a measured length from the coil of silver about his wrist.

'Two to one on the king, master,' replied the boy, thrusting out a hand to accept the silver.

'I say we back the wild man,' grumbled another. 'Gilgamesh is a burden on us all nowadays.'

'And what if it's a draw?' asked one, wiping the sweat from his brow.

'A draw!' exclaimed the boy, his grin broadening further as their silver vanished into the depths the pouch. 'Oh, that means everything goes into - er, into the temple bank. But don't worry, master; someone has to win. That's the way things usually are!'

'You'll not see your silver again,' muttered one man as the boy was swallowed by the crowd, 'that's another thing I'd wager on but not with him. I wonder how he got hold of that ring.'

'It's worth risking a snip or two just to stand here and watch,' replied his companion as the drummer passed by.

The drumming ceased. The drummer stepped aside and called out, 'All hail the Lord of Uruk!'

The king glanced about. A few voices in the crowd responded half-heartedly, 'Hail, Lord of Uruk!' Once there would have been universal cheering. Once the people would have pressed forward in their enthusiasm to see him. Most now remained silent as before. Ahead of Gilgamesh stood the entrance to the House of Marriage. Through his mind ran images of the fallen star and the great axe of his dreams. But nothing lay in his path as he walked on toward the timber-framed portico beyond which, virgin fresh, the young girl waited in trembling anticipation.

'Let them begrudge me my dues,' breathed Gilgamesh. 'Without me they'd be sweating under the yoke of Kish. A harsher burden by far. Let them be sullen but by the gods I'll break the skull of any man who offers me insult.'

From the deep shadows of the portico a figure emerged.

Gilgamesh halted. A tide of murmuring rippled through the crowd as sunlight fell upon the stranger. Dressed in a kilt of stitched hides, he was one of solid, muscular build and they saw in his eyes the look of a hunter. A hunter of men as well as of wild beasts.

'Ah!' cried Gilgamesh. 'Who is standing in my way? Has the wild man crept out from the shadows at last?' Gilgamesh strode forward, an equal glint of resolution in his eye. 'Step aside and I'll deal with you in due course!'

Arms folded, Enkidu stood his ground, placed a foot across the entrance and declared, 'Not so!' in a voice that carried across the crowd. 'You'll go no further, Lord of Uruk! This is not the place for you today!'

'Is it not!' countered Gilgamesh, hands placed firmly on his waist as the two narrow-eyed each other. 'Well, rustic, move aside or it's a day *you* will regret!'

The followers of Gilgamesh stepped forward, spears at the ready as one declared, 'Give the word, my lord, and we'll drag this oaf up to the city wall and heave him over the side! Or would you have us put him to death now?'

Hardly had he finished speaking when the crowd parted. From their midst strode Sheshkalla the metalworker with his blackened and burly company close behind, each armed with bronze hammer or thick metal bar. 'You'll drag no one nowhere!' growled their leader with a look in *his* eye that chilled even the staunchest of the royal companions. 'Let the newcomer have his say!'

Someone in the crowd muttered, 'Sheshkalla's taking a chance isn't he? Gilgamesh won't let this one go.'

'Think about it,' responded another. 'No king, not even ours, can afford to get on the wrong side of Sheshkalla and his lads. They make the weapons we need to fight with. No one else could.'

'Lay your spears aside!' Gilgamesh commanded his youths. 'Let no man interfere!'

The companions did as they were told. Seeing this, the metalworkers laid down their weapons also - but remained where they stood.

'Well my fine friend,' declared the king, turning back to Enkidu, 'it seems you have a dedicated following. No mean achievement for one

113

only this day arrived within the city wall! You must be proud of yourself. Enjoy it for the short time it's going to last!'

A cry arose from the crowd as Gilgamesh bounded forward to seize Enkidu. But Enkidu was ready and with a growl of the beast, grasped him hard. Locked together, both spun around, only to collide with the timber post of the portico, splintering it with a crack that echoed over the square. The two parted, each to regain his balance, each to avoid the collapsing structure. Eyeing one another with eagle stare, they crouched, shifting from side to side, each man manoeuvring to gain advantage over his adversary.

Gilgamesh regarded Enkidu, thinking, 'He's as big as I am but has no training in the ways of combat. I'll have him down in no time.'

Enkidu regarded Gilgamesh, thinking, 'He's as big as I am but has no experience of survival against the beasts of the wild. I'll have him down in no time.'

Once more they closed and grappled.

On all sides the crowd heaved as those to the rear scrambled upon whatever they could find so as to obtain a better view. Gilgamesh and Enkidu, each with back bent, breath shortening, bodies glistening, pivoted around, each grasping the shoulder of his opponent, both locked as bulls in combat. In the wavering pool of their own shadows they spun, feet parrying as each attempted to throw off balance and hurl the other to the ground. On they went. Neither man seeming able to gain advantage over his adversary.

From amongst the people came shouts of encouragement - some for the king but as many for the stranger. Then cries of 'Aaah!' as Enkidu lost his footing and was thrown down to the dust. Gilgamesh would have leapt full upon him but Enkidu sprang aside, catching the other man with his foot, bringing him down also. Bruised, visibly much angered, the two leapt to their feet and were once more locked together, sweat-streaks glinting sunlight. Around they struggled. Gasps and oaths rose in the torrid heat of the square. Teeth gritted, faces creased with the mighty effort of a contest showing no sign of resolution.

Pressing in, the crowd began to jeer as the two fell rolling in the dust where pigs and dogs scavenged for offal thrown down by the market traders. First one man appeared to prevail, then the other, until the eager onlookers, seeing them dishevelled, foul and begrimed, were hard put to tell which was the noble lord and saviour of Uruk and which was the man from the wild lands beyond the reach of the city.

On their feet again, limbs grazed and blood-smeared, they parted for a moment to regain their breath, then each cried out and made a lunge for his foe, each man determined in this grim, final embrace to wrest the strength and subdue the will-power of the other. The crowd began to chant loudly - some for Gilgamesh, some for Enkidu, their voices growing as the struggle continued. But the sun was traversing its arc and everyone could see both men were nearing exhaustion. Most realised the gruelling struggle must soon end but still Gilgamesh and Enkidu grappled in suffocating heat, hair matted about sullied faces, veins defined in arms and legs. Neither was willing to succumb, neither able to conquer. The two swayed, staggered, gave each other a final heave, then both were down on their knees in the dust head to head, mouths agape and craving breath.

'Damn you!' gasped Gilgamesh, supporting himself on one arm and wagging a finger in his opponent's face. 'I will not – I will not have you better me!'

'Nor,' panted Enkidu, supporting himself in like manner, 'nor will I be beaten by you!'

Silence fell. The crowd waited to see who would rise up first but each man remained on his knees. Each gazed long and hard at the other. With supreme effort they struggled to their feet, breath passing hoarsely, arms swaying, legs unsteady. Reaching out as if to embark upon a further round of exertion, Gilgamesh instead appeared to support Enkidu with a hand on his shoulder as Enkidu appeared to support Gilgamesh.

'I've little strength left in me,' gasped Enkidu, 'but if you wish to go on -'

'Oh - then I thank the gods for it, wild man,' wheezed the king, wiping sweat from his eyes. 'I, too, am almost spent. Furthermore, I've no wish to entertain this idle mob any longer when they should be about their business. And - and apart from that, I think we must look a sorry pair.'

People began to murmur and one blurted, 'Surely they'll go on. I placed five pieces of silver on the king to win.'

'And I had ten on the stranger,' responded another. 'I've a feeling our wagers are about to vanish like smoke on a strong breeze!'

Had their attention not been so closely focussed on the contest, some might have observed the boy quit the market place, his dusky face set in a grin of satisfaction, the box containing his clay slab clutched hard under one arm, bare feet pitter-pattering as he gained the entrance to the sacred precinct of Inanna's temple. Swift of foot he hurried up the temple steps with, swinging from his shoulder, a leather bag weighted by the folly of others.

In the market square, silence had again taken hold.

'I will shake your hand,' breathed Gilgamesh, wearily.

Enkidu eyed the open hand with suspicion.

'It is a custom of the cities,' said Gilgamesh. 'It means I offer my trust in return for yours. I think at present there is little else either of us can do unless one of us is willing to concede defeat and by the gods I will never do that.'

'Nor I,' replied Enkidu, grasping the hand, 'but I'll accept your trust for now.'

Shouts of approval arose from some members of the crowd, though one was heard to remark, 'See what's happened - neither of 'em can thrash the other. Now we'll have two bringers of tribulation instead of one!'

The chatter grew louder and Gilgamesh said, 'Enkidu - I know that is your name - Enkidu, no man ever fought me to a standstill. You are worthier in strength and courage than any I know. If you care to accept, I offer you my friendship.'

'I – yes, I will accept and I offer you mine,' replied Enkidu. 'But you are lord of Uruk and until today I never stood within any city.'

'Enkidu, lord of Uruk or no, I have learned a lesson here in the market square. Many were with you and wished you to better me. I would rather have you as a friend on that account as well.' Gilgamesh turned to his herald and ordered, 'Have the people disperse! We are finished!' Then to Enkidu he said, 'You and I are defiled by the filth of the street and that I despise. There's a pool in the courtyard of my palace - at this moment it is my one desire in life!'

Shamkhat lowered the reed blind. Alone in the dim silence of the room she sat to think hard about Gilgamesh and Enkidu. She and only she knew both men as intimately as any woman could. Something stirred as a tiny flame at the back of her mind. It was a notion so strange so bizarre that even should it grow to haunt her, as eventually it must, she would not be able to share her thoughts with anyone. At least not until -.

The streets they trod to the palace square were all but deserted. Stooping, weary of limb, they were seen only by children and slaves who wondered at this oddest of sights. The guards at the palace entrance stared speechless as the two blundered by.

'Never has the pool been so welcome, friend Enkidu!' Laughed Gilgamesh as water sparkled in the sun to stream away dirt and sweat from their naked bodies. 'At least not since I routed the army of Kish.'

'Welcome, yes,' replied Enkidu, 'but afterwards, what? I came to Uruk with a purpose but now it seems I don't have any – unless you can think of one.'

Gilgamesh pushed wet hair back from his cheeks. 'Purpose! Yes – I'm certain there's a purpose though it will need some explaining. But now we've proved ourselves against each other you should be my companion. I harbour none of the malice or contempt toward you as I confess I did before we met. My initial feelings are washed away with the dirt – you must believe that. I can only hope you feel likewise.'

'Perhaps my being your companion will benefit both of us,' replied Enkidu. 'Perhaps it will also benefit others. I gladly accept.'

'Then let's apply cool oil to ourselves and then dress. You must appear before my household as a friend of the king. We can talk a while, eat, drink and take our rest away from the afternoon heat. You must tell me about yourself and your life, and I'll describe fully the portents that I feel gave meaning to your arrival here in Uruk.'

'Portents?' queried Enkidu.

'Aye, my friend, portents! But only now do I fully understand. Only now do I see what those dreams predicted. You were never meant to be my enemy. Never! And later, when the sun goes down we'll take ourselves about the squares and streets. I will show you the pleasures of Uruk. The temple woman who came for you – ah, she has many sisters and you must have your choice of them! Tomorrow, I will show you every corner of this great city then we'll ride out in my chariot. There's ready sport to be had and I'll wager in a short time you'll want to join in and outdo those boastful men of mine in the games where they fancy themselves a cut above all others.'

'Lord Gilgamesh,' replied Enkidu, stepping from the water, 'I am a stranger yet you offer me much. I may not be used to the affairs of men but you offer with a suddenness that bewilders me. It's as if we had known each other all our lives. I cannot say how I will account for myself since the ways of the city are new to me.'

'You'll find out all you need in good time, friend Enkidu - of that I'm certain. No one will prevail upon you to do otherwise because you are your own man - and remember, you need not address me as your lord except when common people are present. And as for your being a stranger – well, you are not as strange to me now as you imagine, though I find this almost as odd as you do.'

Gilgamesh stood by him in radiant sunlight and Enkidu said, 'This is your domain and you are lord whether I choose to call you such or not. I will try to be the companion you desire but I will have to find answers to my own questions. Time is what you have offered and time is what I will need.'

'But you'll not be here just for my sake,' replied Gilgamesh as they walked to the shadowed arcade surrounding the palace courtyard. 'You have lived away from mankind. You have no friends and no -.'

'But the girl of the temple,' interrupted Enkidu. 'She is a good friend to me.'

'Oh yes, the girl of the temple,' laughed Gilgamesh. 'She is a good friend to many men, I can assure you of that.'

Enkidu frowned at the remark but Gilgamesh failed to notice and continued, 'Friend Enkidu, even as we fought in the market square I also felt I knew you - as though – as though you were here when I was a child. As though you had gone away for all these years but have returned like a twin brother from distant travels.'

'I have no answer to that,' responded Enkidu. 'True, we are close in appearance but I spoke to no other man until we met the nomads and I know of no brother in any city.'

They stood talking a while longer then Gilgamesh retreated into thought for a time. Enkidu watched in silence the man who a short time before had ridiculed then confronted him with ill intent. When at last Gilgamesh spoke there was another surprise in store for the newcomer.

'See now friend Enkidu, you - you have no family and that's a bad thing. We must talk with my mother, Lady Ninsun. She has vision beyond that of other people. I believe she will look upon you as her own – as one returned from a long journey. Then you will belong. Then you will have a family and people of your own and I will have not just a companion but a brother in truth. I think that would be right.'

'I am unworthy of your offer,' replied Enkidu. 'I came to Uruk as your enemy and I would have humbled you had I been able.'

'Quite so,' smiled Gilgamesh, placing a hand on the other's shoulder, 'and humble me you did.

Until today no man ever faced the king of Uruk and brought him to the dust - neither in battle nor in sport. But think about this as did I whilst we bathed at the pool; what if the gods had not sent you - for surely they did? Why, the people would have risen against me. I realise it now from the way they behaved. That would have pleased a good few, not least the Man of Kish. His cohorts would soon have been clamouring at the city gates and ready to storm us - of that I have no doubt.'

They continued on through the cooler air of the arcade and on reaching the narrow door at the rear of the king's apartments, Gilgamesh said, 'Believe me, friend Enkidu, never have I put so much trust in another and in so little time. It is as though I am guided from above. It makes me wonder how much a hold we have on our own affairs.'

'Then there is much I must live up to,' Enkidu replied. 'And much I must take heed of now my old life is gone. But if I am able I'll be as true a companion as ever a man had.'

***

They entered the palace of Egalmah, the house of Ninsun. A realm of silence. The noise, the dust, the odours of the street - all were left behind. The inner room to which the slave girl conducted them had small, high windows and was dimly lit. It held a peace, a profound stillness Gilgamesh had experienced nowhere else in the city, not even within the shrines of the great temples. The air was laden with perfumed incense. The girl departed without a word, leaving the two before a bead curtain that swayed almost imperceptibly. Now accustomed to the subdued light, they became aware of a figure seated behind the curtain. A voice announced, soft and calm, 'Gilgamesh, Enkidu, I will speak with you both. Please enter.'

Gilgamesh stepped forward to push aside the curtain. Enkidu followed.

On a couch of patterned hide and inlaid cedar reclined Ninsun, dressed in a gown of finest linen. A gown woven in intricate pattern. In her hair, delicate ivory combs held coiled tresses in place. At her ears hung precious stones set within exquisite wire nests of silver and copper.

'I bring you greetings, mother,' said Gilgamesh.

'I offer mine also,' said Enkidu.

'I welcome you both,' replied Ninsun, rising from the couch. 'I heard about what happened in the market place. You, Gilgamesh, you, Enkidu - each met his match in the other and through this test of strength each has found a friend. In this I see the hand of the gods. Enkidu, we have never met but even as you stand there I know you and I am much pleased because of it.

You, Gilgamesh, never had a true friend. Not amongst the young men who follow you is there one worthy of your whole trust. They respect you as their lord, as do the common people of Uruk. They respect you because you are strong but respect is not friendship. Nor is it trust. Respect may come and go with the birds of the air. Friendship - true friendship, is like a rock and remains whether the waters rise or fall. Whether the crops thrive or wither.'

'It is true,' replied Gilgamesh. 'Whilst Uruk prospers I have the people's respect, if not their love, but in none of them could I find a true companion.'

'My companions were the wild beasts,' said Enkidu. 'Humankind I hardly knew until the temple girl brought me to Uruk. When I tasted the apple she offered me, a new vision opened.'

'Then the gods have served us well,' answered Ninsun. 'They have brought Enkidu – open and true as the skies and the hills, to Gilgamesh, who walks the path of mankind but must always beware the pitfalls of deceit and malice.'

'But I have you and the others of my family,' said Gilgamesh. 'Enkidu has no one of his own and that is not right. I am his companion as he is mine but he must also have kinship as I do – as do all people.'

Ninsun raised her arms and placed a hand upon each of their rough cheeks. A smile touched her lips as she spoke. 'Yes, Enkidu must belong. He should not burn as a flame alone in endless night. In looks he could be your brother. It is as though I had borne twins. As though one had been taken by an eagle at birth only to reappear in full manhood. Enkidu shall become mine as a son because you wish it and because I sense the same blood running through the veins of you both.'

'I can find no words for your kindness,' answered Enkidu.

'You need look for none,' said Ninsun. 'I will have your name recorded in Anu's temple and your time of birth will be the same as the time Gilgamesh was born. Gilgamesh is king, for only he can be, but you will be his right arm. You will be one upon whom he will depend in times of need.'

'I wish no power for myself,' said Enkidu. 'I want my shadow cast by the sun as any man would but not to darken the path of others.'

'That may be so,' replied Ninsun, 'but when your shadows are cast together, neither will diminish the other and you both will be stronger for it.'

As Ninsun spoke to Enkidu, Gilgamesh recalled his own childhood. Had he ever been much closer to his mother than Enkidu now was? There had always been servants, always slaves. There had been his tutor in the House of Tablets, the training in fitness and combat that had served him so well of late and had done so even before his adolescence. Yes, he had known her presence throughout his life but never truly realised what a mother was. Her office, her sanctity, had been a barrier.

As for his father, the unknown priest of Kullab, his name was never mentioned. He existed only in rumour. And what of the hero-king who had held power before Gilgamesh himself; the man referred to as 'Devine Lugalbanda?' He, too, was cited as the husband of Ninsun. There were shrines to his memory throughout Sumer though he had died in Gilgamesh's early years and the elders had ruled Uruk until Gilgamesh came of age. Should Gilgamesh have questioned Ninsun about his parentage? Until of late he had considered it a subject never to be raised.

It seemed to matter now Enkidu was here. Perhaps far more than it ever had before. Words swelled within his mind. 'Yes - that's why I had to forge my own way in life. Maybe until now there's been no one to tell me I shouldn't keep on pushing. At least no one I'd care to hear say it.'

**

Their voices echoed across the darkened palace courtyard. Each, in fine robe, walked with a silver goblet of wine in his hand.

'We'll hunt gazelle and lion,' laughed Gilgamesh, 'and man of the country you may have been but I'll outdo you. See if I don't!'

'Oh, I doubt that, brother Gilgamesh,' smiled Enkidu. 'I doubt your boisterous fellows will be happy with the outcome should they wager their silver on you.'

'Then we'll hurl our spears and I'll show you the better distance there!'

'You might at first,' responded Enkidu, 'but I'll find your measure in time and you'll need all the gods on your side to better me afterwards. And your asses - I hear you use the lash when racing your chariots. I'll speak kindly to the beasts that pull mine then you'll see how much swifter they'll go because of it.'

'Well before long,' boasted Gilgamesh, drinking deeply from the goblet whilst Enkidu took a modest sip from his, 'we'll find ourselves among the women. Now there's a sport where I won't be beaten. I admit I have an unfair start, brother Enkidu, but I intend to take full advantage of it and never let you catch up with me.'

'So you say, brother Gilgamesh, but the girl you yourself provided me with was a good teacher, and the gods have given us the same desires. I expect I'll learn to savour those pleasures just as I learn to savour your wines. In the few short days I have spent in Uruk, I even find myself taking an interest in the pieces of clay upon which you and your scribes make those odd signs.'

'Ah!' responded Gilgamesh. 'Then there I have you! Not all the prowess, strength and cunning in the world can make up for the time it takes to gain an understanding of the scribe's art. But say the word and I'll see to it you are given the tutor I had as a boy. He's an old man, now, but still occupies himself teaching. I'll see to it also that he's given a wooden rod to encourage you. That's what it takes to learn and I should know. I suffered at his hands for many a year.'

'A rod!' laughed Enkidu. 'If any man tries to strike me with a rod, tutor or no, he'll hobble away with it poking out of his backside!'

'Then I'll send along my old tutor just to watch you do it,' responded Gilgamesh, draining the goblet. 'No man better deserves such a fate! If it wasn't for repeated intercessions by my mother, I'd have had him castrated, flogged or put to death years ago. Let's grab ourselves more wine. I have the thirst of an ox and I have a feeling the women may soon be here!'

About to follow him, Enkidu hesitated to look above the courtyard wall. Low in a peaceful sky glowed the bright star of Inanna, just as he recalled it from his time in the wilderness. Remaining for a while he gazed out and felt a sadness uncoil within. He fancied a voice called from far away - a part of himself he had abandoned to the distant shadows of the night. He liked the brash and boastful Gilgamesh but he, Enkidu, could never become one like him. The wilderness, the sky and the stars held a meaning the likes of his new-found brother would never understand. He must never let that go.

'Come along now, brother Enkidu!' called the king. 'There's fresh wine brought in and the women have arrived!'

CHAPTER 4
THE CEDAR MOUNTAIN

Has no one seen him?' asked the king. 'Has no one seen my brother today?'

'He's not passed this way, sir,' answered one of the two guards standing within the narrow entrance to the palace.

'We've not seen him since yesterday afternoon, Lord Gilgamesh,' confirmed the other.

Gilgamesh nodded, turned away and walked across the hall toward an arched doorway at the rear. This led to the palace scribes' quarters, which in turn looked out through the arcade and onto the palace courtyard. As he approached, a figure in white linen kilt emerged through the arch, bearing clay tablets on a wooden tray.

'Wait!' called the king as the young man hurried by with gaze fixed downwards. 'You are not with my scribes. What is your business?'

'I serve with the scribes of Lady Inanna, My Lord,' answered the young man, lowering his head. 'I was sent to collect these tablets.'

'I see,' muttered Gilgamesh. 'Tell me - some weeks ago, when Lord Enkidu came into our city, I sent a slave boy of the temple to their scribal house for instruction. Does he progress well? Does he progress at all?'

'If you mean Shannu, My Lord,' replied the young man, not daring to look up, 'he does exceedingly well. Not once have they used the rod, so I am told.'

'Not used the rod!' responded Gilgamesh. 'Then he must be diligent indeed. I know of no pupil who ever escaped at least an occasional taste of it. Were he not a slave of the temple I'd suspect he was touching their palms with silver.'

Gilgamesh looked down at the tablets. They recorded transactions between temple and palace workshops, nothing more. 'When you have delivered these,' he continued, 'I want you to ask in the temple if anyone has seen my brother today. Be discreet. When you have spoken to the priests and she who supervises the women, return here with your answer. Take my ring as your authority and be quick about it.'

Hurrying by the two guards, the boy made his way out into the palace square. Gilgamesh, much preoccupied, turned aside, walked slowly back to the stairs and ascended to his audience room.

'The Lord of Uruk is not happy,' observed one of the guards. Both had stood impassively at their posts, ears straining to catch every word.

'It looks that way,' agreed the other, 'and he parts more readily nowadays with that bronze ring than I ever knew him to. First to that shifty little bugger from the temple - now to a runner for the scribes. And he's little knowledge of either of 'em if you ask me.'

'He's got things on his mind,' said the first guard. 'He's a worried man.'

'Oh, is he now,' responded the second. 'Well he can swap places with me if he cares to. It's an easy job with no real demands. What d'you say?'

'I'll go with that, and his darling brother can have my place. He's looked even more miserable than the king these last few days.'

'If you ask me, they've fallen out.'

'Fallen out over what?' asked the first.

'A woman,' came the reply. 'That's what it usually is. A woman.'

'A woman! What, when the king picks up whoever he fancies whenever he fancies?'

'Not lately he hasn't,' replied the second guard. 'He's not been putting himself about as much since the other one turned up. Everyone's noticed it. I reckon he's got his eye on some little tart in the temple and she prefers his brother. I reckon that's where our Enkidu's gone – off with her.'

Speculation continued until one of them glanced toward the entrance and said, 'Watch out - here comes the answer on two scrawny legs. Better call for one of the attendants to take him up.'

With the bronze ring clasped in his hand, the youth found himself conducted in some haste to the upper floor then into the king's presence. Rising from his seat by the window, Gilgamesh dismissed the attendant and asked, 'Well, what news d'you have?'

'My lord,' answered the youth, bowing whilst reaching nervously out with his hand, palm upward, to give back the ring. 'My lord, I spoke to our priests. They told me they had not seen Lord Enkidu since he left the city on foot yesterday when the sun was low. They say they have not seen him since. I asked also amongst the temple women but they could tell me nothing. Then one followed me as I left and took me aside. She was the one who came with him into the city. She told me he had gone out alone along the track by which they had entered Uruk. She said he had gone beyond the fields and that your lordship should set out to find him if he had not yet returned. Er – that's all, my lord.'

Gilgamesh's expression remained fixed as he said quietly, 'You have done as I asked. Return to your duties.'

***

Hearing the rumble of wheels, hearing the snort of asses, people hesitated. Their gaze followed the king's chariot as it lumbered by as though heading out to the field of battle. But they saw the lord of Uruk was alone - no spearman shared the small space within his wagon. As he clattered through the Southern Gate, pigs and geese scattered in raucous panic from his path. Scribes, traders and citizens stared and wondered. Never had they seen Gilgamesh set out from Uruk without at least a handful of his companions or men-at-arms to escort the royal person. Those near the gate began to speculate as they watched him cross the bridge then press on through orchard and gardens toward the fields.

They continued about their affairs, passing in and out under the great arch. Of late they no longer needed to avoid or to shun the sight and stench of the maimed and dispossessed - the heaps of filthy rags that had scavenged with the animals. They, the cast-offs of humanity, were absent. They had acquired tasks, nourishment and refuge. They had found some comfort in their wretched lives because the man Gilgamesh now sought had determined they should.

132

***

The cultivated fields and irrigation works were far behind him. The sun blazed high overhead when Gilgamesh found himself leaving the pastures where livestock grazed. Soon he was riding into sparser lands where the timbers of his cumbersome chariot protested at the uneven ground. Beneath the wide skies he was reminded of that second momentous dream where he had come upon the great axe laying across his path. This was the first time he had entered open country without his men but with sword at his belt, with axe ready to hand Gilgamesh was not afraid.

But there were gods other than those of Uruk here.

A while later, in the heat haze, he spied a water hole surrounded by palm trees and small bushes where wild birds swooped. His gaze strayed over the flat lands beyond but something drew back his attention. A patch of white fluttered against one of the bushes. He lashed the asses onward and, drawing nearer the pool, made out the pale form of a cloak with embroidered edge – a cloak much like that he presently wore over his own tunic. He knew there was only one other like it because both had been made at the house of Ninsun – one for himself and one for his brother. Gilgamesh brought the chariot to a halt and dismounted.

By the pool sat a figure, naked, still and silent. Gilgamesh strode forward, calling, 'Enkidu! Brother Enkidu!'

Birds spiralled up in panic. The figure stirred but did not rise as he approached, merely glancing up to say, 'Oh, so you have found me.'

133

'Brother Enkidu, why have you come here? Why did you leave Uruk and say nothing to me? Until this morning I thought you'd found some diversion in the city. A woman, perhaps.'

'No, I had no business within the city. I set out yesterday. I have remained here ever since.'

Putting aside his own cloak, Gilgamesh sat down close by Enkidu. 'But why - I don't understand? And I don't believe I've seen you looking so unhappy as you have of late.'

Enkidu stared a while at the reeds and the water before answering. 'I came from the wild places into the world of men. I came to Uruk with nothing and I had nothing to give, yet I have drunk in full from the cup of your generosity. It is in part the spectre of my own selfishness that chides me.'

'No!' exclaimed Gilgamesh, placing a hand on the other's shoulder. 'No, I won't hear this! There was never a man I could call my true friend. Never a companion in whom I could confide my thoughts. Enkidu, I'm lord of Uruk - I do as I will, but not all the wealth of palace and temple could gain me the trust and the friendship you have so freely given. The people see how you have offered hope to the poor and abandoned - those I rode by in disdain because I loathed their presence. For that they adore you – which I believe is more by far than I could claim for myself nowadays. How can you not feel pride in the good service you have given to our city?'

'If I'm to feel pride in anything,' replied Enkidu, 'it must be because a man in your position should consider me so important. What I fear now is that I might seem to lack gratitude when another in my place would judge himself the luckiest of men. The trouble is, brother Gilgamesh, unlike the birds and the insects I see about me, I have no path to follow. I find my life without purpose. As though in endless procession about the city wall, when in my dreams I still roam free over the rivers and the hills. The wine of the city muddles my thoughts because I am persuaded to take too much - and all too often cannot remember what I have said or done. And the women - why, they would keep me in bronze fetters to satisfy their lusts. In the beginning they were like - like water to a man with great thirst but now I feel myself drowning in their attentions. There's only one woman in whose company I find true happiness. Only one. She is the girl, Shamkhat – the girl who turned my fate with the offer of an apple and the pleasure of her body. She is always in my thoughts – her eyes, her smile. I'm bewitched by her.'

'Then take her for your own,' laughed Gilgamesh. 'I suspect she'd like nothing better and she'd beguile the gods themselves with her beauty. Why she's the woman I would choose for myself if I thought the time right, though I must say it seldom occurred to me until after you arrived in Uruk. I swear, though, I'll not stand in your way. She'll find no better a man than you, I stake my worth on it.'

'The time is not right for me, either,' sighed Enkidu. 'I feel there is much I should do but I've not the wits to see which path I might take. The city is becoming a prison. It oppresses me, but the world beyond no longer welcomes me either. There are feelings I could express but I have no wish to cause you offence.'

135

'No, Enkidu, but you might well cause offence by keeping your concerns from me. Look, I'm king of nothing and no one out here. I'm just another man but still your brother. Sharing your burden with me now will make matters easier.'

'Very well, then consider this. I sit here gazing across this pool. I see sunlight on the water. I see the reeds, I see the trees reflected there. I watch the creatures come down to drink then go on their way. I watch the birds that pause a while on their long journey. Even the insects that skim the water seem to do so with a purpose of their own. Gilgamesh - I don't know what it all means any more than I understand the stars in the sky, but it is part of something greater than we know. It has a harmony beyond our perception. It would speak to us if only we knew how to listen. Oh, how I know it would.'

As he spoke, a flock of herons passed above. Both men watched them and Gilgamesh said, 'But the priests of our temples, they understand the order of things. They sacrifice to the very gods who have decreed the affairs of this world.'

'Yes, I have listened to the priests and watched them at their ceremonies. I have to tell you, brother, I feel there are far greater truths passing before my eyes as I sit by this pool. It is a place of much consolation.'

Lost for a while in thought, Gilgamesh also contemplated the water and the reeds, then at last said, 'Yes, perhaps the priests are as blind to the nature of things as are the common people. They can speak for the people, as I do as head of the priesthood, when I take the trouble. But I think they – we, are calling into a great darkness. Most of the time we don't even know if we're heard. But now you have confided your thoughts I'll tell you mine. Since you arrived I'm gaining less pleasure than I once did when out hunting or pursuing futile sports. Like you I find myself wishing I could leave Uruk altogether for a time. I want to breathe a different air. Just lately I feel the city wall contains me like a stockade. Perhaps the flame of freedom burning within you lights a new path for us both.'

'If so, 'responded Enkidu, 'let's hope our path has a worthwhile destination.'

'It may well have,' replied Gilgamesh. 'I'll tell you what I have so far discussed with no one. Now Uruk is at peace, now Kish is subdued, I crave a greater challenge than Sumer is able to offer – at least until our friend Agga, the Man of Kish, gets back on his feet. I think then I will finish the job and kill him, but for now -.'

His attention roused, Enkidu listened as Gilgamesh continued. 'You must have heard about those who travel far to our north. Traders who visit a world where there are mountains and endless forests of cedar. We could take ourselves there. We could fell some of those trees and employ the timber to further enhance our city. It's well known the rivers that bring water to our crops arise in those same mountains. If that is so then they would carry the cedar logs down to Uruk. Think about it, brother Enkidu; it's an enterprise we could undertake together - with a few of my armed companions, of course. It would keep them out of mischief as well. Once there, you and I could take ourselves off. We could be alone in wild and strange places where beasts roam, beasts the people of Sumer never laid eyes on. The whole world would be ours. There's nothing to stop us!'

'Ay,' answered Enkidu. 'It's an enterprise in which I'd gladly play my part. I would be your equal in it and each of us would be as spear and shield to the other.'

'Now that's what I wanted to hear!' laughed Gilgamesh, seeing the light of enthusiasm kindled in his brother's eyes. 'I've heard tell of a great mountain rising above the river where the finest, the tallest of those trees grow. They say there's a guardian appointed by Enlil himself to protect them and because of that no man dares go near the place. It's there we should take ourselves, brother Enkidu.'

Enkidu frowned then looked him in the eye. 'You're talking about the Cedar Mountain. And the creature you refer to, the creature that stalks those forests, is called Huwawa. When I roamed the wild places I went to that mountain and I saw him. Gilgamesh – I'm no more afraid of danger than you are and you know it. But believe me when I tell you, Huwawa is the stuff of nightmares - yes that's exactly what he is.'

'Nightmares! Then by the gods if he's a greater nightmare than the Man of Kish then it *will* be a challenge worth facing. And I take it, then, you know the route through the forests to his lair.'

'Gilgamesh, listen to me if you will. I first saw him from a distance drifting like a black shadow in the dusk. Huwawa is a fearful being. No man in all Sumer ever encountered his like or would wish to. Neither lion nor bear has the courage to approach him because they know he'd tear them apart. Such a creature as Huwawa is not of this world and that I also know!'

'But if he lives on this earth then surely he can die on it,' responded Gilgamesh. 'Could he have grown more terrible in your thoughts with the passage of time? Surely you're not saying *you* would be afraid to go there?'

Enkidu closed his eyes then replied, quietly, 'You hear Huwawa before you see him. You hear him growl like thunder on the horizon. One night I lay asleep in the forest close to the mountain when something roused me. I heard breathing in the darkness - the breathing of something evil that moved unseen among the trees. I could smell corruption as he passed close by. My skin felt alive with crawling ants. I'm only here now because I remained still and silent. Perhaps the gods were watching over me, I don't know. But even as we sit in the heat of the sun with the blue sky above and the wide land about us, I am chilled to my bones by the thought of that damnable creature. Even now I feel his breath sweep about me as a cold shroud. I want to banish him from my thoughts.'

'Well, brother Enkidu, your demon of the woods sounds a troublesome opponent and no mistake.' Gilgamesh studied shimmering sunlight on bright water. His expression, his voice brimmed with resolution as he continued, 'There's more to this, Enkidu, I tell you. It's more than just another challenge. Every king of every city, at least those who last long enough, has his name stamped on the bricks of his foundations. Yes, and if he's able, carved on monuments of stone. Uruk is strong again through her victories and through my leadership.

But in Sumer, as you know by now, power and glory are granted first to one city and then another as the gods see fit. The Man of Kish boasted he would prevail and our own elders would have offered him homage had I not determined otherwise. Who's to say which town the gods will smile upon tomorrow or the day after? I sometimes wonder if it isn't a kind of game they play with humanity. But I must go beyond Sumer to make my name. I - I wish to do what no other man has done or could do again, so when the walls and temples of Uruk are ground to dust they will remember the name of Gilgamesh.'

'That is vanity beyond reason!' chided Enkidu. 'Really, brother, it's unworthy of you.'

'I hear what you say, Enkidu. I do hear it! But when war came I stood my ground for Uruk and risked my very life. Is it so wrong of me now to build upon that victory? Or do I continue as I was and risk the alienation of my own people? It was after all your arrival that opened my eyes to what was happening within our city.'

Enkidu made no reply so Gilgamesh continued, 'I have my men to support me but your companionship on such a venture would be of much greater worth. I tell you, Enkidu, if there's glory to be had then I'd prefer we returned home to share it equally. And what if I went up to those mountains alone? What if I died there? Who would know what happened? Who would know my last thoughts? The truth would be lost like the unread message of a clay tablet ground underfoot.'

'What you propose is an errand of utter folly,' insisted Enkidu. 'Huwawa watches the forest. He never sleeps. He hears goats bleat, he hears pigs grunt from far across his domain and he knows exactly where they are just as he'll know exactly where we are if we venture there.'

The afternoon was becoming hotter. Insects still buzzed but there were fewer birds to be seen about the pool. Gilgamesh clasped hands about his knees and both men gazed at the water. After a while Enkidu turned to Gilgamesh. 'I remember the route to the Cedar Mountain. I have seen the greatest trees. And, in answer to your proposal, brother Gilgamesh, I say yes, I will make the journey with you. As much as I fear Huwawa I could not face the people of Uruk if they believed your fate was a result of my cowardice.' He placed a hand on his brother's arm. 'Apart from that, I'd not be pleased to have you fixed in the minds of the people as a hero, dead or alive, whilst I languished with too little purpose in the city. Perhaps in this case an errand of folly is better than no errand at all.'

'Ah, now that's more like it,' smiled Gilgamesh, slapping him on the back. 'And for my part I'd be ill-suited to undertake the task without you. I'm too much a man of the city. I'd most likely find myself lost after a day or so beyond civilisation.'

'I'll teach you the ways of the hunter, brother Gilgamesh. You must learn how to make fire and set traps so you can survive without the luxuries of your palace. Call out or clap your hands in the wild places and it won't be a servant you'll attract but possibly a bear or worse.'

'Then I'll learn whatever you need to teach me,' declared Gilgamesh. But for now we should take my chariot and return to Uruk. On the way we can discuss how we're to go about this foolish enterprise.'

***

Gilgamesh had gone to the elders and not the elders to Gilgamesh. They had gathered in the House of Assembly, close by the Eanna precinct. There the lord of Uruk stood proudly before them with Enkidu in unassuming dignity at his side.

'Our king proposes an expedition to the far mountains of the north where the cedar forests lie,' began Kuraka. 'We trade our grain and our manufactured goods for timber as we do for metals, but both pass through many hands so that Uruk gains poor measure for her labours. In other words we pay a high price to obtain that which the gods have created for the benefit of all.'

'That is so,' declared Gilgamesh, stepping forward in his robes. 'We pay dearly for what others take for nothing. Until recently it was the king of Kish who controlled the main trade routes to the north, now we find them in the hands of others of whom we know little or nothing. I say we gather what is there for the taking and let Uruk and her people enjoy greater benefit from it.'

Kuraka regarded the king coolly and resumed, 'Such an enterprise, it is recorded, was undertaken by others in earlier times for *noble* purpose.' Few failed to notice his emphasis on the word 'noble' as he eyed Gilgamesh. 'It is known,' he continued, 'that timbers from the northern mountains will carry down the river to Uruk unless others prevent it. Much passes by our city on the river - bodies of the dead from distant places and creatures the like of

142

which we have never seen walking this land. They pass on through the marshlands until they reach the Great Water to our south. I see no reason why logs of cedar and pine could not be ours if we diverted them to our quay when they drifted close.

Now our king and his brother, Lord Enkidu, propose to go to the Cedar Mountain, sacred to Enlil. But we consider that even though the gods have blessed both with strength and courage, they should not venture there. Many have passed on tales of this creature, Huwawa. They say he is set by Enlil to watch over the tallest trees because the god will not have them plundered. They say no one can stand against Huwawa. They say his breath is fire and his jaws are -.'

'They say - they say - they say!' interrupted Gilgamesh, mockingly. 'They said,' he went on, staring directly at Kuraka, 'that Uruk could never prevail against Agga of Kish until I took up arms and rallied our people! They say what they say, and whilst *they* stand idly by and say it, I take up my spear and my axe and I prove them wrong! My men are preparing to go and no one will stand in our way – no one! Not the dog of Kish, not the men of the north and not this Huwawa you talk about but know only from the gossip of others who are themselves peddlers of hearsay!'

Several noticed Enkidu frown deeply at his words.

'I speak for everyone, I'm sure,' continued Kuraka with measured calm, 'when I say that I hope our Lord is right. I'm sure, also, that every citizen of Uruk will wish he and his noble brother success. However -.' There was a pause as Kuraka glanced about at silent faces, 'the Man of Kish will hear about this enterprise soon enough. He will know we are without some of the strongest and fittest of our men. He will no doubt appraise the weakness of Uruk and deduce it to be in his favour.'

'He won't be the only one!' put in another of the elders. 'The Man of Larsa is ill disposed toward us at present because of our dispute over the canal running between our borders - and Larsa is of less distance to Uruk than is Kish! It's reported their envoys have been much busier of late scuttling from one town to another. They may well be in collusion against us.'

'Ah!' exclaimed Gilgamesh, 'So you think that when I, my brother and my companions are gone from the city our enemies will close in.'

'It would hardly be surprising if they did,' replied the elder. 'Were our Lord the King to find himself in their situation he might well be tempted to do very much the same.'

'So I might,' agreed Gilgamesh, folding his arms and turning with a smile to Enkidu. 'Well, brother, where does that leave us? Do we forego our aspirations?'

'Since you have asked me, Lord Gilgamesh,' he replied, 'I feel we should not abandon the people of Uruk in these uncertain times. What would any venture be worth if the city was taken during our absence? What consolation would a thousand logs be to the dead and defeated?'

A murmur of agreement arose but a flash of defiance crossed the king's face and his voice rang out. 'By the gods, I'll not be turned aside from this enterprise! My companions and my captains will remain here. I've no wish to risk our city being pillaged while my back is turned. I will go alone if I must, though -,' he glanced at Enkidu, 'there is still one man I'd prefer have by my side, otherwise I might achieve little for my efforts.'

'I'll be with you, brother,' declared Enkidu, 'have no fear of that.'

'Then there will be the two of us!' declared Gilgamesh. 'And we will accomplish the task of a hundred men if needs be!'

'We'll cast and forge new weapons for you if you wish it, Lord Gilgamesh!' called a rougher voice and Sheshkalla the metal worker pushed forward. 'We'll forge the strongest blades a man could have. We'll take the grey metal that fell from the sky to the fields of Uruk many years ago. It needs great skill and is difficult to work but when it's finished and sharpened no blade will match and no armour resist its bite. I reckon there's more than enough to equip two men in all their needs.'

'Then maybe the gods do smile on our venture,' said Gilgamesh. 'They have sent this metal from heaven and given you, friend Sheshkalla, the skills to fashion it. I suggest you begin your task very soon. I will visit your workshops later today and we can discuss in detail what is to be done.'

***

'There was no other way,' said Gilgamesh as they left the House of Assembly and stepped into sultry afternoon heat. 'That tiresome man who speaks for the elders is right about our enemies all the same. If they saw Uruk weakened they'd gather like hungry jackals at our gates. This may prove quite a handful for only two of us but how could I admit to fear in front of them?'

'Can any man avoid knowing fear?' asked Enkidu.

'Maybe not but the likes of you and I should never let others be aware we know it. Even so, we must take ourselves to the palace of Egalmah where Ninsun waits. I will not ask the priests to intercede on our behalf - that would speak of uncertainty, though they will doubtless do so of their own accord. But the Lady Ninsun will make her appeal to the gods in private with little ceremony and, we must hope, to greater effect. She is closer by far to that other world than any mortal I know of.'

***

They waited alone in the silence of her dimly lit chapel. Two small ceramic lamps burned on a table in one corner, casting their shadows large on walls hung with richly patterned fabrics. The air was heavy with exotic perfume. The slaves and women of the house had been dismissed. When as a shadow Ninsun appeared from behind the curtain she wore a long gown and gold tiara set with precious stones that enhanced her beauty and confirmed her holy status.

'I have heard about your enterprise,' said Ninsun, sitting down on a wool-cushioned bench and bidding them do likewise. 'I expected you would make your way to my house.'

'Enkidu and I will go on this journey together,' said Gilgamesh. 'We have to find our path through wild places and dark forests. And it would seem we may encounter this Huwawa in his lair before we can help ourselves to the best cedars.'

'Not *may* encounter,' declared Enkidu, 'but *will* encounter! So we ask you to pray for us alone at your altar. I don't doubt we'll need it.'

'Tales of Huwawa are truer than most people know,' replied Ninsun. 'He is a creature of deceit and darkness. It is a pity such a one should serve Enlil. The lord of daylight and justice loathes Huwawa, even though he himself fostered the creature. Were it not for the sacred trees Enlil would evict Huwawa from his domains, if not destroy him altogether. I will call upon the sun, upon Utu, glory of the day, to protect and preserve you both. I will burn incense and pray you return unharmed to Uruk. I will beseech Utu to draw aside the thirteen winds who might otherwise conspire with Huwawa against you. I will ask that they instead gather against him should he endanger you both.'

'Then,' replied Gilgamesh. 'We'll go about our task knowing it is not just the two of us who are confront this so-called guardian of the forests.'

'I hope it works,' added Enkidu. 'My heart is heavy because I have seen Huwawa but perhaps now I'm less certain we are stepping out to meet our deaths.'

'Now that's positive thinking,' smiled Gilgamesh. 'I say it will also help us through.'

'Gilgamesh,' said Ninsun, 'I'll ask you to leave us now and wait outside. Before you go there are a few words I wish to have with Enkidu alone.'

When Gilgamesh had left the chamber, Ninsun said, 'Enkidu, I speak as mother of you both. Gilgamesh is as impetuous as you are steadfast and neither could have at his side a better companion than the other. I ask that you counsel and watch over him because he will listen to you when he ignores all others. Show him the wisdom of caution. Bring him back to Uruk safely.'

'I will preserve his life as I would my own,' replied Enkidu.' I swear it.'

'Then wear this as a token of your pledge.' Ninsun arose from her seat to place a copper chain bearing a small silver amulet in the form of the sun, about his neck. 'I would give this only to a child of my own - you will have seen that Gilgamesh possesses another like it. Let it remind you, should doubt arise, that you belong to my house and that you are cared for in the same way as he.'

'I have not doubted it since the day you accepted me,' answered Enkidu. 'If I say you are my mother I do so from my heart and not because it is expected of me. I could not face you if harm befell my brother Gilgamesh through my neglect.'

Ninsun watched him leave and considered her feelings toward both men. She had never been the mother she ought to have been for Gilgamesh - yet now she cared for him and for Enkidu more deeply than she could have expressed. The thought that either or both of them might fail to return would be a burden she feared she would be unable to face. A tear glistened in her eye.

***

'I've counted the days with thinning patience, brother Enkidu,' said Gilgamesh, setting aside the silver goblet and rising from his couch by the window. 'Today at last we take ourselves to the metalworkers. As soon as their messenger arrives we'll be down there to see the weapons those fellows have prepared for us.'

'I'm certain Sheshkalla and his men will do all you have asked of them,' remarked Enkidu. 'They're proud of their skills.'

'Oh yes, but that's not all – I gave Sheshkalla my authority to draw upon whatever resources he saw fit in order to fulfil the task in hand – including the temple craftsmen. The weapons they forge will reflect our status. They must bite deep into those timbers, they must strike down our adversaries, but they must also be fit to hang in the hall of my palace as a reminder to all of our deeds.'

'Do you believe the metal from the fallen star was destined for us?' asked Enkidu.

'Perhaps, brother Enkidu, and I once had a dream that suggested it. But I've heard such metal is found elsewhere in spite of what that old rogue, Sheshkalla, claims. I'm told the people of the hills far to our east know about it but I doubt their skills equal ours in its working and embellishment. Sheshkalla himself made the bronze spear and axe I carried into battle against Kish. Yes, his very name sounds like the clash of weapons. Blunt he may be in his manners but no one would say that about the blades forged in his workshops. Had he beaten us, the King of Kish would have forced our metalworkers into his service.'

'It's as well we have them,' replied Enkidu. 'Afterwards, I'll visit the palace stables to ensure our chariots and provisions are ready.'

'Good, I will order the elders and priests present at first light tomorrow and my companions will be ready to depart with us.'

'Your companions!' exclaimed Enkidu. 'But that isn't what we agreed.'

149

'Ah, I'm not going back on my word, brother, but we must not make our intentions clear to our enemies. My men will leave the city with us, fully armed. You and I will dress as they do so that no one will recognise us from a distance. We'll travel north past ancient Shurrupak, holy Nippur and beyond Kish. Once out of their sight, my companions will circle about and pass by Kish again on their return to Uruk whilst you and I go on alone. Agga will think our men have been sent to keep an eye on him. None of his merchants have traded here since the war so he may not know for some time that you and I are absent in spite of inevitable rumour.'

'There is so little trust between men,' sighed Enkidu, picking up his cloak. 'And I think it will always be that way. I'm sure the people of Kish want to get on with tending their fields and their flocks, and trading their wares in the same way as the people of Uruk.'

'Well at least there's trust between brothers,' smiled Gilgamesh, slapping Enkidu on the back. 'Come on, let's take ourselves to Sheshkalla's workshops now, messenger or no. My patience crumbles like dry clay and I will not wait any longer for the messenger.'

***

As they approached the street of the metalworkers they were surprised to see the bear-like Sheshkalla in his kilt of scorched leather already waiting at its entrance.

'Welcome, My Lords!' he exclaimed with hands clasped momentarily to his chest. 'Please follow me.' Sheshkalla's bow was slight. He served

Uruk well but was never a man of servitude. He led the way, swaying as he walked as though on the deck of a boat. A barrage of hammering assailed them as they trod the narrow street. An acrid haze all but obscured the far end.

'I trust we have not caught you unawares, friend Sheshkalla!' called Gilgamesh above the cacophony.

'No, My Lords, the boy was already on his way to inform your lordships. When he saw you coming he returned to me at once. Everything is ready.'

They followed him through drifting smoke to the harsh chime of hammer on bronze or stone anvil. To the wheeze of leather bellow beneath brick crucible of molten bronze and the coughing of workman and slave confined for too long within the heat of blackened forges. At length they entered the small courtyard where stood Sheshkalla's own workshop with his home on the floor above. The clamour of the street spilled over his walls but Sheshkalla's workplace lay still. By one wall of the courtyard was grouped his rough company of men and thick-haired urchins, their kilts of hide stained with sweat and seared by flame. Some betrayed soot-daubed apprehension but all gazed through smoke-reddened eyes at the King of Uruk and his brother. With nervous glances, they clasped hands to their chests and bowed as the two approached. Against the wall where they waited stood the mud-brick bench where Sheshkalla laid out his finished wares. The bench was covered with drapes of coarse wool and upon it, gleaming in the light of the sun were arrayed the new weapons.

Though presented by Sheshkalla and his men, what Gilgamesh and Enkidu saw was not the work of their hands alone. The artisans of precious metals had also applied their delicate skills. There was silence as Gilgamesh and Enkidu stood before the bench. Sheshkalla moved aside, arms folded, jaw set firm.

'By the gods, what fine work this is!' proclaimed Gilgamesh, taking up one of the two great axes and holding it high to test its weight. 'Never have I seen its equal!'

'And this spear!' declared Enkidu, lifting and holding at arm's length one of the splendidly wrought but formidable shafts. He stood with legs braced apart, raised the spear and balanced it in his grip as though making ready to hurl it through the air.

'In my mind's eye,' declared Gilgamesh, 'I see our worthy Kuraka standing exactly where your spear is to strike!'

The faces of the metalworkers displayed an almost tangible relief and they relaxed as one, whilst a glint of satisfaction lightened Sheshkalla bushy eye. Gilgamesh tilted the axe about, hands caressing the sturdy shaft of cedar, his gaze moving with admiration over the smooth lines and intricate inlay of silver and copper that adorned its lower end. Running a thumb lightly over the curved edge of the blade he announced, 'This would cleave through an ox with one blow. Yes - I'd face ten men with it!'

'Only ten?' smiled Enkidu. 'That's not the Lord Gilgamesh I know.'

'All right then,' laughed Gilgamesh, 'I'll make it twenty!'

The waiting men echoed their laughter.

'The metal is heated, hammered and quenched many times to give it greater strength,' declared Sheshkalla, with enthusiasm. His workers were grinning broadly as he continued. 'It has the edge of a bronze razor but will not yield as does bronze. It does not glow as copper nor has it the sheen of bronze but its value in weight is greater than silver or even gold. Nowhere in Sumer, I say, has anyone found the secret of its marriage to those elements that bestow such flexibility and strength. Only the men of *my* guild have that knowledge and we hold it as dear as our own children!'

'Fear not, friend Sheshkalla,' responded Gilgamesh, 'I'll not ask you to reveal any of your secrets.' His attention fell to Enkidu. 'I hope you are as impressed as am I, brother Enkidu. I'll be amazed if you're not.'

Turning the shaft in his hands, Enkidu appraised the flawless lines, the sensuous, lethal form of the spearhead. 'You are a better judge of such things than I but yes, I doubt any mortal foe would stand his ground before such potent arms and they look to me also as objects of rare beauty.'

The king turned to the chief of the metalworkers. 'Friend Sheshkalla, you and your men have accomplished miracles with this strange metal.'

'Well, My Lords,' replied Sheshkalla, 'I'll admit the craftsmen of your palace added a few touches – the fancy work and all that, but what are the trappings without the substance and the soul that we created?' Sheshkalla stepped to the bench, adding, 'And there's more, My Lords,' At its rear he pulled away the cloth to reveal what lay hidden beneath.

Two polished leather scabbards gleamed in sunlit splendour; each banded with intricately braided copper and replete with a gold and silver rosette ornament of striking artistry. Attached to each was a broad belt of patterned ox-hide fitted with a finely engraved bronze clasp. Upon the belt were fitted plates of intricately engraved bronze inlaid, as was the clasp, with silver and lapis lazuli. Within each scabbard nestled a short sword. The metalworker picked up a scabbard in each hand, presenting the first to the king, the second to his brother. 'Perhaps My Lords, you'd care to test the balance of these weapons as well.'

Gilgamesh and Enkidu eyed the pommels of gilded bronze, each set with a precious blue stone. Each placed a hand upon the hilt of boiled ox-hide bound with braided copper wire. Each withdrew the double-edged blade from its snug enclave and each balanced the deadly, glinting form in his hand.

'I wager no finer blades have seen the light of day in this or any land,' boasted Sheshkalla. 'They are, as you see, straight - not intended just for slashing as are the swords our men use, but for thrusting. I myself have tested these blades – they will pierce the strongest bronze scale.'

'You have excelled yourself, friend Sheshkalla,' answered Gilgamesh, stabbing at empty air, 'and any man would be rash indeed to dispute it. I'll consider it a great injustice if we do not find good sport for these splendid implements.'

'I think it more than likely we will,' breathed Enkidu, fingers gliding over the flat surface of his blade to find it smooth as polished obsidian.

'When would our Lords wish to take formal possession of their arms?' asked Sheshkalla.

'I'm loathe to part company with them now,' replied Gilgamesh, 'but at daybreak tomorrow we intend to leave Uruk. We must have possession by then.'

'In that case,' declared proud Sheshkalla, 'I ask that my men and I present them to you before the elders and the people. Unless - unless that is, you'd prefer the elders to do it.'

'What - Kuraka and his cronies!' responded Gilgamesh. 'No my friend you'll do it. But make sure you clean yourselves up first!'

Hardly had the king and Enkidu departed when one of the metalworkers remarked to Sheshkalla, 'Let's hope his new arms don't lead our king into further mischief in these parts.'

'Not whilst his brother is around to keep him straight,' replied Sheshkalla. 'On the other hand, let's hope these fine and fancy weapons don't fall short of their expectations - for all our sakes!'

***

The air was cool with the breath of retreating night. Much of the square before the palace was in shadow when they assembled beneath the gaze of Inanna's star. It might have been a day like any other, when market traders set out their wares and people streamed off to their labours through the city gates. But it was not a day like any other. Rumour had scurried through the streets and alleyways like cats in the night. The king and his brother were to

155

leave Uruk. People hurried on their way through the shadows; nobles, priests, artisans and slaves.

On a raised platform in front of the palace steps, upon the throne of precious inlays that had borne his predecessors, sat Gilgamesh. By his right side stood Enkidu, solemn and likewise simply dressed in belted tunic of pale linen. To either side and directly before them on the hard ground were seated the senior priests of Anu, of Inanna and of the lesser gods, the elders and other worthies of the town. Around the square, on the walls, at the windows and about the parapets and rooftops of surrounding buildings, wherever space permitted, people waited. The restless breeze of their chatter passed back and forth over the square. But when the drum sounded, when the king arose to speak, they became silent.

'I Gilgamesh,' he began, his strong voice carrying over the square, 'will go with my brother to the forests of cedar. I cannot say how long we will be absent but my companions and men-at-arms will keep watch from the wall and about the boundaries of our fields and pasture lands. In the forest we will cut down trees and have the men of that place haul them to the river. The timbers will follow the river along its course toward the Great Water. The people of our city must be vigilant. They must watch for them throughout the days and nights. They must go out and guide the logs to the quay of Uruk then bring them within the city wall. The people of the mountain country will know our city and our gods. I will make known the name of Uruk and they will know the name of Gilgamesh!'

Already the crowd had begun to voice its approval but the king's herald sounded a sharp roll on his copper drum and they again quietened.

'We will go up into the Cedar Mountain,' continued the king. 'There we will seek out Huwawa, the creature set down to guard the forests, of whom many speak with fear in their hearts. He, too, shall know our arms and our might and all Sumer will hear of it!'

The crowd began to stir but now one of the elders stood up; a lean, stooping man of many years and few teeth but one whose voice was still strong. 'Our Lord the King is young and no one could doubt his courage. But he and his worthy brother should not venture where Huwawa lies in wait. Those who speak of Huwawa say he is not mortal and cannot be harmed by the weapons of man. Why must our king and his brother risk their lives against one who cannot be defeated?'

'Am I to stay my hand for the sake of rumour?' asked Gilgamesh. 'Am I to languish in fear of something no man here has even seen?'

Enkidu's glance fell sharply on him because Gilgamesh spoke as rashly now as he had in the House of Assembly. But the king was presented with a greater distraction as the priests arose together and one of their number stepped forward. 'Lord Gilgamesh, prayer is already being offered and sacrifice made in your name and that of Lord Enkidu at the shrines of Great Anu and Lady Inanna, and at the altars of the lesser gods within our city. Each and every day our supplications will continue until you are both safely returned to Uruk. But when you find fresh water to drink, either from the river or from the wells you dig, always pour a little of it in the name of Utu, the sun, who we pray will light your way and guard you from harm.'

'I thank you and the holy ones for your concern,' replied Gilgamesh. 'I'm sure we will prove ourselves worthy in the face of danger – with your prayers to aid us, of course.'

Turning aside, he nodded and lifted a hand. From close to the palace wall at his left stepped a small group of men led by Sheshkalla, each of them bearing an object wrapped in white linen cloth. These they proceeded to unwrap so that now were revealed to those close enough to observe the arms fashioned for the king and his brother. With subdued chanting the priests of Inanna and of Anu blessed in turn the axes, the spears and the swords. And as they did, Sheshkalla, incongruous in plain woollen robe, took them up one by one, held them out and placed them at the feet of Gilgamesh and Enkidu. Gilgamesh rose from his throne to hold up his scabbard and sword to the crowd. Enkidu did likewise. Both fastened them about their waists then each took axe and spear in his hands and raised the weapons above his head. Cheering broke out across the square and echoed down from those arrayed about the rooftops.

When the weapons were lowered, three of the city elders stepped forward, the foremost being Kuraka. Though his voice did not carry well it was he who spoke as the second elder presented part of their offerings to the king. 'The Council of Elders wishes our lord to take these on his journey for we believe they will serve him well.'

'You offer me the bow of Anshan!' exclaimed Gilgamesh as the third elder - the one who had earlier advised caution - lifted up the arrows in their ornately gilded quiver.

'Indeed we offer the bow of Anshan,' replied Kuraka. 'One of our worthy ancestors carried it to Uruk from the land of the eastern mountains when he forged our links with distant Aratta and brought us their trade in metals. It was presented out of respect to the city elders of his day. It has hung until today in the House of Assembly as a symbol of truth and justice amongst the people, for *he* cared greatly about their welfare and contentment.'

All within earshot were struck by Kuraka's innuendo. Without change of expression, without comment, Gilgamesh listened as Kuraka continued. 'No man in our land possesses such a bow. Only one of great strength can pull it. Let the gods guide our king's judgement when he raises this bow, as we pray they will guide him in all else!'

'And I know where the first arrow should take root,' muttered Gilgamesh.

As he accepted the bow with a cold eye on Kuraka the third elder spoke out. 'My Lords, please consider this for all our sakes. If you must go to the Cedar Mountain, let Lord Enkidu walk before the king. We hear he knows the forest and its secret pathways. Let him guard and protect our king who is a stranger to these wild places. Let us pray to the gods that they succeed in each and every task that falls upon them!'

'If prayers and advice were to give us strength,' breathed Gilgamesh to his brother, 'I think the two of us alone could take on an entire city.'

'They are concerned for your well-being,' answered Enkidu. 'They wish you to return safely.'

'And they hope the Man of Kish doesn't become too restless in our absence,' added Gilgamesh, nodding to his herald then adding, 'Mind you, brother Enkidu, so do I.'

The drum spoke again - now harsh and insistent. From the far end of the square where the palace stables lay arose a commotion and with it the crowd began to part. The king's drummer ceased but another sounded out in slow, steady rhythm from where the crowd had opened. The drummer appeared with behind him, issuing from beneath the stable archway, the first of the king's companions in their war carts. The gruff snort of asses, four to each wagon, and the rumble of heavy wooden wheels grew louder as they streamed into the square. The chariots bristled bronze spears with the bright pennants of Uruk swaying from them. The chariot men wore patterned white tunics, fringed red cloaks, rounded and delicately engraved bronze helmets. Trudging behind came the less pretentiously attired footmen with plain bronze helmets, spears and square wicker shields faced with boiled ox-hide. Following the drummer they moved in loose parade toward the platform where Gilgamesh and Enkidu waited. The two leading chariots held only one man apiece, whereas each of those following carried two. Along with the footmen plodded a number of asses hung with wicker panniers whose contents included jars of beer.

Not since the war with Kish had so many armed men paraded through Uruk, though anyone with the ability to do so would have counted no more than five hundred.

The drummer and the leading carts halted before the platform. Remaining silent as the drum stopped, the people watched whilst attendants attired the king and his brother with red cloaks and presented them with bronze helmets which they lifted and fitted themselves. Each took his spear and axe. Each let himself down into one of the leading chariots. Joining the drummer who had led the parade, the king's herald now placed himself in front of his master's chariot and, given a signal by Gilgamesh, both drums began to beat in steady unison. The column began to move. People pressed forward, waving their arms. Once more raising their voices. The King of Uruk - *their* king - was leading his men from the city as though to do battle. And by his side, equal in strength and prowess, champion of Uruk's poor, rode his brother.

It hardly concerned them that no army was clamouring outside the city wall, no hoard advancing in raised dust over the plain, no enemy awaiting their arrival behind strong defences. That there was a challenge beyond the city was all that mattered. This was the Gilgamesh of old - Gilgamesh the warrior who had humbled Agga of Kish and made Uruk strong.

The drummers and chariots continued on. They would leave Uruk via the Nippur Gate at its north and not from the Southern Gate on the side where the river flowed. It was not because the route to the latter wound through narrow, congested streets via the market square and the Eanna precinct. No, the Nippur Gate, through which pilgrims passed on

161

their journey to the holy city itself and the temple of Enlil, was closer. Just as important, kings of Uruk had traditionally led their men to battle from that gate.

People streamed noisily behind the procession, some scrambling over rooftops, others making their way along the city wall, following it around as sunlight spilled into the city.

There was one, more agile than most, one who had managed to thread his way through the crowd. One who knew as well as anyone which direction the king and his men were to take. He knew also that at the Nippur Gate they would be moving slowly because the gate was narrow and the crowd would be pressing close. The great copper-banded, cedar doors were creaking ponderously inwards when someone yelled above the clamour of voices, 'Great Lords - hear me!'

The men in the leading chariots glanced about, some looking up at the high square towers either side of the gate. There they saw him perched within an empty niche to the right of the main arch and well beyond the reach of anyone below.

'I have something for our mighty king's brother!' he called, holding out a small leather pouch. As the procession eased by, Shannu gazed down on the two chariots almost directly beneath, his hand poised as if about to hurl down the pouch, his eyes darting with uncertainty from one to the other.

'He cannot tell which of us is which!' laughed Gilgamesh. And true enough, the temple boy, seeing both men dressed alike and with bronze helmets covering their heads, was about to throw the pouch down to the king, whose attendant held up his hands in expectation. Then the light of recognition glinted in the boy's eye and grinning widely, he changed his aim. Enkidu's hand shot up, grabbing the pouch in mid-flight before it could land beneath the wheels of the cart. Passing under the arch Enkidu's chariot had slowed further to fall in behind that of the king. By the time he emerged from the shadows he had opened the pouch.

'What did the boy give you?' asked Gilgamesh as Enkidu's wagon drew alongside his.

Enkidu glanced over his shoulder at the people gathered on the city wall before answering. 'It's a lock of her hair.'

'You mean the temple girl, Shamkhat - she has sent you a keepsake?'

'That she has,' he replied, tucking the pouch into his tunic. 'I looked hard amongst the crowd but I couldn't see her. She must not have come down from the temple.'

'No, Enkidu, Inanna's maidservants do not mix with the commoners at such times. She will have watched from the temple but now you can be certain her thoughts are with you on our journey.'

'By the gods, I will miss her company,' sighed Enkidu.

***

Shamkhat gazed out from the temple platform, a tear on her cheek. She had seen the boy throw down the purse and wished now she had been closer to Enkidu as he departed. So strong had her feelings become for him that she would no longer accept the company of other men, despite the censure of her

163

superiors. But the priesthood could do nothing because her champion was no common man.

***

Under a brightening sky they passed through the drifting smoke of a camp whose occupants were already setting up for trade by the Nippur gate. By now, the noise and bustle of the city had given way to the ass's snort, the thump of hooves and the creak of wheels. Trailing loosely in their wake, the king's companions chatted amongst themselves. Behind them strode the footmen. To their right, the sun cast long shadows across their path from slender palm trees. Ahead lay the fields, the pastures, a few rustic hamlets and the dusty plain.

***

Utu's warm rays bathed the small shrine above the palace of Egalmah. From the altar a tang of burning incense sweetened the morning air. Ninsun watched the glint of bronze amidst rising dust as armed men moved away in the distance. Then she turned her face to the rising sun. Her tiara sparked sunlight, her long robe glowed warm colours as she raised her hands to the light of a new day.

'Utu, why did you give Gilgamesh so restless a soul? Never will the city and the people fulfil his desires or give him contentment. Now he leaves Uruk with his brother for the forests of the Cedar Mountain. They will challenge Huwawa, the one you and all the gods loathe. Let the days remain long. Shield them with your glow. Let no harm come to them by day or night. Guard them from the evil Huwawa. Cause the thirteen winds to confound that terrible creature so their weapons may prevail.

Let my sons add glory to your name and let them return to Uruk in triumph!'

CHAPTER 5
BEAST OF THE FOREST

'Well we've made it this far,' said Gilgamesh, gazing across sparse land that rolled away from the greener banks of the river. 'I've never been so long away from the city. Never in such an empty land as this. It seems only the river gives it life. And I'd no idea how many skills would be needed to set up camp and live off the land the way we have. I never gave a thought to making fire until I saw you at work with those dried sticks or pieces of flint. Now I can make fire like a man of the country and I'm more proud of it than I could ever have imagined.'

'I watched the country people do it often enough,' said Enkidu. 'Once I applied myself, it seemed second nature. So now even a king can do it.'

'Yes, even a king.' Gilgamesh relaxed against the grassy bank, hands clasped behind his head, eyes part closed. 'Ah, I feel we've passed these many days moving in and out of our dreams. It's as though time no longer mattered. We could have travelled five days or fifty as far as I'm concerned. Though if we had a mirror we might guess how long from the growth of hair on our faces.'

'Until I set out for Uruk,' commented Enkidu, sitting close by, 'I had no need to count anything. Sunrise and sunset were all that mattered. My only judge of time was my stomach.'

Smoke coiled into the morning air. The crack and hiss of their fire Gilgamesh found reassuring, in part because his sleep had been disturbed these last few nights. High above circled buzzards, black specks against a sky draped with loose skeins of white.

'This is such an empty land,' said Gilgamesh. 'At least there are fish in the river.'

'There's plenty of life hereabouts if you know where to find it,' mused Enkidu, 'otherwise we'd not have fresh meat. And see over there – jackals and vultures are feasting well on the carcass of the gazelle you killed.'

'You're right of course and loathe as I am to admit it, I should be thankful to our elders for giving us that bow. Even that damnable spokesman of theirs. But as for life, dear brother - it seems scarce enough for one used to the presence of the court and the coming and going of so many people.'

Enkidu stirred the fire and turned the skewered meat. Fat dripped into glowing wood, causing it to hiss and flare. 'As you say,' he smiled, 'You're a man of the city. You don't find comfort in solitude any more than I found it in the clamour of Uruk.'

'Quite so,' answered Gilgamesh, sitting up, 'but I am beginning to understand how you felt about the city. I've seen how readily you took to the wilderness that was once your home, though until this moment I never cared to remind you of it. I've watched you follow tracks I wouldn't have noticed if I'd passed by them a hundred times. I've watched you set your traps at night and I marvel at your skill and cunning. I'm beginning to appreciate the wild places in a way I never thought possible.'

'Just as I'm beginning to think there is some good to be said about the city now we're far away from it,' grinned Enkidu. 'And I, too, feel we are drifting in some strange realm. When I roamed alone distance was hardly important. All that mattered was that there was food and water to be had. This journey seems far greater than I recall because I now carry my share of mankind's burdens.'

Gilgamesh asked him, 'Reckoning the days that have passed by since we left the city, d'you think there could be as many again before we reach the forest?'

'No, the days will be fewer. See how the river has grown narrower. Look at how it flows more rapidly and cuts deeper into the land. And feel how fresh the air is. I'll wager if we make good progress the rest of today then tomorrow will find us in the hill country. If so, we'll have sight of the mountains by midday.'

'Oh, so you'll wager!' laughed Gilgamesh, lifting a skewer from the fire. 'Enkidu, you've become more a man of the city than you realise!'

**

'Now about this wager of yours yesterday, brother Enkidu. The sun is already high and I don't see any mountains. What is it you care to wager or have you put aside your expectations?'

The asses snorted, the wagons jolted over uneven ground. Enkidu considered his answer. 'To wager with you now would be churlish in spite of your impatience. The sun is high but still some way from its zenith and already I can smell the air of the mountains and the tang of the trees. Have your senses given you no clues as to what lies ahead?'

'They certainly have! I smell the asses since they're directly in front of us and my aching bones make me wonder how much longer our chariots will survive this rough ground before they break apart beneath us and end up as firewood. It's as well we have the river to carry us back home.'

'Over the next rise I'm sure we'll have sight of the forests,' said Enkidu. 'If we do not, I'll ease my brother's journey and stop his grousing by washing his feet at every stop as a penance.'

'Now that sounds highly pleasurable but on this occasion I'll not commit myself to a wager because I fear you may be right. No, I don't fear it – I desire it!'

They carried on, moving away from the river as its banks became steeper and overgrown with shrubs. Rocky outcrops already impeded their progress. The land rose steadily until the river, now some way below in a ravine, disappeared from view. The sky was clear, the sun hot and the air buzzing with insects when they crested the rise and came to a halt.

'See over there!' cried Enkidu with a triumphant wave of his arm. 'There are the cedar forests! And rising directly beyond are the mountains!'

Across the wide valley spread beneath them the river snaked like a ribbon, disappearing where the hills rose muted in a soft haze.

'I've never seen such grandeur,' declared Gilgamesh, shading his eyes from the sun. 'Never so much greenery.'

'Ay, it's green, and it's cooler, brother - you'll see!'

'Then let's go on as far as these chariots will take us. After that we'll have to walk so the asses can carry our provisions.'

'Our chariots ought to make it across the valley if we go carefully,' assured Enkidu. 'There are hunters and woodsmen about the forests. If we offer them silver they'll help us in our work. We'll need many willing hands as well as their oxen to get our timber down to the river.'

'It's as well my companions and armed men returned to Uruk. They're willing enough to cut our enemies down on the battlefield but I doubt the task we've set ourselves here would please them.'

'Nor will it please us,' said Enkidu, 'I sometimes watched the woodsmen at work. They have cruder implements than ours but they are skilled in ways we have yet to learn.'

'Oh, I never imagined we'd brought along these fine axes just for chopping wood,' answered Gilgamesh. 'I expect from what you've told me we'll meet dangerous creatures in those woods - not to mention the one you say will be waiting to murder us.'

'You'll not be disappointed on either account. The finest cedars grow on the flanks of that mountain directly ahead. Streams gush through its valleys on their way to feed the great river. The trees stand undisturbed because no one has so far been foolish enough to venture there. Or if anyone ever did then they never returned to tell the tale.'

'Then let's see if the woodsmen find their misgivings outweighed by our silver,' smiled Gilgamesh, 'especially if we set them an example by leading the way.'

'I doubt they will but we should go on without delay and hope our wagons will take us as far as the forest edge. Once there we can bathe in one of the streams and set up camp. In the morning we will find men thereabouts and they'll have a chief with whom we might strike a deal. We could offer these asses to them as part of it - theirs will not be so well bred.'

'And maybe tonight,' sighed Gilgamesh, 'I'll rest and be free of the dreams that have troubled me these last few nights.'

His brother noted the remark. He recalled how Gilgamesh had slept badly of late. Recalled hearing him talk incoherently in his sleep. Enkidu had thought more than once to ask what had been disturbing him but decided for the time being it might be better to have his brother volunteer the information.

Their progress across the valley was becoming more difficult. Apart from brittle shrubs and frequent ruts, bare rocks protruded like the clean-picked bones of a cadaver to slow them further. Some way across, both men dismounted, joining their own beasts on foot in an effort to haul the protesting chariots to their intended destination.

'Well,' observed Gilgamesh, breathing deeply as they came to rest, 'it is cooler here as you said it would be, and a good thing too.'

'Yes, a good thing,' replied Enkidu, 'but the forest hides creatures that will envy us our food. Some might even see us as their next dinner. Once we're refreshed we should secure our camp whilst there's still light then I'll prepare our fire and meal.'

'We can burn the chariot timbers,' suggested Gilgamesh - they'll be of no use to us now.'

'Yes, and we'll need to cut and trim branches for a palisade. The forest has to be our servant, not our master.'

***

A river of stars bathed a moonless night sky. Within the small camp two figures sat facing one another, their faces reflecting the red glow of their fire. A crack of wood and living embers danced amidst coiling smoke. Adrift in the vastness of night, their oasis of light seemed all that mattered in an unfathomable world.

'I won't claim to be dissatisfied with our venture,' mused Gilgamesh as the fire spat, 'even though Uruk is a long way away, even though our realm is shrunk to a space hardly more than two steps across. And yet my harpist and the company of Inanna's girls would not go amiss this evening.'

'Your musician and the temple women would not be happy so away from the comforts of the city,' replied Enkidu. 'And right now you and I hardly present an image of courtly bearing.'

'Yes,' reflected Gilgamesh, running fingers across a bristled face, 'I dare say you're right.'

'Speaking of women, let me say once more how much I miss the girl who befriended me. At night I see her eyes and hear her voice. I'd make my way back to Uruk for nothing other than her.'

'You're in love with the girl, Enkidu. I've suspected it ever since we sat talking by that water hole the day I rode out to find you. Admit it.'

'Love is a subject I know little about but I think you must be right.'

172

'Then I'll gladly confess something to you. The day before we left I summoned the boy who brought you the lock of hair and ordered him to look after her – discreetly, of course. He's a wily young rogue and no mistake, but for reasons beyond my understanding I have placed my trust in him. I do not think I'll find it betrayed.'

'I'm grateful to you for doing that,' smiled Enkidu.

'Ah, well, wild forest animals or no, I find our situation pleasant enough and the air here is sweet as wine. I'll sleep tonight as soundly as I would in my own bed – with a bit of luck.'

'Yes - you spoke earlier of dreaming,' said Enkidu. 'You mentioned you had been much troubled but you never said why.'

'No, I said nothing because I feared the dreams might be a portent – as were those I had before you came to Uruk. I thought that – I thought if I told you about them, you might conclude I was having a change of heart. I assure you I am not.'

'Nor would I think so,' replied Enkidu. 'I know you'd never want to return with our task unfulfilled. But why not tell me what troubled you so in those dreams? We've eaten well, we're at peace by our fire so this is as good a time as any to unburden yourself.'

As though transfixed by memories, Gilgamesh stared into the glowing microcosm of landscapes their modest fire had become. 'These last five nights I have dreamed,' he said at last. 'Each time I thought I heard you call my name but when I woke up, when I looked about, you were still asleep. Each time I imagined I'd left your side, that I had passed through some kind of portal. In the first dream I found myself climbing the Cedar Mountain through a ravine. The sheer scale of the place made me feel small as an insect. I was overwhelmed by its immensity. The ground shook - it started to heave and I looked up to see the walls of the mountain crashing toward me. I thought I was done for but then - then a figure appeared and snatched me from death. It glowed so brightly I was dazzled. Then it set me down safely, and offered me water. The face I could not see but this being was oddly familiar, like a friend whose name you cannot quite recall.

In the second dream I was higher up on the mountain but as in that first one, the ground began to tremble like a living thing. Rocks started to fall about me then the earth yawned open as a black chasm. The ground where I stood was sliding into it. I tried to scramble clear but it was no use. I was about to be swept into the bowels of hell but again he, that same figure, came and saved my life.'

Firelight shone in his eyes. Gilgamesh became silent once more, turning over in his thoughts the scenes he was about to relate.

'And the third dream?' asked Enkidu.

'Yes, the third dream. Yet again I was on the flanks of the mountain but this time flames burst from its summit and the ground bellowed like thunder. The fires increased in violence. Smoke spread over the sky. Smoke so thick it shrouded the sun until it was blotted out entirely. A darkness fell that was blacker than any night I ever knew. A kind of ash drifted thickly on the air. It touched my flesh like moth wings. Lightning began to flare and in its raging madness I saw black rain. Black rain, brother

174

Enkidu! What d'you make of that? If I asked our soothsayers, would they say this venture of ours was doomed?'

'That I cannot say. But describe the other dreams before I consider my answer.'

'In the fourth dream I wandered in a bare, open plain. On the horizon I saw an immense dark bird rise into the air like a thundercloud with wings that beat as the great drum of Inanna's temple. It soared above me so large I could not escape from beneath its shadow. Its mouth was agape, I tell you - and glowing with fire. I knew it had seen me when it circled about and began to descend. I knew the thing would have me because there was nowhere to hide. No bush! No rock! Nothing! But as it swept down, the stranger leapt out from nowhere, seized the bird by the neck then wrestled it to the ground!

In the last of those dreams I stood confronted by a monstrous bull that snorted like a gale. It bellowed. It beat the earth. It threatened to crush me, rising up such a cloud that it, too, spread and obscured the sky. When I tried to get away I was thrown to the ground by the tremor of its hooves. But yet again, even as the thing towered over me, that same one, that same guardian hurried to my rescue. He drove the creature back and yet again offered me comfort and cool water. What d'you see in all this, brother Enkidu? You came into this world with an understanding not given to others. Those dreams - those messengers in the night - were they a warning from the gods? Or is it because I find myself in a strange land? Or could they be the dreams of a child who sees demons in every household shadow. Sitting here enclosed by utter darkness anything seems possible.'

'I can only offer what my instincts tell me,' breathed Enkidu. 'To me those dreams foretell a struggle in which the powers of nature as well as the gods play their part. But in all of them no harm befell you - and you were aided by one who must have been your guardian. Your – our mother, Lady Ninsun, would understand far better than I. Perhaps it is her prayers that manifest themselves in these visions. Perhaps it was Utu, lord of the day, who descended to save you from harm.'

'Perhaps,' sighed Gilgamesh. A reptile hiss, a lolling tongue of flame and the fire's blinking red eye flared to illuminate his bristled face. 'But so real were those dreams, so odd is the night in this land we have entered that afterwards I began to question my own reality. Am I in the world of the living with a brother of flesh and blood who once belonged in a world beyond ours, or have I now entered that world?'

'It's quite unlike you to wax pensive,' smiled Enkidu. 'It must be the effect of our long journey. In troubled sleep your mind became a deep well in which the images of that other world found their home. If you hear sounds tonight it will be wolves and bears scavenging about but our camp will be proof against them and I will remain alert even in sleep.'

'I thought the land of Sumer contained all that mattered. I think, Enkidu, your understanding of the world is much greater than mine although you came to know mankind and the city only of late.'

'I claim nothing other than what has been given to me,' replied Enkidu. 'But it's time to put out the fire and rest. At first light we can find the woodsmen and begin our work.'

'I imagine it will be difficult to make ourselves understood,' yawned Gilgamesh.

'Oh, I know their language,' said Enkidu, settling back and drawing up the sheepskin cover.

'You know their language? Enkidu, how can you know their language?'

'I know it as I knew your own when Shamkhat first spoke – when she offered me her apple. The understanding was with me from the beginning.'

'The understanding was with you from the beginning,' breathed Gilgamesh, laying back and closing his eyes. 'How strange the world has become. And ever stranger.'

***

'Those timbers are magnificent!' exclaimed Gilgamesh. 'Do you not agree?'

The cries of the loggers carried through the forest. The screech of tormented wood shivered the air as another tree crashed through standing foliage to shake thunder from the ground.

'I'd be happy if *you* agreed we had enough,' replied Enkidu, 'but I know you will not.'

'No, I still say we help ourselves to a few of the very best before we leave. I want Uruk to be the envy of all Sumer. That was always foremost in my mind.'

For six days they had played their part in felling the cedars. They had watched the great trunks shorn of their branches then dragged by oxen down the slopes to the riverbank. They had seen the logs set adrift on turbulent water to carry southward on their journey to distant Uruk. They stood now on a rise, bathed in the rays of late afternoon sun, each with axe slung over his broad back, each with a stout spear in his grasp and sword hanging ready at his side. Their weapons gleamed deadly light, their shadows cast dark pillars over the grass. The breeze stirred their long hair. The two brothers, more wild men in appearance than citizens of Uruk, were lords of the wide land. Heroes gazing across to the forested mountain that soared in deceptive tranquillity.

'I hope the people of Uruk are vigilant,' said Enkidu, 'and that the people of the many other towns on the river are not, particularly those of Kish.'

'We have carved the names of Gilgamesh and our city on those timbers,' he replied, gesturing to where the oxen dragged their burden on lower ground. 'If they understand what they're seeing they'll think twice before laying a hand on any prize we have set ourselves to win.'

As Gilgamesh spoke, they were approached by a stocky, course-featured man in rough tunic of stitched hides topped by loose-fitting leather helmet. Trudging up the grassy slope with the aid of a gnarled walking stick he stood before them and addressed himself to Enkidu. Enkidu then turned to Gilgamesh. 'He says the end of this day will see them finish their quota. Tomorrow we must pay them more silver if they're to continue.'

'Then tell him,' answered Gilgamesh, regarding the narrowed brown eyes set in a ruddy face as bristled as the hills, 'that tomorrow we will go up

178

into the Cedar Mountain and wish to hire four of his woodcutters together with four good oxen.'

On hearing the message related by Enkidu the man became excited. He babbled rapidly, gesturing with his stick to the higher land above the forest and the river.

'He says neither he nor his men will go near the Cedar Mountain,' related Enkidu, 'and if we want his oxen we must buy them from him before we go. What he asks is considerably more than their real value even though he accepted our asses and their harnesses as part payment.'

'Then offer him a good deal less,' replied Gilgamesh, looking down at the man. Then resting a hand on the pommel of his sword, he added, 'And say it is my only offer and that we go in the morning with or without his miserable beasts.'

It was evident, after further animated gesturing and skyward glances of mock despair by the forester, that an agreement of sorts had been reached.

'He still demands more than their true worth,' said Enkidu, 'but I insisted we choose the best from his herd so that our oxen are strong enough for the task. He agreed to that but says we are fools to go up into the Cedar Mountain because it is protected by an evil beyond all understanding. That message should come as no surprise, brother, and I have the impression he expects his oxen to return without us - if they return at all. He wants payment in advance for their next labours, nevertheless.'

'Does he indeed. Well, put it to this boorish oaf that we pay only for what we take and that he gets nothing more until we return. Once we get started

179

we'll probably work up a great enough appetite to eat his damned oxen. Tell him we'll need his men as soon as we come down from the mountain. Tell him also that should he not co-operate when we return, I will personally skewer his arse with that stick, cut him up and feed him to the dogs. After that a thousand men will come out from Uruk armed as we are and seize his entire herd!'

The steely gaze and ample stature of Gilgamesh were sufficient to render the man wide-eyed and speechless even as Enkidu sighed, 'Ah, that's more the Gilgamesh I know.' But it was evidently enough when Enkidu added, 'They won't give us any problems. He says they only wish to go about their business as we wish to go about ours. Except that - except we're more likely to finish up dead.'

'Very well, let's choose our beasts and plenty of strong rope. Then we can return to our camp and offer fresh water and grain to the sun before he leaves the sky. After that we ought to eat, get our rest and be ready to set off at first light.'

***

Gilgamesh halted to peer skywards through spreading branches. 'Only in those dreams I spoke about did I see anything like this. But it truly exists.'

'The trees hereabouts are older,' replied Enkidu. Untouched by the woodcutter – of course.'

Morning sunlight slanted through ranks of trees; dark sentinels that towered high above the two men. Bright splashes shimmered on the sombre, cone-strewn forest floor. Now and again they halted the plodding oxen to stand and gaze about. On doing so a silence descended more profound even than that of the deserts. There was no breath of wind. No cry of birds. They spoke in lowered voices as though in the hallowed sanctuary of an ancient temple. They had climbed some way further, treading softly, when Gilgamesh said, 'Hold, Enkidu. Do you sense a presence or am I troubled by the trees that crowd in on us and the shadows they hold?'

'A presence, brother? Yes, there is a presence. It listens but I'm certain it is not close. No, not yet it isn't. It will have known of us even before we quit our camp. Right now it probably wonders why we have dared venture this far. We should waste no more time. Beyond the next ridge, if my memory serves me, we'll find some of the best trees and we can begin our work. We've learned enough from the woodsmen these last few days to give a good account of ourselves.'

They urged the beasts on until they at last reached the top of the rise. Enkidu noticed that though the sun was high above, it had become veiled by a thin, white mist that drifted from the mountain. He made no comment. Ahead was open, rocky ground that levelled out for a short way only to sweep upward again to a thickly forested higher level.

'I'm certain those ahead of us are the greatest of the cedars,' said Enkidu.

'Then that's where we'll take ourselves!' declared Gilgamesh.

'If you insist,' replied Enkidu, glancing up at the pale sky with a frown his brother observed but chose to ignore.

'Let's make our camp here and see which of them will be the first to fall,' said Gilgamesh. 'My axe and I are impatient to get started!'

'I agree. The sooner we begin, the sooner we'll be finished. The thought of that will give greater strength to my swing - do not doubt it.' Under his breath he added, 'Yes, finished for good.'

'Oh, give strength to your swing will it!' laughed Gilgamesh, following Enkidu up the rise. 'I'll have my axe bite into these so-called sacred trees at least as eagerly as yours! Aye, it will keep me fit for when Uruk next goes to war! I'll wager now that before the sun goes down I will have -.'

'Wager, brother! Not here! We may soon find we have enough on our hands without wagers.'

They laid their axes and spears on the ground then led the oxen aside, tethering them some distance away. 'The exercise will keep us warm,' remarked Gilgamesh as they returned. 'We must be close to the sky here. I'm chilled and I see the clouds are descending around us.'

'The weather changes quickly in these mountains,' said Enkidu, gazing up again through the few remaining gaps in the canopy high above to observe a sky that now had become sunless and pallid as a shroud. 'You'll seldom find the warmth and clear skies of your land in this part of the world.'

'*Our* land, brother; or are you forgetting the rich fields of Uruk and the pleasures of the city?'

'No, I'm not forgetting but I live with other memories as well you know and this place is -.' Enkidu hesitated. Enkidu stared hard into the massed trees.

'What is it?' asked Gilgamesh.

'I thought I heard -. Wait!'

Again there was silence and both men peered into an obscurity of shadows.

White mist oozed from amidst darkening trees like the overflowing vapours of a cauldron but heavy and cold. A dull grating that might have been one slab of stone dragged against another echoed from deeper within the forest, followed by a mist-deadened crack of timber.

'Hear that!' exclaimed Gilgamesh. 'It seems we're not the only ones about today. Others are working in the forest. Or perhaps it was a bear going about his business.'

'There are no other men here whether you choose to believe me or not,' countered Enkidu. 'And what you heard was no bear because there are no bears here either. That you *can* have my wager on and if you're right then I'll pay it tenfold. Something approaches within the mist – sooner than I expected it might. Something that is not here to welcome us. D'you not smell corruption in the air?'

'So the guardian of the cedars has got up off his arse at last. Is that what you're telling me?'

'Gilgamesh, we might still have time to take our possessions and go - or d'you still not accept what I say? It moves quickly. It draws near even as we talk.'

Tethered some distance away, the oxen snorted and stamped. In growing terror they attempted to free themselves from the coarse rope that kept them attached to a tree trunk.

'Accept what you say, brother? Perhaps - perhaps not! Yet, I do sense danger. I feel the hairs

183

of my flesh stand up, though I wonder if that is not because of the cold and because this forest is so alien to me. Whatever the cause, I do not intend the priests and the people of Uruk should wail for my soul just yet!'

'Brave words, brother Gilgamesh, but very soon we'll have to look to our weapons and put our trust in those amongst the gods who are with us!'

'Then,' responded Gilgamesh, his expression one of grim defiance, 'I will take up my axe and spear and I will stand alone against your demon because I insisted on our coming when I might have heeded your warnings. Whatever the danger I do not intend to turn and run. Threats, bad dreams or demons of the forest - I stay and I fight!'

'You're more reckless than any man should be!' declared Enkidu. 'But you'll not stand alone. That I swore on my oath to Ninsun and I'll be true to it though the horrors of the netherworld confront us. But the air grows colder still, and listen – can you hear it breathing? Take up your weapons, brother Gilgamesh! Take them up now!'

Gilgamesh shouldered his axe, as already had Enkidu and both men grasped their spears in readiness. A swish of branches then a hollow thud from something as yet unseen shook the ground. From the gloom of the forest echoed a crack of splintering timber and a low growl that seemed to drive the mist before it. Amongst the trees moved a shifting form, vague and indistinct - seen then unseen - now a looming darkness amidst the paler mists. Louder the breathing grew and Gilgamesh said, 'Enkidu, my flesh crawls as though the breath of the grave wafts over us.'

As he spoke, a wild cackling shivered the air. A darkly fearsome image burst from the trees. It lurched from side to side, jerking its head as though amazed by the sight of the two men. Round yellow eyes, large and speckled with black, stared out from a mask of shining black fur. Spider-palp jaws quivered red, framed by curved white tusks that must serve only to grasp its victim close to the terrible mouth. In the creature's wake scampered a gibbering turmoil of lean and foul, white toothed, red eyed and long clawed black little scavengers, eager to bloody their noses in the remains of their master's kill.

'By the gods!' cried Gilgamesh. 'What monstrous thing is this?'

'It is Huwawa, brother, and he has come to take us!'

The creature hooked one limb about a tree and raised itself higher, spilling an insane howl of triumph over the two men. 'You came to defile the forest!' it screeched. 'Your time in this world is ended! Ended!'

'He speaks to us!' cried Gilgamesh, though the mocking howl rang much louder in his mind than in his ear.

'Indeed he does.' replied Enkidu as both backed away. 'He speaks the language of all men for whatever good that will do.'

'You!' shrieked Huwawa, his head shaking fitfully as his baleful gaze fell upon Enkidu. 'I know you well! You were at one with the forest but have chosen betrayal! You wandered free even here and I allowed it! When you grovelled in the earth I could have seized and devoured you! You have become a

185

hireling of this vain and boastful man. You do his bidding for your daily bread! You will share his fate as will any foolish enough to follow you and defile the sacred groves of Lord Enlil! The trees you sought to destroy will remain as a testament to your arrogance and I will shit on your remains!'

Huwawa lurched forward, his several white-clawed limbs gouging earth and flailing air. In a moment the two brothers would writhe within his deadly grasp.

'Remember your boasts in Uruk as I remember my promise to Lady Ninsun!' called Enkidu, raising his spear high.

With a shout of defiance from Gilgamesh, with a fierce cry from Enkidu, both men hurled their spears as the creature sprang. Enkidu's spear struck Huwawa in the shoulder - that of Gilgamesh below the slavering jaws. Huwawa screeched insane rage as the two darted aside to avoid his rush. Flashing a clawed arm at Gilgamesh, who leapt back to avoid it, Huwawa hesitated momentarily, employing others of his limbs to grasp the spears in an attempt to wrench them from his body.

'He fears the metal of our weapons!' cried Enkidu, once more fixed by the malice of those baleful yellow eyes. Huwawa sprang at him with an ear-splitting howl. Axe at the ready Enkidu prepared to meet the onslaught as with jaws agape the creature reared over him. But Enkidu caught his foot against an exposed root, staggered and fell sprawling on his back. With a shriek, Huwawa was astride him. The jaws might have done their grisly work at once had not Gilgamesh rushed forward to seize and thrust harder on the spear that swung wildly from the creature's short neck. This momentary torment distracted Huwawa as intended but both men were now within his reach and a black-furred limb shot out to seize Gilgamesh about the waist. Enkidu was back on his feet and raising his axe with a cry whilst Gilgamesh wrenched at the spear. Enkidu's axe hissed to strike Huwawa between the eyes with a blow fit to sever the head from an ox. Gilgamesh tore free and raised his axe, seeing blood-matted fur and thinking Huwawa must be sorely injured and ready to retreat.

'Strike him!' shouted Enkidu, wrenching his own axe free and raising it again.

Before either could strike, Huwawa lashed out a limb and flung Enkidu back to the ground. Gilgamesh he seized again, then the fallen Enkidu. Huwawa raised up, his grim, gore-spattered head shaking rapidly from side to side as he sneered, 'Pitiful little men! Pitiful - pitiful - pitiful!'

Both men drew their swords, each striking through Huwawa's dense fur but finding no vital spot. The creature steadied itself ready to impale one or the other man on his tusks whilst the drooling jaws gaped wide to exhale a blast of putrescence. But as the two struggled for their lives in Huwawa's grasp, something distracted him. The mists began to swirl as if stirred by some great, unseen hand. The swirling rapidly became a vortex. So sudden, so violent was the buffeting that Huwawa released his grip, rose up to his full height with a howl of anger and glanced fitfully about whilst striking at the air with his forelimbs. Each man hacked at the limb holding him until it loosened its grip. Freed from his grasp Gilgamesh and Enkidu fell to the ground, rolled aside then scrambled clear to join one another by a sturdy tree. The wind struck them with a demon's shriek even as it struck and beat at Huwawa. So strong was the vortex, so fierce its pummelling of Huwawa, so rapid its changes in direction, that he flailed about, not knowing which way to go in order to escape the turmoil. His grim entourage, seeing their master's plight, dashed to and fro in confusion then fled screeching into the mist where they promptly vanished. The sturdiest trees groaned in protest. Timber cracked as the two men, fearing the wind might tear them away, held hard to a stout branch close above their heads.

'Utu has sent the winds to aid us!' shouted Gilgamesh above the commotion.

The frenzied Huwawa, no longer concerned about his intended victims, raged at his new foe - a foe he could neither see nor grapple. The power of the winds grew further still, shaking the great trees to their very roots. Huwawa, two limbs locked about adjacent trunks, jaws quivering, held fast against a fury that centred on him as a shrieking whirlpool, a fury that seemed to draw away his energy.

'Look!' yelled Gilgamesh close to his brother's ear. 'Our spears have shaken free! He cowers in terror! We should strike him now!'

'We'd be swept away!' called Enkidu. The winds are strongest close to him! Wait!'

Huwawa, wailing aloud, fell to the ground. The mists began to swirl apart - an expanding, disintegrating vortex torn into fragments that wavered for a time then drifted slowly skyward.

'The sun!' shouted Gilgamesh above the creature's howling. 'There is the sun!'

'Look at Huwawa!' cried Enkidu. 'Look at him!'

Gilgamesh saw, too. 'He's growing smaller or do my eyes deceive me!'

'They do not!' gasped Enkidu as the wailing died to a whimper. 'The winds have sucked away his strength. And the sun - its light will make him a creature of this world who no longer has the power to destroy us!'

The remaining winds blustered away, the air calmed, the light of the sun fell in bright shafts through the trees to spread warmth across the clearing. The two men released their hold on the branch then, still regaining their breath, still shaking, leaned for some moments against the trunk.

'We should leave this tree standing,' said Enkidu, 'as a token of our gratitude.'

Slumped in the shadow of a cedar, his upper limbs folded across his face, Huwawa appeared silent and still as the two strode away from the tree that had given them sanctuary, hesitating only to recover their weapons and sheath their swords.

'Look at him now!' exclaimed Gilgamesh as they approached. 'Look at the fearsome beast who rules the Cedar Mountain. He can hardly face the light of day!'

'We are fortunate the Lord of Light heeded the appeals of Lady Ninsun and our priests,' cautioned Enkidu, 'otherwise you and I would have been his next meal - ripped to pieces and our blood mixed in the ground.'

'Well that's what our appeals to the gods were for, dear brother. I saved our mother and the temples when Kish moved against us. The least they can do is help out at such times as this.'

'Such times as this?' Enkidu groaned aloud. 'Gilgamesh, we have escaped death only through their pleading, in spite of our stupidity. Surely you can admit the gratitude we owe them.'

'All right, Enkidu, I -.' But before Gilgamesh could finish his words a cough distracted them. Huwawa stared up reproachfully with diminished eyes and Gilgamesh said, 'Is this a man or some contemptible beast? His limbs now only number the same as ours. If I saw him from a distance I might mistake him for a large bear or some travesty of mankind thrown together at a cruel whim of the gods. What are we to do with him?'

'We must kill him,' was Enkidu's terse and uncompromising reply.

'Oh, you'd have him dead,' responded Gilgamesh, studying the vanquished Huwawa. 'Well I have it in mind we could bind him and -.'

'We must do nothing other than what I say!' interrupted Enkidu, angrily. 'We kill him!'

'Well, brother Enkidu - and I thought you were the compassionate one. As I was about to say, we ought to -.'

'Er, pardon me, if you don't mind,' interrupted the voice. Huwawa stirred and began to rise awkwardly from the ground.

'We must kill him now!' insisted Enkidu, thrusting his spear into the ground then unshouldering his axe.

'I really feel I ought to have a say in this discussion,' continued Huwawa, his voice conspicuous by an absurd calmness. To Gilgamesh the voice was one of contented amiability in spite of the grotesque mouth from which it issued.

'Now,' insisted Enkidu, raising the axe. 'If you don't, I will!'

Gilgamesh lifted a hand to stay his brother and looked on perplexed. Enkidu gasped with impatience but lowered the axe part way as Huwawa continued, 'Please hear me out before you make any rash decisions. I appreciate we haven't seen eye-to-eye on the occasion of our first meeting and, oh dear, a bad start is a bad start. But I wasn't having a good day when you arrived and, whether people like it or not, I *am* expected to keep up appearances and do my job. Do say if I'm not making myself clear, won't you.'

'I can hardly believe my ears!' exclaimed Gilgamesh. 'He speaks to us now as if we were sitting at ease with our elders in the House of Assembly. It's as if we have moved from one state of awareness to another, just as I did in my dreams.'

The look on Enkidu's face and the purposeful manner in which he renewed the grip on the axe gave no doubt as to his feelings. But Huwawa eyed him nonchalantly and spoke again. 'Enkidu, dear fellow, you are upset - I can tell. You want to destroy me even though I allowed you freedom of the forests when you were a man of the wild. I know perfectly well you have returned here to help yourselves to some of the Lord Enlil's trees and - and I have to admit it is the best timber in these

191

parts so I can't blame you. Oh no, no, no, I'm sure I'd do exactly the same if I were in your shoes.'

To the consternation of his brother, a smile crossed Gilgamesh's face as Huwawa busily scuffed earth from his fur and went on. 'But I know for a fact Lord Enlil doesn't go around counting the trees - not one in his position. No, he leaves that sort of thing to me and er, just between ourselves the forest would benefit from a little thinning out in places. I ought to have mentioned it when you first arrived. So - what say we have a friendly bargain? I could show you the really good stuff a bit further on and help you get it down the slope at night when there's no one around to notice. In return I'd expect to avoid, em, whatever unpleasantries you have in mind - naturally.'

'By the gods!' declared Gilgamesh, 'A short time ago he would have murdered us - torn us limb from limb and fed us to his minions. Now he's offering to help us make off with his trees! I find this gross creature quite entertaining in his duplicity.'

'Brother, you vex me,' responded Enkidu. Look at his face. Can't you imagine those eyes fixed on you after the sun has set and darkness falls? Hatred burns there even as he speaks.'

'I hear you, brother Enkidu and yes, he is still loathsome and what's more has a stench about him that all the incense in Sumer couldn't disguise. But - what say we bind him? What say we make a strong cage of timbers and take him back to Uruk? I'll have a bronze ring fixed in his nose, or somewhere suitable since he doesn't appear to have a nose, and tether him at the Nippur Gate. We will have

192

conquered Huwawa who they claimed could never be conquered and his presence will advertise our deeds as nothing else could.'

'Ah, that isn't quite what I had in mind,' responded Huwawa in a voice that now swished as gravel shifted about by lapping water.

'No, it isn't quite what *he* had in mind,' mocked Enkidu. 'When the light has gone and the sun no longer holds his power at bay, he will be again the Huwawa we saw come out of the mists. If we leave the forest now, whilst he is pacified, he will find our trail when night falls. He will fall upon us in the darkness by the river or in the desert. Even if we make it back to Uruk he will follow. He will stalk the streets at night until he finds us. That is what he was created to do. He is a creature of vengeance!'

'You are wrong,' said Huwawa, rising to full height and even now taller than the two brothers. 'You are wrong,' he repeated, rolling his grim head from side to side. 'Wrong, wrong, wrong! You, friend Enkidu, should grant me the forbearance and understanding Uruk offered you when you were without kith and kin. I have no such blessings so you mustn't blame me if I get a little tetchy now and again and make heavy going of a situation. None of us is perfect, I say.'

His voice a high-pitched rasp, Huwawa gestured a hooked limb over to the tallest trees. The mouth quivered. The pallid tusks gleamed beneath pools of soot-flecked yellow. 'Let's put our differences aside. Let me show you the secret places of the forest where no man ever trod. An afternoon of leisure and a little sightseeing will do us all good.'

'And let this deceitful bastard of a creature lead us to our deaths!' exclaimed Enkidu, laying aside his axe and turning to Gilgamesh. 'Brother - strike! All the glory of the deed can be yours as far as I'm concerned. I never wanted it in the first place!'

Huwawa crouched ominously. Gilgamesh backed away and turned to Enkidu who had picked up his spear, 'I see, brother, your renowned qualities of mercy are not to find expression here.'

'Mercy is a gift we should prize,' replied Enkidu, meeting his gaze, 'and it's the greatest of all when offered to those we hold within our power. But mercy is not the granting of life to one who will repay us with destruction. D'you see anything other than the planning of our deaths in that creature's expression? His malice is too great to be confined. It carries on his breath. It seeps from his pores!'

Gilgamesh regarded Huwawa's eyes and gruesome jaws. His blood chilled. 'I hear what you say, brother Enkidu and – yes, I no longer feel inclined to argue.'

His hand fell to his sword. It closed about the hilt. A hand's breadth of blade had drawn from its sheath when like a monstrous spider, Huwawa crouched lower, opening wide his mouth to slice the air with a fearsome hiss. 'Upon you, Enkidu,' he growled, 'I call down the wrath of heaven. I curse your body and soul!'

Seeing Huwawa about to leap, Enkidu stepped back with spear raised but Gilgamesh sprang forward to plunge his blade deep into the short neck. Drooling venom, the cackling Huwawa would have seized him in his claws, would have impaled him on curved tusks had not Enkidu rushed forward to thrust his spear hard into the creature's side. Gilgamesh dodged the claw and wrenched free his own blade. But it was Enkidu who, dragging out the spear, plunged it with all the strength he could summon into that part of the creature's body where he believed the heart to sit. Rattling from deep inside, head jerking, jaws shaking - Huwawa sank to the ground, shivered convulsively, then lay with his limbs drawing slowly in.

They were wiping the gore from their weapons on the grass when the wind that had earlier abated sprang up once more to pass through sighing trees. It seemed as if the gale was returning, then as quickly as it had begun, the wind ceased and calm returned to the forest.

They regarded the stricken Huwawa, his blood oozing freely over the ground. Then to Gilgamesh's surprise, Enkidu picked up his axe and braced himself beside the creature, saying, 'Stand clear. You'll not want his foul blood on you.' Metal glinted in the sun as the axe flashed in deadly arc. With one stroke, the head was severed from the torso to tumble aside where it came to rest on blood-spattered grass, jaws gaping wide, eyes staring blankly into a blue sky. 'There, it's done!' declared Enkidu. 'Now he can feed the worms if they'll have him!'

'Not all of him!' responded Gilgamesh stepping over to haul the gruesome head up by its matted hair. 'We'll take this back to Uruk in case no one believes us. Maybe I'll present it to Kuraka. Maybe I'll make him hold it up in the House of Assembly.

But for now, there's a rock over there where it can rest a while. Once those oafs down below see what has become of their forest demon they'll fall over themselves to co-operate.'

'That they will,' agreed Enkidu, 'so let's get to work. Let's do what needs to be done.'

'There is one tree I fancy rises above the rest,' gestured Gilgamesh as they approached. 'I see no other to match it.'

'Ay, brother, it looks the tallest of them all but it should be our offering to Enlil for what we have done here. The timbers should go to Nippur and be used there to glorify his temple.'

'Hm, I'd rather see it put to use in my palace or at least in our city but if that's your wish, brother, then to Nippur it must go – with the name of Uruk carved on it, naturally. The people of the holy city and the pilgrims who visit should know how it came to be there.'

'We could sail with the trunk as part of our raft,' suggested Enkidu. 'That way we can ensure it arrives safely.

'Good, then we'll enter Nippur as conquerors. *And* it will remind people of Uruk's hegemony in case those attending Enlil's shrine from other parts of Sumer have allowed it to slip their minds. I suggest we fell the big tree between us, brother Enkidu, then we can each choose our own to cut down over the next day or so. When we're done we can weigh up who has cut the greatest amount of timber. I wager I'll account for more than you before we quit the forest!'

'Ha - we'll see about that!' retorted Enkidu. 'You may have longer acquaintance with the axe but I know better than you the methods of the woodcutters. But what d'you have to wager out here that would be of any use to me? I've nothing that would be of use to you.'

'I'll - I'll wager my sword and the belt with it.' declared Gilgamesh. 'How about that? And you could wager yours.'

'Wager our swords! You know quite well neither of us would need two swords or care to be without one. That's nonsense.'

'You're right,' answered Gilgamesh, kicking aside a cedar cone as they readied themselves before the largest tree. 'It must be something meaningful - so how about my chariot - I mean my best chariot against – er, let me see now - against the girl of the temple?'

'Against the -! Absolutely not! She's worth more to me by far than ten of your chariots.'

'But, Enkidu, the girl will get older whereas the chariot will serve you all your life.'

'If I treat her well, so will Shamkhat,' smiled Enkidu. 'And that's exactly what I intend to do. You didn't mean a word of that wager and we both know it. But even if you did, even if I had none of the feelings I do have for that girl, I've not the slightest desire to parade through Uruk in a fancy chariot when I can get about far easier on foot. If you *must* wager,' he added, readying his axe, 'let's agree the loser takes charge of that revolting head until we're on the river.'

***

Shouts echoed through the light of an early morning. The last of the Cedar trunks was pushed out from the riverbank to drift southward.

197

Gilgamesh and Enkidu looked back at the forest and the muted colours of the Cedar Mountain. And though Huwawa's body remained to feed the earth, his head lay packed in dried grass within a box of rough planks; a grisly testament to the valour of his slayers.

CHAPTER 6
THE BULL OF HEAVEN

Word had gone ahead by messenger from Nippur; an account of the timber dedicated to the temple of Enlil and the two men who had brought it. In the heat of the afternoon people had abandoned market, workshop and field, to swarm about the Southern Gate and Uruk's quay. They had scrambled onto the city wall and to the tops of the gate's twin towers until Uruk looked to be under siege. The only space clear of people was the route kept open by the king's companions for his entry into the city. Along this route, passing in procession beneath the high arch and the great timber doors, came the elders and worthies of the city, distinguished in fine robes and caps, and bearing their emblems of office. There, too, were the portly priests in woollen kilts, all shaded like the elders beneath linen parasols held above their heads by slaves of the temple or town.

Those perched above the gate were first to see the raft of logs enter that branch of the river passing close to the city. 'The king!' they called down. 'The king and Lord Enkidu are coming!'

Soon they were able to make out the two figures, each with a hand about the makeshift mast to steady himself. They watched oarsmen cast off from the quay in swaying boats to meet and guide the raft in.

Enjoying the festive mood as much as any on this day was Shannu. Since the king and his brother's departure he, with a helper of even lesser

199

stature and fewer years than himself, one often burdened by the weight of a disproportionately large, pine-framed writing board, had sidled through the crowds of street and market. But Shannu had carried the reed stylus and weighty shoulder bag.

Wagers had been offered on the number of days that might pass before the king's return. A small number of citizens had placed their silver in favour of one or both of the royal brothers never returning at all, or of their death being announced before the year's end. Having ventured their silver, few appeared to benefit from the investment on the day news arrived, though coloured banners swaying in a warm breeze above the quay spoke only of celebration.

The people had been filled with curiosity when the first logs were reported drifting down the river. Elation had taken hold in the streets when more appeared over the following days. Enough to keep the carpenters, builders and artisans of the city busy for years to come. Uruk basked in pride for her king's exploits now he and his brother were coming home. Not even the defeat of Kish could have bestowed more prestige upon the city. The girls of Inanna's temple, normally reclusive in the heat of day, had set out in ox-drawn covered wagons that presently stood grouped on the riverbank at a respectable distance from the quay.

One among them had waited more anxiously than her sisters. As she gazed along the river, her heartbeat matched the drum of welcome that sounded across Uruk from the roof of her temple.

'What a sight, brother Enkidu!' cried Gilgamesh as the small boats drew close, as the people cheered, some waving coloured flags, some holding children high. 'The entire city is out to greet us and look – there are some of our timbers stacked on the quay - and there are the men with my chariot waiting to escort us through the streets!'

'Yes, a fine sight,' replied Enkidu, shading his eyes from the sun to see if the one person he most wished to see was in evidence. 'And what a fine sight we must be - a pair of wild men in filthy rags that would shame a ditch digger. I hardly think we'll present ourselves as the heroes they seem to be expecting. Though I recall, brother, that's how I must have looked when the girl found me.'

'Well our deeds will more than compensate for our present appearance, Enkidu, you'll see. And the first thing I'll have done once we're off this raft is get that foul smelling head out of our sight, then we'll make our way directly to the palace. By the time we appear before the people we'll be minus these beards, cleaned up and looking the part in our finery. Our friend Kuraka will be obliged to deliver formal greetings in gracious manner, though he may choke on his words.'

Ropes had been cast and secured, the raft was in tow and approaching the quay. From the quay or from the city wall, few could fail to notice the object spiked on the pole at the rear of the raft. Long days spent festering in the heat of the wooden box had done nothing to lessen its loathsome aspect. The cheering died to a babble as the king and his brother stepped from the raft and onto the quay where the priests and elders met them, the latter receiving back the great bow of Anshan and quiver of arrows. Having no desire to loiter, Gilgamesh and Enkidu mounted the waiting chariot with their weapons and set off side by side through the gate.

'How hollow it makes people's voices sound,' remarked Enkidu, looking up at the arch as they rode beneath its shadow. 'It's as if we are mocked in our time of triumph.'

'As hollow as my stomach!' responded Gilgamesh. 'I could eat an ox! And mock us, you say? No, even Enlil wouldn't begrudge us our acclaim now.'

With the royal companions marching at front and rear, they passed on through the city. People followed noisily through street and alleyway, many hesitating to regard with varying degrees of revulsion Huwawa's head being set up on its stake before the temple precinct. The slaves whose task it was, would have hurled the putrescent object into the river had they not toiled under the gaze of two armed men. Flies in the heat of day and rats at night were to be Huwawa's acolytes. He would lack nothing in the fervour of their devotions.

'Scrapers and oil!' ordered Gilgamesh above the snorting of the asses as they clattered to a halt inside the courtyard. The palace attendants, already on hand, were about to hurry off when he added, 'And bronze mirrors! And razors! And regalia worthy of our appearance before the people!' As the servants scurried away he turned to Enkidu. 'On the day we fought each other, we washed the grime away here in this pool. I think another appointment is well overdue. What d'you say, brother?'

'Aye, it seems more than just a luxury right now.'

'A necessity without doubt! I've never felt so vile and unwholesome. I feel my skin and my hair crawling. I'll be in the water before you!'

'No you won't!' responded Enkidu, ripping off his befouled tunic as he dashed away from the chariot with his brother closing behind.

In the cool waters of the fountain they refreshed tired limbs and washed away the grime of their journey. At length the girls appeared with perfumed oils in glazed jars. Theirs was a task Gilgamesh was never inclined to hurry, nor would he regard it a lesser pleasure for Enkidu, but for once it was done in haste because of the crowds thronging before the palace. The priests chanted thanksgiving at the shrines, imagining themselves in part responsible for the success of the expedition though the city elders anticipated the king's first attentions. These latter stood idly, exchanging small talk so as to gloss over their impatience at not being summoned sooner to the royal presence.

When the herald's drum rattled, when the king in regal attire and his brother in plainer robes stepped out before the palace, the crowds fell quiet. Priests ascended the steps with incense burners and flasks of water, sanctified at the shrines to bless the homecoming of Gilgamesh and Enkidu.

Enkidu's thoughts, not wholly occupied by the ceremony, were distracted further by the furious waving of someone who had pushed out from the crowd and dashed to the side of the stairs. The mop of thick hair and bright-toothed grin he at once recognised as a palace guard approached with the intention of driving the intruder away. Enkidu gestured the guard to let him alone and leaned over to speak. 'Shannu, what's so important that you need interrupt me now?'

'A quick message, Lord,' the boy replied, stabbing a finger toward one side of the square. Enkidu followed his gesture and saw her. Shamkhat watched him from an upstairs window. Her head covered, her eyes bright. A loving smile on her face. She raised a hand as Enkidu nodded and raised his. Soon they would be together.

Gilgamesh was party to none of this. Gilgamesh was idol of his people. Gilgamesh basked in the light of their adoration. Their voices once more rose, ignoring the drum that demanded silence. Not the clatter of the drum, not the chanting of the priests or the proclamations of the elders could most of the crowd hear.

Only when the day was waning, only when the weapons that had served the king and his brother were held up by their attendants for everyone to see did the babble subside. There were the spears that had dealt the first blows to Huwawa. There the sword that had pierced his body and the axe that had struck off his head. People gasped as its blade gleamed in the setting sun. Sheshkalla and the men of his forge looked on with a special pride of their own.

Set about the periphery of the palace square and the Eanna precinct as darkness fell, were braziers and stalls laden with food and beer for the evening's celebrations.

'It's time to take ourselves away,' Gilgamesh remarked. 'The people will welcome the food and drink you have so amply provided.'

'In your name, brother,' smiled Enkidu. 'It has to be in the name of Uruk's king.'

'Whether in my name or not, I doubt if they'll ascribe such generosity to me. The gesture was yours, brother Enkidu, and will be recognised as such. I'll bid them farewell and be with you.'

In a deepening sky Inanna's star shone above the city wall. Her star was always bright but this evening it was unusually so. Gilgamesh found himself distracted by its pure and steady radiance. As he raised a hand and prepared to take his leave, the light of the star glowed in his eyes. It entered his soul. When his chief attendant appeared close by to lift the edge of his cloak, saying, 'Is My Lord ready to go?' Gilgamesh remained oblivious to his voice. It fell to his brother to touch his arm, something few other men would dare do, and repeat the man's words. Even so, Gilgamesh remained some moments longer gazing out to the sky.

***

'Who is there?' he breathed in the sultry obscurity of the room. He thought a voice had called his name from beyond a dreamless sleep. Something – someone, had roused him. To one side of the window glowed a faint light. As he emerged to full wakefulness, he imagined it was Inanna's star hanging in the sky beyond his room but quickly realised it was only the small flame of the oil lamp glowing from above its bronze stand. The window by which it stood was curtained with matting that obscured the night sky. He gazed about the silent room. His fingers closed about the hilt of the sword at his bedside; the sword that had pierced Huwawa.

From somewhere beyond the palace square drifted the yapping of dogs.

Gilgamesh raised slowly up and leaned back against the cushions. The sound of his breathing seemed to echo from elsewhere within the room. Perhaps it was a trick of the night, though he did not recall it happening before. On the still air hung a delicate, sensual aroma the nature of which tantalised and eluded him. Was there an offering of perfumed oil being made at some shrine close by?

He would have let down the sword and would have closed his eyes but a vague shadow fluttered across the wooden beams of the ceiling. The small wick, suspended in its flask of oil, shivered fitfully as though disturbed by a draught. The lamp held his attention. He wondered now if a moth had entered the room and, attracted by the light, had flown aimlessly about before vanishing into the shadows. He was musing on how far away the morning might be when her voice touched his ear, 'Gilgamesh.'

Unsheathing the sword, he swung from his bed to peer about the room. 'Who is there?' he asked once more. 'Who calls my name?'

As he spoke, the lamp by the window brightened to cast a warm glow about the bed and the walls. She was standing to one side of the window.

Gilgamesh stared hard. 'By the gods – how did you get in here?'

The girl watched him intently with a hint of amusement in her eyes. For a time she said nothing more. She was beautiful. Very beautiful. Her full-lipped, sensual face was framed by hair that fell across her shoulders and about her breasts with obsidian sheen. The fringe at her forehead was set above eyes deep as fathomless pools. Eyes that regarded him from beneath fine curved brows with an expression of wanton desire. All but naked and quite hairless, her slim body was adorned at the arms with ornate, delicately wrought bangles of gold and silver. Small jewels set about them glittered as stars. Around her waist hung a fine chain of gold from which was suspended a gleaming ruby set in an ebony cameo that rested against the smooth flesh directly above her sex. As she shifted her weight from one gilded sandal to the other, her lips held a voluptuous smile.

Gilgamesh studied her, his initial caution subverted by lustful desire. 'I take it I should know you,' he breathed, laying aside the sword.

'Oh, yes,' replied the girl in a voice that caressed his ear with carnal promise. 'You should know me very well, darling Gilgamesh.' Her perfume invaded his senses - subtle wraiths - tentacles of erotic delicacy. She raised hands above her head and began to sway like a reed in a gentle breeze, turning from side to side, moving her feet in a dance of sensual provocation.

'Or should I assume,' he continued, 'that I'm asleep. That I'm dreaming on through the exhaustion of my labours and that once I wake up you will be gone.'

'Dreaming or not dreaming, Lord Gilgamesh, what does it matter? I am here and we are alone in this room together. Quite alone. Time and the world beyond these walls are now the illusion. They are now the dream.'

A dark passion seized Gilgamesh. Blood raced hot, but in the depths of his mind a red spark of warning glowed. Here was a woman of compelling beauty who, by means unknown, had entered his room to seduce him by her wiles. Why should he not take her as he had taken so many women? She knew him. He must know her, yet did not recall her from among the girls of Inanna's temple or from those among the women of the city who he had taken for his own pleasure.

No - he did not know her. No - he could not know her. And the shadow she cast toward him might be that of an assassin. Even a daughter of Kish!

She lowered one hand to cup a firm breast, moving splayed fingers slowly down her stomach to stroke the hanging jewel. She continued to gaze at him with lips parted. Her whisper coiled disembodied about the room to caress him in a vortex of desire. 'You are a conqueror of men. You have slain the beast all others feared. Uruk shines in your light as it does in the light of Utu the sun. All Sumer is awash with talk of your deeds. But Gilgamesh, just as Utu has his consort, you also should have a queen. A queen worthy to stand by your side. A queen worthy to share your bed. I will be that one, darling Gilgamesh. Why do you wait? Touch me. Feel the heat of my body.'

With the grace of a gazelle she moved to the low couch that stood by an adjacent wall. Relaxing against the woollen covers, she spread herself wide to his gaze. A hand dropped to her sex and, closing her eyes with a sigh, she began to caress then to stroke herself intimately. His youthful desires furnace-raged at the sight of her but still he did not move though her words brushed his ear like burning moth wings. 'Gilgamesh, kneel and worship at this temple of love. Taste my passion and let me taste your seed. Rise up and ride me like a frenzied bull. Let me feel your strength deep inside. Gilgamesh, no part of my body is denied you.'

The warning spark within danced. The spark brightened.

'Say first who you are!' demanded Gilgamesh, an all but unbearable lust stayed only by the flimsy reins of nagging caution. 'Say now!'

'Oh, how well you know me,' she sighed. 'I have been your strength in love and war. When the girls of town or temple cried with passion in your arms, that passion was also mine. When you took up spear and axe, when you set the fire of your anger against other men, that fire raged from within me. When your blade cleaved flesh and bone, I revelled in the blood that soaked the earth through your might. Grant me your passion and your seed, Gilgamesh. I am all the women you ever knew - all the battles you ever fought. Oh, how I ache for you. Make me your bride on earth and in heaven.' Her sighs grew louder. Her fingers moved with greater urgency. 'Come now, Gilgamesh!'

'Yes, I know you!' he exclaimed, reaching for the sword. 'Whether I dream at present or not. Yes, I know you very well!'

'Then know also that the pleasures I give will be a thousandfold any pleasure you have known. Power beyond imagining shall be yours. Men will cross desert and mountain carrying tribute to Uruk. Your chariot will be drawn by lions in gilded trapping. The lords of other cities will eat the earth when you appear before them glorious as the blazing sun who is my own brother. Let us revel in the flames of our passion, Gilgamesh. Let us revel in the flames together!'

'No, I will not!' he declared. 'Any flame of your making will become my funeral pyre. Hear me! You are venerated by the people of Uruk. The treasure house of your temple is brimming full and neither your altar nor your priests are found wanting at times of sacrifice. That must be enough. I can offer no more and nothing will I take from you!'

Inanna raised herself from the couch and started toward him but Gilgamesh levelled the sword at her, saying, 'Stay! The writings tell us of your past consorts. The priests teach us about their fate. They tell of your first love, Dumuzzi, the king whose wife you became. What did he gain for his devotions? Why, he was thrown down from your world to begin a cycle of death and resurrection as regular as the seasons. And what of those other mortals who fell prey to your deceit? Once you tired of their affections they were cast aside to dwell among the lowest creatures of the earth. You are insatiable. No man or men will satisfy you for long.'

'Worthless oafs - all of them!' she cried, recoiling from him. 'And as for the great Dumuzzi - what did he do when I was dragged into hell and none thought I'd ever return? Did he show remorse? Did he grieve for me? No he did not! He strutted around in his finery and saw fit to entertain other women when he should have mourned for me, his queen. When he finally ended his days down there he deserved all that befell him - as did the rest of them!'

Gilgamesh watched her face cloud with anger as his own voice rose. 'I hear what you say but I will not eat your poisoned fruit! Lady Inanna, you should leave now. Some claim the gods are within me but we both know they are wrong. I'm just a mortal man and that would make my fate all the worse. Go from my room. Forget you ever came here!'

Rage blazed in her eyes. Her mouth set tight. By the window the lamp flared up with wildcat hiss to glare like the sun. In that last dazzled glimpse he saw her mouth and hands fouled with gore, her face a grinning mask of death and decay. With a cry of, 'Damnable bitch!' Gilgamesh let fall the sword and threw hands across his eyes. In his mind her image remained but as quickly as it had burst out, the light was altogether gone.

It took a while for him to adjust again to the darkness. Eventually, he groped his way to the window and lifted aside the reed blind. A full moon hung in the sky, casting pale rays across the floor. The room was once again silent and he knew he was alone. Returning much troubled to his bed Gilgamesh lay with eyes closed but the comfort of sleep eluded him through the remainder of that night.

***

She sped as a whirlwind through formless voids, through shimmering towers of creation. Her cries echoed through spectral caverns of radiance and shadow, rising, falling, echoing in torrents of discord. 'Father Anu! Father Anu! Father Anu!'

Seated in contemplation of infinity was how she found him when she swept in. His chin rested upon a fist, his eyes were half closed. He seemed unaware of her presence, in spite of her calling his name. When at last he looked up, she hovered before him in angered disarray. Her face was distraught, her hair wild and unkempt, her gown torn and hanging loose from one shoulder, damp with the tears that streaked her face.

'What now?' he sighed. 'What brings you to me in such a sorry state? Really, my dear, what am I to make of it?'

'I am grievously offended,' she sobbed. 'I am mocked by one to whom I would have granted the highest favours. Gilgamesh, the king, the arrogant King of Uruk threw insults at me the way an ass kicks grit into the face of the meanest peasant!'

'Oh, you offered to marry him, did you?'

'I offered what mortals barely dream of. I offered pleasures even he has never known despite his victories, despite the women he calls at a whim to serve him in his bed. I offered power that would have had all Sumer, yes, all Sumer and the lands beyond grovelling at his feet.'

'And he didn't appreciate your generosity,' breathed Anu. 'Well, my dear, you don't have the best of reputations when it comes to fidelity and you do put yourself about rather freely.'

'Well that's *my* business isn't it!' she cried. 'Some might consider him part divine but not to me he isn't! No – he's a mere mortal and no man should reject me and live!'

'Nor can any man accept you and live,' he responded. 'I can understand his point of view,

212

philanderer though he may be. But I left their petty squabbling behind to study greater things. You should talk to the others. They still concern themselves with the human race. They will, I'm sure, give advice as to what you should do.'

'Give *me* advice!' she cried out, clutching her gown as though about to rip it apart. 'It is not advice I came for! I came here to ask for what only you can grant! *That's* why I came!'

'Anything for a quiet life,' he muttered, lifting his eyes to those pillars of eternity where stars were born and died. 'Tell me what it is you want.'

'Father Anu, give me Gugalanna! Give me the Bull of Heaven!'

'The Bull of Heaven,' he replied, turning to her with a frown. 'Would you punish all humanity in your spite? I don't consider that a good idea.'

'I will use him to destroy Gilgamesh!' she serpent-hissed. 'I ask you again, father. Give me the Bull of Heaven!'

'And I ask you to reconsider. His stamping and bellowing will bring nothing other than pain and sorrow to mankind. Why take things so far?'

'Why?' shrieked Inanna. 'You ask *me* why?' Gasping in frustration, she twisted her head from side to side with raised fists clenched. 'You know why! What greater affront could any man offer me, a daughter of the gods! His vanity soars like an eagle! It knows no bounds!' She lowered her arms then with narrowed eyes she stepped closer. Her voice hardened. 'Father Anu, give me what I ask or I will break down the gates of the underworld. I will speak the names of the dead. I will raise them rotting from the ground. They will wander foul and hideous in the streets and markets of the cities. The world of mankind will become a hell upon earth. The dead will feed on the living as the living feed upon the beasts.'

Anu shook his head in sadness but with wild eyes and bared teeth, she cried out once again, 'Father Anu! Give me Gugalanna! Give me the Bull of Heaven!'

Anu saw burning deep within her the fires of grim determination. At last he sighed and raised a hand. 'Very well, I find this whole affair tiresome but you shall have your wish. I will give you the Bull of Heaven. Now please leave me alone.'

***

New shoots had sprung from the earth. People went about their tasks in the shade of narrow streets and under the open skies beyond the city walls throughout the land of Sumer. But those whose labours did take them outside the cities knew all was not as it should have been. Soon the people of all the towns knew it and, day by day, began to talk among themselves in square and tavern.

At Uruk the elders were gathered in the House of Assembly.

'The situation has become obvious to all,' declared a wizened, toothless figure seated amongst those on the low bench that ran around the wall of their dim room. 'It has been unusually hot and dry. The river that sustains us has not risen as it should at this time of the year, nor has the great river to our east. Both are at their lowest within living memory. My living memory that is, and I can count more years than most of you. Even when Agga's men

214

attempted to divert a part of the river in order to intimidate us, things did not look so ominous.'

'Since our lord the king has been back within the city,' said another, not quite as advanced in years, 'he has concerned himself with little more than the supervision of building works. We are replete with timber, and all credit to Gilgamesh and his noble brother I hasten to say, but we face a shortage of water. I for one hold no doubts as to which of those commodities is of greater importance to our well-being. The rivers supply water that is blood to the veins of our land.'

'Judging from the facts I have gathered these last few days,' said Kuraka, rising from his seat at the head of the room, 'it is Uruk's land that will suffer most because our canals have not been properly maintained.'

'That is true,' declared another. 'The people of Larsa often complain because neglect of our waterways and our dykes has affected land of theirs. The priests of Inanna reported a delegation sent to Uruk months ago by the Man of Larsa to address this very matter. It was set out on hard clay for our king. Even now, we believe, no official reply has been dispatched from Uruk.'

'The canals,' continued Kuraka, 'should have been cleared long ago. They must be deepened to bring more water from the river to our fields before it is too late. Our noble king has never granted such maintenance works the priority he sees fit to give other matters such as grand adventures and the temple women. Fortunately, throughout his reign the waters have always risen and our crops have flourished. We need his authority to get more men working on the canals and ditches, though I doubt his fine-feathered companions will be eager to get their hands dirty for the common good.'

'Unless sufficient water is brought to our fields,' remarked one, 'the next harvest is likely to be a poor one.'

'I have spoken to those who work my own modest lands,' responded Kuraka. 'They say it will be worse. They say that if nothing is done soon, we will have little harvest at all. That means scant bread for our tables and no grain with which to trade!'

A murmur passed through the room then the eldest of them declared, 'We must voice our concerns to the king. And if he is not available or if he will not listen then we might find a more ready ear with his brother. Lord Enkidu may not be a man of the city but he's shown much concern for the people of Uruk, not least by his care for our poor and dispossessed. Why, he has shown compassion even for the common criminal and those awaiting execution.'

'Indeed he has,' agreed Kuraka, 'but the king will take offence if we venture to address anyone other than himself – even if it is his worthy brother. There's only one man holds authority over Uruk but I will approach him when the two of them are together. We must hope for once he will take note of our needs. The coming weeks will be critical for all of us.'

***

'D'you think they'll succeed,' asked Enkidu, a hand lifted to shade his eyes from the sun. From the roof of the palace they could see much of the town and surrounding country. Only the upper works of the two great temples, the houses of Anu and Inanna, rose high enough to overlook them.

'My hopes are with the people,' sighed Gilgamesh, 'but I fear the confidence I had when work began has fallen with the level of the river. Still, the situation can't last forever. But this heat – I've never experienced its like.'

'It's worse below in the city,' commented Enkidu. 'The streets are almost deserted; even the babble of the market has gone. Labour in many of the workshops has all but ceased.'

They were well aware that except for the very young, the old and the infirm, most men and women were outside the city wall. With little shade from the date palms they toiled in canal and ditch, wheeling pick and spade or carrying earth to and fro in baskets amidst foul odours and torrid heat. Sunlight reflected dully on shrunken, muddy pools where long ribbons of water once mirrored the sky. Even townsman not accustomed to plough, hoe or sickle noted how the barley and the wheat no longer stood strong and upright. They saw how fruit had begun to wither on the orchard trees and how listless and dull-eyed were the sheep and the cows. Only pigs and goats that roamed the town and accounted for much of what was discarded by the inhabitants appeared so far unaffected.

'Hm,' observed Gilgamesh, 'some of Anu's priests are bending their backs next to citizen and slave. They've quit praying and put their faith in the humble spade. I noticed earlier, though, Inanna's priests still have enough worshippers to keep them about their duties.'

'What about your companions?' queried Enkidu. 'I've seen nothing of them for several days. What are they doing to help?'

'Most of them leave Uruk before dawn each day to hunt whatever game they can find. They bring a little fresh meat into the city and they drive away anyone who might regard our livestock as easy prey.'

'The men of our neighbouring cities will be doing likewise. Let's hope their paths don't cross or their spears will be put to even bloodier use.'

'Yes, let us hope,' replied Gilgamesh. 'It seems there's much unrest in Sumer. And as I expected, Larsa has lain accusations at our door yet again.'

'Even they cannot blame us if the rivers fail to rise or for a lack of clouds in the sky,' responded Enkidu.

'No, but they say we have made matters worse through our neglect of the canals and dykes - as though they're devoid of fault when it comes to the upkeep of the waterways. They may believe that but I don't. What I do believe are reports of their collusion with Agga, for all the good it will do them. The Man of Kish will use any situation to serve his own interests.'

'I'm puzzled as to why you let him live after your victory over Kish,' remarked Enkidu. 'If I may say so, it seems out of keeping with your character.'

'Quite. It was his younger daughter who prevailed on me to do that. She has many talents. I tell you brother Enkidu, she was most persuasive.'

'Yes, she must have been,' smiled Enkidu, returning his attention to the heat-hazed fields

218

below. 'But now it's time I was seen amongst the people again.'

'I'll join you then I'll take myself and my remaining armed men to the canal bordering Larsa's territory. If they're looking for trouble, we'll be there to settle matters our way.'

'And what if our labours don't succeed? I look at the canals and it seems to me there's little point in much more digging if the river gets any lower. What if the waters fail to rise and the rain does not come? More praying? More sacrifices? I wonder if the gods have not deserted this land.'

'We can only wait and see,' replied Gilgamesh. 'If this cursed enemy could be defeated by the might of our arms as was Huwawa - we'd soon have people dancing in the streets.'

'Huwawa's defeat as I recall,' responded Enkidu, 'was not entirely by the might of our arms.'

***

'Some may have lost count of the days that have passed since our lord the king returned and this affliction beset us,' declared Kuraka, 'but I have not!'

'Nor we,' voiced a number of others amongst those seated within the House of Assembly. Several breathed heavily in the oppressive heat. Reed fans quivered as agitated moth wings. Flywhisks wafted the sullen air as swooping birds.

'We can hardly blame the king for the onset of a drought,' objected one. 'All of Sumer is stricken. The good years cannot last forever and nor can the bad.'

'There are many who believe otherwise when it comes to allocating blame,' responded Kuraka.

'They observe those cedar logs stacked in the palace square. They notice the king's workmen still cutting timber to embellish his palace whilst the majority of our citizens are obliged to take their food in ever decreasing measure. In the past we traded for timber with the produce of our fields and our workshops. That we saw as legitimate trade. Now, rumour is afoot that we are paying the price for what was taken from the Cedar Mountain and for slaying its guardian. *I* do not claim to know the truth of it but if that's what people are saying then we can do little to banish it from their minds.'

'It is obvious,' declared one, 'that people are becoming increasingly hungry. As in all times of misfortune they look to their king, as one in charge of the priesthood, for a remedy whether he has the means to address the situation or not. He who was once their saviour they will see as having betrayed them, though he can do no more than lead the priests in offering and sacrifice, as he already does.'

'At least his brother goes amongst the people to offer what comfort he can in their time of need,' remarked another. 'So far only a handful have died and from what I hear, many of these were amongst the sick and infirm to begin with. Even so, our citizens grow more restive with each passing day and this damned heat doesn't help. It smothers Uruk like the hand of some devil.'

'The stench from the canals,' said Kuraka, 'permeates every street and house – I dare say even the royal palace. The flies torment us all. The wells within the city are foul. They are drying up and our cisterns are not being replenished. Water for making beer is brought from the river but grain is getting scarcer. On top of that the fishermen who supplied our market no longer find their nets filled. Milk from our herds is not as forthcoming because the beasts themselves cannot obtain enough food and water.' Kuraka hesitated, letting his gaze drift in slow deliberation across airless gloom. 'Today I went to the temple warehouses to examine our stocks of grain. I do not wish to cause further alarm but I saw what I saw and it is not good news for Uruk. There ought to be enough to feed the city for some time yet but that is not the case. What we have left is infested with mice and other vermin. Soon there will be nothing – unless the people can eat cedar logs.'

'Surely the king is aware of this,' remarked one elder, wearily mopping his brow.

Kuraka raised his hands. 'Aware of it – aware of it, you say! He never goes near the granaries! The priests and overseers do not have the courage to inform him either since their negligence, so I find, is largely responsible. They pray and make sacrifice with growing zeal, hoping this drought will end before matters get any worse.'

'It would make precious little difference if they did inform him,' arose a voice from the far corner. It was the elder who had on the occasion of their previous meeting suggested a representation to the king. 'I recall a time like this when I was a boy and I tell you, the people's hunger will become acute sooner than you realise. When the fish, the grain, the dates and the poultry are gone, when our orchards are stripped bare, they will eat the sheep and cattle. After that the pigs and the dogs, unless the poorest amongst our citizens have already

221

accounted for them. Then the cats, rats and mice if they can catch them. Pestilence will tread close in the footsteps of hunger as surely as night follows day. Few will escape its crossing of their threshold, serf or noble. Not the stoutest door, not the highest wall will suffice to keep affliction at bay.'

'We thank you for those reassuring words,' breathed Kuraka. 'I take it there are no suggestions we might put to our king in order that -.'

Noises from the square outside caused him to glance aside. A commotion had begun. Voices were raised in anger. Two of the less elderly members rose to their feet, gathered up their gowns, pushed by their fellows and left the hall. Kuraka remained silent as the elders, murmuring amongst themselves, looked anxiously about. Soon the voices of the men who had just left could be heard mingling with those outside, though no one within the hall could ascertain what was being said. At length the voices subsided and the two reappeared, entering the hall but remaining by the arched door rather than returning to their places. 'The people outside wish to speak with us,' said one raising a sleeve to brush sweat from his forehead. 'They will not go away until we agree.'

'Is there someone chosen to represent them?' asked Kuraka, dryly.

'It's difficult to say but it might be as well if you went outside to hear them before their anger is turned on us.'

'Turned on us?' repeated Kuraka with a look of misgiving. 'Why on us? It's not with us the blame lies.' After some moments in hesitation he headed for the door.

He emerged, lifting a hand to shield his eyes from the sun, at once aware of many pairs of eyes fixed on him. About him hovered twenty or more citizens, farmers, fishermen, artisans and others united by hunger and vexation. One of their number addressed him; a stocky, balding man of moderate status who owned grazing land adjacent to Kuraka's own. 'I speak on behalf of these people because you and I know each other well and I hope you'll not take lightly what we have to say.'

'I will listen,' replied Kuraka as a handful of others followed from the House of Assembly to peer in narrow-eyed curiosity over his shoulder.

'You and the elders,' he began, 'do not frequent the taverns the streets and the squares as often as most of us do. There's a rumour about - a rumour you might do well to heed, though I'd be surprised you and the rest of 'em in there haven't heard the odd whisper.

'We are aware of many rumours,' replied Kuraka, 'but do go on.'

'This rumour has it,' he continued, perspiration glistening on his face, 'that this drought has been sent with a purpose. It has been sent because our lord the king, bless 'im, has offended the immortal gods so grievously they've seen fit to punish the entire population of Sumer.'

'Oh, and where did this rumour arise?' enquired Kuraka. 'Was it in one of the taverns?'

'The taverns breed rumours as the ditches breed flies,' came a remark at his rear.

'No,' the man replied angrily, 'this rumour isn't from any tavern. It's said to come from the priests of Inanna themselves. A number of people not

223

involved in digging out the ditches have gathered at her temple since dawn expecting further revelation and their mood is not good. They think it's wrong our king does not show 'imself more often to the people the way his brother does, and – and, we say, make greater sacrifice at the shrine on our behalf.'

'Heaven knows,' replied Kuraka, 'I seldom find myself applauding the conduct of Lord Gilgamesh but as things are I can't imagine what further sacrifice will achieve.'

'That isn't what people think,' asserted the man. His companions began to mutter, to nod in agreement as he went on. 'They're saying that so grave is our king's offence that the gods have sent the Bull of Heaven against us. If that's true then what we see now is only the beginning. Plague will follow drought and hunger and for seven years we'll suffer hardship and misery. The king needs to make amends before this goes yet further.'

'Make amends!' retorted Kuraka with a sardonic laugh. 'Gilgamesh could no more apologise for offending the gods than he might beg forgiveness from Agga of Kish after decorating our city wall with the bodies of his captains. The man's pride casts too great a shadow for the seeds of humility ever to thrive.'

'If he does *not* act,' growled the spokesman, 'the people will turn against him and his hangers-on because they see in his actions the source of their suffering.' There was further agreement as he went on. 'You must tell him what's happening. You're supposed to be in office for the good of Uruk and its people. You are the king's council. It is *your* job!'

'We are the king's council in theory and according to tradition,' responded Kuraka. 'In practice he consults us on nothing of substance. He values our advice much as he does the passing breeze.'

'Well, friend Kuraka, if he doesn't listen to your voice he'll have to listen to that of the people and their voices will rise such a tide as to drown him! A modest number have died so far but if you look up at the skies, you'll observe how the vultures circle. It seems *they* know what the king does not know and does not wish to know!'

***

'Make amends!' laughed Gilgamesh, striding to the window from where he gazed out across the palace square. For a time he studied the few people still to be seen. People who no longer went about their business with purpose but stooped as though they carried some invisible burden. Where shade could be found they gathered, broke up and reformed into small groups that lolled about in subdued conversation. Dogs that once yapped busily about the streets lay torpid and silent.

Turning back to the room, he faced the group who waited by the entrance; Kuraka and his two colleagues, bearded and white robed, and three shaven-headed priests in layered kilts. All members of the delegation except their spokesman bore an expression of nervous disquiet. Kuraka, by contrast, retained an aura of detached authority. He sensed Gilgamesh was ill at ease.

'You dare come here to suggest,' resumed Gilgamesh, waving a finger before them, 'that *I* have somehow brought this drought upon a people

225

and a city that *I* have risked my life to preserve? A city *I* have strengthened and glorified for the benefit of you and all our people? I am amused at what you say. I am amused because if I were not amused I would be angry and I would prefer for all our sakes not to be angry!'

Kuraka appeared agitated by his tone and replied, 'No one, least of all ourselves, would suggest our lord the king could know this might happen. We realise the gods are fickle. We know they take offence all too easily. But we say that they might be persuaded to once more consider the well-being of those who gather at the temples – of those who hold them in reverence.'

'Lord Gilgamesh, we must also speak,' ventured the first priest. 'We can never be certain why the gods punish mankind unless they reveal it to us. It seems a harsh penalty indeed for the taking of a few trees and the demise of that abominable creature whose head is now reduced to bone. Nevertheless, they *have* decided to punish us. They have sent down the Bull of Heaven. They have set him astride our land. Our augurs have studied the signs and they confirm it. With his breath he scorches the pastures and dries up the reed beds and the marshes. He drinks dry the rivers and the waterways. With his hooves he tramples our crops, wears bare the earth and cracks it open. He is at large in the land to vent his mischief on all Sumer.'

'On *all* Sumer as you say!' responded Gilgamesh. 'Upon our enemies as well as ourselves. Upon Kish, Larsa, Ur and Lagash - even holy Nippur. Unless I am misinformed, *all* suffer as we do. Have they contrived to offend the gods at the same time and in the same manner? No! The reasons are not as you suggest and I will not supplicate myself before the altars in acceptance of a guilt that is not mine. What say you, brother Enkidu?'

They had been aware beforehand of Enkidu's presence but until that moment he had sat aside in the shadows where he listened in silence. Now he rose up to speak. 'I, too, am puzzled as to why this affliction should have befallen us. I share responsibility with my brother for what was done, but what we took from the vast forest was no more than a few grains from a field of barley. Further, I doubt the immortals, would wish to wreak such terrible vengeance over the likes of Huwawa.' Glancing at Gilgamesh he continued, 'I sense there is more to this than we know. I sense there are deeds not spoken of that have aroused the anger of the gods.'

Gilgamesh regarded his brother with an unease that did not escape Kuraka's notice as the king turned to the others. 'Yes, there is much we must consider. My brother and I will discuss the matter in due course. You should leave us now.'

Kuraka's eyes held an expression of barely disguised contempt as he offered a formal though slighter bow of respect than the rest. Once the sound of their footsteps had gone the king turned to Enkidu. 'As you see, brother, the people now regard me as siring all the ills of the land. Well, that makes a change. Before you came they attributed half the bastard children in Uruk to me and I was content to let them think so. But this draught – I'll not have them unload the guilt for it at my feet.'

227

'Perhaps it's because they look first to their king in times of crisis, not to the city elders. You cannot blame them doing so now, even though this enemy is beyond the reach of sword and spear.'

'Ah, you try to console me with the best of motives, dear brother.' Gilgamesh moved back to the window and, in a gesture of anger, pulled across the blind to shut off the outside world and plunge the room into shade. 'I'm well aware how anger simmers amongst the people. I don't need to visit the taverns or walk the streets of this town to know what's being said. Resentment is obvious in their bearing, in their glances, yes, in the very manner of their walking and breathing.' He grasped the blind again as though intending to pull it aside then let it fall back before turning once more to his brother. 'Enkidu, there may be truth in what they say. Perhaps they're right and what I have done has - has -.'

'What *we* have done, brother,' put in Enkidu. 'If there is guilt then a half portion of it is mine.'

'No!' Gilgamesh shook his head and waved a hand dismissively. 'No, there is something I've not spoken about. Not even to you. Something that -.' He hesitated and looked hard at Enkidu. 'What torments my thoughts may have been no more than – no more than a dream; perhaps a dream with less substance than a jackal's cry in the night. We should continue our attendance at the temples but - but I will go to the altars at night to pray and make my offerings. If this brings relief to the people then well and good, though I doubt it will.' He seated himself on the couch then added, 'You at least have your consolations. I take it your temple girl is well?

228

She seems to occupy your thoughts most of the time.'

'Shamkhat is well. I see to that as best I can. And young Shannu is at hand to wait on her in my absence. But I must say that of late she has expressed her concern over you more than once.'

'Tell her I'm grateful,' he smiled, 'and tell her I'll think on it and find comfort whenever I hear the voice of that tiresome fool, Kuraka.'

'He expresses his concern for Uruk, as he should,' replied Enkidu.

'So you say, but if I thought he meant me ill I'd take my sword and -. No, perhaps I read too much in his manner, though I cannot forget how his negotiations with Kish would have ended in our ignominy had I not intervened. I would have treated that man as a traitor had not the elders spoken out for him. I still feel I ought to have –. No, I mustn't go on. Brother Enkidu, I grow impatient because I cannot prevent what is happening. I find it difficult to contain my feelings, as you see.'

'I'll come with you tonight when you visit the temple, if it will help.'

'There are few occasions when I'd not be glad of your company as well you know, but it will be to speak of something that must remain private for the time being. Perhaps I'll discuss it with you later - and with our mother. Give me a few days to think it over – that's all I ask. Just a few days.'

***

The day had been one of silence in Uruk. Early evening saw Gilgamesh alone with his brother in the shadow of the palace arcade. His voice was troubled. 'The heat of day is unrelenting. It adds

229

greater torment to the people's suffering. Uruk lies helpless under the burden.'

'In early morning,' sighed Enkidu. 'I go with them as they strive to bring water from the river to fill the ditches. They take whatever containers they can lay their hands upon but it can never be enough to revive the crops and orchards.'

'Throughout the town even children cower in the shadows,' said Gilgamesh. 'It is the rats who venture into the light of day in their quest for food. I listen at my window at night. I hear people going by as they take their dead outside the city for burial. At least that is what we must suppose they are about because I see fires burning beyond the wall and dare not ask why. The gates are no longer barred after dark nor are they even guarded.'

'At least we have no human enemy to fear,' reflected Enkidu as they paced the arcade. 'There can be little enough left to feed an army in all of Sumer.'

'Nor enough beer to quench its thirst,' added Gilgamesh. 'I walked the streets alone today and what I saw caused me greater unease by far than when I faced the men of Kish in battle. The poor and the starving sat huddled in their doorways. Some were eating the vermin plucked from their own hair and bodies.' He gazed beyond the wall at Inanna's light, seeing not an image of pleasure or valour but a baleful eye, crystal hard, unmoved by the sight of suffering. 'I think,' he breathed, 'it's time for me to make my confession. We must take ourselves to the palace of Egalmah. I'll send a slave ahead to announce our coming.'

***

230

'So you scorned her,' said Ninsun, eyes reflecting the glow of a flame that swayed in the small pottery lamp set by her couch. 'Most unlike you - but what else could you have done, knowing the fate that sooner or later would have been yours had you accepted her advances.'

'Yes, mother, as you say, most unlike me. I imagine the gods must have intervened. Yet I could have known greater fulfilment than any man. The name of Gilgamesh would have been branded upon the face of the Earth and all Sumer would have been spared this suffering.'

'You say all Sumer would have been spared,' put in Enkidu, 'but I'm assured such disasters have occurred before and will do so again long after we're gone. You should not carry guilt for what it seems to me the gods dispense at a whim.'

'The Queen of Heaven serves mankind well,' reflected Ninsun, 'but when she's angered her spite, her desire for revenge, defies all reason. Your rejection must have induced her to call down Gugalanna, the Bull of Heaven, even if the other gods did not approve. You, Gilgamesh, had little choice in the matter. A lesser man would have drunk from her cup of temptations and paid the penalty.'

Ninsun looked into his eyes and into the eyes of Enkidu who sat by his side. A smile crossed her lips. Here were her sons; two brothers strong in arms; one boastful and rash, loving the pleasures and challenges of this world - the other steadfast and compassionate, wanting little for himself other than life's necessities but always ready to offer his strength and courage for the good of others. The ember that had glowed in the thoughts of Shamkhat on the day the two men met in combat had become, in the mind of Ninsun, a flame of understanding she dared not reveal. For a time she remained in silent contemplation, then once more spoke. 'There may be a way to defeat our enemy but it is one of such terrible danger I fear the risk may be too great.'

'A way to defeat Gugalanna!' exclaimed Gilgamesh. 'If there is a way then you must tell us!'

'That is so,' agreed Enkidu. 'There is already pestilence in the city. Soon the plague will visit every home. Whatever the risk, if it will bring about the salvation of Uruk and the lands beyond, then the decision has to be ours.'

'The Bull of Heaven,' said Ninsun in a low voice, 'has been called down many times as a scourge of mankind. He is an instrument of torment set free to run amok so as to leave the hands of the immortals unsullied. But the creature itself, I assure you, is not immortal.'

'Mother,' breathed Gilgamesh, 'are you saying the thing can be killed as was Huwawa?'

'He can be killed,' replied Ninsun, 'but not the way Huwawa was killed.'

'How can that be done?' asked Enkidu. 'He stalks the land unseen. He passes like the desert wind, drawing moisture and life from the air and leaving the cities beleaguered under empty skies.'

'Enkidu is right,' said Gilgamesh. 'The Bull of Heaven manifests himself only in the suffering and misery he brings - just as the gods speak in thunder and lightning without themselves being manifest. Gugalanna was never flesh and blood in our world.'

'That is true,' breathed Ninsun, pushing aside the lamp so as to lean closer to them. 'He lives in a space and time between this world and the unreachable realms of the immortals. I have seen it in my dreams. It is a strange place where our rules and where our understanding no longer apply. It is a crossroads by which the gods pass back and forth. There our world of imagining becomes one of reality and the world we now occupy becomes itself the dream. In that place Gugalanna is flesh and blood. There he does not have the power he manifests in ours. With my help you can cross the threshold as if in body as well as in mind. In our world you will be as clay but in the domain of Gugalanna you will become flesh and blood. But be warned – you must have Gugalanna come to you, as he surely will. Any mortal stepping beyond that domain can never return.'

'Then show us the way,' insisted Gilgamesh. 'Show us how to enter the portal with our weapons and by all I live for we will destroy him!'

'Return to your palace,' she answered. 'Each of you take up the weapon you feel will serve best then return here. I will make preparation whilst you're gone. I will send to the priests of all the temples in Uruk and tell them what we are to do. I will have them pray and sacrifice whatever they have left to sacrifice. It may distract the gods from what you are to do but understand - if our voices and the weapons you carry are not enough, I will never see you both in this life again. Go now. I need time to prepare, but return before the night is done.'

***

233

'I feel my strength and hope renewed,' said Gilgamesh as they hurried through fetid darkness, each wearing a kilt of leather, each bearing at his side the sword fashioned by Sheshkalla. 'I cannot wait to pass through that gateway. I want to carve the flesh of that beast for bringing such ruin upon us!'

'We have our swords and our courage, brother Gilgamesh. We must do our best.'

Where the narrow street opened into the square before the temple of Inanna, they hesitated. There were voices. People and priests hurried with purpose where until now all purpose had been usurped by hunger and despair. Oil lamps glowed on the steps that led up to the temple platform. More lights drifted as though disembodied from the surrounding obscurity. The two continued on, keeping out of view, saying nothing until they were once more alone.

'The people, too, have hope,' said Enkidu. 'It's the first they've known for many days.'

'If we do not fulfil their expectations, brother Enkidu, I have no wish to return. I'll not face the citizens of Uruk in defeat. Never!'

'And I'll not come back alone,' responded Enkidu. 'Our swords were forged together and I'd not wish to have them parted.'

No one was to be seen outside the palace of Egalmah but at a window above, like a star in the night sky, a solitary flame burned where Ninsun waited.

She stood alone in her gilded robe to greet them as they entered to find the air within the curtained room charged with incense.

'Are we in good time?' asked Gilgamesh.

'You are in good time,' replied Ninsun. 'Follow me.'

At the top of the staircase where her shrine stood open to the night sky, two candles burned steadily on the small altar of carved limestone. At each side of the altar a bed of sheepskins and a pillow of soft leather had been prepared.

'Throughout the city,' said Ninsun, 'they pray to Enlil who watches over humankind, to Enki the wise and to Utu who lights the day. They - we, say the people have suffered enough and ask that none intervene if you pass the portal into the middle world. Remember, much of what we see as passing shadows in our world will there have substance. I cannot say if the gods hear our pleas and I cannot say what the Lady Inanna will do, even though our priests offer the finest wines and precious grain at her sanctuary.'

'How do we step through this portal?' asked Gilgamesh.

'You cannot pass through in the conscious world,' she replied, reaching for two small silver goblets that rested between the candles. 'It may only be attained when the mind is set adrift from the body. Take these and drink. They contain the distillation of a plant from beyond the mountains to our east. It will free your minds. When the cups are empty, lay quietly with your eyes closed until you are cast off from the world you know.' She watched them lift the goblets then said, 'I will stand close by and pray you cross in safety. After that, my very precious sons, I can only wait and hope.'

'The liquid is bitter,' said Gilgamesh, replacing his empty goblet on the altar.

'I know the plant from which it was made,' said Enkidu, placing his cup likewise. 'It promotes deep sleep. It induces vivid illusions.'

'Yes,' said Ninsun, 'deep sleep. And it will come soon. But the illusions will be very real.'

Each man lay down, Gilgamesh to the right of the altar, Enkidu to the left. Seeing them close their eyes, Ninsun waited until she was certain both had drifted into sleep. Then she stepped to the altar, fell to her knees, clasped hands across her chest and began to recite under her breath those ancient verses long forgotten by the temple priests. The candle flames, steady until then, swayed and danced, though no breeze touched Ninsun's cheek. Their light steadied then intensified, spreading wider until the altar and the space about it seemed to float in a sea of blackness. The two men began to stir, their heads rocking gently from side to side, their mouths uttering soundless words.

***

'Enkidu, are you there?' His voice reverberated with deep chasm echoes.

'I'm here, Gilgamesh! Wait - I'll be at your side!'

'By the gods!' cried Gilgamesh. 'What is this place! What have we done!'

Both men gazed about in awe. 'It's like a great hall!' exclaimed Enkidu. 'No, not a hall. It's open to the sky - if that is the real sky up there!'

'I can't tell if it is the sky,' responded Gilgamesh, 'or if that's the sky we see beyond those arches in the far wall.'

'If that is the sky then I've never seen the like of it,' replied Enkidu, gazing upward. 'It's awash with flame and lightning yet there's no crash of thunder - just the sound of gusting wind, yet there is no wind. Look there - look at the odd slant of the floor and those walls – can you tell if they go up or down? I can't make out which are close or which are distant. My eyes are deceived!'

'Mine too,' responded Gilgamesh, 'but perhaps it's through those arches we have to go if we're to face Gugalanna.'

'No – remember our mother's words? We should not go beyond them in case we find ourselves stepping into a void from which we can never return.'

'Yes, but -.' began Gilgamesh. Someone was laughing. A woman's laughter echoed all about. Now close. Now distant. 'There's someone standing beneath the end arch,' he said, pointing across. 'See – there's a woman and she's watching us!'

'Yes, I see her,' responded Enkidu. 'And there are shadows drifting like a mist through those columns. They're spreading across the floor. They're playing tricks with my eyes. They approach and recede at one and the same time with the sound of some - some monstrous breathing. Should we go further? Should we approach to speak with whoever is waiting there?'

'No!' snapped Gilgamesh as they advanced a few steps, 'That is not a woman with whom I wish to converse. I tell you, she is not watching out of concern for our well-being but for the sake of crass entertainment. It would be better if we -.'

His words were cut short by a roar that shattered the air as a clashing gong. Where weird images had ebbed and flowed below the arches there loomed a form darker than the shadows. The creature emerged, stamping and bellowing. A vision of grim and threatening aspect.

'What have we here!' cried Gilgamesh, drawing his sword. 'It is Gugalanna! Yes, he sees us!'

'A formidable beast,' observed Enkidu, fitful light catching on his own blade. 'But remember, this is not a chimera like Huwawa. This is a creature of flesh and blood.'

'Then I never saw a mightier piece of flesh and blood!' responded Gilgamesh. 'And do I imagine it or is that damnable thing growing larger as we stand here? His eyes are glowing embers - look at them fix upon us. I can feel already the heat of his breath!'

'Yes,' replied Enkidu, 'and the gleam in his eye is not the light of friendship. I'd say, dear brother, he's about to come at us and you'd better watch for those horns!'

Emerging fully from the shadows, the bull hesitated, head swaying from side to side so as to judge the men's distance. A snort rolled through the bizarre hall like the massed drums of an advancing army, then with a blacksmith's hammer blows his hooves rang on the stone floor. Gugalanna lowered his head. Gugalanna charged, thundering toward the two men in unstoppable fury. The great horns swung aside to impale them but they leapt apart, spun about then with loud cries dashed back to plunge their swords hard into his flanks. The beast

238

let out an explosive snort as he clattered to a halt. Enraged by pain his bellow tore the air then, jetting white vapour from flared nostrils he pounded the floor, swinging about to fix a gaze of bloody hatred upon his adversaries. The two men were some distance from one another as Enkidu, sheathing his sword, called out, 'Gilgamesh – he is sorely wounded! If he escapes us we may not get another chance!'

'Sorely wounded you say,' replied Gilgamesh. 'Well the big bastard seems unaware of it! Nor does he look inclined to escape!'

'I know this beast as I once knew others,' responded Enkidu. 'He is maddened. His judgement will give way to baser instincts. I'll get behind and distract him. When he turns about, leap astride! Get where you can strike into his neck behind the horns!'

'Leap astride him,' muttered Gilgamesh with a grim smile. 'What greater folly might I attempt before ending my days? Ah, well, here I go.'

Both men circled at a prudent distance whilst Gugalanna, snorting fitfully, swayed head and horns. His eyes gleamed baleful light, his gaze shifted from one man to the other whilst he determined which of them would be impaled first then tossed aside in bleeding ruin.

Shouting aloud, brandishing his sword before the beast, Gilgamesh strode forward. Gugalanna eyed him, bellowed, stamped then lowered his head. He would have started as a rushing wind toward Gilgamesh but Enkidu, crouching low, had slipped unnoticed to his rear. Seeing him there, Gilgamesh sheathed his sword and sprinted forward. At the

239

same time his brother seized the creature's tail and braced a foot hard against its hind leg. The bull attempted to turn on him but with grim resolution, Enkidu held tight, pivoting about, not daring to lose his balance.

So distracted, Gugalanna shed all thought of his other adversary until Gilgamesh seized one of the horns and gripping hard, heaved himself up with a cry to land astride the massive back. Lurching violently, the bull would have rolled over to crush his unwelcome guest but Enkidu released the tail and springing up before him let forth a growl then straight away seized the horns. There he stood rock solid, arms and legs akimbo, muscles rigid, jaw set firm, his whole body seared by Gugalanna's furnace breath as Gilgamesh with a shout of triumph raised his sword high and struck! The blade plunged deep. Deep as if to impale the flowing ribbon of time, for in those moments the beast set rigid as a clay idol. Gilgamesh held fast on the sword hilt, uncertain as to the effect of his blow. The horns still firmly in his grasp, Enkidu stood his ground, fearing to release them in case his brother's blade had not entered deep enough to kill Gugalanna.

There was no heaving. There was no bellow of rage. Only a long, rattling sigh that issued from deep within as, very slowly, the great bull sank to his knees.

'Done, brother Gilgamesh!' cried Enkidu, releasing the horns and promptly stepping back.

'Done, brother Enkidu!' laughed Gilgamesh, wrenching free his sword then jumping to the ground moments before the bull toppled heavily aside. 'The Bull of Heaven is dead! We have destroyed him!'

Their voices boomed about the vault while outside, beyond the pillars, the clouds and lightning had begun to subside. The sky, once seething lurid, brightened now to burnished gold. Falling through each of the arches in turn, a shaft of light pierced the void as Gilgamesh placed a foot against the carcass. 'See - Utu greets us! We must give thanks because he watches over us here as he did in the Cedar Forest. We must offer him the heart of Gugalanna!'

'Aye,' agreed Enkidu, 'if that's your will then we must.'

Gilgamesh plunged his blade into the dead creature's side so that warm blood gushed over the floor to soak their feet. With their swords, both men carved through the flesh, bloodying their limbs, laying open the white bones of Gugalanna's rib cage until the heart was exposed, glistening fresh. Both wrenched apart the bones but it was Gilgamesh who reached inside to cut the heart away from its gore-spattering vessels. It was Gilgamesh who wrenched out the drizzling organ. Gilgamesh who held it high to greet the sun as it burst forth to illuminate them in a pool of silver light.

As he let down the heart they recalled the figure that had watched from beneath the arch. Both looked aside to find she was no longer there.

A low cloud swept in to obscure the newly brightened sky. From the darkness above emerged a snake-hiss. It sped through the air to circle them in a vortex of malignant sound. 'Gilgamesh! You who insulted me - you have slain the Bull of Heaven!

With reckless folly you have destroyed the instrument of my vengeance – the one created by great Anu to humble mankind! Your arrogance exceeds that of all other mortals!'

As she was speaking Enkidu seized a hind leg of the bull, hacking through muscle and bone with his sword until the limb could be ripped free at the thigh. Stepping away he let fall the sword, raised the gory haunch with both hands then hurled it into the darkness from where the voice had issued.

'There!' he cried, 'There is my gift to you! I'd gladly robe you in Gugalanna's entrails for what you have done to the people of Uruk and to all of Sumer in your spite!'

There was no reply but a cacophony of whispers seethed amidst the vapour as many chattering forms flitted invisibly back and forth. The sound grew, issuing from the gloom to pass over their heads as a flock of birds in agitated flight. The air was suddenly cold and Gilgamesh, smearing redness across a shoulder with soiled fingers, exclaimed, 'Oh, there's blood all over me!'

'Over me, also!' cried Enkidu. 'Could it be from the limb I threw?'

'No – it's coming from above. It's raining blood!'

'Blood - yes!' replied Enkidu. 'It's all about us! Blood! Everywhere there is blood!'

Their voices echoed, reverberated, ever louder, 'Blood! Everywhere blood!' until they were swamped by a booming mockery of their own words.

'No, not blood,' came her voice through a confusion of spinning lights. 'Not blood but water!'

'What!' Shocked into wakefulness, Gilgamesh opened his eyes to stare about in confusion. Enkidu shook his head and groaned, 'Wh – what's happening?'

'Rain is falling,' laughed Ninsun, raising her arms as the altar lamps spluttered out. 'When the morning heavens should have brightened, clouds spread over the sky. When the rain began I knew you had destroyed Gugalanna.'

'Yes, at last,' responded Enkidu, rising unsteadily to his feet to find himself soaked with water. 'But why did we think it was blood?'

'What does it matter,' answered Ninsun. 'The affliction is lifted from us.'

'It may be too late for our crops,' said Gilgamesh as the rain beat down. 'But at least our herds, our orchards and our date palms will survive.'

Ninsun backed away to shelter beneath the arch at the head of the stairs.

'The rivers will rise and the fish will return,' said Enkidu. 'New crops will spring from the earth in good time.'

Gilgamesh stood, face raised to the sky, hair matted about his shoulders. 'Listen to the beating rain. In it I hear the applause of ten thousand people and many, many more. The acclaim of Uruk! Of all Sumer!'

'And the air,' smiled Enkidu, 'has it ever tasted sweeter? This could be the morning of our world. The very first of days.'

'Let's take ourselves through the town,' said Gilgamesh, 'and when all is settled I'll have Sheshkalla make a pair of bronze horns as big as those of Gugalanna. They'll take pride of place in my audience room. They'll remind our visitors who they have to thank for their salvation.'

Enkidu said nothing though the words crossed his mind. 'This was too easy. Too easy by far.'

They passed through the streets of the town, now awash. People hurried about, splashing along, hardly concerned to avoid water that sluiced down from drainage holes below the parapets. Most took themselves to the precinct of Eanna where they danced about, hands raised, in the deluge. But from Inanna's temple, above the pummelling rain, drifted voices of dire lamentation. Enkidu hesitated. 'D'you hear that, Gilgamesh? It hardly sounds like a chorus of thanksgiving.'

'I cannot explain what we hear but we'll find out this evening - you'll see!'

'This evening?' he queried as they splashed their way from the precinct.

'Yes - this evening. I'll send to the temple and summon the girls whilst our meat roasts on spits. We'll break open jars of the finest wine; the harpists and the flute-players will entertain and we'll have ourselves fine sport when the light is gone. Enough of suffering and misery! What d'you say, brother Enkidu?'

'I wasn't aware you and I had suffered at all,' remarked Enkidu, 'nor a few others I can think of. Only the common people really suffer, so it seems to me.'

'Ah – there is disapproval in your manner. D'you think I'm insensitive to their misfortunes?'

'Not entirely,' answered Enkidu, 'but the rain will not wash away hardship. Many will carry their burden through the year and far beyond - more so the poorest. And as much as we craved the rain it will be a mixed blessing to those whose wretched dwellings of mud crumble about their ears.'

'They will quickly rebuild at the cost of no more than their labour,' said Gilgamesh. 'The humbler buildings of the city may also suffer but those I will renovate to greater advantage.'

On approaching the palace square they stopped beneath an arch that bridged the narrow street and there took shelter between curtains of water. Gilgamesh placed a hand on his brother's shoulder. 'As always, you concern yourself with the well-being of others but our abstinence would benefit no one. The people will go about their tasks whether we choose to indulge ourselves or retire for the night as penitents. You must admit we have cause to celebrate; we've risked our lives and our very souls for them, have we not?'

'Aye, brother, we've cause enough, but it would pain me to see some go without their bread when we live amidst plenty.'

'Then I'll open the palace stores and dispense much of what remains to those whose need is greatest. Our stores are kept for times of war but I doubt Uruk will find herself under siege for a long time. The temples must also give some of their grain to ensure no one in the city lacks bread and beer - and it has to be done in your name.'

'Then,' smiled Enkidu, 'I'll gladly celebrate with you tonight. Not just for what we have done but for the compassion that of late is finding a home in your heart. Ah - I see lights at the palace windows and though the square is awash I'll reach the steps before you no matter how hard you run.'

'By the gods you will not!' laughed Gilgamesh, and the two braced themselves for the dash.

***

'D'you wish to join them?' asked Enkidu in the darkness. Her cheek rested warm and sensually soft against his own. 'I told Gilgamesh I would be with him this evening but I'll not go without you.'

'We'll join them if you wish,' she sighed, 'but I would be happier to stay alone here with you. Gilgamesh celebrates in ways I know you find not always to your liking.'

'Well I don't begrudge him that,' smiled Enkidu. 'He's their hero again – almost a god incarnate. People are thronging the square below even though the rain still falls. The serving girls of the palace vied for his attention. They bared their breasts without shame when he returned. Even some who considered Gilgamesh the scourge of Uruk are full of praise for him now.'

'Nothing will please him more,' replied Shamkhat. 'He thrives on adoration but once that's gone the emptiness might well return. Only you have made him see reason, dear Enkidu. He never listened to any man as he listens to you. You deserve equal praise but I know you'd not desire it as Gilgamesh does.'

'He can be boastful and vain, perhaps, but he carries less malice in his soul than some I have encountered. When he hurts others it's often because he doesn't understand the result of his actions.'

'But you give him that understanding,' she whispered. 'When I first knew you it was strange, but afterwards, after we travelled over the desert together, after you fought with Gilgamesh in the market place, it was as though -.'

'As though -?'

Shamkhat remained silent for a time then said, 'I - I can't explain. I cannot find the words because what haunts my mind is so unreal - as it was in the temple at daybreak after the rains began.'

'Ah, I felt something must have happened there to upset you. When we passed by the temple we heard your voices. They seemed to be raised in mourning whilst the voices of Uruk's citizens were full of joy. What was the reason?'

Her fingers spread across his chest with adoring touch. 'I will tell you but I ask you to repeat none of it - not even to Gilgamesh. Perhaps especially not to him though I don't intend deceit.'

'If that's your wish then I promise I won't repeat anything you tell me.'

Shamkhat again hesitated, gazing aside with troubled expression before speaking. 'We woke at first light and we saw clouds billow above the horizon. When the rain began I and the other girls were so glad we joined the priests and hurried to the shrine of Lady Inanna to offer our thanks. We thought salvation had been granted with her blessing because she presides over our city.' Enkidu groaned inwardly and closed his eyes as she continued. 'We'd hardly gathered about her altar when she appeared to us - but her image was not the one we expected her to hold - not one of radiance and pleasure. No, it was an image of utter dread.

She was naked with wings spread at her back as if she had swooped down from the sky. Her feet were bird's claws that gripped the base of the altar and – and they screeched horribly against the stone. Her body, her face and hands were spattered with fresh blood. At her feet lay the bleeding haunch of some great animal and we knew you had slaughtered the Bull of Heaven. She pointed to it and screamed at us. She demanded our lamentation instead of our gratitude. We raised our voices in fear of her wrath. But worse, dear Enkidu, her eyes were afire with hatred and she cursed the two of you dreadfully for what you had done.'

Shamkhat was tearful. From the chamber below chimed laughter. A girl cried out in the grip of her climax. Then more laughter. The servants and musicians had been dismissed some time before, though a call for more wine meant the king had at least one attendant still on hand.

'I fear for what Inanna might do next,' sighed Shamkhat.

'Think about it no more,' he whispered, kissing her lips. 'The rains have come and you are by my side. Right now I care about nothing else.'

CHAPTER 7
VENGEANCE OF THE GODS

'How long must I wait?' she cried with arms raised. 'I have lost count of the times I have asked the question!'

Her bright-eyed female attendants, voluptuous, bare-breasted in bejewelled splendour broke off their intimate caresses to nod their agreement. The mist that swirled all about might have been a procession of spectres.

'Be patient, lady,' rolled back the voice. 'The gods go about their affairs and cannot be summoned at a whim. Not even by you!'

'Is that, Lord Enlil?' she asked, turning her face up to gaze at the pillars of cloud towering up to merge with twilight heavens.

'It is I,' drifted back the voice.

'Then if you are here, the others must soon follow.'

'Yes, they are beginning to arrive. Anu himself will be last to join us.'

'Father Anu?' she questioned. 'Did he need to be called down from among the stars now you are here?'

'You have set matters in motion and there are grave decisions to be made. At times like this he will sit as ultimate arbiter. There must always be one whose wisdom guides the final word and records it in the annals. You should know our traditions as well as anybody, Lady Inanna, even though you have contrived to alter the order of our proceedings on occasion.'

'Oh, I know our traditions!' she retorted as his outline became more distinct. 'But I so often find myself occupied with other matters. More down to earth matters, you might say.'

'Yes,' replied the Lord of the Winds, eyeing the subtly suggestive manner of her small entourage, 'I had noticed. This appears as much your doing as anyone else's. You should exercise more self-discipline in your affairs.'

'Me! Me exercise more self-discipline as you call it! *I* didn't make them traipse off to the cedar forests - *your* cedar forests – remember? *I* didn't tell them to start hacking down the trees then kill *your* guardian. *I* didn't have them cross the threshold and slaughter -!'

'Wait!' called Enlil, his bearded form materialising fully in gilded robe and gem-studded headband. The breeze of his arrival dispersed the mist and swept wisps of raven hair about Inanna's crescent moon earrings of jewel-set gold.

'My!' he exclaimed, 'don't you look your enchanting self. I'm surprised the king of Uruk didn't rise to the occasion and pledge himself body and soul without a second thought. Unless you were wearing that as well. Were you?'

From the shift in his gaze she knew he referred not to her dress, a gown of finest kidskin that exposed her right shoulder and breast. It was dyed shining black and sewn together by her handmaidens to fit tightly the curves of her body and impart to it the sheen of a slithering snake. No, it was the belt at her waist or rather what was attached to it that had caught his attention.

Inanna's expression hardened. Long, ruby-nailed fingers stroked lightly over the jewelled hilt of the dagger whose cruel blade of curved bronze nestled in copper-banded leather sheath. A deadly serpent poised in its lair.

'No, I wasn't wearing it,' she replied. 'If I had been I might have been tempted to -.'

Something else was happening. The cloud-pillars were rising. They were drifting apart. They had begun to diffuse into a rapidly darkening sky. More figures were appearing, more were gathering about, whilst the space had taken on the aspect of a vast spectral enclosure open to the stars. As the later arrivals approached, Inanna recognised Enki, Lord of the Deep. Now appeared silver-attired light of the day, Utu the Just. Behind him drifted gold-clad Nanna whose serene image ruled the night. She next observed Ninhursag, consort of Enlil, in her horned head dress, but averted her gaze from the next arrival, muttering, 'And *that* abomination is my own sister.' She had caught sight of Ereshkigal, Queen of the Underworld, the one afraid of light, the one who had once held Inanna herself prisoner in her grim domain. In her wake followed Namtar, her grotesque minister who spawned the demons of sickness and misery. Inanna shivered, hoping to avoid their baleful gaze. She spotted Dumuzzi, alone and standing aside from the rest. In distant times a king of Uruk, he was most notable of the lovers she had taken only later to reject and cruelly punish. He stood mute in the shadows that had become his lot. All but one of the great and all of the lesser immortals were there to witness the convocation. Drifting about, they formed themselves into a semi-circle before a dark, slab-like rock that lay revealed as the last of the mists vanished.

Something caught their attention high above. Against the sweep of the stars one light grew to outshine the rest. It moved across the sky until hovering directly above. It began to descend, expanding, fading to a shimmering red. It paused, steadied, then continued down to envelop the rock, growing ever larger until it had inflated to a dull vapour that passed outward and through them as a warm breeze. In moments it had altogether gone.

Upon the slab they perceived the grey bearded figure everyone knew but seldom witnessed.

'Father Anu - greetings!' called Enlil. 'We thank you for leaving your realm of contemplation to join us!'

'This is a matter I cannot ignore,' rolled across the reply, 'though I find it petty and irksome. At first I was inclined to put it aside but upon reflection it seems the mortals have transgressed beyond what we - what I consider acceptable. This is a matter demanding my judgement.'

'And a judgement it must have,' declared Enlil. 'The King of Uruk and his brother have treated us with contempt.'

'And hurled gross insult at me personally!' cried Inanna to the nodding agreement of her girls.

'Yes, my dear,' responded Anu, fingering the end of his beard, 'we have been over that and we're all aware of the outcome. Even so, the depth of your bitterness I still find puzzling, given the reverence and sacrifice offered you by the priests of Uruk.

Why, you get a deal more out of them than I do - not that I let it play on my mind.'

For some time discussion continued, centring mainly upon which of them received his or her fair share, or less of it, from the altars of humanity. Enlil, exasperated by the drift of their dialogue, raised his arms. 'We are here to determine the punishment of the two concerned. I maintain the whole of their arrogance is more than the sum of its two parts. Gilgamesh troubled only humanity when he was alone. Now the two of them together bring their contentions close to our own realms.'

'Remember you stood back and allowed them to slay Huwawa,' put in Enki, 'and Lord Utu himself was instrumental in their success. We must be fair.'

'Huwawa?' responded Enlil. 'Yes, I'll admit I let that one go. None of us liked the wretched creature even if he was one of ours.'

'One of *yours*, actually,' someone put in.

'More so one of ours was the Bull of Heaven!' declared Inanna.

'Yes,' breathed Anu, 'more so the Bull of Heaven and I wish I'd never agreed to it.'

'I'm sure we all appreciate the seriousness of this affair,' said Enlil in a no-nonsense manner.

'We cannot do otherwise,' replied Anu, to a general murmur of agreement. 'The gods always have to make known their anger as we do our pleasure. What's the point in being gods if we don't.'

'Which means?' asked Inanna, tilting her head aside.

'Which means one of them has to die,' answered Anu, wearily.

'Then it should be Enkidu,' said Enlil, ignoring the gasp of disbelief that issued from the Queen of Heaven's reddened lips as she and her girls mouthed, 'No - Gilgamesh.'

'Aruru fashioned him from water and clay,' Enlil continued, 'and we breathed into him the gift of life with a purpose that has not well served us.'

'But Enkidu is the least guilty of the pair,' protested silver-clad Utu. 'It was Gilgamesh who struck the death blow in each case - not his brother. I say neither should suffer and no tablet should record their guilt. What Gugalanna brought to Sumer was punishment enough.'

Enlil turned in anger to the Lord of Light. 'If we were to inscribe a tablet of culpability then it would have to bear your name, also. Had you not interfered, matters might have taken a different course and we would have been spared this inconvenience.'

'Exactly,' responded Anu, 'and I assure you this is the last time *I* get involved in their wearisome transgressions.' Again he fingered his beard then looked directly at Enlil. 'In future *you* can deal with the whole sorry lot of them - starting from now.'

'I doubt he'll make a better job of it,' grumbled Inanna under her breath. 'It ought to be the other one. What wouldn't I give to torment *his* soul.'

'We are all – or nearly all – agreed,' announced Enlil. 'It must be Enkidu,' 'His was never a full life but his brief existence has given far greater meaning to the life of Gilgamesh. Because of that, it is upon the king of Uruk that the real burden of punishment will fall. That is my verdict!'

***

The hand of misery is lifted from Uruk,' said Gilgamesh. 'The streets and squares are washed clean and corruption is swept away. The air of the city is more wholesome than I ever remember.'

'Aye,' answered Enkidu, hands spread on the parapet as he watched the people in the square below hurry about with renewed purpose. 'The city is purified and the land will be green again.'

'Yes, the land,' continued Gilgamesh, moving to his side. 'Our pastures are growing afresh so our herds will soon regain their health. I never thought to welcome the glare of sunlight on our waterways or the sight of fishermen at the quay but I do now. Their nets are hauled in full. Their catch gleams more precious than silver on the market stalls.' He breathed deeply, placed hands on his hips and gazed across the fields toward the desert. 'Before long you and I must join the hunt and show those fellows of mine the skills we employed in vanquishing Uruk's afflictions. Yes - we should leave tomorrow at first light and head out to where the gazelles and the lions roam.'

Enkidu stepped back from the parapet and passed a hand across his forehead. 'Not tomorrow. Maybe some other time.'

'I sense you are ill at ease,' said Gilgamesh. 'I've noticed these past days how tired you look. Whatever troubles you, I'll gladly share the burden unless it's your girl of the temple keeping you awake at night. If it is then I'll pry no more.'

255

'No,' replied Enkidu with a pale smile, 'it is not the girl. Trouble is the last thing she brings to my bed.' His fingers strayed to the amulet given him by Ninsun before he and Gilgamesh set out to the cedar forest. He looked his brother in the eye. 'But since you ask what troubles me, I'll tell you for all the good it might do. I have begun to avoid sleep. No – more than that – these last few nights I have come to fear it.'

'To fear sleep! Are you disturbed by dreams? I thought I was the only one who suffered their visitations, though they've not bothered me of late I'm glad to say.'

'You ask if I'm disturbed. No, Gilgamesh, I'm not disturbed, I am tormented! I speak about it now when the city glows in sunlight and the land spreads out under a clear sky. On a day like this the ghosts of the night are far away and seem not so important. But when the shadows lengthen, when darkness closes in - then -.'

'Why have you not mentioned this before?' asked Gilgamesh. 'My physician will prescribe a potion to calm your sleep. Could it be the fault of those who prepare our food?'

'I don't think so,' sighed Enkidu. 'These are stranger than any dreams I ever had. As strange as yours but very different. They're dreams in which I play little part. They're dreams of events to which I am a secret party. It's as if I stand listening in darkness behind a curtain whilst others discuss matters of great importance. Always they are the same - as though time is repeating itself.'

'Then I suspect you're suffering from boredom again, brother Enkidu. Otherwise, how could these dreams give you such cause for apprehension?'

'How - I'll tell you how.' He turned aside for a moment, arms hanging loose by his sides. 'It's because I hear them speak my name in a manner that gives me no comfort.'

'They? Who are *they*? And who would speak your name other than in praise?'

Enkidu looked down and considered the question before replying. 'Their voices are all about but nowhere at all. I see nothing yet I know they're there. I know they are not the progeny of my own mind. Gilgamesh, I see this is a dark premonition. I believe I hear the dialogue of the gods themselves as they sit in judgement over what you and I did on the threshold of their world.'

'If there's one upon whom they pass judgement then it surely cannot be you. It was my decision to go to the cedar forest. It was my blade sealed the fate of Huwawa. It was I who rejected the one we're pleased to call Queen of Heaven and it was my sword that struck dead the beast she sent against us. If there's wrath to fall upon either of us it's more likely they'd single me out for vengeance.'

'Oh, perhaps what you say is true. Perhaps I'm creating a feast of woes from a few scraps of discomfort. That's so much easier for me to believe as we stand here. Perhaps it's the spectre of guilt returning to haunt me in the night.'

'Guilt, Enkidu! And what guilt do you bear? Or is there guilt in being a true and steadfast companion to me and to the people of Uruk? Why, if each of us wore our misdeeds as a garment of clothing, you'd need to commit more than one offence just to hide your nakedness!'

'We all carry guilt but do not easily see it unless by the light of another's wisdom. Still, why should it matter? Maybe we're set upon Earth only for the amusement and diversion of the gods. Perhaps we dance to the beat of their drum whether we realise it or not.'

'This is unlike you, brother Enkidu. You're darkened by sadness at the very time you should be glowing with pride. I have been asked by the priests and elders of our city to preside over a ceremony of thanksgiving to be held at the temple of Anu. I'll accept and we will make offerings also at the shrine of Utu as well as the lesser gods. I dare say the Queen of Heaven will expect her portion in spite of everything - and hopefully we'll keep our peace with those who determine our fates. The people can rejoice and you, brother, can ensure the poorest among them receive their share as you have done in the past. Take heart now. Think over what we have achieved and look to our future.'

'Very well,' smiled Enkidu, 'I will take my wine and my pleasures in full tonight, and in the morning I'll be at your side.'

***

The shadows were long, the streets and squares still cool and cupping darkness when they began to gather in the precinct of Kullab, before the temple of Anu and before other shrines throughout the city. Gilgamesh would tread the dusty streets of Uruk resplendent in red robes, preceded by the high priest of Anu. Behind would follow a line of near-naked priests, strung out like beads in the wake of majesty and bearing the offerings of field and workshop. Pipes, drums and cymbals would play as he ascended the steps to the platform and to one side of the great cedar doors would wait the chorus of bangle decorated, naked female acolytes ready to sing in praise of his deeds. He would stand with his brother before them and the citizens of Uruk would see Enkidu as a hero in his own right.

At the palace square the herald's drumbeat began the procession. It moved slowly through the streets, amidst a cacophony of people, until uniting with the file of priests within the precinct. At the temple steps, Gilgamesh paused to glance about. Continuing to the top, bathed now in the radiant sound of the girls' voices, he again hesitated to look about - this time for a little longer. People continued to stream into the square, massing until it could hold no more. They gazed on him from window, wall and parapet. Their babble surged as a rising tide of sound. Gilgamesh made no gesture because it was not yet time. First the affairs of the temple must be concluded and then, with Enkidu by his side, he would emerge from his solemn duties within the shrine to bask in sunlight and adoration.

Perhaps Enkidu had been delayed. Yes, delayed, but his brother would be with him soon.

***

'Where is my brother?' he asked when emerging from the rites to halt within the filtered light of the vestibule. 'Where is Lord Enkidu?' He glanced about, then his eye fell upon a nervous figure hovering by the part-opened door. Recognising him as one of the palace slaves, Gilgamesh was about to summon him when the

259

man, hands clasped tightly together at his chest, tottered forward to speak.

'S - Sire,' he stammered, 'Lord Enkidu sent me to beg your forgiveness. He says he is unwell and - and cannot be present.'

'Unwell!' exclaimed the king. 'What is wrong with him?'

'I - I do not know, Sire,' answered the man, hoarsely, all but wilting in terror, 'but he - he said you should not concern yourself and - and that his thoughts are with you. That is all - lord.'

'All right, man – return and say I will be with him soon.'

As the great doors groaned aside on stone sockets, Gilgamesh stepped into the light of a newly arisen sun with words tumbling through his mind. 'Unwell! No - he cannot be unwell. Not Enkidu. Not now!' But the cheering, the intermittent thunder of drums and clash of cymbals filled the air. They drove away his thoughts as he let slip the ceremonial robe, as he raised his arms to reveal himself once more as the warrior his people wished to see.

'Gil-ga-mesh!' they began to chant. 'Gil-ga-mesh! Gil-ga-mesh! Gil-ga-mesh!'

Before long he was aware of another name issuing from the mouths of the artisans and the poorer people. 'En-ki-du! En-ki-du! En-ki-du!'

Gilgamesh raised his arms again but as the tide of voices ebbed, someone called from a nearby parapet, 'Where is Lord Enkidu?'

This seemed to lull the people closest to him and Gilgamesh knew he must provide an answer. Stretching out a hand to command silence, he addressed them. 'Lord Enkidu bids me greet you! He bids me thank you all in his name as well as in my own! He bids me say that, out of modesty - the modesty of a true hero, I say, he wishes to remain aside from pomp and ceremony! He wishes to be at one with the people of Uruk and not to stand above them as my own office demands! My brother and true companion will soon be among you! You have my word as your king!'

Renewed cheering told him the message was enough to satisfy most of the crowd but the king of Uruk, focus of admiration before his people, wished for nothing more than to hurry back and ascertain what had prevented his brother's appearance.

***

'It's an inconvenience,' sighed Enkidu when Gilgamesh entered the room to find his brother rested upon his mattress of sheepskins and part covered by the lion skin he had brought with him from the wild lands. 'I shiver as if a cold wind blows down on me from the mountains but sweat as I did a while back when labouring in the heat of the ditches. I think the rich food of our celebrations and an excess of wine have also taken their toll. I regret I was not at your side, today, yes - today of all days, but jut now this body of mine wants to behave contrary to my will.'

Now accustomed to the low light, Gilgamesh saw how bright his brother's eyes were. Perhaps too bright. Enkidu's forehead glistened with sweat. He stirred with a restlessness that spoke of considerable discomfort.

'You cannot be unwell, brother Enkidu,' said Gilgamesh. 'I forbid it.'

'Ah, I'd gladly comply with your royal decree on this occasion. I'm not one to suffer ailments as you know. I'm sure a little rest will serve to drive away whatever troubles me.'

'Troubles you?' asked Gilgamesh, with undisguised concern. 'You appear to have a fever.'

'Perhaps I employ the wrong word,' said Enkidu with a faint smile, pulling the cover closer about himself, 'but I'll still call it no more than an inconvenience.'

'Has my physician not attended you? If he's failed in his duty he will regret it.'

'Gilgamesh, you must not be angry with him. He came here earlier to offer his services but I sent him away. I wish for the attention of no one at present. Silence and the company of my own thoughts is all I ask.'

'Enkidu, I -. Oh, very well. I'll leave you but I insist a servant remains outside your room. He will bring you food, beer or wine whenever you need it. Meanwhile, there are matters needing my attention.'

Before leaving he glanced about the chamber. Apart from the low wooden bench upon which Enkidu rested, there was a pinewood chest to contain his clothes and close by, an ornate copper stand supporting his one oil lamp. Little enough, thought Gilgamesh, to suggest that the occupant was hero and brother to the king of Uruk, or even a member of the royal household. 'I'll return before evening,' he said, then pushing through the arched doorway, hesitated to glance again at Enkidu before letting the reed-curtain fall back into place.

Treading ill-lit stairs to the ground floor, he again considered that austere room. It was all

Enkidu had ever wanted - hardly more than some of Uruk's poorer citizens might enjoy. A suite of the royal palace could have been his, complete with retinue of servants and slaves. More - a mansion of his own had he wanted because there was space enough within the city wall. But Enkidu desired only modest accommodation. Apart from the pleasures of sport, he also eschewed other diversions Gilgamesh found so gratifying, especially hunting wild beasts. His simple desires, his attachment to the girl who had brought him to Uruk, Gilgamesh found oddly touching. No one had ever stirred that sentiment within him other than Enkidu - the Enkidu whose smile a short time ago had not quite concealed a pain to which he would not admit.

That afternoon there were petty affairs to discuss with the chief of his household staff. Correspondence from the elders of Nippur awaited his reply regarding further donations to the Temple of Enlil – as though the great cedar log and other gifts sent before the drought occurred had not been enough. These were matters for which Gilgamesh had little enthusiasm. Worse, a herald from Larsa had earlier announced the forthcoming arrival in Uruk of yet another delegation.

'What do they want to discuss now?' Gilgamesh asked himself. 'The same problems they always turn up here to complain about, for sure.' As he crossed the main hall of the palace he muttered, 'Get well, brother Enkidu. Raise yourself up so we can ride out again beyond the city wall for good sport with our bows and our spears.'

***

Thin clouds streaked the morning sky and though the sun was scarcely risen, the still air presaged a day of sultry heat. The pleasure Gilgamesh found in the cool waters of the palace pool would have been all the greater for the company and conversation of his brother. But Enkidu was not there.

Attired in patterned, belted robe and sandals, Gilgamesh had set aside his first meal of the day and hurried to his brother's room. Beside the door sat a trusted servant, one who had attended Gilgamesh since he was a boy. The man rose to his feet to clasp hands at his chest as the king spoke. 'Has Lord Enkidu left his bed? Has he called for food or beer?'

'He has not left his bed, Sire,' replied the man. 'He is sleeping now but he suffered a night of much unease. He called out often but when I attended he would have nothing but a little beer. He insisted I should not report to you though I desired otherwise. He says he wishes to see no one.'

'Very well, but I'll see him all the same.'

Gilgamesh eased aside the matting then stepped through. Within the subdued chamber he hesitated, expecting Enkidu would greet him, but no word came. From the figure lying motionless on the bed only a shallow, rapid breathing could be heard. Moving to the window, Gilgamesh hooked aside the reed curtain to allow in morning light. From the bed came a low groan as Enkidu stirred.

Gilgamesh moved forward, saying, 'It's only me, brother Enkidu. I'm very much concerned over what ails you.'

As if pained by the effort, Enkidu raised himself, coughed harshly and placed a hand to his head before opening his eyes. 'Forgive me - I should have been up and about by now.'

'No,' responded Gilgamesh, reaching out to him. 'You must stay where you are.' Glancing back to the door, he called to the servant, 'Tell my physician to come here at once!'

'Physician?' responded Enkidu, coughing once more as he struggled to raise himself higher on leather pillows. 'I need no physician. I suffer a minor discomfort that will pass as soon as I -.'

Again he began to cough and when it had passed, he closed his eyes and let his head fall back.

'He *will* see you,' responded Gilgamesh. 'I insist on it and I'll not hear otherwise.'

Little conversation had passed between them when Lelu the physician entered, his sinewy, stooping form accoutred in long, belted gown of fringed white linen. Of hooked nose and pale, searching eye, the bearded Lelu cradled in his hands the small lacquered box that accompanied him on his duties. The box contained his instruments of copper and bronze.

'Examine my brother,' ordered Gilgamesh. 'Use the skills you so often boast about and discover the nature of his ailment, for ailment he has whether he will admit to it or not. And when you are done you will bring your report directly to me.'

With that he was gone and the physician, somewhat hesitantly, approached the bed.

'I need no physician,' objected Enkidu, hoarsely. 'Leave me in peace. The city is full of others in need of your services.'

'My Lord,' he began, setting his precious box down close to the bed, 'I beg you - let me do as the king asks. If you refuse, his anger will fall upon me and that I do not relish.'

Enkidu looked at the man, closed his eyes and sighed, 'Very well, if you must, but do not have me move about unduly. My body aches and a demon capers within my head though I've touched no wine these past two days.'

'I thank you, My Lord,' answered Lelu. 'I will be brief and then I'll leave you in peace.'

***

Deep in thought, Gilgamesh was standing by the window of his private room when the physician's arrival was announced. The man was ushered inside, handing his box to the slave who had conducted him there. At first the king seemed unaware of Lelu's presence. He remained with his back to him as if peering through the reed blind to observe the comings and goings of the people in the square below. Lelu hovered uncomfortably, afraid to speak without first being addressed. He was preparing to clear his throat when Gilgamesh turned to look directly at him. 'What have you to tell me?'

'Sire,' began the physician, clasping hands briefly to his chest, 'I find Lord Enkidu much fevered. He is troubled by an aching of body and limb. He suffers, too, from a lethargy that prevents him rising from his bed. I will -.'

'Just tell me what is the matter with him,' interrupted the king.

'Sire, I would tell you the truth but I fear it in case your anger should fall upon me.'

'By the gods my anger will fall upon you if you don't!'

'Sire, it is an ailment usually brought down as a curse by the gods upon the poor, though it can afflict any among us.'

'Are you saying this is no trivial matter?'

'It is no trivial matter, Sire, no - I fear it is not.'

'Then how will you treat him, for treat him you must, and quickly?'

'My Lord,' replied Lelu, glancing nervously down then interlocking fingers across his chest to prevent their trembling, 'I will prescribe dried and powdered herb extracts. These must be dissolved in his beer and will ease his discomfort but -.' He hesitated as though afraid to say more.

'But what, man? What!'

'Sire, you would not wish me to be anything other than honest.'

'No I would not! Tell me what you need to tell me!'

'Sire, the affliction he has -. I - I am saying that many do not recover. I am saying there is no remedy known to any physician in this land. No remedy at all.'

The king's eyes remained hard on him.

'Sire,' continued the physician, his voice steadying, 'he should remain alone and not have the company of anyone other than those whose business it is to attend his needs. I will prepare a balsam to soothe his body and we must burn incense day and night to keep the air within his room pure. Others may suggest incantations and the placing of amulets about his room but I have little faith in these so-called remedies.'

'Very well,' responded Gilgamesh. 'You and a trusted assistant will between you attend him day and night. I will visit his bedside as often as I can. He must lack nothing until his health is restored. I know him better than any man. He has the spirit of a lion and his time in this world is measured as is mine.' Gilgamesh pulled a ring from his finger and handed it to Lelu. 'Here, take my seal as your authority. Go and gather everything you need. We will speak later.'

With a small bow, the physician left. Collecting his box from the slave, he made his way quickly from the palace, speaking to no one, ignoring the guard at the entrance when the man raised a hand to ask, 'Physician – who in the palace needs your hand?'

From the window above, Gilgamesh watched him hurry, his gown billowing, across the square and out of sight. The square was busy with traders, merchants, slaves and the occasional scribe clutching his tray of wedge-worded tablets. A group of arm-waving urchins careered noisily by, circled by yapping, wiry black dogs with bright eyes and wagging pink tongues. But in the mind of Gilgamesh was the wild land and the great river, with beyond it the forest of cedars rising up the slopes of the green mountain. He recalled the place where he and Enkidu had sat over their fire at night. The place where they had strode proudly as brothers and true comrades together.

***

268

The physician's assistant, a small, balding man with short beard, rose up from his seat by the door, finding barely time to offer brief homage as the king approached to ask the inevitable question, 'How is my brother today?'

Bowing a second time, the man replied, 'He remains much unsettled, Sire, though my master has been with him throughout the night.'

Gilgamesh pulled aside the reed matting and entered the semi-darkened room. The air was heavy with burning incense. He had no need to repeat the question. Enkidu lay on a bed of disarray, his eyes closed, his mouth slightly open, his breathing hoarse. The physician, in the process of arranging the lion-pelt cover into some order, turned to the king, his eyes wide, his voice a whisper. 'Sire, he has been sorely troubled throughout much of the night but he sleeps at present. I much regret his fever has intensified.'

'How long is it now?' asked Gilgamesh, 'Five days? Six? Each day Lady Ninsun and his temple girl come to visit him but I hear he will see neither - and I think you have encouraged him in this. Even to me he has spoken little.'

'He knows it is better for others not to enter this room,' answered Lelu. 'For now, I have cleansed him with oils and given an infusion to ease the coughing.'

'I'll remain with him for a time,' said Gilgamesh. 'You should take your rest and return later.'

'Very well, Sire, I will return before -.'

From the bed issued a muffled cough, then a voice. 'Who is there watching me?'

'I am here,' answered Gilgamesh, gesturing the physician from the room then moving closer to the bed. Enkidu had opened his eyes and, his face wet with perspiration, struggled higher against the pillows. Gilgamesh saw how this simple act caused him much difficulty and took hold of his arm to give assistance. His brother's flesh was cold and damp.

'I'll stay by your side,' said Gilgamesh, seating himself on the low stool used by Lelu. He was deeply troubled by the sight of a gaunt and spiritless Enkidu.

'I see them in the night,' breathed Enkidu, weakly. His eyes were fixed ahead as if gazing beyond the walls of the room.'

'Who is it you see?'

'I see them in the night. The world below. I walk amongst those who dwell there.'

'It's no more than a bad dream brought on by your fever,' assured Gilgamesh, 'It will pass and when you're well again it will be forgotten.'

Enkidu seemed not to hear him but continued, 'I walked in the place of dust and shadows where they dwell and - and I saw. They stood in darkness, clothed in garments of bird feathers. They did not speak. I heard only the rustle of their feathers and the scamper of unseen creatures. On a throne of clay was Ereshkigal who rules that dreadful realm. Her eye was upon me and in her hand she held a tablet. Upon that tablet was my name!'

'Brother Enkidu, this is not you but the fever speaking.'

For the first time since Gilgamesh had entered the room, Enkidu looked sharply at him. 'Ah, brother, you are here to see me but should not be here. It is quite unlike you to approach the afflicted.'

'Of course I'm here. I'll never be far away while you remain unwell and confined to your bed.'

'Unwell, you say? Yes, unwell. I can no longer claim possession of my own body. It is turning to clay. I feel I am an unwanted tenant.'

'Nonsense. The sickness weighs heavily on you, that is certain - but it will pass. Our mother and your Shamkhat, come each day to ask about you but our worthy physician insists there must be no visitors. I think he's overcautious but since he errs on the side of your well-being I see little harm in complying with his wishes. At every altar in the city prayers and offerings are made for your recovery. The common people, too, ask about you and await your return.'

'You must thank them for their kindness but -.' Enkidu coughed and his breath shortened so that it took some time before he was able to continue. 'Yes - thank them but no other must see me so indisposed. This is not the Enkidu they knew.'

He eased himself down until his head rested once more on the pillows, then he closed his eyes. Gilgamesh waited, hoping Enkidu would speak again, but the regular, hoarse breathing told him his brother had lapsed into unconsciousness.

Passing from the sick room and down to the main hall of the palace, he observed a figure by a mosaic pillar. Her eyes, wide and alert, peered from beneath the cape of a white linen gown that covered her to the ankles. 'Shamkhat,' said Gilgamesh, 'how long have you waited here?'

271

'I came at first light,' she replied. 'Your physician rushed past me but would say nothing. I worry constantly, Lord Gilgamesh. We are forbidden to see him - even Lady Ninsun, though she says it's for the best.'

'It is Enkidu's wish as well as that of my physician,' answered Gilgamesh, placing a hand on her shoulder. 'My brother says you are to wait until he is well and strong again. He will not risk passing his sickness to others.'

'How soon before he's well?' she asked. 'Please - I need to know the truth.'

'No one can say,' breathed Gilgamesh, 'but I'll send to you each day with news until the crisis has passed. In the meantime, how d'you fare? Tell me and I'll pass your message on to him. I'll be voice and ear for you both.'

Shamkhat raised the back of her hand to her lips. A tear glistened on her cheek. 'Tell him I'm well and want for nothing, yet have nothing until he's well again.'

'If anything troubles you then send to me at once, no matter what the hour. I will have a slave of the palace placed at your disposal day and night.'

'There's no need for that,' she answered. 'Shannu – the boy you sent to learn the scribe's art - he has remained in my service because of the favour you bestowed on him and the kindness shown to his people by dear Enkidu. Whatever I need he will bring and he will hurry to you if I ask him.'

'Then tell the rascal he can expect a reward from me for his service.'

'I think fortune has already rewarded him,' Shamkhat smiled. 'He seems to want for little and will accept nothing from me.'

'What, and he a slave - the one who knelt in the dust to grasp the wheel of my chariot? Perhaps I'd better not question the source of the boy's good fortune.'

'I'll go now,' she said, pulling the fabric of the gown across so that only her dark eyes showed. 'I'll work at my loom and remain with my thoughts until you send me news of my Enkidu.'

***

Three days on and late afternoon sun filtered through the matting to scatter moths of light across the rich hangings of the king's room. At the door appeared an attendant, hands clasped in due respect. 'Sire, Lord Enkidu calls your name.'

Rising from his window seat, Gilgamesh put aside one of a number of tablets he had been studying then strode to the door. 'Has my physician returned yet?' he asked as the official stepped promptly aside.

'No, Sire, but his man remains on hand.'

Passing through the corridor, Gilgamesh noted the tang of incense drifting from the direction of the room where Enkidu lay. It was stronger than before. By the doorway waited the physician's assistant, dutiful as ever though with eyes agitated and hands clasped before him in a manner that betrayed considerable unease. Wisps of pale smoke drifted lazily upward from one of the small pottery censers that had been placed on the floor outside.

'Sire -.' began the assistant, in a dry voice, raising the clasped hands to his chin.

273

'I'm told my brother has called for me,' the king said.

'Sire,' repeated the assistant, 'he has twice called your name but I - I think he is delirious because he also calls the names of others. I have added more pillows to his bed for comfort but he coughed frequently in the afternoon and I fear he is much weakened.'

A cry sounded from within the room. Gilgamesh swept the matting aside and stepped across to find Enkidu sitting upright, lodged part against the pillows, part against the wall beside the bed. His mouth quivered. His eyes stared bright into some imagined space beyond the confines of the room.

'Enkidu, I am here,' whispered Gilgamesh, leaning close. There was no sign of recognition - no acknowledgement. 'Brother Enkidu, it is I!' he said loudly, reaching out a hand. Still there was no response. He noted how, in spite of the burning incense, an odour of corruption tainted the air.

'I curse them,' muttered Enkidu, lifting a hand as though to address spectral forms that passed before his gaze. 'I curse those who changed my life.' His voice grew louder. 'I curse the trapper who made me known in Uruk. Let his snares and his nets fail him. Let him return to his home with empty hands. Let him know privation and sickness! And the harlot who blinded me with her wiles – she who lured me to the city. May she be cast into the street by her own kind. May she offer herself at the crossroads and in the shadow of the city gate where drunkard and serf will use her!' His voice began to falter as he ended, 'Let her – let her never know the pleasures of hearth and home.'

Falling silent, he remained with eyes fixed as Gilgamesh looked on in speechless dismay.

'He speaks to the gods, Sire,' came a voice from the doorway. There stood Lelu the physician, a leather pouch clutched in one hand, the other raised close to his mouth as if to say, 'Hush, do not speak too loudly.'

'Yes, to the gods!' cried Enkidu, though his brother could not be sure if he was aware of anyone's presence because his expression remained unchanged. Enkidu appeared to concentrate, as if listening to faraway voices. His lips moved once more, silent at first, then the words came hoarse and broken. 'Shining Utu, y-you ask me to repent, to - to lay aside my curses.' For a time there was silence, then, 'Yes, I will do it. I will do it because it brought me a brother and true friend. It brought me Lady Ninsun who took me as her own son. Yes – oh, yes, I will repent. I will ask for your blessings to fall upon the hunter but - but above all upon the girl who loves me. Give them happiness and long days. Give it to them for my sake!'

Enkidu closed his eyes then dropped back against the pillows, his head falling aside, his breath rasping harsh and uneven. Glancing at the king as he stepped closer to the bed, the physician placed a hand on Enkidu's brow and with a thumb, lifted his eyelid. The expression on his face did nothing to reassure Gilgamesh. 'There is no lessening of his fever. I have brought a distillation of herbs used in such cases by the physicians of Nippur. When Lord Enkidu wakes, I will have him take it with his beer.'

As he spoke, his hand moved to Enkidu's chest. 'His heart grows weaker. Tomorrow I will bring a potion to quicken it.'

'Lelu,' said the king, gravely. 'I do not question your abilities as a healer but we must consult others on this matter. We must add their knowledge to yours so that we prevail in the fight against my brother's sickness. I'll send my agents through all of Sumer. If necessary, they will go to the spice lands beyond the Great Water and across the deserts to distant Egypt. We must overlook nothing in our search for an answer. Nothing!'

Lelu stammered, 'Sire, I - I ask to speak with you alone if you will permit it.'

Gilgamesh looked in silence on the prostrate Enkidu before turning to the physician. 'Very well, follow me but have your assistant remain here to watch over him.'

Before departing, Lelu addressed his assistant, 'Bathe his head with cool water and have fresh beer ready for when he awakens.'

Neither spoke as Lelu shuffled along in the striding wake of his lord and master. On entering the audience room the king turned to face his physician, who remained standing nervously just inside the doorway. Conscious of the man's unease, Gilgamesh sat down on the couch and bid Lelu sit close by, saying, 'You may talk freely now we are alone, friend Lelu. Have no fear unless you have concealed the truth from me.'

Lelu cleared his throat nervously. 'Sire,' he began, sitting rigid with fingers clasped on his lap, 'I would not have you think of me as negligent or unworthy in my calling but I have consulted with others and regret to say again that – that all agree, there is no cure for Lord Enkidu's ailment. In my travels through other lands as well as here in Uruk I have encountered many such afflictions and all I - all any physician can do, is administer his medicines and try to ease the suffering. I – I regret it is so, My Lord.'

'I see in your eyes you fear my brother will die,' said the king, gravely. 'He cannot die.'

'Forgive me, Sire. No one can be sure of that. Such wisdom, alas, is not given to us.'

'I say he *can-not* die,' repeated Gilgamesh. 'He is - was, the fittest and strongest of men. Why should this malady strike him and no other hereabouts? Why?'

'Forgive me, Sire,' answered Lelu, trembling visibly, 'but this terrible sickness is our master. It will run its course whatever we do. I swear upon my life that is the truth. The crisis will come long before help can be summoned from elsewhere – it is already close at hand. In the time that is left we must offer prayer and sacrifice for his recovery. For now I will return the ring you gave me.'

Gilgamesh stared at him, accepted the ring then sighed, 'Lelu the physician, you are a good man and I cast the net of my anger wide because I see my brother laid low. Lady Ninsun also has persuaded me on the severity of his illness and she insists I follow your advice. Do all you are able for his sake. Never be far from his side and whatever you require will be

brought to you. Return now and tend him whilst I remain with my thoughts.'

***

Four more days passed, then came late afternoon of the fifth day - a day when Gilgamesh was occupied by the arrival at the Nippur Gate of a large caravan from Aratta, the town beyond the mountains of Anshan, far to the east of Sumer. Except in times of war, each had supplied through trade what the other needed and had done so since long before written records began in Uruk. Relations between Uruk and Aratta had never been easy. They were not about to become so now.

'The merchants of Aratta demand tenure within Uruk rather than their usual camp outside the city wall,' declared one of the small delegation of Uruk's elders and guildsmen, the latter represented by Sheshkalla. 'They also demand the right to set up market within the city and to trade freely as do the men of Uruk who are established in Aratta.'

'Oh, demand do they!' replied Gilgamesh, seated in gilded and belted robe upon his regal chair of cedar and ivory. 'Their time for making demands upon me is ill chosen if only they knew it.' The tinge of contempt that coloured his response was not lost on any of those present. 'And how do these men of Aratta find it in themselves to make demands when they ought to consider themselves our vassal? Perhaps they fail to recall how Uruk responds to the demands of others - not with empty words but with keenly sharpened bronze!'

'Lord Gilgamesh,' said Sheshkalla, stepping forward with a noticeably understated gesture of respect, 'they've brought ingots of tin, silver and copper for our workshops. We've need of these due to the lack of trade these last months. Some of my lads are standing idle and that's no good thing.'

'They in turn,' resumed the elder, 'request grain and manufactured goods we do not yet have in sufficient quantity because of the drought. And because we do not have enough to spare, they demand the concessions instead. They have expressed their intention to go elsewhere in Sumer if we do not agree to negotiate.'

'Oh, really,' smiled Gilgamesh, 'and how will it serve them to do that? They'll still find no town in this land with surplus grain.'

'No, Sire,' replied the elder, 'but if we allow it to happen, another town, perhaps Kish, will accept them. After the next harvest we may find our monopoly of trade with Aratta and its lands has been lost. Our merchants there may be placed at risk. The men of Aratta know this perfectly well and they are not in the least concerned about it.'

'Unconcerned are they,' breathed the king, rubbing his chin before turning to his chief attendant. 'Take my seal. Have twenty of my companions gather with their arms in the courtyard.' Turning back to the delegation, he continued, 'We will allocate to the merchants of Aratta their own enclave just as they require. My men will escort them and see to it they unload their goods and set up their quarters in a manner that suits both parties. Once established, they may find it more difficult to uproot themselves than they imagined. I will personally see to that and - wait!'

His eye had fallen upon the balding, bearded figure of slight stature that had appeared at the entrance to the audience room. The man tottered anxiously toward them. 'My Lord,' he croaked with hands clasped so hard at his chest that his knuckles had whitened, 'my master begs urgently that you attend Lord Enkidu!'

'Very well,' replied Gilgamesh. Rising to his feet, he pulled the newly returned bronze ring from his finger and handed it to his attendant. 'You have my authority to do as we have discussed. Have the elders determine where best to lodge the men of Aratta together with their goods. Have them brought within the city before the sun goes down. I'll attend to other matters later.'

Moving aside to let him pass, they watched in silence as Gilgamesh hurried from the room, aware that in the presence of others he usually avoided haste for the sake of dignity. He arrived at the room where his brother lay to find Lelu waiting by the door. 'What's happening?' he asked.

'Lord Enkidu dismissed me, Sire, and asked for you to join him. His fever has grown worse and I fear he -.' The sentence remained unfinished as Gilgamesh swept aside the matting and entered the room.

Unshaven for many days, a gaunt, visibly wasted Enkidu lay against his pillows with the lion skin clutched to his chest. The air within the room hung ever more corrupt in spite of abundant incense. Of the fact that Enkidu was fully conscious, there could be no doubt. Eyes even brighter than before, he looked directly at his brother, saying, 'Ah, how many men could demand the king of Uruk's presence? His speech was hoarse as the grating of metal in a stone socket.

'Enkidu, you are awake and alert,' smiled Gilgamesh. 'Is that why you sent for me? Has the sickness run its course?'

A feeble smile touched Enkidu's lips. 'Brother, I have missed your company. I have not known myself. My mind has been confused but now, yes, my thoughts are clear. You must know I cannot manage the workings of my own body. This bed has become a pit of foulness I can no longer bear.'

'Your health will return, I am sure, especially now we can talk again. Soon you'll be on your feet, free of this bed, and when you are your girl, your Shamkhat, will be overjoyed. I have much planned for us as well. You and I will set out into the wilds once more. Our swords will glisten in the sun. Our spears will cast twin shadows as they cleave the air together!'

But beneath those words of optimism Gilgamesh knew matters were dire.

'To step out into the day at my brother's side,' breathed Enkidu, 'to see my girl of the temple with a smile lighting her eyes - these things I desire above all else. But they're no more to be mine. I see only a dark path before me.'

'Nonsense, I'll not have it!' rebuked Gilgamesh. 'We're the fine pair who conquered the Cedar Mountain and its guardian. We're the ones who entered the realms of Gugalanna to strike him down and lift his scourge from our land. We'll set ourselves against any challenge. No enemy in all of Sumer will prevail against us!'

'There is one that can,' breathed Enkidu, sinking into the pillow, 'but whilst I'm able, there is something I must ask you.'

Inwardly distraught, Gilgamesh leaned closer as his brother spoke. 'Whatever my fate, you must not turn your anger against anyone because of it. I came alone into this world and alone I must leave it. I brought nothing and nothing will I take away. Do you understand, brother Gilgamesh? I know you will grieve but be glad for the blessings bestowed on me by Lady Ninsun. I had your friendship and the love of my beautiful Shamkhat. These have been the treasures of my life and they are greater treasures than any man had.' His fingers moved slowly up to close about the amulet that hung from his neck. 'Promise me, brother Gilgamesh. Promise what I ask. Place a hand on this token our mother gave me and swear.'

Gilgamesh raised a hand to the cool metal at Enkidu's chest. 'I - I swear I will turn my anger on no one as you ask - but -.' He watched his brother's eyes glisten and close - watched his hand sink back to the bed and waited for him to speak again.

Enkidu did not speak. But still, Gilgamesh waited.

A sound caught his ear but he did not observe the reed matting move aside as the physician entered. The man stood silent until the king turned to address him. 'My brother is resting now. See to it that he stays comfortable. Send for me again when he awakens.'

Lelu stepped over to the bed, leaned close to place an ear above Enkidu's lips and touched fingers lightly beneath his jaw. He remained there for some time before rising with solemn countenance. 'Sire, I fear he is gone from us.'

Moving forward, Gilgamesh placed a hand on his brother's chest, held it there for some moments then turned to the physician. 'I feel no heartbeat but we cannot know for certain. You cannot know! I have heard the heart may slow greatly in sickness to preserve its strength. My brother cannot be dead. I say he cannot! We will wait and see and I will return to him later.'

When Gilgamesh had gone, Lelu the physician, with sombre deliberation, pulled away his stool to place it against the wall opposite the bed. There he sat, deep in thought.

***

The sky had barely lightened, the shadows of the date palms had not yet slanted across the city wall when Gilgamesh awoke from a troubled sleep. By the light of bronze lamps that remained lit about the palace corridors, he made his way to the room where incense still arose from smouldering pots. The physician was huddled on a sheepskin in one corner but stirred as the king entered. The figure in the bed appeared exactly as it had the previous evening. Gilgamesh reached out a hand to touch his brother's shoulder. Some time passed before he said, 'My brother is cold as clay taken from the river.'

Lelu struggled to his feet and stood in silence. Gilgamesh said, quietly, 'Go to your home. I will have the priests lay him out for his final rest.'

He stood alone in contemplation of Enkidu's corpse, pallid and shrunken in stature as it had been these last days though Gilgamesh had refused to acknowledge it. He wanted to call out - to rouse Enkidu from the bed and make him walk. He stared hard at a face that no longer knew life. When Gilgamesh next spoke, it was softly; so softly that the words barely formed on his lips though they blazed in his mind. 'No life should end this way.

Brother, you are gone from me after so short a time. I have sported with the women of the temple. I have set myself against the best of men in every contest. I have prevailed in arms against the strongest of my enemies. Yet never was my heart lighter than when you and I set out into the world beyond Uruk. Never more than when we walked together by the great river through desert and woodland. We stood side by side in the face of danger and were strong as a thousand men. Never was I more contented with my lot.'

He paced back and forth with quickening step, clutching at his robe, shaking his head, becoming ever more agitated until he tore the fabric. In anger his voice filled the room, 'Why did you have to leave this world? I am alone! I am a broken vessel!'

For once in his manhood, the king of Uruk wept.

The matting across the door moved aside. He turned to see her standing in her white gown with the shawl about her head. He was about to order her away but the words were stillborn. He looked aside, saying nothing as she entered the room.

'Lord Gilgamesh, I saw the physician leave. I saw his face. He had no need to tell me.' She gazed upon the still, silent figure and her cheek glistened tears. 'I loved him as he loved me. He was so kind, so gentle in all his strength.'

'Lady Shamkhat,' said Gilgamesh, placing an arm about her shoulder, 'he desired no one but you and only you were worthy of him. In his name I will ensure you want for nothing as long as we both live.'

'He was a new sun that shone in our lives,' breathed Shamkhat, looking into the eyes of Gilgamesh. 'A sun that arose for but a day and just as quickly set. But the light that he brought was greater than we knew and has not left us. Now I fully understand. Lord Gilgamesh, there are truths still to be revealed.'

'Truths? What d'you understand?'

'I - I cannot talk about it. Not here. Not yet.'

'We should leave him alone now,' whispered Gilgamesh. 'Let's take ourselves to the courtyard with our thoughts.'

In the cool shadows of the deserted arcade they walked, saying nothing until Gilgamesh asked, 'Will you return to the temple? Will you stay in mourning for him there?'

'No,' she answered abruptly, stopping to face him. 'I have decided what I'll do if you will help and give me your blessing.'

'Then ask me.'

'I will leave Uruk. I will return to the wild land where he lived. I was the first woman he knew and because of me he came to Uruk. I will return to the pool where I first saw him. I will call to the beasts that gather there. I will tell them Enkidu has left this world. I will tell them - and after, I will sit by the water and I will think about our days and our nights together.'

'Perhaps his spirit has returned there,' said Gilgamesh.

'No,' she replied, gazing into his eyes as she once gazed into those of Enkidu, 'it has not returned there.'

'You seem certain of that.'

285

'Yes, but still I have to go; I have much to think about.'

'Very well, I'll give you all you need for your journey. My men will escort and protect you. But now I have to send for the priests. Enkidu must lie for a time so the common people can wish him farewell though I regret it has to be in Inanna's temple'

***

'It is not right,' declared the first priest. 'It is not right that the mortal remains of Lord Enkidu should lie with us for so long. His tomb was marked out close to the precinct of Eanna days ago and still awaits the king's permission for its excavation.'

They sat within the temple vestibule away from the heat of the day with their plates and beer jug set out before them on rush matting.

'He should have been laid within the earth days ago,' agreed the second priest.

'Five days ago by my reckoning,' chewed the third, averting his eyes momentarily from the stick of skewered lamb and dish of boiled lentils which until then had occupied his attention.

'I have watched the king each morning,' resumed the first priest, laying aside a date stone before pulling himself upright on his sheepskin. 'He walks to the precinct alone each day before sunrise. He ascends the stairs to the temple in a robe of course linen and enters the chapel to look upon his dead brother.'

'Always we must burn incense to keep the air wholesome,' said the second priest. 'It is not at all good in this heat.'

'We'll need it burning everywhere before long,' grumbled the third, his corpulent edifice rolling forward as he inserted one end of his drinking tube into the jug and moved his mouth close to the other. 'Something ought to be done now. Immediately.'

'I heard him call out more than once,' continued the first priest, glancing at his companion whose face looked about to disappear within the rim of the jug. 'He called to the gods not to take away his brother. He cannot accept that the soul has long departed and all that remains is rapidly corrupting flesh.'

'He *must* accept it,' answered the second priest as the third drew beer noisily through the copper tube. 'It's of no benefit to anyone for the body to remain in our chapel. Even people in the streets are remarking on it.'

'I will approach the king and speak with him today,' said the first. 'It cannot go on.'

'He may have little inclination to listen,' replied the second priest. 'Perhaps if we go together he will take notice.'

'Tomorrow,' said the third, rising from the beer jug then reaching for a pastry. 'Tomorrow will be the sixth day. We ought to leave things until then.'

'But you just now suggested it be done immediately,' said the first priest.

'I did, yes, you're quite right, but I didn't expect to be taken quite so literally. The king has already been and gone and I've no stomach for a confrontation with palace officials in order to get an interview.'

'You've a stomach for just about everything else,' muttered the second priest.

'We must be on hand at first light when he appears,' declared the first priest. 'There will be no palace officials to get in the way and we'll be on our own ground. When he leaves the chapel we must speak to him. He may be angered but he *must* listen to what we say.'

'Tomorrow it shall be,' agreed the second priest.

'Mmm, tomorrow,' mumbled the third, closing his eyes as he relaxed against his cushion.

***

No one crossed his path as he approached the temple steps. Though the sky was lightening to the east, the kingdom of night still held sway in the streets and courtyards of Uruk. Pigs that grunted and foraged in the shadows, the wail of unseen cats, the yapping dogs - none of these were of concern to Gilgamesh as his sandaled feet trod the cold stairway.

There was always a night-time guard within the temple vestibule whose duty it was to ensure no unauthorised person entered the building within the hours of darkness. His was a solitary task. His few comforts were a dish of bread and beans, a flagon of beer and a small oil lamp as his meagre source of light. Having little to hold his attention other than the owl's hoot and the unwelcome whine of mosquitoes, the man had consumed all his beer ration and fallen asleep long before the night had ended. He was on this occasion unaware of the king's approach. He stirred as the great door rumbled open then fully roused he scrambled to his feet, bowing rapidly, clasping hands to his chest as the king walked by. Gilgamesh ignored him.

288

Trembling in guilt at his laxity, the man watched his lord and master pass through the inner doors and knew where he was headed.

The brick-vaulted chapel where his brother lay was cramped but as he stooped to enter there was light enough to see in the incense-laden air. A small lamp glowed yellow at each corner of the brick bench where the shrunken husk that had been his brother was covered to the neck under a shroud of pale linen. In the sparing illumination of that austere, claustrophobic space, Enkidu appeared as one who could never have been a living, breathing man, as if the touch of a hand against his waxen cheek would cause it to crack like an eggshell. Beneath the shroud, Gilgamesh knew his hand still set as a rigid claw about the leather pouch that had been thrown to him as they departed the city on a glorious day that seemed so long ago. The pouch must still contain a lock of her hair.

'Why were you denied what is enjoyed by the peasant whose day is bounded by the tread of his ox and the length of a furrow?' Gilgamesh paced slowly about the altar. 'Did one steeped in malice ordain your death? Who would do it?' He paused to look down at the face. 'I have asked that question often these last days yet the answer was never in doubt. Why, if that accursed bitch stood before me now I'd lay her open with my sword and feed her remains to the dogs!' Raising an arm, he poised fingers above the face of the corpse. 'But that would not bring my brother back. No, that would not bring you -.'

Beneath the fingers something moved. From the nose wriggled a small white form, a loathsome worm of decay that glistened pallid on his dead brother's cheek. Gilgamesh recoiled. The flames wavered to incite fitful shadows that swayed in macabre choreography across the walls and vaulting. His cry rang to mocking echo about the chamber. 'It cannot be my brother upon this cold altar! No, it cannot!'

They watched him emerge from the temple and hesitate by the doors, and because the day had lightened they saw at once how dishevelled was his hair and how grim his expression.

'This is not the time,' croaked the third priest.

'I'm inclined to agree,' added the second. 'Our king looks in no mood to hear us.'

'It has to be now,' hissed the first priest. 'There can be no better time than this.'

Huddled together, they edged their way across the open space toward the stairs down which the king now hurried. It caused the three acute misgiving when Gilgamesh, observing their presence, changed direction and strode directly toward the spot where they stood rooted like a trio of hares in the shadow of a swooping eagle. Clearing his throat, the first priest stepped forward as the king drew close. 'My Lord, forgive our intrusion in this time of sadness but we must speak with you.'

'It's about my brother is it not?' snapped Gilgamesh.

'It is, Sire. We feel we must -.'

'You're waiting here to tell me he should be buried. I know that's your intention.'

'It is only proper, Sire,' murmured the first priest.

'Only proper!' responded Gilgamesh angrily. 'If only your prayers had persuaded the gods to spare him! That would have been proper!'

He turned his face to the brightening sky and for a moment they thought he would continue on without further comment. Then he looked hard at them and exclaimed, 'Yes, damn you all! I will begin preparations today then tomorrow you may bury him.'

CHAPTER 8
THE FINAL CEREMONY

Ninsun watched as he stood at the parapet, gazing into a clear night sky. A breeze swayed the flames of the two lamps on her small altar. The city glowed pale in moonlight. From it now and then, drifting on the air as lost souls, arose the distant nocturnal calls of unseen creatures.

'Perhaps I should regret having shown you the way through that portal,' said Ninsun. 'But how many thousands would have died had I not? What was right – what was wrong - can anyone say?'

'The workmen toiled on his grave until after dusk,' said Gilgamesh as though not hearing her. 'I have issued summons to the elders, priests and guildsmen. Criers went out into the town and the fields to tell all the people of Uruk. Tomorrow no one will lift a hand in labour nor pass silver in payment. They will gather to see Enkidu depart and I will address them from the temple steps.' Turning to face her, he continued, 'I have broken the seals on the palace vaults and marked those treasures of value to offer the gods for his journey. With him will be buried his sword, his spear and his axe. Everyone will see what is provided before he is laid to rest.'

'You know as well as I,' said Ninsun, 'he wanted nothing from this word. Gold and silver he cared for less than the clay beneath his feet. Why place with him in death what mattered to him so little in life? The birds of the air and the stars in the night sky are what gave him pleasure.'

'Yes, but if what the priests say is true, he must have precious objects in order to pay his fare on the long journey.' Gilgamesh touched her arm. 'The amulet I have worn since I was a child - I placed it about his neck together with the one you gave him. I hope you're not offended.'

'That,' smiled Ninsun, 'will be worth more to your brother than all the treasures of your palace. Wherever his soul should wander it will be his pride and comfort for a part of you will be with him, though -.' Her eyes looked deeply into his.

'What is it?' he asked.

'Gilgamesh, do you not sense a presence? Perhaps you will think me foolish but - but I feel he is close by, waiting.'

'If only that was so, mother. If only. He died before my eyes and for days I wouldn't accept it. No, Enkidu is gone. I feel no presence.' Gilgamesh moved away from the parapet. 'Now I have to leave you. Tomorrow I have to rise early and prepare myself.'

***

Before morning light the people had started to gather. Their voices were low - their gestures few. Incense smoked in the earthenware pots placed about the square. The female mourners assembled in gowns of course linen. As the square filled, a sea of faces looked to Inanna's temple, their whispers passing as a breeze in the palm trees that lined deserted waterways.

The great drum on the temple roof boomed out. Startled birds arose to circle against the dawn sky. Scarcely had the sound faded when the heavy, copper-banded doors of the temple grated part open.

293

Again the drum shook the air and at this second signal, red-cloaked men with stout spears came into view and began to move people back from the base of the stairs. The doors opened further. A third time the drum sounded and now the doors stood wide.

From the darkness emerged a line of priests with rams horns held to their mouths. They sounded a plaintive braying that seemed to endow the temple sanctuary itself with a hollow voice. Even before the last of the priests appeared, the appointed female mourners, hair loose and dishevelled, surged with outstretched arms toward the temple doors, their anguished cries rising high. Directly behind the priests came six of the king's companions, each clad in red tunic and bronze helmet. Each man grasped his spear in one hand, and each with the other hand supported the cedar-wood bier of Enkidu.

The great drum began to beat in slow, measured rhythm, punctuating the harsh call of the rams' horns as the procession started in measured tread down the stairway. The mourners cried ever louder, throwing up their hands in wild abandon then falling to their knees where they began to rip the cloth from their breasts. Just as quickly they were on their feet, treading the stone steps, milling about the bier upon which everyone could see the shroud of linen that enclosed the corpse.

Next appeared the king himself, humbly robed, his eyes fixed ahead. He seemed unaware of the crowd, whose laments began to echo those of the mourners. Behind Gilgamesh followed Kuraka and the elders of Uruk in their long gowns. With them came the priests whose task it was to carry those offerings that would accompany the deceased on his journey.

On reaching the bottom of the staircase, the leading priests turned to their left where a way had been cleared in the direction of the precinct wall. Their horns were silenced so that the wailing of the mourners sounded all the more intense. Above all the steady beating of the drum rolled through the air of a dawn that promised only sadness.

Clear of the temple steps, the main part of the procession passed through the waiting crowd as others joined it at the rear. The mourners, hurrying on ahead to incite the onlookers by their theatre of grief, had already reached the brick-lined, rectangular pit. Here they continued in flagrant remorse, hands raised to the heavens or splayed across ochre-smeared, tear-streaked faces as if the sound of the drum itself beset them with torment.

As the bier and its solemn entourage reached the pit, Gilgamesh looked at the mourners now spread about it. And though Shamkhat was not amongst them he knew she would be close by, perhaps with Ninsun, perhaps seated alone at a window overlooking the square. Neither she nor her grief would be on public display. Her sadness was a desert flower whose roots threaded deep to tap the dark waters of sorrow.

The mourners calmed somewhat as the bier was conveyed down the timber ramp into the shadows of the pit, their cries becoming whimpers, their hands clutching torn garments. Louder echoed the drum as the body came to rest. Then with shocking suddenness the booming ceased. Not even the workmen spoke as the chest containing Enkidu's modest possessions was manhandled down to vanish from sight. Next came his weapons, sword, spear and axe, bundled together in reed matting to be laid at his side. The offerings of food set upon precious dishes and the goblets of gold and silver might have been expected, as, too, might the small harp of rare wood, its frame and ram's head ornament inlaid with silver, seashells and lapis-lazuli.

In silence the workmen emerged from the pit then began to pull out their ramp and ladders. As they backed away Gilgamesh strode forward, reached into the mound of rubble by the grave, took up a handful of dirt and threw it inside. Workmen returned to the pit with copper shovels in hand to begin the task of final burial. And if that was a signal to the workmen, it was also a signal to others. Three times the deep voice of the temple drum rolled out. As it did so, the entourage and the mourners stepped back some way to leave the king standing by the grave; alone except for the workmen who went about their labour, ignoring all about them as if they toiled alone in a distant field.

Gilgamesh turned to face the crowd, raising his arms high to speak in a voice that carried strongly. 'I say farewell to my brother and companion. I say farewell to the best of men. I say farewell to one that leaves Uruk beneath a shadow of sadness now his light is gone from us. Let all the people of the city mourn him; the priests and the elders at altar and office. Let the young men of the city who bear arms and face our enemies mourn him. Let the artisan and the craftsman at his bench, mourn him. Let the harlots of palace and temple mourn him. Let the moulders of clay and the makers of pots mourn him. And those of the field - the ploughman at his furrow and the herdsman with his staff; let them also mourn him. Let the hunter with net and spear and the fisherman on the river mourn him. Let the birds of the air, the beasts of the field, the wild creatures of the plain and of the distant hill mourn him. Let the great river where we walked together and the distant cedar forest where our deeds were done - let them also mourn his passing.'

In the silence that followed, only the swish of shovel and clatter of earth could be heard. Gilgamesh glanced aside at the workmen then turned to the waiting priests, his hand raised in gesture. The priests lifted their horns to sound a long, harsh blast that reverberated throughout the precinct. Again silence, then a distant squealing and snorting caught their attention. Eyes turned toward the wide passage formed where the wall close by the grave pit ran parallel with the façade of the temple platform. Along it approached a group of six men, two of them priests but the others of rustic appearance. In tow behind the latter were an ox, a sheep and a goat. Behind the ox bobbed the unkempt head of another man whose stick swished back and forth against the rear of the unfortunate beast with every few plodding steps. Closer they came and armed men pushed aside those few of Uruk's citizens who had found their way around to that side of the pit. The king, too, stepped back from the grave and announced, 'This is but a small offering I give to him, though in his humility my brother would have wished for none at all! But our customs and the gods demand it! Their wishes also I must address!'

The crowd pressed forward, though those further away without a vantage point could make out nothing more than the backs of others likewise straining to see. To the priests' chanting and the blare of the horns, the sacrifice took place. The priest's knives cut deftly, the lifeblood of each quivering beast being discharged over the edge of the part-filled grave. And no sooner were the lifeless bodies lowered down to earth drenched with their own blood, than the workmen once more took up their shovels.

Maintaining the solemnity that had marked their arrival the priests and elders re-formed themselves into line before returning to the temple with the king following close to the rear of the procession. At the base of the temple steps they halted, shuffling aside so that Gilgamesh could continue by and ascend alone.

The sky had brightened to a full and clear day when he turned to face the people. Sunlight reflected from the offerings of the royal treasury that had been carried out of the temple and stood in full view. Sunlight bathed the city so that the walls of temple and rampart glowed white yet a grey dusk was all the king of Uruk knew.

'These precious things,' began Gilgamesh with a gesture toward objects of gold, silver and bronze, of rare woods inlaid with delicate intricacy, 'I offer to the gods who see all, for the sake of my brother's soul and for his memory. May the gods welcome him amongst them as did you, the people of Uruk. May she to whom we offer reverence -.' here he hesitated and set his expression to suppress rising anger. 'May the Queen of Heaven accept these gifts and walk by his side. May great Anu who rules eternity, accept these gifts and walk by his side. May Ereshkigal who is queen of the underworld accept these gifts and walk by his side. May Dumuzzi who is the turning of the seasons, accept these gifts and walk by his side. May Namtar who presages death, accept these gifts and walk by his side. May the shining Lord of the Day, accept these gifts and walk by his side -.'

His voice carried over them like the wind as he enumerated the gods, great and less than great, who protocol demanded he should entreat to comfort his dead brother's soul.

***

Twilight had returned when Gilgamesh made his way to Egalmah, as Ninsun knew he would. There was nowhere else for him to go and no one else in whom he might confide. Much of that day he had spent alone with his thoughts. Earlier he had gone up to the rooftop to gaze out across the city and the fields. It was from there he had observed the wagon bearing Shamkhat out beyond the river with an escort on her long journey into the desert. Her face, her soft lips, her deep eyes persisted in his mind for a long time. Longer by far than seemed proper.

'When he lay in the chapel, I saw my own image. I saw myself in decay and corruption.'

Ninsun listened in sympathy then said, 'It is the fate of all humanity.'

Gilgamesh stood before the couch on which she rested, her eyes bright in the glow of the lamps. She

299

looked by him and saw the lamps had cast his shadow twofold upon the hanging curtain behind. Once more it seemed as if his brother stood by his side.

'When the mound above his grave is finished,' continued Gilgamesh, sitting by her, 'I have ordered a likeness of Enkidu to be placed above it. Tomorrow, the artisans of Uruk will begin their work. It will be an image to surpass all others - an image of bronze, gilded and finished with precious inlays. They'll come from far away to admire it and the image will be known throughout all Sumer.'

'Gilgamesh,' whispered Ninsun. 'You should not do that. It will be a false image - a soulless idol to be stared at by the indolent and the envious. Its shadow will fall across the memory of the Enkidu who lived and supplant it with a travesty. Must we weigh his memory against such things? Let his image live within ourselves. It will speak louder than a thousand statues.'

'I wondered if you'd disapprove,' he sighed.

'Yes - well, it's not what I would choose for him but I suppose you'll do as you wish. You always do as you wish and that's why Uruk is strong.'

'And perhaps why my brother is dead. But I'll think over what you've said, though we surely must give substance to his memory. A simpler effigy, perhaps.'

'Yes, think it over,' answered Ninsun, rising up to place an arm about his shoulder. 'Today has not been easy but in spite of what has happened you still have your responsibilities. When the sun rises tomorrow it may light other paths that have remained hidden from you over these dark days.'

'Other paths,' he sighed. 'If only there were other paths. If only I could see as clearly as I once did. Yet I cannot close my eyes and be content.'

'All remains as it was,' consoled Ninsun. 'Your perception of the world has changed but the world itself has not changed.'

'No, it has not. I'm told a delegation from Larsa will arrive tomorrow with more complaints. If they knew what was in my thoughts they'd stay well clear of Uruk. There's ample space above the city gates to display their damnable heads if the Man of Larsa wishes it. My axe craves employment!'

'No, let your anger free in the field of sport as you once did. Do not unleash it upon others - even though they test your patience.'

'I no longer care for those futile games,' he answered. 'Why should I seek to attain a hill when I – when we, once conquered a mountain?'

'It is yourself you must conquer. You must conquer grief and anger. That is your real challenge now. Both are a greater foe than any mountain.'

'Are they, mother? Are they?' He looked at her across flickering lamps as she returned to her couch. 'I know where the greatest challenge lies though I've presently no wish to talk about it. But I will think over what you say. Perhaps you're right and in the morning I'll see things differently.' He pushed aside the curtain and left her, muttering grimly, 'And perhaps I won't.'

Stepping into the night air, Gilgamesh was soon crossing the open space before Inanna's temple where the moon in ripe fullness bathed the square and buildings about it in ghostly light. He might have continued on but instead hesitated, then walked instead to the steps where, earlier that day he had followed behind the body of Enkidu. With only the eyes of skulking creatures to witness his progress, Gilgamesh ascended the steps and, finding one of the heavy doors ajar and the feint glow of oil lamps spilling cobweb light across the limestone threshold, he entered.

He was not surprised to find the man whose task it was to guard the vestibule, asleep and snoring. The beer flagon that lay on its side close by his crumpled form was obviously empty. What would have been his reaction had he known the king had passed close by to observe yet again his neglect of so simple a duty? In earlier days he would have earned himself a public flogging, or worse, but Gilgamesh moved on through the columned hall, preceded by his own shadow, until he reached the chapel where his brother had lain.

In the small, vaulted space, a single pottery lamp burned on the bare altar to dimly illuminate encroaching walls of burned brick. Incense no longer smouldered. The air was laden instead with a brooding silence. Gilgamesh remained still, devoid of conscious thought. The world outside seemed altogether excluded from this sombre place, as if the chamber had been cast adrift into fathomless night. In one corner a dull, black beetle groped with nameless purpose across the stone floor. Gilgamesh watched it with simmering despair. A despair of one seeing no exit from that tiny cell. A cell whose walls closed upon him as the innards of his own sepulchre. It mesmerised with secret whisper, 'Here is the beginning and here the end.'

'No!' he cried, his voice ringing close. 'This cannot be the measure of my life! No - I cannot have corruption triumph over me!'

Stooping to wrench aside the reed matting he strode into near darkness intending to return the way he had come when a fleeting movement caught his eye.

'Who is there? Show yourself!' His sword swished from its scabbard. His voice echoed and re-echoed through darkness amidst stout, mosaic-clad pillars.

'Lord Gilgamesh,' came the reply, 'I am a priest of this temple.'

'Ah, then I must have seen you on occasion. And what duties d'you discharge at this hour? Were you listening by the chapel door? If so that is not to my liking.'

A gowned figure emerged from the shadows, fragile, aged, supporting himself with a long stick of ebony that tap-tapped on the limestone flags. Approaching Gilgamesh he stooped not from veneration but under the burden of years. 'I perform no duties, Sire. I walk the empty places because sleep eludes me in the heat of the night.'

'Sleep eludes me also, holy one,' replied the king, slipping back his blade, 'but the heat of the night is not its main cause.'

The old man regarded him with pale eyes, a smile moulding his toothless mouth. 'Sleep is not always our best companion.' His gaze remained fixed upon Gilgamesh. 'I heard you, My Lord, but I was not listening. Had I been thrice the distance away still I would have heard. Your voice is strong. It carries far. It was so when you were an unruly child.'

'You address me with familiarity yet I don't recall we ever met in close conversation.'

'No, Lord Gilgamesh,' replied the priest, 'we have never spoken so. As for fear, I have seen it drain away with the years. No man can take from me the wine I have already drunk. What is left of my life offers rather less than a repetition of what has gone before. As for familiarity - that I rightly claim. I pronounced incantations at your birth and read the auspices there. I saw no portent of my demise in the conduct of your future.'

'Oh, and what of my future? Was it written down on clay tablets, in sheep's entrails or in the stars above? If it was, then so should have been the death of my brother, yet none of you came forward to mention it.'

'There are many possible futures,' answered the old priest, gripping his stick. 'Sometimes we are able to choose; sometimes we are not. You now desire that which no one, or perhaps almost no one, ever achieved.'

'Really! And what is it you've concluded I desire?'

'Why,' he smiled, 'you desire what is beyond our reach. You wish to cheat death. You wish it because of what happened to your brother.'

'Wouldn't any man? Wouldn't you seek to do that?'

'I think not. For most of us, one life of toil and tribulation is quite enough. Whether life is measured by the furrows of the plough, by the beat of the hammer or in weighing silver, it is still measured as the gods decree.'

'But when you spoke of cheating death, you said *almost* no one had managed it. What about the one who did? His name is focus of a moral tale but is surely nothing more than that.'

'Ah,' smiled the priest, 'then you know his name. You know of Ziusudra.'

'Of course I do,' frowned Gilgamesh, 'everyone throughout Sumer has heard of him. Like every child I was taught how he escaped the great flood.'

'Yes, and the man himself is a legend because a legend is what people made of him. And though most believe he was a man who long ago lived as you and I live, the passage of time has served to recast our memories of what he once was.'

'And by what means is it claimed he eluded death?'

'Of that I have no knowledge other than vague traditions,' answered the priest. 'We only see Ziusudra now through a dark veil of long vanished years. The myth of today is now greater than the man of yesterday.'

'But should he still live, he'd no doubt speak of it. And if he did then I'd want to hear the account from his own mouth.'

'Maybe he would speak of it if indeed he does live - who can say? But you will recall from what you learned as a boy that his voice can never be heard in the land of Sumer. It is taught how he left behind the tribulations of mankind, how he travelled far beyond our realms to cross the Great Water. Tradition amongst our priesthood has it that his departure was recorded on clay tablets. Some believe it never was but others claim those tablets have lain hidden for generations somewhere beneath this very temple. I never met anyone who could actually say where. And you will appreciate, Lord Gilgamesh, that unless the tablets were baked hard they will long ago have turned to dust.'

'But if those tablets do exist,' breathed Gilgamesh, 'we must find them. And when we do we will read them together, and if I consider their message holds any truth then - then I'd have to find this fortunate man. I'd seek him out and I'd know the means of his immortality.' He placed a hand lightly upon the frail shoulder. 'It may be no accident that brought you to me this night. Perhaps through you the gods have illuminated the path I must follow.'

'Forgive me, Sire,' smiled the priest, 'but I do not think it is what the gods wish. Even if the tablets still exist, even if they could be read, the path you speak of will lead to a greater sadness than weighs upon you now. Perhaps to misfortune and despair.'

'Misfortune and despair I already possess in full measure,' declared Gilgamesh. 'That vessel is filled to the brim so there's no one can add further to it.' He turned away, was silent for a moment, then spun about with a light of passion in his eyes. 'This could be my greatest challenge! If so I will take up arms against it. I will set out from Uruk with the image of my brother and the sound of his voice within me and we will pour our laughter and our rage into the world! We will march against the mountains and the sky if needs be until death himself flees before us! Come now, help me discover where these tablets lie hidden!'

CHAPTER 9
THE QUEST FOR ETERNITY

'Everyone within the city and no small number beyond' declared Kuraka, 'must be aware of the fact that our revered king left Uruk three days ago. He was observed at dawn riding out through the Larsa Gate then heading eastward in a chariot drawn by two of his prize asses. We are given to understand he was attired in a lion's pelt and equipped with axe, spear and sword as though intent upon violent conflict.' His gaze drifted over the silent faces of the elders then to the guildsmen and others whose presence in the heat of that afternoon made the House of Assembly more a place of stifling discomfort than it usually was. 'What the citizens of Uruk ask – yes, what *we* are assembled here to ask, for it presently eludes us, is the reason for his quitting the city in such haste without even the royal household being informed. Had he been escorted by his precious companions we might be forgiven for thinking he had returned to his former ways in spite of his brother's recent demise. We are told, however, that he was alone and I in turn am assured he has not yet returned.'

'He certainly was alone,' put in one of the elders, wiping sweat from his brow with a corner of his linen garment. 'I myself saw him leave as I took the morning air upon the city wall although I assumed he would soon return. As for his intentions - well -.'

'I personally called upon Lady Ninsun to find out more,' Kuraka went on, 'only to be informed that she was absent. That I much doubted. Nevertheless –.'

'The king has his reasons,' interrupted a voice from the rear of the hall. Members of the gathering looked about, puzzled as to where the voice had come from. Kuraka, standing on his speaker's platform observed a slight, stooping figure in long kilt ease through the press and make his way forward.

'Ah, holy one,' said Kuraka, 'it is unusual to see one of the priesthood among us.'

'Quite,' replied the old priest, 'but then there is no shrine here to warrant our presence. However, you voice concern about our lord the king do you not, and I dare say I'm the only one in Uruk able or willing to inform you of his intentions. He asked me not to reveal it until now though I doubt you will wish to accept my account.'

'You must tell us what you know,' remarked one of the elders.

The priest gathered up his kilt and, aided by several hands as well as by his ebony stick, stepped onto the low platform to join Kuraka.

'Why has the king not returned?' asked another voice. 'Do you know that?'

'I fear the king may not return for a long time,' he replied, leaning on the stick to peer down at them. 'He has set out from Uruk and intends to leave Sumer for the world far beyond. He has gone to find Ziusudra - the one they say was granted eternal life.'

Uncomprehending silence followed until, looking down his sharp nose at the old man, Kuraka said, 'You are not a confidante of the king. What can you possibly know of this unlikely escapade?'

'I know of it because he enlisted my help. It is the king's one and only desire to seek out the immortal man and to learn his secret, if there is any secret to be learned. You may believe me or you may think otherwise. It makes little difference as far as I'm concerned.'

'Little difference to you, perhaps,' responded Kuraka, turning from the priest to the rest, 'but we have to address this situation whatever the cause.'

Kuraka gazed back and forth over attentive faces, bearded and beardless, dark-haired and hairless, toothed and toothless. Sooner or later they must express the conclusions he had already reached.

'Is the holy one suggesting that the king has left the people of Uruk to their own devices?' asked an elder.

The old priest merely shrugged.

'If what the holy one says is true,' commented another from the back of the gathering, 'it would appear the king has without question turned his back upon us. Is that not so?'

'Deserted Uruk!' called one.

'Abandoned his city and his people!' called another. 'Perhaps the death of his brother has affected his mind.'

'A most likely conclusion,' agreed Kuraka. 'His loss must be quite unbearable – enough to shake apart his wits.'

'Whatever his shortcomings,' came a gruff voice from near the entrance, 'I doubt he'd so easily give up what he'd fought for - not him!'

'Ah, Sheshkalla,' responded Kuraka, 'you speak now in favour of the man against whom you earlier made complaint. That is commendable indeed.'

The metalworker smiled, folded his arms and leaned back against the wall.

'What are we going to do about it?' asked another from the opposite side of the hall.

'What are we going to do?' repeated Kuraka. 'Well it's an odd state of affairs without doubt but our metal worker may be right and the king may soon return. Our noble lord may simply have left Uruk for reasons he did not wish to disclose and given the holy one a convenient story. He is king after all and generally does as he pleases – as we all know. Perhaps over the next few days will be revealed the cause of his -.'

'As I have already told you,' interrupted the old priest, 'he will not soon return. In fact, the way I see it, he may never return.' The man's voice carried the authority of age and the assurance of one who had no need to speak falsely. 'I was in the temple through much of the night before he departed. I encountered him leaving the chamber where his brother had lain and the subject of Ziusudra was raised. Gilgamesh was fired with enthusiasm over the possibility of our finding ancient records about this man. We each took up a pair of lamps and I was with him as he explored those ancient passages lower down within Inanna's temple, some long disused.'

The old priest now had their full attention as he continued. 'Our king was utterly determined in this task. He left me there for a time and returned with a

311

bronze crowbar. I stood by tending the lamps as he levered aside those stones or bricks he thought might conceal a passage. At last he revealed one hidden behind a plastered wall where stood a small altar, otherwise this was a dead end. It was something even I never dreamt might exist because it had been so carefully hidden. Here was concealed a narrow, rubble-strewn staircase leading down to a much earlier level within the foundations of the present temple. We made our way to the bottom with some difficulty and there was a stout timber door sealed fast with pitch long ago gone brittle. Gilgamesh forced it open and behind it we discovered a small, vaulted chamber with mouldering walls, cold and streaked with damp. Stored within copper banded wooden boxes placed upon a brick bench were baked clay tablets and cylinder seals left there by those of our ancestors who served the temple in ancient times. Why they had been left there I cannot say but it seemed to me they were never again intended for human eyes. The tablets were written in an archaic style, most difficult to comprehend, but he insisted I try. I was able after a time to fathom their message, though not in complete detail. It was, nevertheless, what he had been looking for. The tablets told of Ziusudra and the place to which he went.

It was as though, in the gloom of that secret place, a great enterprise was revealed to him. His mind is much affected by the death of his brother. He fears for his own mortality. All other considerations have fallen by the wayside. His road was pitted with anguish but in those tablets he perceived salvation. In them he perceived the conquest of death itself!'

There was silence for a time then, 'A fine tale to present us with,' voiced Kuraka.

'If this is true he's taken by madness,' grumbled one of the elders. 'The death of his brother has stricken his senses.'

'Madness - yes!' called out another. 'If some demon has usurped his mind then we must take action must we not?'

Murmurs of agreement spread throughout the hall.

'It would seem appropriate,' declared Kuraka, 'that we first pray and make sacrifice for the speedy return of our beloved king. Do we agree upon that?'

'Aye, pray and make sacrifice,' they concurred.

'Then,' he continued, 'we will assume our absent lord and master will recognise the folly of his actions and soon find his way back - but, and I say this with reluctance of course, we must consider seriously what the holy one has told us and decide what has to be done.'

'That's right!' declared a guildsman. 'If the king fails to return then we must take measures to ensure the safekeeping of our city. If the king of Larsa, or worse, the king of Kish hears about this, they'll lose no time in finding an opportunity to gain advantage over us.'

'Quite so,' agreed Kuraka, 'if those two form an alliance against Uruk and act when we have no leader - well, we need not set *our* thoughts down on tablets of clay. Remember also, our king in his wisdom saw fit to bring the men of Aratta within the city wall and they're not renowned for their

313

loyalty to anyone. If the elders gathered here consider it proper, I will approach one of the king's companions to command our armed men. Through our council they will take responsibility for the preservation of order and security - in the name of our worthy lord, naturally.'

'You've changed *your* tune since we last had difficulties with Kish!' taunted Sheshkalla. 'You were all for breaking bread with 'em as I remember - or was that *your* twin brother?'

Kuraka regarded him coldly. 'In those days, you may recall, we stood some chance of negotiation. Since our last conflict, bitterness and a desire for vengeance have pushed aside all reason. The fact that two of their captains of war and one of the dignitaries our king so dutifully had executed were Agga's close relations has not helped matters. We must now assume the Man of Kish will want to show the world he can do better. Any in Uruk who oppose him he will hang on hooks from the city wall to feed the birds and the worms. He will add to his wealth mightily from looting our coffers. He will defile our people and our sanctuaries. He will seize the statues from our temples to adorn his own shrines. He will cut out the heart of Uruk and anyone who cannot see that is a fool!'

'And as you've put yourself in charge, you'll be the first 'e'll 'ang!' leered Sheshkalla.

'Why some people cannot be agreeable at a time like this is beyond me,' responded Kuraka, uncomfortably. 'The minds of others will soon turn to the king's absence. Yet another delegation from Larsa is to visit Uruk. If the king is still absent it will fall upon our council to deal with them. That in

314

itself may cause offence if they bring royal documents. Armed men must be seen in our streets and squares as though the king himself has ordered it.'

'I'll be agreeable all right,' replied Sheshkalla. 'My men and I will play our part as well as the king's companions as long as you keep a grip on our affairs while he's absent. Uruk needs a voice whether it be yours or someone strong in arms like Gilgamesh. The latter choice would be mine.'

'We the council shall be that voice,' answered Kuraka, dryly. 'Meanwhile, we should consult our soothsayers. Their comments on the matter ought to be of interest.'

***

The city he had restored to greatness in his short years of rule lay far away. Only once did Gilgamesh rein in the asses so as to look back. From across the fields and orchards he gazed at distant Uruk, bright in the early morning sun. His keen eyes observed people going about their day's work amongst the fields and waterways. In those moments the shadow of remorse darkened his path and he had asked himself aloud, 'Who will rally the people when trouble comes? Who will step forward to champion Uruk now I'm gone? They'll say I'm possessed. Am I indeed possessed? Are the gods playing some devious game with me? If they are then I'm absolved from guilt. If not then I cannot return and live with indecision and failure.'

The asses snorted. They tugged impatiently, shaking him from his thoughts. Grasping the reins, Gilgamesh drove them on.

***

He had long since waded the shallows of the great river to the east of Uruk and the flat plains had given way to a rolling land of semi-desert and outcrops of pale stone. In the first days of the journey he had spotted only nomads but even they were no longer to be seen.

No human life had he encountered for three days when a caravan appeared, travelling in an opposite direction between himself and a low range of distant hills. Observing him, the caravan halted and two of its riders set out toward him. Gilgamesh ignored them and continued on. Seeing he showed no interest in them the riders stopped then returned to their companions.

The going was difficult and he suspected the ground would before long become so broken and rutted that he would have to abandon the cart. The two asses he would keep for a time. After that he would be alone and on foot. In his mind shone the message of the tablets though their light cast shadows of ambiguity. The ancient signs could be read in more than one way. They spoke of the days in one direction and then in another that the traveller had to go - long days and nights beneath the passing phases of the moon. They described the direction of the sun, the flight of the birds and of a deep mountain pass through which shining Utu himself must travel to begin his daily progress across the sky. Over this pass it seemed the gods had placed guardians.

They spoke, too, about the Great Water that mortals may never cross.

In the wilderness of night he imagined the shade of Enkidu was close as he whispered into darkness. 'In the skills I have learned to set my traps, to make fire, to cook my meat and dig wells to find water - in all these things, brother, your hand, your patience guide me. Do you see me now looking up at the stars as I rest here by the embers of my fire? I turn my head and there is the star of Inanna bright above the horizon. How can I help but see it though I wished never to set eyes on her again?

***

Soon after first light the next day, distant mountains appeared as the morning mist dispersed but his progress was becoming more difficult. Stopping when the sun was barely clear of the horizon, he took his weapons from the creaking chariot and laid them on the ground. The asses he tethered to a bush as there was work to be done and use could still be made of them. Taking his axe, Gilgamesh strode to the chariot and stood before it. With a loud cry, he raised the axe and swung it down to split the timbers apart. The rending wood startled the asses. Nearby birds rose up to circle and swoop about the bushes in noisy trepidation. Morning sunlight flashed on the axe as it fell several times more to complete the destruction.

When he had done, the chariot and its four sturdy wheels lay about in splintered ruin. The larger timbers Gilgamesh lashed together in bundles, fixing them across the backs of the asses. The rest, including copper and bronze fittings, he gathered together but abandoned where they lay.

'There now,' he said, addressing the two beasts, 'at least I'll not be short of fuel for my fire over the next day or so.' He raised his eyes to a cloud-matted

317

sky and smiled, 'I'm not doing too badly so far, brother Enkidu. What d'you say? I think I might learn to live off the land as well as you given a little more time.'

Another day and the mountains loomed closer but in spite of his plans, the loaded asses conspired unwittingly to slow his progress. By evening, when pine-wooded slopes and stone crags rose about him, their peaks emblazoned by the setting sun, Gilgamesh unloaded the remaining timber and drove the asses away. 'Go! Find your way back to the city or take to the wild as you please.'

For the first time since his journey began, Gilgamesh felt he had entered a land as strange as that of the cedar forests, but quite different. As the sky deepened he took his flints and a quantity of dried grass gathered from close about to use as kindling. Once the flames were dancing he placed wood from the chariot carefully about them. When the fire blazed up, dusk was well-advanced and steep hills reared as formless shadows against the stars. The fire was his testament. The flames consumed and the smoke carried away any lingering regrets he harboured over quitting Uruk. In the lurid glow he stood, sword at his belt, axe across his shoulders, spear grasped ready in his hand. 'As this fire defies the night so I will defy the mountains and the waters in my quest. Tomorrow when I enter those high hills no man will bar my way!' Raising his spear high he called into the night. 'To neither man nor beast will I yield! Not to the likes of Huwawa! Not to the likes of Gugalanna!'

With his words the timbers cracked, flaring brighter, gushing up a shoal of animated sparks to join the stars above. The fire glowed as a beacon in an endless dark sea. But somewhere beyond his domain of light the cry of a beast rang out as if the night answered his call. When the flames lessened, when the timbers settled to a fading glow, when he finally lay down to sleep, the night was silent, until -, 'Why do you wander here?'

Her voice was no more than a whisper. Was it close to his ear or was it far away? He could not tell. He raised himself, reached for his sword, peered into obscurity. 'Who's there? I heard you speak.' The night air was cool. His once living fire had shrunk to a feeble glow. 'Are you a spirit of this place? Show yourself.'

Again her voice, like wind in the reeds. 'You wander far. What is it you seek?'

'Why - I seek Ziusudra, the one who was granted everlasting life.'

Immense walls and buttresses towered about him, darker than the starless darkness beyond. 'This is not the land I entered,' breathed Gilgamesh. 'This is some great hall I find myself in. Is it the hall where we struck down Bull of Heaven? How far away are its walls? Are they close? No, I think not. I think they are very far away. I think they are boundless yet, ah, I see ahead of me a great portal like a city gate. What lies beyond? Where does it lead? I must know. I must pass through it.'

'You ask where it leads. Where would you have it lead?' As he moved forward her voice shivered on the air. It caressed his cheek, though he felt it had travelled very far.

'I'd have it lead me to the eternity of the gods,' he answered. 'I will hasten to pass through it. I will go on until I reach it. I will pass through the gate!

'Enkidu.' It was the voice of another. A dry, reverberating echo in the darkness.

'Who calls my brother's name?'

'Are you not the man called Enkidu - the one who walked the wild places?'

'My brother Enkidu is dead. I am Gilgamesh. I am king of Uruk.'

'Gilgamesh,' repeated many unseen voices. 'Gilgamesh, King of Uruk.'

'I am Gilgamesh and I will pass through the gate. I hurry on yet it seems no closer. I will go on. I will run hard until I reach it. See - not a fleeing gazelle will outpace me. I run and yet - still it is no closer. It is far away but I will go on. I will go on forever!'

***

The sky was brightening when Gilgamesh awoke. The fire still smouldered with a thin wisp of smoke spiralling into calm, cool air. He eased himself up on chilled, aching limbs to see vultures some distance away. They circled as dark motes, silent, ominous against a cloudless dawn. There was no sign of the asses as he gazed about. The humble asses and the chariot had been a remnant of his familiar world. The beasts knew the streets of the city. The chariot had been built by the hands of Uruk's craftsmen. Now they were gone.

Then there was the dream. He could not recall how or even if the dream had ended. He whispered into the silent morning. 'Who spoke to me in the night? Who mistook me for my dead brother?

320

Perhaps the spirits who rule this place in the darkness watched over me whilst I slept. Well, for now I'm alone as I have chosen to be.'

Taking a little of the meat he had cooked the previous day, together with a few dried dates, both kept in a soft leather pouch carried over his shoulder, Gilgamesh ate whilst surveying a brightening land. 'Ah, beyond where those vultures soar, between those two great mountains there may be a valley. Perhaps that is the portal I saw in my dream. Then that's the way I'll go.'

The ox hide flask contained enough water to quench his thirst. He knew well enough how to find water in the lowlands of Sumer. Water was seldom far away - beneath the earth if not in sight. Here the ground yielded none.

'There must be fresh water ahead,' he breathed, buckling on the sword-belt then slinging the axe across his back. 'Nearer those mountains there has to be a stream.'

Spear in hand, he set off across broad, gradually rising land, thinking that before the sun had passed its zenith he would be close to a passage through the hills.

'Those vultures,' he breathed, 'it cannot be me they regard as their next feast. Whatever is holding their attention must lie close by my route.'

The sun had not reached a quarter of its arc when he saw them across a gentle slope of pale grass and scattered shrubs. There were three lions, a male and two females lounging amidst bushes where the land rose abruptly. About their tawny forms scampered a number of playful cubs. Even as he watched, the male eyed him then, yawning widely, rose to his feet. The females, too, stirred. One of them rose lazily whilst the other picked up in her jaws the cub she had been licking and placed it aside. Striding to higher ground, Gilgamesh saw what had at first escaped his eye but was surely reason for the vultures' patient circling. Amidst the big cats lay a bloody, half-eaten carcass. The remains of their victim he imagined he recognised.

'So, you have killed one of my beasts,' muttered Gilgamesh. 'And now you're looking to complement your fare with my flesh!' Even as he expressed his thoughts, one of the females stepped away from the others to stand rock still and alert with her eyes fixed hard on him.

'Not so!' cried Gilgamesh starting briskly toward them. 'I've not set out on my travels to garnish your table!'

The three adults watched his approach with interest. This man's behaviour was not in the nature of humans, especially when alone. But on he strode and if he did not stop he would soon be in their midst. Stretching her limbs, the closer of the two females started toward him with a low growl. The male skirted to one side but kept his distance whilst the second female, glancing over her shoulder, ambled with scant enthusiasm in the wake of the first before stopping, reluctant to leave behind their young. One alone would be enough to deal with this impetuous man.

Weighing his spear with practised care, Gilgamesh watched the tail-swishing lioness approach. Moving quickly, she came on with purposeful gait, panting hard, breaking into a trot, paws thumping hard as his pounding heart. Closer she came and he saw the light of triumph in her eyes. Closer still and he knew she would at any moment gather speed then make her leap. With the grass dry and firm beneath his feet Gilgamesh sprinted forward, spear raised high, until man and beast were fearful moments apart. Now came the final, bounding dash. Her claws ripped the earth, her fangs glistened white, her growl cut the air. With all the strength at his command, with a cry of, 'Fly true!' Gilgamesh hurled the spear.

Too late she saw it. Already committed to the final leap, she had barely time to turn aside when the weapon struck. Her claws sprayed grit as cold metal drove into her shoulder. Howling rage at the skies she crashed to the ground, the momentum of the charge causing her to roll violently so the blade tore her flesh, letting blood vent freely as she came to rest on her side. Gilgamesh was over her with sword raised and, seizing the spear shaft to hold the quivering beast down, plunged his blade deep into her neck.

Whether she died at once or lingered a while he hardly cared, for other considerations were at hand. Wrenching free both spear and sword he turned to size up his other foes, expecting soon to meet their advance and wondering if he would repeat the next kill with equal facility.

They were not closing on him. The lion had begun to circle but was keeping his distance. The remaining female had returned to her young and showed no sign of following her mate. Sword and spear in hand, Gilgamesh started grimly toward the male, intending that this creature's blood should mingle on his blade with that of his fallen partner.

When the lion hesitated, Gilgamesh felt relief vie with disappointment, neither gaining over the other.

'Is the king of beasts to quit the field of battle?' he shouted, raising the spear high. At the sound of his voice the lion gazed at him, turned and trotted away, having altogether lost interest. Switching his attention to the other female, Gilgamesh observed her also in retreat with her young bobbing playfully behind. As for the slaughtered ass, dark shadows scurried over the hillside as the hungry birds swooped low in anticipation of their next meal.

'Go, then,' muttered Gilgamesh, eyeing the lions as he wiped his weapons clean on reddened grass. 'Yes, go!' he called, rising up with spear held high. 'Go and tell them Gilgamesh will have nothing stand in his way!' Wings spread as billowing black shrouds, the vultures descended. They began to strut about, swaying, craning their ugly heads whilst closing in for their grisly banquet of raw flesh.

There was no visible path yet his way was guided by the twin mountains ahead. They rose higher than the rest - great crags that seemed to pierce broken clouds that drifted placidly above. Yet whilst the lower hills formed a continuous, undulating ridge, these appeared, as he suspected they might, to enclose a deep valley.

The day wore on and the sun was low when he found himself entering boulder-strewn terrain. Ahead lay the mouth of the valley, obscured in darkness where it vanished into grim mountains. Peering toward it he said, 'My brother would caution me. He'd say only a fool would enter that valley of shadows now. And yes, I would agree with him. The darkness in there might swallow me forever.'

A short way on and the welcome sound of tumbling water reached his ear. 'I see amongst those rocks a stream coming down from the mountain. That's where I'll make my camp and set my traps. The air is cool but pleasant with the aroma of pine, and there's dry wood to be had for my fire.'

Gilgamesh moved closer to the busy stream. There he stood a while watching water sparkle, seeing star-crystals shiver and dance amidst the stones. 'Oh, how cold this water is,' he breathed, kneeling by the edge and cupping his hands to drink. 'Cold and pure you are. And to where do you hurry? To the rivers of distant Sumer from where I came? Will you carry back my thoughts? Will you tell them Gilgamesh lives?' Raising up, he peered again into the valley. 'Tomorrow when the day is new my valley of shadows will fill with light. Utu's hand will guide me through its depths. For now, I'll set my traps and hope the night brings my breakfast.'

His gaze turned to where the sun poised red on the horizon, casting long shadows from rock and bush. With the name of the deity on his lips he let water spill to the ground with a silent prayer, just as he and Enkidu had done on their journey to the Cedar Forest.

In the night his dreams returned. There were more voices. People he could not see. People he could not know. Always they whispered, 'Where are you going? What is it you seek?'

Always he answered, 'I seek the man who was granted immortality. I desire his secret.'

Always they said, 'Then seek to touch the heavens. Seek to hold the stars.'

But it was not voices he heard as he awoke. To the east, above the hills, the sky was brightening though the stars to the far west were not entirely vanquished. Spear in hand, Gilgamesh rose to his feet. The plains below were a sea of grey mist merging with the horizon. His fire had long since died and his limbs were stiff with cold because he had not thought to bring a woollen blanket. But what had he heard? What was it other than the chattering stream that had alerted him?

'Surely something moves out there beyond my vision. I did not dream it even though -.'

A series of clicks followed by a hollow rattle reached his ear. He gazed into the shadowed obscurity of the hills but could see nothing to account for it. 'Ah, I think those sounds are not close by but coming from the valley. Perhaps stones were dislodged from the slopes above by some creature that wanders there.'

Smoke drifted lazily on the morning air, spluttering yellow flames cheered him. Once his fire was established he walked over to check the traps he had set close by the stream. 'Good! I see a hare is fouled. I'll cook and eat its flesh with the last of my dates. With a bit of luck that'll be enough to see me through the pass.'

His meal finished, Gilgamesh returned to the stream and though at first daunted by the breath-taking chill of the water, he bathed and washed as best he could. In the morning light he strode on and was soon below slopes of sparse vegetation that rose more steeply to either side as he went. The once green valley was becoming a rocky gorge that soared ever higher ahead of him. Shattered rocks lay about in chaotic disorder where they had crashed down from the heights. Gilgamesh saw that it narrowed further ahead to a chasm of fearful aspect penned in by sheer cliffs that defied the light of the sun. Here was a sombre, forbidding realm that offered no promise of easy passage.

'I will not be deterred!' he said aloud, though his voice echoed mockingly from bare walls. A few more steps, then - 'What is that?'

A scraping noise. Then a clatter of stones came from a short way ahead followed by that odd clicking he had heard earlier. Gilgamesh hesitated, looked about, his hand firm about the spear's shaft. Exactly where the sounds came from he could not tell. Echoes passed to and fro like confused birds. Then he saw it - black and glistening. An object moved amongst the rocks ahead, swaying back and forth, appearing - disappearing.

'Show yourself!' he called. 'Show yourself now or I'll seek you out and you'll feel the kiss of well-honed metal!'

'Nasty, nasty, nasty,' rasped the voice. The echo that followed might have been just that but was not. A second voice called forth an echo of its own to mingle with the first. 'Nasty, nasty, nasty.'

'Show yourselves!' he cried, striding onto a broad, tilted slab.

From behind a cluster of boulders emerged the oddest of heads. But though the face was flattened and the eyes oddly blank and bulbous, it was nevertheless a human head - of sorts. Something swayed behind the hidden body, its tip showing

327

above the boulders. He wondered at first if it was a black-painted spear with curved obsidian blade. But the object appeared to be hinged and the segmented shaft not straight at all. In his mind it was familiar but so out of place it refused to give itself a name. Another, similar face appeared to the opposite side of his intended path, its body likewise obscured by boulders, again with that odd protuberance quivering in the air to its rear.

'It's a man,' declared the first head, in a voice that sounded like the turn of an ill-fitting bronze hinge. The voice was accompanied by that same odd clicking.

'You're right as usual,' answered the second in similar manner. 'It's definitely a man, and he's alone.'

Both at last emerged into the clear area some twelve paces from him, limbs tapping against the boulders as they went. Seeing them fully revealed, Gilgamesh raised his spear and cried out, 'By the gods, what manner of creatures are you?'

'Manner of creatures?' squeaked the first, black rear limbs scraping against the stones. 'We're *our* manner of creatures and always have been. We guard the pass through the mountains of Mashu, if it's all the same to you.'

'That's right,' added the second, smugly 'we guard the mountain pass. 'It's the only way through, you know.'

'Yes,' agreed the first, raising up on its back legs, 'it's the only way through the mountains of Mashu and we have to guard it.'

'That's exactly what we're here for,' whirred the second, 'so you'll have to go back the way you came.'

'Yes, I get the point,' responded Gilgamesh.

'But *we'd* rather not get the point if you don't mind,' said the first. 'So please don't throw your spear at us just yet.'

'If you don't mind, dear,' repeated the second, 'don't throw it at all. We're simply not used to that kind of treatment.'

Gilgamesh kept the spear raised and pointed at each of them with his free hand. 'Pardon me saying so but you're hideous to my eyes! You're not men but scorpions with the foreparts of men! You are the spawn of nightmares yet you speak my tongue. Am I still prisoner of afflicted sleep or am I awake and confronted by beings of the lower world? Tell me that at least!' But in his thoughts passed the words, 'No, Huwawa was worse by far than these two.'

'Hideous!' exclaimed the first creature, indignantly, arching its sting to quiver menacingly. 'Did you hear what he called us? Hideous!'

'Hideous!' repeated the second. 'Spawn of nightmares! Oooh - he's got some nerve - I'll say. We try to introduce ourselves and what does he do - waves his spear at us and calls us names. I don't call *that* in the least bit civil and, anyway, it's *he* who speaks *our* tongue.'

'I don't call it civil either,' agreed the first, gesturing a forearm toward Gilgamesh, 'You're not much to look at yourself, dear. Pink and smooth, actually. At least most of what wanders by here has a decent coat of hair, yes, and a tail to call its own.'

'Pink and smooth,' agreed the second. 'Now that's what *I* call ugly.'

'Quite repulsive,' clicked the first, 'But tell us, apart from demonstrating a fine aptitude for insults, what brings you here dressed up in some poor creature's skin and armed as though you bear a grudge against the whole world?'

'All right – maybe I overreacted. I am Gilgamesh, King of Uruk. I seek the one called Ziusudra who was granted immortality. I'm in a hurry and I'm in *no* mood for idle conversation.'

'Oooh!' exclaimed the second creature. 'King of Uruk! Whatever next!'

'King of Uruk,' chirruped the first, 'and us not looking our best. But if it's immortality you're after - well, that's a complete waste of time, we can tell you.'

'A waste of time - definitely,' agreed the second. '*We* are quite sure of it. You're obviously possessed by demons.'

'I'll be the judge of that,' answered Gilgamesh, drawing back the spear in readiness to cast as both shook their lethal tails and advanced toward him. Stopping some eight paces away, they settled their rear ends on the ground and continued to regard him with vacant stare. Lowering the spear, Gilgamesh asked, 'Why do you guard this valley? Why don't you want me to enter what you call the mountains of Mashu for enter it I soon will?'

'We guard the way because we were told to guard it,' replied the first creature.

'We're guards, you see,' added the second, sarcastically. 'Guarding things is what guards do.'

'But why?' insisted Gilgamesh. 'On whose orders?'

'Why? Who?' repeated the first creature, turning to its companion.

'Don't ask me,' chirruped the second, folding its arms and rocking its head to and fro. 'It's been such a long time. I thought *you'd* remember. Something to do with the sun, I thought.'

'You expect *me* to remember everything,' responded the first, turning back to Gilgamesh and adding, 'Yes, it's been so long we, er - we don't remember.'

'Then let me through. I grow impatient and I *will* continue my journey!'

'I suppose we could let the man through,' said the first creature. 'He must be quite insane to want to go in there but why should we ruffle our scales over it?'

'Quite – why should we,' agreed the second, 'but that's not being a guard, is it? We wouldn't be doing our job if we let him through.'

'You're right – we ought to give it serious thought before we reach a decision.'

'My patience wears thin as a pauper's blanket!' exclaimed Gilgamesh, raising the spear again and bracing himself. 'Out of my way - now!'

'He's going to throw his spear!' called out the first creature.

'Nasty man's going to throw it - yes!' repeated the second, and both scuttled backward to shelter behind the boulders.

'Well, now do I go on?' asked Gilgamesh, lowering the spear.

The two faces reappeared, glanced at each other then regarded him. 'Oh, yes, yes, yes,' grated the first creature, its small mouth twisting into the semblance of a smile. 'You can be the first one since - since - I don't remember when.'

'The first for, ooh - ages,' added the second.

'Then stay clear of me!' called Gilgamesh, bounding from the slab, reassured by the sight of their continuing retreat. Both scuttled up the slope a short way to his right, turning with arms folded to sit back on curved tails and watch in silence from beneath the cliff. Wary of their slightest movement, he strode over the spot where their clawed feet had scuffed the ground and continued past the boulders that had earlier concealed their bizarre forms.

'If I were you -!' called the first creature.

'If *we* were you, dear,' added the second, both voices echoing ahead of him, 'which I'm glad to say we're not.'

'If we were you,' continued the first, 'we'd get a move on and no mistake.'

'It's not as easy as you think,' declared the second.

'Oh, no,' called the first, 'it's not easy at all!'

Gilgamesh hesitated to look back. Both remained seated. Each bore an unmistakable smugness on its face as the first creature called, 'You'll have to pace yourself against the sun, King of Uruk! You'll need to reach the other end before the sun completes his passage across the sky!'

'Once darkness falls,' added the second, rearing up on its back legs, 'you'll not leave the valley alive! It will swallow you and Uruk will have to find another king!'

'Another king!' mocked the first creature and their laughter rattled along the walls like cackling crows, passing by as if to alert malignant spirits that lay in wait ahead.

Had they spoken the truth? Gilgamesh was sure they had as he hurried on. 'Damn you and damn this place!' he called back but the bizarre pair were no longer in sight and his voice thunder-rolled through the chasm. Hurrying as best he could along broken ground that sloped this way and that; clambering over loose rubble and skirting shattered slabs, Gilgamesh used the butt of his spear to help keep his balance. The cliffs towered in sombre, chilling gloom but onward he went while wondering how far above the horizon the sun might have risen. 'They think I'm possessed by demons and they may be right. I ask myself if this is real. But was Huwawa not real? Was Gugalanna not real? And did we not defeat them - my brother and I? If only you were by my side now, brother Enkidu. I think you'd lighten my burden of fear.'

Always his attention was fixed on the ground ahead. To stumble, to catch a foot in jagged rocks, to wrench a muscle or worse, could mean his end. When at last he paused to glance upward it was to observe the sky narrowed like a pale river meandering far above. Gaunt and cold, the walls pressed in to steal away his warmth. A chill breath coiled about him and Gilgamesh knew he must not slacken. 'I have to go on. There is no other way. No other way! I swear this place would crush the soul of any man and needs no guardian. Each stone I kick echoes to awaken whatever lies ahead. No matter how I hurry I'm like a beetle groping my way in some ancient vault where the living were never meant to tread. There's no life here - no sunlight. Not weed nor thorn grows amongst these barren stones. And does the chasm grow darker? Is the sun already getting low or are the shadows on those walls high above cast by my own disquiet? Ah – the ground further on appears more even. Now I'll make better progress. Yes, it looks like sand for some way so -.'

Something in the gloom of a rocky overhang ahead caught his eye. Something pale that did not belong. As he slowed his pace, as he drew near, the sight of it chilled him to the heart. The bones of a human hand reached upward from the ground in mockery of a command to halt. And by the side of a fallen rock, unseen until he drew close, lay the stark-white horror of a partly buried skull. Sand spilled from empty sockets where once shone living eyes and from open jaws that grinned skeletal humour.

Gilgamesh froze before this icon of despair. Here was a vision that proclaimed the end of hope and life. 'Who were you,' he breathed, 'you were once flesh and blood like me? How long have you lain alone? What fateful mission brought you to this place?'

Silence descended about him as a shroud. Cold fingers touched his back and the breath caught in his throat. In those moments of hesitation, in that confining bubble of stillness, of frozen time, the white skull blinded his vision to all else. It breathed phantom words into his ear, 'Stay, my friend. Stay a while and take my hand. Let your warmth and your words caress my bones. In the countless years I have waited, no one has passed this way.'

Gilgamesh reached out a trembling hand then backed away. The skull seemed to shift in the ground then to turn a hollow gaze upon him. The rotted mouth opened wide in soundless laughter. Words drifted from below the overhang, exhaled from deep within cold rock - the mournful lamentation of a woman - a voice of compelling, exquisite beauty that drew his gaze beneath the dark stone whilst it rose up to swirl about him as a wraith. 'I sang a tune of doleful air - I sang it to my heart's despair. Now you are here. Leave me not. Leave me not.'

And though his flesh crawled, though tentacles of fear pierced his innards, Gilgamesh desired nothing more than to see her. Her voice mesmerised. It convinced him utterly of her beauty. In his mind appeared her image, young and pale, her eyes sapphire blue, her full lips crimson-red, her hair cascading silver over naked shoulders. If he stayed longer, just a little longer, she would stand before him. Yes, just a short while – no more. She would stand there. She would reach out a hand to touch.

A burst of laughter swept down to shatter his reverie. A hammer-strike against a bronze anvil then a voice he knew well. 'Brother Gilgamesh! That wailing old hag will eat your soul! Let's get on our way! I wager I'll be out of here before you!'

Startled, he looked above the empty ledge from where the voice had called. 'What – out before me!' he exclaimed. 'By the gods you will not!' He glanced at the skull, crying aloud, 'And the years will turn you to dust before some other fool passes you by!'

Around tumbled rock, over tilted slab he scrambled, his spear serving to aid his progress as he leapt from side to side. 'I'll go on. I'll go on because my flame of life burns bright. This valley of shadows will never claim me. My axe has become a burden but I won't lay it aside. No I will not! What d'you say, brother Enkidu? Will this valley ever end? I know you wouldn't falter. You would find a way through and so will I. Yes - so will I!'

With heart pounding, with breath passing harsh, he looked only ahead though the hollow echo of his footsteps was a beast that followed close. His thoughts were of his brother and the days of their exploits. The spirit of Enkidu was close at his side. Once more they laughed together and his strength was renewed even though the day had been long and must soon draw to a close.

When Gilgamesh looked up at the sky the clouds were tinged rose-red. 'The sun is going down and I have still not reached the end. Yet the chasm looks to be widening. Yes, it widens! And unless my eyes are playing tricks, the cliffs are not so high. Perhaps I'm through the worst of it.'

The gorge had begun to widen and his progress was becoming easier. Walls that once provoked dismay by their vastness seemed at last not so overwhelming. 'Ah, there are shrubs and ferns further along the path. Once I'm over the rise ahead I may see my way out of here.'

He clambered upward, scattering stones and rubble until finally reaching the top of the rise where he halted and breathed deeply. 'There! There beyond the cliffs. The sun is close to the horizon and I see grasslands. I see a forest of trees and - yes, there is a stream with gazelles drinking at its banks. Once I'm down there I'll set up my camp and - oh.' Gilgamesh lifted a hand to shield his eyes. 'Beyond the woodlands there is water. A great expanse, vaster by far than the rivers of Sumer and I see nothing beyond it. Did anyone from Sumer ever journey this far? Did any ancestor of mine stand where I now stand? No – I alone have passed through the valley of the shadow of death!' Turning for the last time to the darkened chasm he raised his spear and cried, 'I have triumphed! You will never claim me!' His voice rattled through the chasm until swallowed by its sombre depths.

With spear held high, he half scrambled, half ran down the rocky slope, glad of a gentle warmth from the lowering sun and the lazy buzz of insects. In the air hung a tang of pine and soon he trod grass underfoot. In the time it took to reach the banks of the stream the sun had almost set and shadows crowded over the land. 'My new companion is now tiredness and I don't imagine he'll leave my side until the morning. I'll set my traps before darkness then I'll find a place to make my bed. And in the morning - yes, in the morning, I'll head through those woods and beyond until I stand at the edge of the Great Water.'

On reaching the river he laid aside his weapons, drank, bathed then sat to nurse aching feet. Here was a bank of soft grass close to the stream and Gilgamesh, intending to rest a while before setting his traps, lay back beneath his lion skin. The air was calm and remained pleasantly warm. He found the lapping water a source of comfort after the menacing desolation of the pass.

Before night had cast her net of stars over the land, he was adrift on a gentle river of sleep.

***

'I hear birds singing. Did I dream or did I not dream? Did I really talk with those bizarre creatures and pass through that damnable valley yesterday? Well, this grass is real enough - and my aching limbs are also real.'

He got up slowly to find his sword, spear and axe resting where he had laid them. 'Ah, last night I didn't set any traps. Now I'm without food.' So saying he reached for the leather pouch, pulled it open and peered inside with a frown. 'What would you say to this, brother Enkidu? I doubt you would have let it happen.'

Fastening on the lion skin then gathering up his weapons, Gilgamesh looked toward the pinewoods. 'There's a track I didn't notice yesterday. Perhaps the gazelles have made it. Maybe it will guide me through the woods.'

Within the woods the path was not so clear but morning sunlight slanted low through the trees to dapple the trunks and splash the ground with colour. 'How pleasant this place is,' he sighed, walking on. 'I sense there's no evil here. Only hunger stalks me now and for that I've only myself to blame. There is life - I feel it all about though I see and hear nothing except the birds. Before the sun is overhead I'll reach the Great Water and I'll stand on its shores. Then what shall I do? What if it's a barrier I cannot cross? My journey will have come to nothing unless

-.' He stopped, gazed ahead through the bushes then took three more steps. 'By the gods, what have I come upon?'

Gilgamesh found himself standing before an orchard garden. There were orchard gardens in and around Uruk and he knew them well – but not in all the land of Sumer could there be one like this - not even in the outlandish tales the travellers told. In awed silence, he moved slowly forward.

Here were no growing things, no green bushes, no swaying flowers, no soft fruits. About him stood an assemblage wrought in exquisite image of nature but not in nature's hues or in her substance. Here was a vision of shimmering light, of crystal starburst - intricate saplings, leaves, branches and stems of shining copper, beaten metal. Flowers of shining gold and silver sprang motionless from the ground, their delicate petals having centres set with precious gems that sparked vivid colour.

'What have I chanced upon?' he whispered. 'There's the stillness of a temple sanctuary here yet this is a place of glorious light. And such - such artistry! This surely is beyond the skill of mortal hands. No palace, no temple in Sumer could possess its like - yet it stands untouched. If this is not a preserve of the gods then my mind has been ousted altogether from the confines of reason. What would you make of it, brother Enkidu - a garden where jewels outshine the stars in the sky and their radiance rivals the glory of the sun? It was your way to contemplate things of beauty and know their worth when I was blind to them. See, I lay my finger upon flowers of lapis-lazuli, pearls and gold. Ah, they quiver at my touch and I hear delicate chimes. Who tends this grove of treasures? Who delights in such unearthly beauty? Does this mean no mortal inhabits the land? If so then I'm truly alone. I am tempted to stay here and explore further, to revel in these wonders, but I have to go on. If I remain longer I'll forget the purpose of my journey, I know it, and this fabulous garden will claim me as the chasm of Mashu never did. I'll touch nothing more; I'll take nothing from here - nothing except the images I have witnessed.'

He continued on, glancing back often, more than once tempted to return, until finding himself surrounded again by greenery. On turning for a final look he could no longer see the garden.

***

She was alone about her business, singing to herself, sweeping her doorstep with a straw broom when she caught sight of him emerging from the woods with spear in hand. The stranger had evidently spotted her tavern, close to the shore, and with head shifting from side to side in the manner of a prowling vagabond, had set his course toward it.

Siduri hastily gathered up her long skirt, hurried down the steps and across her small courtyard to the arch set within a white-plastered wall. He was approaching rapidly, about to stride across the path by her vegetable garden, so grasping the edge of the door she pushed hard. It was made of ancient timbers, stout oak with bands and fittings of bronze but having lain wide open for some considerable time the door at first resisted her efforts to force it shut. Siduri heaved and the door moved, pushing up a ridge of fine earth at its base. Then it was free and, in the instant before it

340

slammed, she glimpsed him only a few paces away, eyes bright and determined. Bronze bolts screeched into stone sockets as she made the door fast, then having leant against it for heart-beating moments Siduri hurried back across the courtyard and up the steps where she entered then closed the tavern door with a thump before securing that as well.

Outside the courtyard, he pushed against the door to find it unyielding. Twice he beat against it with his fist and called, 'Hello!' but there was no response. He cursed aloud and was about to strike the timbers with the butt of his spear when a voice called from above, 'Who are you? What d'you want?'

Gilgamesh stepped back and glanced about. Then further back still until he was able to peer above the wall. He observed her slender figure on the roof of the tavern, hair red as polished copper drifting about her shoulders in the warm breeze, hands placed defiantly on her waist as she stared down at him. 'Well,' she called, 'you seem to have a voice in your head so use it!'

'Yes,' he declared, puzzled for a moment over how readily he understood her tongue. It was surely not the language of Sumer or any of its close neighbours, 'I do have a voice, woman, and I would have used it to speak with you had you not bolted your door against me! I have travelled a long way with little company other than the creatures of the wild!'

'Well if I may say so,' she answered, leaning over the parapet and eyeing him sternly, 'you look like one of 'em yourself! You come rushing out of the woods, armed to the teeth like a bandit - what d'you expect me to do - get out my best dishes and goblets?'

'Dishes! Goblets!' he responded. 'Woman, I am Gilgamesh, King of Uruk! I dine off gold and silver whenever it pleases me. If I wanted to break into your house I'd reduce this door to firewood with my axe! Right now I'm of a mood to do it! I tell you I'm footsore and hungry.'

'King of Uruk!' she laughed, folding her arms. 'Uruk! Yes, I've heard of Uruk - that's in the land of Sumer on the other side of the world. No one comes here from Sumer except the occasional sailor. You'd have to pass through the mountains of Mashu. No one's done that - not within -.'

'Not within living memory. Is that what you were about to say?'

'More than that – no one ever heard of it being done since the great flood. They say after that the gods put a guardian over it so no one could follow Ziusudra.'

'Oh, so you do know of him! Well Ziusudra's the one I hope to find. I want nothing from you but beer, a little food and to know which way I have to go.'

'Do you really,' she answered. 'Well don't demolish the door just yet - I'll be right down.'

Keeping clear of the door so as not to cause her further alarm, Gilgamesh leaned on his spear and waited. A muffled scraping and the bolts were drawn back. The door opened a short way to reveal the fox-eyes of the woman peering warily at him from beneath long lashes. 'King of Uruk is it, dearie? I've heard a few travellers' tales in my time but no one's claimed to be a king yet.' She smiled, pulled the door wider, stepped aside and gestured him to enter. 'Still, you don't sound like a villain in spite of your appearance, nor like a hunter of bears or lions though you look big and strong enough. Whatever you are, you don't look to have eaten properly or seen a decent bed in a long time, either. You could be an old man behind all that growth on your face but up close I see you aren't.'

'I have lived off the land since leaving Uruk,' he replied, entering the courtyard then turning to face her. 'I am who I say and that's the truth. See this ring on my finger - see these weapons I carry – do they look like the arms of a common man?'

'Hm, I suppose not,' she answered thoughtfully, looking him up and down, noting the belt at his waist and the inlaid and finely worked hilt of the sword, 'but I can't imagine any man owning such fine possessions would need to live as rough as you. And, phew, that lion skin – does the thing come running when you whistle?'

'This,' he responded touchily, prodding the skin, 'this was taken years ago from a beast I slew when out hunting. A beast everyone said no man would dare confront.'

'Well,' she responded, folding her arms, 'it looks as though it's getting its own back now and I don't want it frightening the goats. Still, my house is here for the comfort of travellers and I suppose that makes you a guest. There's nothing a decent meal, a good hot bath and a razor wouldn't put right. Mmm, I'd say in your case the bath ought to come first if only the water was ready.'

'Woman, believe me, I'd be very glad of those things but I've not a grain of silver on me. Is there some task I can help you with by way of payment? Is there some man or – or some beast that causes you distress?'

'Task, dearie? We can't have the King of Uruk or the king of anywhere else do a common man's work. Hmm, even if you're not what you claim, you're surely not a common man. No, I've a copper tub at the back and a well close by. I'll bring you bread, fish and beer in the outer room and while you get your face around that I'll have a fire going under the tub to heat up the water.' Once more she looked him up and down. Once more she smiled. 'We can soak the lion skin as well and hang it out to freshen in the breeze. A month or two might do it. As for payment, diary - I'm sure we'll think of something as we go.'

As he walked behind her across the courtyard he studied her alluring curves, her swaying walk and the gleam of sunlight on her hair. 'How many live here?' he asked.

'Oh, just me,' she answered, raising her skirt before ascending the steps to the tavern door. He followed her through, wondering why such a strikingly attractive young woman should live alone. She gestured to a nearby corner, saying, 'You can leave your fancy armoury propped up there, lovey. It'll be quite safe. I usually bolt the door at night. We never know who might show up, do we.'

As Gilgamesh unburdened himself she turned to him and smiled, 'Er, if you are King of Uruk, or whatever, I dare say there's a proper manner by which you ought to be addressed. D'you care to tell me what it is?'

344

Her features were further softened by subdued light filtering through small windows high in the wall. He looked into her eyes. They were a rare grey-green. 'For now I'm just a traveller,' he replied, 'so you must address me as Gilgamesh and that will do. And your name if you please, as I don't yet know it?'

'No you don't, do you,' she answered. 'My name is Siduri. I keep this tavern for when the boats come to our shores or merchants pass this way. They buy my bread, cheese, and beer - and the wine I make, if they can afford it. I offer them hot water to bathe and a clean place to rest if they need that as well.'

'Is there no man to tend your livestock and make your work easier?' Gilgamesh asked.

'Oh, there was once,' she replied, looking down. 'He owned the grazing land you crossed as well as being a trader. Trouble is he was always on the lookout for new deals. He sailed away with his big ideas, his cronies and much of our silver three years ago and never returned. None of them did and no one hereabouts ever heard what became of them. Pirates had 'em all likely as not. There's a woodsman tends and slaughters my animals when needs be. For that he earns his bread and beer - and that's *all* he gets paid in case you're thinking otherwise. I've needed little more, though now and again I suppose I could do with company.' She glanced up at him and her eyes brightened. 'But, King Gilgamesh, before the day is through, we'll have you looking like a king is supposed to look whether you're a king or no. When you've eaten and bathed I'll take a comb to that untidy hair and a razor to your cheeks - if you'll let me, that is. It'll make a change from milking the goats!'

***

In the light of an upstairs window she worked, passing an ivory comb through newly washed hair before shaving the bristled growth from his face with bronze razor and expert hand.

'I see we've been in the wars,' she remarked, noting the scar that ran down to his cheekbone.

'It kept me busy for a while,' he muttered.

The loosely woven robe of wool she had given him was cool and comfortable. As he sat contented on the pine stool, his reflection eyeing him back from a mirror of polished bronze, he was much taken with her warmth and the perfume she must have applied to herself whilst he was bathing.

She had said little else when Gilgamesh shifted his gaze from the mirror to the window and the woodlands beyond, saying, 'I walked through the forest before I found your tavern. I saw a place of unbelievable treasures. An orchard of gold and silver – all of it wrought in the image of nature. Then it was gone from sight. I wonder now if it was an illusion brought about by days of wandering. Yet – yet it seemed so real.'

Stopping in surprise, Siduri moved back, her eyes wide, her voice little more than a whisper. 'I often walk in those woods but I've seen nothing, nor has anyone I know of. But there's a rumour – no, a legend older than anyone can say. Some people hereabouts believe a temple once stood there - a temple built by gods long forgotten who came to live here for a time then returned to the stars. What you describe is said to be the orchard of those lost

346

gods - a garden never meant for mortal eyes. Others say it never existed at all. How would a stranger like you know about that? If you have in truth seen it then I'd say you are no ordinary man.'

'That's what so troubles me,' he answered, meeting her gaze, 'and it's the reason for my journey. Since the death of Enkidu, my brother, I have come to understand how ordinary and how mortal a man I am. Not kingship, not all the treasures of Sumer can alter that.'

'And in seeking this Ziusudra you hope for the key to eternity.'

'It's why I have left behind the wealth and the pleasures of my kingdom,' he sighed. 'What are those worth when death conquers?'

Siduri resumed her work, finishing with the razor and reaching for a small jar of scented balm into which she dipped her fingers. 'None of us can escape death, dearie; it's foolish to think otherwise. We should make the best of the lives we've got and take the days as they come. If you're a man of Uruk with the power and wealth of a king then you should have little enough to complain about.'

Siduri worked soothing balm into his cheeks and neck with delicate touch. She caressed his flesh. She roused his senses whilst the soft music of her voice and the warmth of her breath tingled his ear. 'And this Ziusudra, love - who can say if he exists? He's just a name that gets aired now and again when people sit around here to drink and tell tales. No more than that.'

Her long hair brushed his shoulder, spreading sensuous warmth through his body. Delicate as moth wings, her fingers stroked his cheek.

'And the pleasures of Uruk - I expect you've missed all those since you left. Still, we're all clean and tidy now - more like a lord than a down and out. I dare say you could saunter back into your fancy palace without causing too much of a stir.' She moved to the window and added, 'You'll maybe want to rest a while so I'll let the matting down to keep the light out. The couch behind you is clean and comfortable. Tradesmen and sailors aren't allowed up here. Only kings.'

'The pleasures of Uruk I do miss – you're right,' he sighed, watching her silhouette against the window as the blind unrolled. 'But I cannot deny the need to finish my journey. It's as strong now as when I rode out through the city gate though in doing that I've put at risk everything I fought for. Am I to blame the gods for turning aside my reason? I don't know, but the day will surely come when I have to face the consequences.'

Siduri returned and, leaning toward him, brushed the back of her hand over his smooth cheek. 'Things compel us for many reasons,' she whispered hoarsely. 'Sometimes we just have to let it happen.' Her lips touched his ear as a soft flame. She did not back away as he rose from the stool to slip an arm about her waist. Their lips met. Her breath was a furnace of passion. Her nails prickled his back through the thickness of the robe. 'Just live for the day, diary,' she breathed, knowing his arousal as he pulled the gown from her shoulders to free her breasts. Her hand fell to his robe and pushed inside. His breath caught as cool fingers slipped about his manhood to begin their voluptuous work. Again her voice. 'There, love, forget eternity. There's only now. There, love - only now.'

In the twilight of that small room his thoughts of yesterday and tomorrow were consumed in flames of pleasure. On the lambswool covers of the couch they played out the fervent game of lust - she gaining the upper hand to straddle her mount, then her new-found lover gaining his to ride her with vigour. Her cries arose as one in torment, the nails of her fingers all but piercing his flesh whilst Gilgamesh groaned, 'Oh, by the gods what a hunger we have. By the gods!'

But theirs was a contest neither could win nor could lose for in the end exhaustion was the victor and they fell asleep in an embrace of warm contentment.

**

The sun was approaching its highest when they awoke. Light filtered through the matting to paint the wall with glowing filaments. Siduri spread her fingers across his chest and whispered, 'It's a long time since a real man entered this house. I mean a *real* man.'

'And you, lady Siduri,' he answered, 'the women of Inanna's temple could teach you nothing though you live far from the arts and intrigues of the city.'

'Then, dear Gilgamesh, stay a while before you continue on your journey. You've travelled a long way and a few days rest will do you a world of good.'

'Rest - with you?' he grinned. 'I doubt I'd get much rest in your company. Even if it was so, I couldn't stay for long. Now I've reached the Great

Water I must find where to take my search next. The tablets I discovered at the temple say Ziusudra crossed the Great Water and that's where I must follow. D'you know of anyone who will take me?'

Siduri gazed down at her hands, unsure as to whether or not she ought to offer him an answer. 'There's only one man dares sail out beyond the sight of land, or so he claims,' she said at last, 'and that's Urshanabi - a miserable old sod and no mistake. Him and his pals get drunk here quite often when they're ashore and leave me to clean up the mess. Still, the drink makes them generous enough with their silver and I suppose that's what matters at the end of the day. As for those who crew his boat – people claim they're made of stone, if you can believe that. Yes, I've heard them talk of the Stone Ones. Dangerous, they say. Ugly and nasty - just like their master.'

'Made of stone,' laughed Gilgamesh. 'That I *will* have to see. And where am I to find this unpleasant fellow and his unlikely crew?'

'There's a cove well under half a day from here where he brings in his boat. It's said no one dares approach him there but I can't see you'd stand any nonsense. By my reckoning it'll be at least a couple of days yet before he's back, then he'll maybe head this way to meet his cronies and booze away his earnings. So there's no need to rush off yet Gilgamesh, dear.'

Gazing into her eyes he said, 'I'll wait here in case he appears. A day or two, perhaps.'

'A day or two,' she breathed. 'And what's a day or two when you're out to find immortality. Immortality won't mind waiting a while longer I

350

shouldn't think. And back home in Uruk - d'you have a woman waiting for you there – or several as you're a king?'

'Yes, I -.' He hesitated, confused over his own response. In his mind had appeared Shamkhat, the girl of the temple. He recalled her as his own lover, though it was in the end to Enkidu she had been so attached, as Enkidu had been to her. 'Why,' he thought, 'why should I see her through the eyes of my dead brother?'

'You were saying?' asked Siduri, her eyes brightly fixed upon his.

'Oh, nothing,' he smiled. 'I meant to say that I have women whose company I enjoy, as would any man in my situation. I cannot say if any of them will be mourning my absence.'

'Really, King Gilgamesh, that does surprise me.'

The touch of her lips on his cheek, his chest and further, were enough to bring him back to the present and she found him once more aroused. Siduri possessed a secret fund of pleasures; pleasures offered before to very few but now bestowed liberally upon her wanderer from far away.

Yet when he rested that night it was the face of Shamkhat he saw in the darkness.

***

Seven days he remained in her company. Seven days she would have made tenfold and tenfold again. They sat together each evening in the warm air and he told her about Uruk. Siduri listened fascinated by his words, by the sound of his voice as he described the city wall, the dazzling temples and the sights of the town. He told her about Enkidu and the perils they had faced together – Huwawa and the Bull of Heaven - then of the grief he had suffered at his brother's death. At night they ate by the light of a small lamp before retiring to the pleasures of her bed.

One morning they strolled hand in hand along the seashore and Gilgamesh marvelled at the water's limitless expanse. Together they walked to the woods and there retraced his steps as far as the stream. Gilgamesh had wanted to show her the wondrous orchard of the forgotten gods and all the precious things it contained but there was nothing other than what nature had bestowed. She was content to simply be with him and cared not at all that the forest appeared exactly as she had always known it. It amused her when he offered water and grain for the sun's protection. No one in her land ever did that but what did it matter if it pleased him?

In morning light Siduri watched him depart as she had watched him appear, from the door above her tavern steps. He had set out dressed once more in the lion skin, axe slung over his shoulder, sword at his side and spear in hand. She had wanted to call after him as he crossed the small courtyard. Wanted to hurry down, to hold him and say, 'Don't go yet, dearie. Stay a while longer - just another day or so.'

Reappearing beyond the courtyard wall, he strode along the path that led to the shore and would soon vanish from sight.

'Don't go,' she whispered, hoping the whisper might swoop as a bird, alight on his shoulder and make him turn about. 'Don't go. Don't leave me.'

He hesitated with a brief wave to her before passing from view. Siduri raised a hand, opening her mouth to call his name, but he was gone. She stood alone. Morning sunlight glistened wetness on her cheek. In those few short days he had been her man and she had awoken each morning to a world bathed in new colours and glorious light. He was the one for whom she had always longed. The pleasures of a life she had never fully known had been hers during that fleeting time with him. There could never be another like her Gilgamesh. Never.

Siduri returned to her tavern. So familiar. So still. So sad and empty. The bright flame that had entered her world had left her abandoned now to shadows of loneliness. The passing days would not quell her bitter tears.

***

He peered out from the cover of the pine trees, tasting in the air an odour of pitch and newly sawn timber. The boat, a sturdier craft by far than those he knew from the rivers of Sumer, lay high and dry on the shingle beach with her mast let down. Working by the side of the boat with bronze saw and clad in a tunic of rough linen with leather apron, was the owner, in appearance much as Siduri had described him. He was swarthy with a broad head, almost bald on top but sporting a thick beard of black plaited hair. Heavy eyebrows sat as dark clouds above a sullen countenance fit to banish even a glimmer of merriment. Not a tall man, he was nevertheless broad of shoulder and endowed more generously still in the girth of his belly. 'Hm,' breathed Gilgamesh, 'the boat looks solid enough, like its owner, though unlike him it's of a graceful and pleasing aspect.'

All this Gilgamesh saw but it was not the boat with its swooping prow or the toiling figure of Urshanabi that continued to engage his attention and cause him, for the time being, to remain out of sight. By the pinewoods on the far side of the cove arose six carved figures. They might at first have been mistaken for the gnarled trunks of dead trees had they not stood in an ordered row. They were equally spaced out and of similar height and breadth, as though placed there by design. Because they were shaded from direct sunlight by trees, it took Gilgamesh a little time to discern their grotesque features. They looked now to be made not of wood but of solid rock. They appeared to have been fashioned in squat parody of the human form - but what individual might have been their precursor he cared not to contemplate. Each stood with folded arms clutching at its body as though in frozen torment. Their eyes were closed tight, their mouths were turned down in expressions of grim resolution.

'By the gods,' he breathed, 'they must be the Stone Ones. They're a misbegotten crew if ever I saw one. I'll wager they keep even the most inquisitive at bay. Huh - wager? I doubt I'd find anyone to offer a contrary opinion. Still, over there is the man I have to speak with, like it or not, and maybe his stone figures are really no more than that.'

Hoping to make little sound, Gilgamesh emerged from the cover of the trees and walked toward the boat. Beneath his feet, however, loose stones crunched loudly enough to betray his presence before he had reached the halfway point. Urshanabi swung about from his task. 'Whad'you want?' he growled. 'No one's allowed down here!'

'I wish to speak to you,' replied Gilgamesh, observing an angry face possessing one eye that appeared unable to align its gaze in quite the same direction as the other, and a twisted mouth whose teeth, where not absent, reminded him of unevenly baked mud bricks. 'I wish to speak to you,' repeated Gilgamesh, 'and I hardly care if I'm allowed here or not since I go wherever it pleases me!'

'Oh, *do* y'now!' declared Urshanabi, jerking his head aside to spit, throwing his saw with a clatter into the boat and glancing at the stone figures. 'You're a big man - big enough to wrestle down an ox, clean-faced or no, but I'll not 'ave no one 'ang about on my patch so bugger off!'

Gilgamesh halted several steps short of the boat. Seeing the intruder was not about to retreat, Urshanabi reached down beside the boat and produced a hefty axe - a large, crude implement but one which Gilgamesh saw he handled as though it weighed no more than a length of sapling. 'Clear off now or I'll chop you in bits!' growled Urshanabi, moving around the prow and advancing hard-eyed. Gilgamesh let down his spear, unshouldered his own axe and stood ready.

Raising his axe high, the boatman dashed forward with a bestial cry and his blade whistled through the air. His intended victim, judging the moment with cool mind and practised eye, leapt aside, bringing down his own weapon to shatter Urshanabi's from his hands then, swinging the shaft around, he struck the butt end hard against the head of his dismayed foe. The man spun about and fell sprawling in the shingle with a loud curse.

'You'll need more than your rustic skills to better me!' declared Gilgamesh, stepping back.

The dazed Urshanabi raised on one arm but, seeing his axe rendered useless, scrambled to his feet and, scattering grit, hastened back toward the boat. Axe in hand, Gilgamesh strode after him. The boat, however, was not Urshanabi's goal for he dashed by it. It was to the Stone Ones he hurried with arms raised high. Gilgamesh sensed there was about to be revealed a far greater danger.

'Aku Sindra!' yelled the boatman, waving his hands whilst jumping up and down before the row of bizarre effigies. 'Aku Sindra!'

He would have uttered the words a third time had not the butt of Gilgamesh's axe once more connected with his head to send him reeling to the ground - this time altogether senseless. Gilgamesh turned to the row of ominous standing figures, assessing each of the six in turn, his hands firm upon the axe. 'What did those words of his mean?' he muttered. 'Ah - did I see them move? No, perhaps the branches swaying above caused the light to shift.'

But something was happening. His attention was drawn to the first figure. Its eyes had opened! With baleful gaze it was watching him! The twisted limbs stirred. The mouth quivered. It drew breath with a serpent hiss.

Gilgamesh sprang forward, raised his axe and brought it down with a terrible crash against the grotesque head, cleaving it to the neck. 'You take on life but just as quickly you'll relinquish it!'

The being shivered. It began to crumble in the manner of dried clay not yet hardened by the sun. But Gilgamesh, in no mood to appraise his handiwork, switched his attention to the next figure. This also had opened its eyes and was beginning to stir. The axe swung a second time to strike with even greater violence and Gilgamesh cried out, 'I will not be thwarted! No damned idol will accomplish what man and beast have failed to do!'

A third, a fourth time his axe flashed through the air, smashing the figures as they stood. The remaining two had not yet shown signs of life but he hardly cared, noting only that when the axe struck they shattered more as decayed stone than as clay, as if their transformation had barely started.

Gilgamesh lowered the axe and leant on it to regain his breath. From the corner of his eye he saw the boatman struggling to rise, one hand clutching the back of his head, the other flat against the ground to keep himself steady. At last he was on his feet, mouth agape in disbelief at the sight of the six ruined idols. 'You - you -!' he blurted whilst staggering toward Gilgamesh, arm raised, fist striking the air. 'D-d'you know what you've done, you meddling bastard! You've destroyed them! You've destroyed the Stone Ones!'

'And preserved my own life, I'm inclined to think,' responded Gilgamesh. Shouldering the axe he stepped around Urshanabi and carried on to recover his spear from where it lay at the other side of the boat. 'Now will you listen in a civilised manner?' he called back.

'Preserved your own life, eh!' called the boatman, tottering after him. 'You could have done that by clearing off in the first place! No one's meant to come 'ere. No one! And now - now the Stone Ones are destroyed! What d'you want - the boat? You wanna smash up or steal the fucking boat? Well take it! Go on - take it you mad bugger! It's little use to anybody now!'

'Steal?' came the reply, 'I've no need to steal anything. I am Gilgamesh, King of Uruk. I would have asked politely for the use of your boat but you didn't have the wits to listen. All you cared to offer me was abuse.'

'Oh, use me boat, was it! And why *my* boat? There are plenty of boats to be 'ad along the coast. Why mine?'

'Because I seek Ziusudra who lives across the Great Water where others will not go - except for you or so I'm told. Is that true or is it not?'

Still rubbing his head, Urshanabi leaned back against the boat, gazed upward then began to laugh. 'Well kiss my arse - King of Uruk! Whatever next! Yes that's true enough but it's only part of the truth. I sail the Great Water, as *you* are pleased to call it but to get where you want we also 'ave to cross the Waters of Death and that's what *everybody* calls it. I carry the things he needs from the outside world. Or did. Only with the Stone Ones could I get the boat through those waters. The gods created them to do just that - but not anymore, no - not after your 'andiwork. If you want Ziusudra for the reasons I think then you've just pissed in yer own beer.' Urshanabi laughed louder still and gestured with his hands, 'King of Uruk, eh! Do kings swim? No? Then maybe you'd better order the waters to part!'

'There must be men enough hereabouts to crew your boat. You can take me to them.'

'They'll cut your throat before they'll set out to cross those waters. You'll find no one to obey yer orders - King of Uruk or king of anywhere else. They'll all stand against you and so will I.'

'By the gods!' declared Gilgamesh, closing on him with levelled spear, 'I have faced perils greater than any man! Perils sent from heaven itself. I'll not see my hopes flow like sand through my fingers. I'll cross the waters in this boat and if its captain is not willing to aid me then he may as well share the same fate as his damnable crew!'

For several heartbeats, Urshanabi directed an eye at him, twice opening his mouth as if to speak. At last he wiped his bulbous, reddened nose on the back of his hand and said, 'Well, King of Uruk, I'm not an unreasonable man, especially when I've a spear shoved at me guts and don't 'ave any say in the matter. But it's a task you'll need to think 'ard on because without the Stone Ones there isn't a crew - whether you like it or not. That leaves two pairs of 'ands to row her instead of six - and she's a hefty craft. Can't be done, can it.'

'Does not the boat have a sail?' asked Gilgamesh, letting down the spear.

'Oh yes, yer lordship, she's got a sail of sorts, y'might say. A small sail.'

'Well, my cantankerous friend, cast in your lot with me and we'll make her a large sail like the ones they use on the rivers of Sumer. You could then ply the waters without need of a crew. What d'you say to that - it's surely preferable to chancing matters as they are?'

Perceiving his life no longer under direct threat, Urshanabi rubbed his bruises, his beard and once more his nose. He pondered over the proposition, glanced aside at the sea, at his demolished Stone Ones, then turned once more to Gilgamesh. 'If it means getting my boat back to work I might consider it.' Again he rubbed his chin. 'All right, we'll need to give 'er a stouter mast and rigging. And I mean *we*. And when - if - we get to the island where he lives, he'll want to know who's buggered up his crew. Even if he doesn't, he'll not care to see you. Ziusudra doesn't want to see or speak with no one. Never did and never will. He renounced contact with everyone a long time ago – especially meddlin' kings.'

'I've come too far to be deterred,' replied Gilgamesh. 'And as for you – you'll need your boat in the future whether you take me on board or not - so let's co-operate for both our sakes and set about doing what we can whilst daylight is still with us. If you furnish rope and cloth for the sail, I will cut timber for the mast and yardarm. It isn't work I'm accustomed to but I've watched them fit out our boats and I dare say you'll be ready enough to correct my errors.'

'Oh, we *are* a man of determination, aren't we!' exclaimed Urshanabi with undisguised sarcasm. 'I wonder you 'aven't made y'self a pair of wings and flown there by willpower alone.'

'Of late, boatman, I think willpower is all I have left.'

***

'Is she sailing well enough?' asked Gilgamesh as they entered open water. Morning sun glittered

360

on a benign sea, the mast creaked and a steady breeze kept the sail taught. The vessel buffeted as they plied on, spray swept across her bow and, benign or no, Gilgamesh found the vast expanse ahead a source of considerable unease.

Seated in the stern the boatman replied tersely, 'Well enough,' as he fixed the tiller at the side of the vessel in position with a cord and glanced up at the sky. 'We'll see how she rides when we're far enough out. That'll be well after midday.'

'Far enough out,' repeated Gilgamesh. 'How long will we be away from the land? What if night falls and the sky is hidden? How will we know our way?'

Urshanabi eyed the sail and tested one of the coarse ropes. From by his side he pulled up a boiled leather flask, twisted out the wooden stopper and took a draught of the contents before replying. 'The Stone Ones knew, whatever the weather or the time of day. Even so, there's a way of finding out if needs be, even in the dark with no stars. Few men know about it – none of 'em kings.'

Not caring to display anxiety, Gilgamesh waited for him to continue but neither man spoke for some time. At last Urshanabi rose from his seat, spat over the side and lumbered along the boat, saying, 'If you want to see something the rest of 'em don't know about, your 'ighness, take a look at this. I'm only showin' you now because we'll maybe need it.'

Swinging by Gilgamesh he reached into a wooden chest that rested amidships and from it lifted a crudely fashioned spindle, hardly longer than a man's hand. It was made of a grey metal

Gilgamesh recognised, the kind of metal that had fallen from the sky near Uruk and from which his own weapons were forged. It was fixed to a thin piece of wood by two cords and the wood was shaped to a point at one end. Urshanabi laid his hand on a copper bowl and, leaning over the side of the boat, scooped water into it. Gilgamesh watched as he held up the bowl on a length of cord and placed the wood, spindle uppermost, into the water. Though the boat rolled a little, Urshanabi was able to keep the bowl steady. Equally steady was the eye fixed upon his passenger as he spoke. 'There, King of Uruk – what d'you make of that?'

'The metal floats because it is attached to the piece of wood,' replied Gilgamesh, steadying himself. 'What am I supposed to make of it?'

'Use yer eyes, man,' scoffed the boatman. 'Better still, use yer finger. Turn the thing around a quarter circle or more then see what 'appens.'

Gripping the side of the boat with one hand, Gilgamesh reached out and pushed the spindle.

'Well,' grinned Urshanabi sardonically, one eye still fixed upon Gilgamesh whilst the other stared disconcertingly past him.

'Ah yes, it swings around to point back the way it did before. How amusing.'

'Oh, 'ow amusing!' mocked the boatman. 'I dare say that's all it would be back in your precious Uruk. But it's more than that 'ere because, you see, it always points in the same direction if you let it. It always tells you which way you're 'eaded, day or night, though it's not so easy when the water's rough.'

'Really, and how does it do that?' asked Gilgamesh, recalling that in Uruk any man who addressed him the way Urshanabi did would be given little or no opportunity to beg forgiveness.

'How, King of Uruk?' he replied, tipping the water overboard and returning to the tiller. 'The gods are in it - that's 'ow. With such a device to guide 'im, a man might go to the ends of the earth and still find his way back 'ome.'

'The ends of the earth. Isn't that where we're headed now?'

'So you might think. Others might think it, too, but I say otherwise.'

Observing him drink once more from the flask, Gilgamesh wondered what it contained. Not water, surely, for he gasped and wiped his lips with each draught.

'Beyond the Great Water I say there 'as to be more land,' Urshanabi continued, sniffing and wiping his nose on the sleeve of his tunic. 'Flocks of birds come in at certain times of the year that must have roosted somewhere out there. Maybe the world goes on forever. More land – more water, then more land. That's what I say whether others agree or not.'

Gilgamesh eyed him uneasily. The land of Sumer was said to be at the world's centre, and in particular the holy city of Nippur where Enlil was venerated. Should the world be so large as this boorish man suggested, thought Gilgamesh, then the status of mankind and all his works must be greatly diminished. There could only be emptiness beyond the Great Waters, even the people of Egypt knew that, though they mistakenly, or so he'd heard, considered their own land also to be at the world's centre.

The sway and creak of the boat, the click of the rigging and thump of the sail, distracted him as a warm breeze sprang up to sweep hair across his face. Gilgamesh looked about, only too aware he was in the hands of the man who had tried to kill him, the man whom he had in turn ill-used. His weapons would avail him nothing under the circumstances because alone, he would have no idea how to return to land. Thoughts of his dead brother entered his mind. 'And what would you say to this, brother Enkidu? Would you advise caution over this journey? Somehow I think you would not though I think you had no more knowledge of the sea than I.'

As if aware of his thoughts, Urshanabi remarked, 'You can't have been this far from land before, majesty. It must seem strange – I mean, surrounded by so much water.'

'Aye, it's another wilderness,' answered Gilgamesh. 'I have travelled many. If you've never seen the deserts, I can tell you they're just as wide.'

Urshanabi spat over the side of the boat, drank from the flask again and looked back at him. Gilgamesh continued to find his gaze disturbing, never being sure from one moment to the next which of the man's eyes was fixed upon him and at which he ought to be looking as they talked. And what *was* in that flask? Not water, not beer. There were terra-cotta pitchers of both, protected by straw and fixed with lashings against the sides of the boat close to the mast. Urshanabi had removed the stoppers to ladle out a little of each from time to time. The boatman noted his interest in the flask and leered, 'The people of our parts distil a good liquor from their fruits. Would your 'ighness care to tickle the royal palette with a little drop?'

Gilgamesh declined. Apart from other considerations, the constant motion of the boat, unlike anything he had experienced on the rivers of Sumer, was causing him discomfort. 'I will tell you about my brother,' he said in an attempt to focus his mind. 'I'll, tell you about dangers we faced together, about the grief his death caused me and how I discovered ancient tablets that led me here. It is my wish that you should understand because I know the bitterness you feel toward me.'

Urshanabi grinned, fondled his beard and said, 'All right yer 'ighness, go on then.'

The afternoon passed into the light-breezed darkness of a star-strewn, crescent-mooned dusk as Gilgamesh explained the circumstances that had brought him so far from home. Urshanabi sat nearby, listening in silence with an occasional gulp from his flask. Of the jewel-laden orchard and of Siduri the tavern keeper, Gilgamesh said nothing, though as he recalled the look on her face the day he departed he experienced, too late, pangs of remorse.

The appearance of Inanna's star and the star-patterns in the sky had offered consolation in their familiarity but beneath the restless water Gilgamesh imagined dreadful, dark forms that might rise suddenly from the depths to devour their now seemingly fragile craft. Such matters seemed of no concern to Urshanabi. At length, Gilgamesh slept fitfully, voices and images crowding his mind; sometimes his dead brother, sometimes Shamkhat and of Shannu, the temple boy who he hoped was watching over her.

***

'You see now it's light enough, 'ighness, the land we left behind us yesterday is gone. Toward the end of this day we'll find the island in sight.'

The words brought Gilgamesh reassurance though his limbs ached from the cramped position he had occupied near the mast of the boat. 'But in between,' continued Urshanabi,' we'll 'ave to go through what 'elps keep Ziusudra safe from the rest of the world. We'll be obliged to cross the Waters of Death.' With a bushy-faced leer he added, 'I do 'ope the royal lungs are up to it.'

Gilgamesh, rising awkwardly and steadying himself against the wooden planking, made his way past Urshanabi to the bow where he gazed into a sunlit expanse. The breeze was fresh and steady, the air clear. 'I see nothing ahead of us,' he commented. 'What are we to fear that gives it such a name?'

'You'll see soon enough,' grinned Urshanabi, his tongue exploring the gaps in his teeth like an inquisitive eel, 'Oh, yes, very soon now you will.'

'If you and that outlandish crew of yours survive this peril,' asked Gilgamesh, 'then why shouldn't I?'

'The Stone Ones were immune to it and they rowed damned 'ard – that's what got me through. Stone arms and stone arses – that's what did it. Without them – well, you'd better pray to whatever gods will be taking notice back in Uruk that this wind stays with us. If it doesn't, we'll end up with the rest of the poor buggers who never made it back to shore.'

366

'Then why can't we sail around this peril?'

'Why? Because it stretches a long way. Because it shifts 'ere and there so you never know quite where it's goin' to be.'

Gilgamesh watched him leave the tiller and produce from the bottom of the boat two lengths of none too clean linen cloth, one of which he held out, saying. 'You'll soon need this, 'ighness. And when I say so, we must go to the pitchers and soak these in fresh water – understand?'

Gilgamesh examined the grubby cloth in puzzled silence - until something else attracted his attention. Across the water ahead drifted wisps of pallid vapour, coiling close above the surface then writhing upward to be swept away by the breeze. As the boat sailed closer, the sea in places appeared white and effervescent, patches forming, spreading, disappearing as the water rose and fell in sluggish heave. An odour, acrid and sulphurous, assailed his throat. It reminded him of the forges in Uruk but soon became worse. Then much worse.

'Now!' called Urshanabi, pulling the wooden stopper from one of the pitchers and plunging in his cloth. 'Soak the cloth and shove it 'ard over your face. Keep it there until I remove mine. Meanwhile, stay low as you can in the bottom of the boat!'

Not inclined to argue, Gilgamesh did just that as Urshanabi scuttled back to crouch in the stern, his face all but concealed by the wet cloth, his hand gripping the tiller. The boat rode on in a keen wind, surrounded now by vapours that scurried about sail and mast. Gilgamesh clasped the cloth tighter to his face but kept an eye on the sail, saying to himself,

367

'May the winds that aided us in the Cedar Forest be with us now.'

He began to gasp and cough, as did Urshanabi, though his face was pressed close to the pitch-sealed planks of the boat where the air was less tainted. There he remained as the vessel buffeted and the timbers groaned by his ear. An eternity seemed to pass before he turned his face to the sky, seeing it still hazed by vapour and realising that before long he would be unable to breathe at all and must surely choke to death. 'My throat,' he coughed, squeezing tight his eyes, 'my lungs – they're assailed by some demon!'

'Hang on, majesty!' came the muffled voice of Urshanabi. 'We're almost out of it!'

When the air began to clear, when at last Gilgamesh could draw breath, he rose gasping to his knees, the wet cloth still held close to his mouth and nose.

'We're safely through, 'ighness!' announced Urshanabi, letting down his cloth.

'Well, my friend,' coughed Gilgamesh, doing likewise and grasping the side of the boat for support, 'if that is something you experience each time you cross these waters then you have my admiration. I should not be pleased to do it again.'

'Sometimes it's not so bad,' said Urshanabi, glancing over his shoulder and stroking his beard. 'I've known it worse but this time I'd call it average. And now we're clear of it I'll tell you a tale I've told no one else. At least you might believe it after what you claim *you've* seen.' One eye fixed Gilgamesh intently, the other peered by as he took a swig from his flask. 'Not many years ago I was passing through where we just was when it began to grow dark. It wasn't long after midday, see, but when I looked up at the sun I saw it bitten into. Devoured by darkness! Never 'ad I been so scared as on that day. So scared, 'ighness, that I ordered the Stone Ones to turn back but they ignored me. They went on as if nothing mattered. The sun's disk vanished altogether. It became like - like a jewelled ring. The sky was almost as night though only 'alf the day 'ad passed. I covered me face as we just did but I 'ad to watch, oh yes, because I thought the end of the world was on us.'

'Hm,' offered Gilgamesh, 'Sounds grim.'

'But there's more,' continued Urshanabi, moving closer. 'I looked over the side of the boat and in the darkness I saw – yes, what did I see? I saw fires burnin' - fires burnin' under the water! What d'you make of *that*, your 'ighness? As farfetched as your tales – eh? And if you expect me to believe yours then I'll expect you to believe mine because it's definitely true.'

'I'll not dispute your tale, friend Urshanabi. You're not the most amiable of men but I believe you're honest. In Sumer, also, we have witnessed the sun blotted from the sky as you describe but Utu is strong and will not be vanquished. Our priests are able to predict when it will happen and claim it is sent as a warning to mankind. As for the fires you saw beneath the water that, too, I will accept because in my travels I also have seen many strange -.' From the corner of his eye, Gilgamesh became aware of something too important to ignore. 'Is that land ahead or do my eyes deceive me?'

'Your eyes don't deceive you, King of Uruk. It's an island surrounded by sheer cliffs and treacherous rocks with only one way in. It's the island you seek. It's where Ziusudra lives!'

CHAPTER 10
VOICE OF THE IMMORTAL

A barefoot, mop-haired boy stood watching, one hand raised to shield his eyes against the lowering sun, the other outstretched to steady himself against the trunk of a gnarled tree. Directly ahead of him the ground fell away in a rutted, bushy slope that swept down to a cove edged by bare rock and short stretches of dark beach. To the left of the cove, like a decaying tusk, the land curved gently downward into a sunlit sea. There, the beach was wider and a wooden jetty reached out dark against the water's glitter. What held his attention was still some distance out, silhouetted against molten silver. The vessel was familiar but there was something wrong. In shape and size, and in the prow that rose and fell to the dance of the waves it could only be Urshanabi's boat. But the sail was not familiar. It was not the small, vivid red and white sail that always signalled his approach but a plainer, much larger cloth. And the oar blades that should have flashed in afternoon light – where were they?

When the boat drew into the bay he moved back until foliage obscured him from view. A little longer he watched then, gathering up the long linen kilt that hung knotted about his waist, he turned and ran.

***

'There's no need to take your weapons,' said Urshanabi, 'There's no wild creatures or no one to steal anythin'. You can leave 'em in the boat.'

'Leave them?' responded Gilgamesh, slinging the axe over his shoulder. The sword belt was already fastened about his waist and his hand fell next to the spear which he held aloft as he scrambled over the side to join Urshanabi on the none too solid jetty. 'No, I'll not leave them. They are my companions. They stay close to me always.' Following the boatman along the rough path, his legs proved less steady than he would have wished. 'But weapons or no, my friend,' he continued, 'I'm mighty grateful to be on dry land once more and I thank the gods for your sailing skills.'

'Why thank the gods?' replied Urshanabi as they began to climb. 'Such skills were passed down through my family. My father, 'is father and those who went before, all sailed these waters and came 'ere. And always with the Stone Ones – until you showed up, that is.'

'Then you have achieved more than they ever did and ought to be proud of it. Now let's get a move on. My journey is almost ended and patience no longer keeps me company. I will confront whatever awaits me.'

'Confront you say!' mocked Urshanabi. 'And what d'you imagine you're goin' to confront oh King of Uruk? Your beast of the forest - your Bull of 'eaven? No, the one who lives 'ere isn't going to leap out with open jaws or come charging at you with lowered 'orns – you'll see.'

During their trek upward, Gilgamesh had ample opportunity to look about. The breeze blew pleasantly warm but the air was fresher than that of his homeland and carried a hint of growing things more exotic than might be found in the orchards of

Sumer. He said nothing as they reached level ground but followed Urshanabi along the path toward a thick cluster of pine trees that part obscured the path beyond. Glancing down to the cove, he was surprised at how small and insignificant the boat appeared and how vast and empty was the sea. 'Brother Enkidu -,' the words passed through his mind, 'if only you were here now to see what I have seen – if only.'

'Ziusudra's place is beyond those trees,' said Urshanabi, 'but it's late afternoon. At this time of the day it's his custom to relax away from the sun. He might not care to be disturbed until dusk – not even by visiting royalty.'

'Is that so!' exclaimed Gilgamesh. 'Well I have not travelled to the ends of the earth to be treated like a common petitioner. Perhaps you jest, friend Urshanabi. If it is a jest then I don't find it to my liking.'

Wheeling about angrily the boatman declared, 'Do you not, your 'ighness! Well I don't jest and *you'll* need to conjure up a little modesty - 'ard as that may be. If you were ever king of anythin', you're king of nothin' on this island! Nothin' at all! This is Ziusudra's realm by decree of the gods and only he is master of it!'

Gilgamesh regarded coldly the less than appealing face that scowled a hands breadth from his. Then pushing by, he hurried ahead through the line of trees with a vexed Urshanabi striding close behind. The path, he perceived, ran through gardens and an orchard where fruits ripened mellow in the late sun amidst the lazy buzz of insects. A short distance beyond the orchard, surrounded by beds of brightly coloured flowers, stood a wooden house of handsome aspect and ample dimension. Green pastures rose up beyond the house toward the centre of the island - a tranquil landscape where cattle and sheep grazed.

'A kingdom of peace and plenty if ever I saw one,' muttered Gilgamesh as he strode on. 'Can there be another like this in our troubled world?'

Seeing no one about, he determined to head straight for the house where he would beat on the door should it not be opened to his call. But in passing a grove of trees to one side of the path, he spotted the boy seated on a rock. To one side of the rock, a shaded hammock hung suspended between two trees. The boy saw him at the same time and rising up, touched the resting figure in the hammock while gesturing frantically toward Gilgamesh, his hands began moving in animated frenzy, fingers dancing over palms. Gilgamesh hesitated some ten paces away as the play of hands ceased and the boy stepped back. From the hammock arose the occupant, letting himself down with considerable difficulty before turning to observe the stranger.

Gilgamesh had approached over half way before stopping abruptly. A gasp of revulsion would have left his mouth had he not caught his breath. Before him in plain, loose tunic of soft wool that seemed to hang in mid-air as though devoid of material content, stood a figure of modest height but shocking aspect. The hairless head appeared little more than a skull enclosed within a shrunken, translucent membrane of blemished skin that, to Gilgamesh, matched in appearance the sun-dried flesh of a desiccated corpse. Set within the pallid mask that was his face, polyp eyes gazed from bone sockets at the stubbled features of the newcomer as if the latter's stature, complement of weapons and garb of lion skin were not of the slightest importance. The boy stepped forward, looked closely at Gilgamesh then once more raised his arms to resume his rapid choreography of hands and fingers. In age and stature he reminded Gilgamesh of the temple boy in Uruk, though whilst Shannu's eyes flashed with mischief, this boy's features spoke more of pain and mistrust.

'You must excuse the child,' grated this grotesque parody of a man, smiling weakly to reveal long, irregular teeth whose gums had receded to the bones of his upper and lower jaws. Gesturing a bird's claw hand at the boy, he continued, 'He was taken as a slave by pirates. It was they who cut out his tongue. When their ship was driven onto the rocks at the far side of the island, only he survived. He is afraid to leave the island and must live out his days here.' He hesitated then added, 'But I have omitted to greet you properly, stranger, even though you have yet to announce yourself.'

For some moments Gilgamesh continued to regard him. The man's blood vessels showed clearly. The pitted bones of the skull itself were discernible. He looked even older than the impression of moments ago – a living carcase – one exhumed after many days beneath the earth. Gilgamesh stepped back in case the man should reach out to touch him.

'I am Gilgamesh,' he announced. 'I am King of – I am from Uruk in the land of Sumer. I am here to speak with Ziusudra. Do I take it you are a member of his household?'

'Oh, then you have come from beyond the mountains of Mashu before setting sail with Urshanabi,' responded the man. 'That does surprise me. You have travelled far and must have suffered much hardship on your journey. No one from Uruk has ever been here. No one at all from the land of Sumer, though they may have tried. But you are care-worn and weary, that is plain to see. My first duty must be to offer you rest and refreshment before you leave our island. You will I trust find our fare worthy of a king's table for I think King of Uruk is what you may well be.'

'Leave!' exclaimed Gilgamesh, thumping the butt of his spear against the ground. 'I came here to see Ziusudra. You should take me to him now!'

'But -,' cut in Urshanabi, stepping forward to point at the one Gilgamesh regarded as little more than a bizarre apparition.

'No, wait!' the man exclaimed. 'Obviously our friend Urshanabi has not made it clear. I am the one you seek. I am Ziusudra.'

'You!' responded Gilgamesh. 'But you are -.'

'Just a frail, unassuming creature,' he interrupted. 'And I gather from your expression not in the least appealing. Ah, well - I do understand.'

'He never asked me what y'looked like,' shrugged the boatman, 'and I never thought to tell 'im. We were too busy with other things – not least sailin' the damned boat.'

'Ah,' said Ziusudra, his mouth broadening to a ghastly skeletal grin, 'so you expected someone of great wealth and power, surrounded by retainers and enthroned in the midst of luxury. I'm sorry to disappoint you, my friend. I have none of those attributes, nor did I possess them in Sumer in those distant times.'

'Yes,' replied Gilgamesh, inwardly confused, 'I imagined you would be a man of high status. According to the tablets and the priests of Uruk – of all the cities throughout Sumer, the Ziusudra I seek was elevated by the gods above all mankind. He was made ruler of his own realms. He was blessed with immortality.'

'Blessed, you say? Well that's another matter. But this island *is* my realm, man from Uruk. Call it my kingdom if it pleases you. You may equally well call it my prison since I am bound never to leave, though nowhere could I find a fairer place of incarceration. Urshanabi carries here those items and novelties of which I would otherwise know nothing and I pay him well in silver. Silver is plentiful on the island but is otherwise of little use to me.'

His attention turned next to Urshanabi. 'And speaking of the boat, the boy says you arrived without the Stone Ones. Why is that? They were created from the very beginning to aid such as yourself in maintaining service to me.'

Urshanabi cleared his throat, remained silent but looked hard at Gilgamesh, who answered, 'I perceived the Stone Ones as a threat. I destroyed them to protect my own life as I would any man or beast that harboured such intent. I knew nothing of their purpose other than that they were your boatman's crew.'

'You destroyed them?' grated Ziusudra, turning his dread gaze back to Urshanabi. 'And you, I suspect, did not allow for sufficient dialogue to avoid this grievous mishap.'

'Maybe I was a bit quick off the mark,' shrugged Urshanabi, uncomfortably, 'but it was for your good. Anyway, no one else is supposed to come 'ere – that's orders, isn't it.'

'That is true but, alas, the rule is now broken and cannot be unbroken. And our visitor – our *royal* visitor as he claims and indeed as he appears to be – stands bemused at our situation. He arrived prepared to wrest the secrets from an unwilling Ziusudra but the Ziusudra who stands before him is not equipped to offer battle in order to protect that which the gods bestowed. Nor does he need to be. What a disappointment for our worthy guest.'

'Yes, I came here to gain that secret by whatever means,' responded Gilgamesh, 'and you should understand why.'

'Perhaps I should understand; indeed I *will* understand, but first -,' he turned to the boy who stood patiently by, 'first I will have my wife prepare bread, meat and wine. And whilst we eat together, I will listen to your tale for as long as it takes to recount.'

Hearing him, the boy hurried off to the house, no doubt, thought Gilgamesh, to convey Ziusudra's wishes in the only manner available to him.

'The sky grows dark and I must tend to my boat,' said Urshanabi, 'I'll keep 'er company for the night. I've 'eard this man's yarns and I've little enough of my own to add.'

***

'So now we are alone, man from Uruk, or should I say, Man of Uruk; alone with the wood fire and the night with which to share our words, and good wine to loosen our tongues. I do not think, though, a lack of wine would inhibit your account. I will listen with patience as it is a commodity I possess in boundless measure. In all these years only our boatman and his predecessors ever came to this island, apart from that poor unfortunate boy, of course. I'm told others have tried to follow but for them the Waters of Death were truly that. Fishermen and pirates from other, more distant lands sometimes approach but the winds and the prospect of those high cliffs deter them. Now you have arrived here with your tale – a man from the world I once knew. You come as an eagle from beyond the mountains to stir for me the waters of a half-forgotten past. I will savour your every word, so I will. Ah, so I will.'

Each sat on a rock with the fire as a barrier between them. It allowed Gilgamesh a degree of comfort since what he least desired was close proximity, let alone the cold touch of Ziusudra's hand.

'My tale is simple and many people know it,' began Gilgamesh, at last able to gaze into Ziusudra's wide-staring eyes - eyes that had seen all that they wished to see. More, perhaps, than they could any longer bear. 'My brother and my one true companion,' he continued, 'the one who stood with me in times of mortal danger and showed me light when I was blind - he was taken by the hand of death. His flame was stifled when it burned brightest. In his death was the portent of my own.

379

When I saw it, the affairs of this world that had so consumed me were no longer important. When it seemed possible that a man really had been given the gift eternal life I wished to know about it in the hope of escaping my brother's fate.' But even as he spoke, uncertainty dogged his thoughts. Could this decayed husk of a man represent the gift of any god other than one ill-disposed to humanity?

Ziusudra placed more wood on the fire. It responded with a crack and a hissing gush of flame to swarm glowing fireflies on the night air. Gilgamesh studied the hollow features, lurid in the firelight's glow but even at a brief glance in the shadiest streets of Uruk, Ziusudra could only have passed for someone with death tugging hard at his gown.

The ancient man insisted on knowing more of Enkidu and the adventures the two had undertaken together, and afterwards, of the journey Gilgamesh had made in order to reach his present destination. In his desire for detail he savoured each phrase as a rare and delicate morsel. Some parts of the account he had Gilgamesh repeat more than once. But all through the narrative squirmed the ultimate question, becoming ever more restless until Gilgamesh could hold it back no longer.

'I have spoken at length about myself,' he said, 'but I'm no closer to the answer I sought than when I first set foot on this island. You know my question well enough. Surely there's no better time than this to answer it.'

'As I listened to your tale,' replied Ziusudra, the bones of his skull click, click, clicking as he went on. 'I considered how best that question might be addressed, but it is not easy. Let me first state what you, what everyone knows: immortality was never intended for mankind. His greatest works may long outlive him but no house, no palace, not even the mightiest of temples will stand forever. When the towns and cities of Sumer are abandoned, what will become of them?'

'I have no wish to think about that,' replied Gilgamesh, still much disturbed yet mesmerised by the spectral horror that was Ziusudra. 'It is you I've risked everything to reach. It's finding the secret of what you have attained that has driven me this far. I have begged nothing from any man but have taken freely what I considered mine by right even though justice and good sense did not always illuminate my path. But you, Ziusudra - I ask in all humility that you recount your tale. If afterwards you tell me to leave - and I'm quite aware that is what you want - I will return to Urshanabi's boat and he can take me away from here. But I must know.'

A dire truth hovered in the night. It wished to enter into the thoughts of Gilgamesh with crushing finality but he would not, dared not, grant it admission.

Ziusudra remained silent, his attention for a time held by the glowing wood. There had been no hint of censure or condescension in his manner, only forbearance. 'I will relate my tale, man from Uruk,' he said at last. 'I will tell it freely with as little diversion as I'm able, although brevity is of little consequence in a desert of years without end.' Logs settled on the fire. They flared yellow tongues. They spilled wavering shadows of the two figures into obscure night as, with a voice of burned brick grating upon burned brick he began his tale.

'I expect you know the town of Shurrupak well enough. It lies on the river between Uruk and Nippur. In my youth it was a populous city but because you have said nothing of it, I assume it must now be of lesser status than Uruk. In my day I saw it grow ever more prosperous, ever more busy until it overflowed with people. They came in from the country, even from the mountains because the opportunities, diversions and pleasures of Shurrupak were many. Always they came until the population spilled out beyond the city wall to consume orchard and field.

I held land and property within the city wall and outside it, passed down by my family through several generations. The dwelling places I let for profit. The demand was unrelenting, though I always endeavoured to deal in fairness with those who needed a roof over their heads. In time I sold most of my land within or near by the city to those who wished to build on it. Because of that I was able to buy greater tracts of pasture further out. That in turn enabled me to increase the size of my herds. Even so, the demand for food was insatiable and the city began to swallow up the fields, and arable land further out. My family and I lived relatively modest lives though I could not help but accumulate greater wealth in gold, silver and livestock.

But it was plain to see how ill-disciplined life within the city had become. The taverns were filled to overflowing. Indeed they never closed, and as a consequence the streets of the city were given over to displays of drunken lewdness. The temples were increasingly neglected until their precincts became the stalking grounds of criminals, outcasts and scavenging dogs. Yes, people squandered their silver on nameless vices whilst the altars of the gods remained empty and silent.

Most of the priests, led by the king himself, had forsaken their duties in order to assuage themselves in every vile manner. And the noise – the clamour! Not just the sound of commerce and revelry but the unending clash of cymbals and the beating drums of trader and entertainer alike. Oh, yes, braying drunkards and barking dogs. There were all too many of them. You walked the streets hard put to avoid treading in vomit and worse. The very earth rang with the tumult of their voices by day and night. Yes, my friend, what should have been a civilised oasis of humanity had become a cesspit – no, a bloated carcase heaving with maggots, ready to burst, to discharge its foulness over all the land. But it was not only Shurrupak, though Shurrupak was then the greatest of cities. With the fertility of the soil, with good harvests, with burgeoning commerce, all the towns of Sumer followed in the wake of Shurrupak and likewise festered in debauchery.

I gave up our home in Shurrupak to find peace and safety for my family - a place where the air was sweet, where the maladies of the city would not taint our lives. I won't pretend we lived as rustics - dear me, no. We had our comforts, we retained our slaves, but nobody could accuse us of ostentation. My sheep and cattle I often helped to tend. In no way did I despise those simple labours. Often, too, I found much pleasure in the company of the honest people who worked under me. Always I did what I could to help if any or one of their family suffered hardship.

One day, I set out walking without even my dogs for company – why, I cannot now recall. Likely enough I simply needed to be alone with my thoughts. Yes, there was much on my mind. After a while I came upon a shepherd's hut, abandoned when the nearby wells became bitter. There, I sat in silence on the earthen bench, sheltered from the heat of the afternoon sun. The air was still and very humid. How long I had rested, I cannot say because I closed my eyes and slept a little.

I was woken up by someone calling my name. It was a deep voice, clear but very calm. Naturally, I imagined I had been dreaming. Then it came again. As it passed through the reed wall of the hut, I felt there and then it was the voice of no ordinary mortal.'

Gilgamesh took up his goblet of wine. The fire spat and flared brighter, shining in the protuberant eyes of Ziusudra as he continued his tale.

'The voice said to me, "I am Enki of the sweet waters, of wisdom and learning."

Such simple words they were, but so overwhelming. I listened, still not convinced as to the state of my mind – still not certain if the world of dreaming had retained a hold on my thoughts. When he spoke again I knew I was fully awake and master of my senses. "Do not fear me, Ziusudra. I come as a friend to bring you warning. The gods are angered. They have turned against mankind. Those created to serve us no longer do so but engage in drunkenness and debauchery to a degree even we find offensive. The clamour of humanity threads the sky with brazen ribbons that coil upward to rattle the very fabric of heaven. Even Great Anu, more distant than the rest, is disturbed. He asks what is the reason for such discord. Enlil, who knows his mind and forges the blade whilst the father of the gods merely contemplates furnace and anvil, has decreed the fate of humanity."

'Fate? I asked. Is there to be a punishment? Are we to suffer famine? Will he send a plague of mice to devour our grain?

"Much more than that," he replied. "Enlil has decreed a flood – a deluge far greater than Sumer ever witnessed. Not the dykes nor the strongest walls of city and palace will hold back the water."

'When I found the courage to question why he had come to the modest abode of a shepherd to warn me of it, he answered, "I speak to you, Ziusudra, because I helped create mankind. I guided Aruru when she cast the forms of man and woman in our own image; and though Enlil is determined to end human existence, I do not want him to succeed. You are a good man, Ziusudra. You have acquired riches without deceit. To those beneath you and to the beasts of the field, you have shown kindness where others would have disdained. Nor have you ever boasted over your wealth and your possessions. It is you I have chosen to preserve the seed of this land. You must sell your pastures and your property then with that silver you must have others build a boat. Into the boat you must take your household, your craftsmen and their women. Take a pair of all the creatures of field and farm so that their line may afterwards continue with yours. Do this, Ziusudra, and you will live on."

'I - I was disbelieving. I asked him how I could ever achieve what he wished. I asked what the king, the elders and the people of the city would think about it. I feared they would mock me.'

"Tell them," he answered, "that the wrath of Enlil is turned against you - that you must take your family, your possessions and leave Shurrupak. It is a halfway truth after all and what you keep from others can be no lie. You will have all the wealth you need to pay the craftsmen and builders. Do as I tell you, Ziusudra. I will not speak to you of this again."

'But, I asked, how was I meant to build such a vessel when I had little knowledge of ships. Apart from that, nothing so grand had ever been attempted. I waited for an answer but there was none. When I arose I began to think that this after all must have been an illusion, or worse, a jest contrived by someone who sought to make a fool of me. Someone who even as I sat there might be hurrying off to tell others how easily I had been duped. The land about the hut was open but when I stepped outside there was no one to be seen. However, there *was* something that truly did astonish me. Close by on the ground lay a clay slab, baked as though in a kiln. It was inscribed with great artistry in both text and diagram. I fell to my knees so I could study it as I knew I had to. On it was set out the manner in which the boat was to be built – its dimensions, the quantity of materials as well as the time that would be needed to do it. I tell you, Gilgamesh of Uruk, for as long as daylight remained, I studied those instructions with, I'm sure, the help of Enki. Had a troupe of grumbling bears lumbered past or a herd of wild cattle stampeded by, I would have remained unaware, so engrossed was I. The sun was sinking below the horizon before I was satisfied that I understood and could remember sufficiently what had been set out so that I could begin the task. Even so, I attempted to lift the slab, intending to return to my house with it in case my family doubted my tale. It was a foolish endeavour. As I struggled to raise it from the ground it crumbled to dust. Yes, it returned to the earth from which it had been moulded.'

'But they believed you in the end,' said Gilgamesh.

'Yes, they believed, or made out they did as I was after all head of our house. Many times I was questioned and often I was obliged to repeat my tale. But with each telling my resolve strengthened. With silver and gold I earned from the sale of my arable lands I bought all the good timber from Shurrupak and other towns nearby. I hired carpenters and craftsmen. I called in the best scribes to set down the details so these could be related to the workmen who were themselves unable to read. They all carried out their allotted tasks because I paid them very well for each day's work to avoid delays or disputes. As the workforce grew, I brought in wheat and barley for their bread and porridge and fruit from my orchards. The luxury of meat they also enjoyed because I had most of my sheep and cattle slaughtered to provide it. Beer and olive oil flowed to them like a river.

Workshops, forges and bakeries sprang up close by as the boat began to take shape. Children hurried back and forth to the town to bring dishes from the potteries and coils of rope from the winders. By the riverbank my boat grew, her hull standing like a city wall thick enough to withstand a siege and supported by stout cedar beams. Long before the decks had been put in place, everyone agreed she could never be dragged to the water, such was her bulk and weight. Certainly I could see that was true but still the work proceeded because I kept on paying for it. Men and boys scrambled everywhere. The boat was a thriving nest of activity. Next came the vessels of melted pitch to seal her planks and tar to coat her hull and decks.

By this time all my properties in the city and much of what I owned outside it were sold off. Seeing how I squandered my wealth the people said my wits had been driven from me by demons. They said my boat was the greatest folly ever conceived by man. Even the most profligate of kings, they claimed, had never set his hand to anything so preposterous. Oh, and I was accused amongst other things of creating a general shortage of good timber. I dare say they were right about that.

Once the boat was completed, I took on board those goods that were of value to myself and my family. Much of what remained of my silver and gold I shared amongst my workers. On the allotted day I took inside the animals with the fodder they would require and all the seed and fruits that had been put aside in the fields close by. Last of all to come aboard were my family, my craftsmen and their women. Once confined to the heat and darkness of the vessel a few of them changed their minds and went away saying, as did many others, that I was possessed and my power of reason turned to chaff. The thought of returning to Shurrupak to squander the silver they had earned was too great a temptation.

During this time, people had come also from Nippur, from Kish, yes, and from Uruk as well as other towns many days away to look at the boat, such was her fame. They camped under the stars in their thousands to witness what most regarded as a monument to madness. Yes, friend Gilgamesh, by then we felt ourselves under siege.

The time given to me by Enlil had arrived. The vessel was completed. Many that had gathered about during that last day began to disperse with some of the vendors and entertainers closing their stalls. In the evening, more of those who at first had joined me left without a word and did not return. A full third of my people had deserted and I feared more would follow because they suffered much discomfort. To make matters worse, rumour was afoot that in a bout of drunkenness the King of Shurrupak had declared the next day a festival and decreed my boat would be burned at the end of it. They said it would be the greatest spectacle Shurrupak ever saw and that he and all the people of the city would gather around to witness it illuminate the night.

I tell you my friend, though I sacrificed to the gods and set guards to keep watch, never was any man so assailed with doubt and anguish. I lay awake in the darkness and considered what I had done with my land, my herds and my estates. I feared I might soon be revealed as the greatest fool that ever lived. I feared I would find myself rendered destitute and rejected by those closest to me. I remember well how it was the night of my profoundest suffering. I dreaded the coming dawn as others dread the horrors of the netherworld.'

The fire burned steadily and seeing Ziusudra refill his goblet, Gilgamesh did likewise, saying, 'What you undertook would test any man's faith to the limit. But if you had faltered, if you had found it too great a challenge to uphold. What then?'

'Yes, what then?' sighed Ziusudra. 'I made up my mind that should the next day bring nothing new I would send every man, woman and beast from the boat, set fire to it myself and remain on board to perish in the flames.' He drank from the goblet, copper scraping against his teeth, then placed it aside to glance up at the stars. 'Before the sun arose that morning the sky was clear. Already, crowds of people were approaching us from the city. At the sight of them I considered my life must soon end and my soul consumed in a pyre of shame.

Then I looked to the north and I saw clouds building on the horizon.' Ziusudra raised skeletal hands to emphasise the vision he wished to impart. 'They welled up dark and ominous like the boiling of some great cauldron. They rolled across to obscure the newly risen sun. They swept on angrily, reaching over the sky like a vast hand to darken the world from horizon to horizon. I ordered the main hatches closed but remained alone inside a deck cabin to witness what was to come next. As I looked on, the wind sprang up. It grew stronger, quickly becoming a gale that cried with the voice of despairing souls. Those coming from the city hurried back to take shelter whilst others still close by our boat fought to hold on to their tents.

As quickly as it had arisen, the wind calmed. For a while there was a tension in the air I cannot describe. Large drops of water began to splash here and there about the deck. Then the rain intensified. Then it was as if the gates of heaven had been thrown open. Flames tore the sky, thunder rolled over us like a thousand armies beating their drums of war. Some of the people below ran to the boat for shelter. They began to call for help but I could do nothing. The sides were too high and the logs supporting our hull were too steep or wet for them to climb. The winds returned, this time with greater fury. The Annunaki, rising from the netherworld, brought fire and the crash of battle to the skies. Ishkur who is the storm, coursed over the land. He filled the sky with his wrath and shook the very timbers beneath us. The rains fell in such quantity that they cut from view the city and the land about it. Errakal, who is ruin and destruction, rode amok to rip trees from the ground and crush the fields of grain. All about our vessel was turmoil. I was witness to a world plunged into chaos!

Throughout that day rain continued in great torrents. Water churned below our boat and I knew the rivers must have long since burst their banks. By the time I judged it must be evening the land was flooded, the water deepening and the storm bestriding Sumer like a raging beast. I quitted the deck through fear of being swept overboard because the cabin in which I sheltered seemed about to be wrenched from its fastenings. I went below to find the sleep that had for so long eluded me but sleep did not come easily. My people called out, cattle bellowed in panic but had they stampeded over the deck, still they would have made less clamour above than did the storm. Sleep visited me briefly but when I awoke the boat was moving! Yes, she was moving, and I knew we were afloat! When I peered through the hatch I could not tell the time of day and saw only that the storm raged as though it would never cease. The currents had taken full charge and they were carrying us to who knew where.

That morning the thunder and lightning ceased but the rain continued unabated through day and night until all hope of salvation was wrested from us. Some declared we ought to have remained in Shurrupak, thinking at least our misery would have been of lesser duration. The boat heaved like a living thing, her timbers groaned aloud and most aboard were sick - some crying out for death. We felt ourselves sacrificed without hope on an altar of calamity. We prayed often to the gods for redemption or annihilation – anything rather than to continue as we were.

Six days and seven nights of tumult we judged had passed during which the boat had preserved her cargo - if not from tribulation, most certainly from drowning. On that blessed seventh day, the storm lessened. I went up on deck to find the wind dying and the clouds thinning. As I watched, the clouds broke apart, allowing the divine rays of the sun to fall across the waters. A calm descended and that empty desert of water, for such it appeared, became flat as polished copper. Here and there floated bodies - human as well as animal. I was certain that many if not all of the people we had left behind must by then have been turned to clay.

Over the following days, not even the tops of hills could be seen breaking the surface. We were convinced the waters must recede, but when – and how long would it take? Our food and our beer were running low as was feed for our livestock. Later, I let free a dove, hoping it would show us in which direction dry land lay. It soon returned, which meant there was no land to be found. Another day or so passed and I released a swallow. That also came back and so more days we waited. Next I freed a raven and we watched it circle about before heading eastward. The raven did not return. After giving thanks to the gods, after making our sacrifices, we hoisted sail and set course eastward also.

Here was the first dry land we came upon, though we did not realise how far we had travelled. When the waters had receded, when we saw we were on an island with no other in sight, we considered we must be the only survivors in all of Sumer. But it is strange how the mind works, is it not? It was our first night ashore and in a dream I found myself at a gathering of the gods in some great hall. I stood to one side, listening to what was said but I was a ghost, invisible to all except Lord Enki, who three times looked at me. When Lord Enlil stepped forward many turned their anger on him for bringing such disaster upon Sumer. A famine or a plague, they said, would have chastened mankind but the flood had gone too far. They spoke my name and said that but for me others might inherit the land – others who did not know the gods of Sumer and their ways. Ziusudra, they said, should be rewarded with something beyond the reach of ordinary men.

When I awoke, I thought I was alone with my wife in the darkness. Perhaps I was still in that other world, perhaps not, but I realised after a moment that someone else was there. From the deeper shadows emerged a figure whose radiance shone out to fall across our bed. My wife, too, was awake but neither of us dared speak as he moved close to look down on us. Oh, I knew who it was. How, I cannot say, but I knew. Even as he reached out, even as his fingers touched my forehead, his name echoed through my mind. Lord Enlil!

'And by that touch,' said Gilgamesh, 'you both were granted eternal life.'

'That is so,' he sighed, leaning back against the rock. 'Yes – ourselves and even our possessions. Yes - life for all eternity or, dare I say, for as long as we wished to carry the burden.'

Footsteps sounded close by and a light showed. A figure appeared out of darkness to place a flagon and earthenware bowl on the ground beside her husband. 'I have brought more wine and some food for you both.' The tone of her voice was that of a woman but it carried no lightness of spirit or youth. It was a sighing voice of weariness. Her head and much of her face were obscured by a soft woollen hood though firelight glittered momentarily in eyes large and staring like those of her husband. It was understandable, thought Gilgamesh as they thanked her, that this immortal wife of the immortal man had kept herself out of sight until darkness came. As she walked away, a ghost in the night, he suspected she had been listening to their conversation from within the shadows.

'You observe how my wife is reticent to show herself,' said Ziusudra, seeming to read his thoughts, 'and you recall just now that I voiced discontent with our lives.'

Even now Gilgamesh was unwilling to recognise the truth of the matter as he replied, 'Yes, you possess what I have gambled my kingdom and my life for yet you express only regret. I watched my brother die. I know the dissolution that faces everyone in this world.'

'I also have witnessed horror and death,' said his cadaverous host. 'Those bloated corpses of man and beast as the waters receded – the stench is something I will never forget no matter how many years pass by. When the gods brought us to this island, I was elated. We thought ourselves the most blessed of people. Everything was here - fresh water, game, pastures and orchards. There was no need to fell timber for our home; the boat supplied more than enough. With the craftsmen who accompanied us we were able to build everything we required. But after a time they, knowing that this truly was and would always be an island, turned their thoughts to Sumer. They constructed a smaller boat and begged me to return with them as their leader but I would not. I would not because I could not. They departed with their women, leaving us alone, though I have no knowledge of their fate. Since then we have lacked for nothing. We fear neither death nor disease as long as we remain on this island. To you it must seem an enchanted place.

There is much here you would find fascinating but our interest was long ago exhausted.'

'You must know this island better than I know my own palace,' Gilgamesh remarked.

'Know it, you say. Oh, yes, we know every pathway, every vantage point. We know every tree, every rock, the sight and sound of every stream. We know the number of paces from any one part to any other. We can set out on the blackest night and walk the circumference of the island knowing exactly where we are, yes, we have done it countless times. Our lives are a path that turns about upon itself. It comes from nowhere and it goes nowhere. That is the meaning of immortality. Yes, that gift we saw as a wellspring of everlasting life now runs bitter and in that bitterness we taste the vengeance of Enlil because of what I did. You see, he never intended eternal life should mean eternal youth.'

One of the logs shifted in the fire. Red sparks whirled as Ziusudra leaned forward, his face a macabre, grinning mask as he said in a low voice, 'Man of Uruk, what I saw in your eyes when we met told me more than any bronze mirror could. We have been spared death but not, as you have observed, the curse of a life that no longer contents us. We carry it as an ass carries its burden, not knowing or caring why. There is nothing for which to strive. Nothing will ever change for us unless we take hold of our fates and put an end to it. Memory, alas, is not immortal. The flood is as clear to us as if it happened only a month ago but much from the years that followed has vanished in mists of forgetfulness. The human mind is like a vessel of measured capacity. If you fill it beyond that measure, the surplus overflows and is lost forever to the earth.'

Gilgamesh stared into the fire, a microcosm of living, mesmerising forms. In it he saw illuminated his own folly. 'I understand all you have told me but at least you have a choice in the matter. A choice denied to all others. A choice I would seek even now if it was there to be had.'

'Alas, it is not within my power to pass it on.'

Gilgamesh continued to gaze into the fire. Only when the glowing wood dropped and scattered red embers at his feet did he sigh, 'Friend Ziusudra, I have travelled for so long over the water, my limbs ache and in the night, the constant motion of the boat caused me great discomfort. On top of that the wine and lack of sleep has dulled my wits. I must rest and think over what I am to do next. If you wish to leave me I'll remain here a while. The air is warm and carries a scent of orchards and gardens I find rather pleasant.'

Ziusudra watched him ease away from the rock and settle down on the soft grass, leaning back against a hummock with arms folded loosely. Soon he was oblivious to the world.

'Ah, King of Uruk,' whispered Ziusudra, 'sleep closes about you as a shroud yet sleep is the lesser companion of death. How could immortality ever be yours?'

Her head uncovered, his wife sat spinning wool by the light of oil lamps set on bronze stands when Ziusudra appeared in the doorway. Seeing her at work he recalled the day they had first set foot on the island, days when she was young and bright-eyed. They had watched each other change throughout remorseless years. He saw in her the languor of one denied too long the ultimate repose. 'Our guest is asleep now,' he said. 'What are we to do?'

'I thought hard about that whilst you were with him,' she replied. 'But I don't know.'

'We hold onto a life without meaning but we still fear death. His coming here means we must decide. If he leaves, he might tell others about us. He might tell them how to cross the Waters of Death. If we are to continue as we are, we cannot allow that.'

'What do you mean?' she asked, wearily.

'His weapons stand beside the doorway,' answered Ziusudra. 'He sleeps exhausted. He will know nothing if -.'

Palc eyes turned, embers within a bone husk, to fix upon Ziusudra. She pushed white hair wisps from a cracked eggshell cheek. 'If what? What are you saying?'

'I am saying,' he answered, leaning over her, 'I am saying we must end his life. We must ensure he does not tell the outside world about us. If he does that, if they find their way here in their ships, they will swarm about us like ants. They will look upon us as the aberrations we have become and view us for their amusement. The alternative we continue to deny ourselves will become our *only* choice. We will have no other.'

'No!' she exclaimed, rising from the seat. 'How could you – you who the gods preserved – how could you suggest such an evil act? Have you forgotten what you once were? Have you forgotten your humanity?'

Ziusudra stepped back, a hand raised to his forehead. 'Yes, I - perhaps I had forgotten, almost. We live for the sake of living but have no lives. Our souls stir within corpses that refuse to sleep. He strives for what we have and I would gladly present it to him were it within my power.'

'I, too, but whether we continue or no, we cannot take away what is so precious to another when we have feasted upon it until we are utterly sated.'

'Yes, I should be ashamed,' he sighed, 'I know that.'

They gazed at each other in silence then he again spoke. 'I'll fetch a blanket to cover him. I doubt he'll wake up until the sun is risen.'

'I pity him as I would a child,' she said as her husband stepped by. 'He is a man of strength yet toil and weariness dim his eyes and trouble his speech. I see him humbled when humility was to him a distant stranger.'

'Perhaps morning light will illuminate the truth in full for him,' said Ziusudra. 'Then he will be reconciled with his lot.'

'The truth is his real enemy,' she breathed, looking across the room at the axe, spear and sword. 'It is a tide he cannot swim against. In the morning he must decide what he will do.'

'Yes,' answered Ziusudra, taking up a richly patterned woollen blanket from one of the seats, 'he will not accept confinement on this island for very long.'

When Ziusudra returned he sat close to his wife, placed an arm about her brittle shoulder and said, 'I think this visit by Urshanabi should be the last now the Stone Ones are destroyed. The world outside has nothing more to offer and we must not risk further intrusion. The boatman I think we can trust. The word was passed down through his ancestors that the gods will destroy any of his line who chooses to betray us. I'm sure he believes it.'

'I agree,' she replied, 'but Gilgamesh will leave our island bitter and disappointed. We should offer him something to compensate for that.'

'Yes, he should not depart without even the illusion of hope, though the burden he carries will be great. We must decide on it now and speak with him tomorrow.'

***

The sun had risen when they emerged from the house. Ziusudra carried a flagon of beer, his wife a bowl containing thin disks of newly baked bread, sliced mutton and onions. Both wore gowns with hoods to shade their faces from the morning sun but more so from the gaze of their visitor. At the spot where the fire had been there was only a spread of cold grey ash. His blanket lay draped over the rock.

'Our guest is absent,' observed Ziusudra, 'though I doubt he will have gone far without his precious weapons.'

'I see him by the slanting tree above the bay,' she said. 'Perhaps he's concerned to know that Urshanabi and his boat are still there.'

Steeped in thought, Gilgamesh seemed unaware of his approach even when Ziusudra spoke. 'Friend Gilgamesh, we have brought out beer and food. Will you return with me to eat?'

Gilgamesh did not reply but continued to gaze out across the bay. Keeping his distance, Ziusudra continued, 'I often used to stand by this tree. In the early days it was just a sapling. Now look at it – ancient, broad and heavy. It leans toward the edge. Someday it will break away and fall.'

Again there was no response.

He had started back toward the house when the voice reached him. 'A man of all eternity – that's what I would have been!' Ziusudra turned to see Gilgamesh stepping toward him. 'I left behind my people and my kingdom to find what you have found. I realise now I should have stayed where I was and asked the gods of Sumer - that at least would have saved me the journey.'

'But if you possessed immortality,' replied Ziusudra, 'do you imagine you could return to live amongst your own people? Could you watch those about you suffer old age, sickness and death? Would others not put your immortality to the test time and time again? Your life would become so intolerable you would have to flee the city. Man of Uruk, you'd not wish to live in a place of isolation – a world where every day and every night were without identity, where even the consolation of sleep eluded you. You could never accept that penalty. You are too much a man of the world that gave you birth. You savour it in full because you must one day depart. And the brother you spoke of who was so dear to you – would he have wanted what you seek? From what you have told me about him, I conclude he would not.'

'No,' breathed Gilgamesh, 'he was too wise for that. I couldn't gather the harvest of his wisdom in ten lifetimes.' In his mind's eye, too, was the face of Shamkhat, though he had only spoken of her briefly

401

so as to complete his account that previous evening. She, too, would grow old and wither before his eyes. That seemed to matter so very much now. He looked upon the desiccated husk that was Ziusudra. 'I will leave this island and return to Sumer. They must by now think I'm dead or gone forever. Uruk may have another king and its people may scorn my name. Still, I must return to the world that nurtured me because there my voice was heard and my arm was strong. I will take my weapons together with those few things I need for my journey then I'll speak with the boatman. My way home will doubtless be long and tedious but if I do not follow it I will wander the wild places until I succumb to age or exhaustion.'

'Friend Gilgamesh, your return may not be as protracted as you fear. There is another way back to Sumer by sea. Urshanabi knows it, though it takes him very far from home. It is the way my people long ago returned to Sumer after the great flood. He will take you around the land and into the gulf where the rivers of Sumer join to enter the sea. We wish him never to return to our island but he will do as I ask because I'll give him enough silver and gold to make him a wealthy man. If he is wise, he will build on that wealth, if not, well – that cannot be our concern. The boat will be provisioned with all you need but you must leave soon. At this time of the year the winds are apt to change and when they do, they will not be in your favour.'

'Are you saying you'll have no more to do with the world outside?'

'That is so - nothing more,' replied Ziusudra. 'I wanted to hear about Sumer and her cities when you

402

arrived but I now realise how little it matters. The world we knew is long forgotten. It is a shadow beyond shadows. It is as far beyond our reach as immortality is to you, regrettable as that may be.'

'Less so than I originally thought,' breathed Gilgamesh. 'I'll eat then I'll look to my departure.'

Seating himself on the rock where food and drink lay waiting, Gilgamesh expected they would leave him alone but Ziusudra's wife spoke from beneath her cowl. 'Husband, we should tell our guest what we discussed last night.'

'Yes,' replied Ziusudra, sitting opposite Gilgamesh. 'King of Uruk, when you first arrived, I doubted you were what you claimed, as Urshanabi still does. But such is your manner and bearing, and such the quality of the arms you carry, perhaps I ought to have believed it sooner. And the ring on your finger – I recall such a ring would be worn only by a man in high authority so it is an ancient tradition. We consider you should leave our island as a man fit to reclaim his kingdom and not as a skulking wanderer. The lion's skin you still wear – no doubt it was once fit for a warrior but now -. We don't wish to give offence but it is worthy only as a cast-off for one whose task is to drive the oxen in his master's field.'

Gilgamesh was aware of how unsightly the garment had once more become as Ziusudra continued. 'We will give you a tunic from amongst the goods that were blessed by Enlil. It belonged to one of the craftsmen who came aboard our boat but foolishly deserted before the storm arose. He was a man almost as tall and as broad as yourself so it will fit well. It is no ordinary tunic.'

The mute boy stepped up to them holding a bundle, white against his dusky limbs.

'It is a garment,' said Ziusudra, 'that will last as long as he who owns it and always it will shed the dust and taint of travel. When you wear it, with your sword at your belt and your axe across your shoulder, you will enter Uruk proud and dignified.'

'Thank you,' smiled Gilgamesh, though the smile sat uncomfortably and did not truly belong.

'But first,' said the wife of Ziusudra, 'the wearer should be made fit for the garment. Beyond our orchards a fresh water spring gushes from the ground and cascades over the rocks before joining the stream. The water is warm and though a little sulphurous you will be purified and refreshed. I know you disdain our touch but if you will allow it I will shave the stubble from your face and comb your hair before you bathe. To do it by yourself would be difficult. Mirrors we disposed of long ago.'

'You'll have a headband and strong sandals for your feet,' added Ziusudra. 'These are far less than you came here to find but you will leave with the cares of your outward journey laid to rest.'

'Laid to rest with my grand illusion,' retorted Gilgamesh. 'Yes, that's the sum of it but I'll not carry that burden back to Uruk.'

Ziusudra's wife looked about to speak, glancing twice at her husband but saying nothing.

'As for the gifts and the service you offer,' added Gilgamesh, 'I gladly accept though I have nothing to give in return other than my thanks.'

'Oh, but there is something you can give,' said Ziusudra. 'You can pledge never to tell anyone about this island and what you have seen here. It is all we ask.'

'You have my promise on that,' answered Gilgamesh. 'I swear on my brother's memory.'

***

Mid-morning sunlight danced on the water as Gilgamesh made his way down the path leading to the jetty. Close behind trod the immortal man and his immortal wife, each concealed by a hooded cloak. The boy followed, clutching in both hands a straw basket filled with fruits from the orchard.

Gilgamesh had allowed her to shave the stubble from his cheeks though during that time neither had spoken. To his surprise, her hand had been firm and steady and more so, he had felt no revulsion at her spider touch whilst aware how but a short time ago he would have recoiled. Afterwards, Gilgamesh had bathed unseen at the pool. No one had observed him sprinkle fresh water to the earth before the newly risen sun or heard his entreaties to the Lord of the Day for a speedy return to his homeland.

Forewarned by Ziusudra, Urshanabi had, with the help of the mute boy, taken on board their provisions and was ready to put to sea. 'My hosts must have worked quickly to assist my departure from the island,' thought Gilgamesh, looking over the boat. 'Perhaps their kindness was no more than a means to that end.'

'So we're leavin' already, 'ighness,' grinned Urshanabi. 'I take it you've managed not to demolish anything?'

At that moment Ziusudra's wife stepped forward to take her husband's arm, saying, 'We

405

should tell him about the plant. It will be little enough after what he expected.'

Ziusudra eyed her with uncertainty. 'Little enough you say, but this man must take his life into his hands to obtain it.'

'What is this plant you speak of?' asked Gilgamesh as the sea breeze ruffled his dark hair.

'There is,' replied Ziusudra, gesturing out into the bay, 'there is a plant, one of the many things peculiar to this island. Like much else, knowledge of it became ours when we arrived here. One of the men who remained a while with us in those first days discovered it. Sometimes we find it washed up on the shore. It possesses the power of rejuvenation - to prolong youth beyond the natural span. It served us for a time when age began to take hold although it can be no path to immortality.'

'But at least it offers something,' responded Gilgamesh. 'Tell me where it grows. If it's within my power to obtain it then I will.'

'And while you're at it you can grab a sprig or two for me,' muttered Urshanabi, dragging his sleeve across his nose.

'It grows beneath the water close to where a fresh stream flows down on the far side of the cove,' replied Ziusudra. 'In appearance the plant is like a boxthorn but it carries spines that will pierce flesh unless you take good care. Good care and haste are poor companions whereas haste is what you will need because the water is deep.'

The immortal woman held out an all but fleshless hand, saying, 'Here is a small piece of the plant I found this morning washed up by the cove. You see now what it looks like.'

'Only with a stone weight will you reach the bottom quickly enough,' continued Ziusudra, 'like the youths who dive for pearls. Then you have to find the plant and return to the surface in time. This may prove too great a risk for a few year's respite.'

'Challenge and risk are no strangers to me,' answered Gilgamesh, turning his gaze to the bay. 'And much as I fear the sea I still have to pass across it for many days.'

Ziusudra said little as Gilgamesh clambered on board the boat. For the last time he regarded the immortal man and his wife, shrouded against the light of day, and the outcast of a boy who had found kindness and security in their bizarre company. The boat drifted clear of the jetty but as Gilgamesh raised an arm in farewell, words slipped through his mind he would not have cared to voice. 'The boy regards himself as your son but could pass through manhood, old age and death before your eyes. Yet I somehow think you'll not outlive him.'

***

The water shimmered lively beneath a hot sun. Naked save for a length of cloth wound about his arm, Gilgamesh breathed deeply, clutched the stone then tumbled from the side of the boat. The stone, attached by a cord to his ankle, he released from his grasp, feeling within moments its downward pull. The water closed over his head and he was sinking rapidly.

As a boy he had dived and swum in the calmer and clearer backwaters of the great river where it was not so deep. There he and his companions had wagered on who could remain submerged for longest. This water was cooler than the rivers of

Sumer but it was of little concern. Into a dreamlike world he descended, seeing tiny, scintillating fish dart here and there whilst larger creatures drifted lazily in the middle distance. The sand undulated below in muted hues, dappled by shifting sunlight from above.

'How far to the bottom?' came his thoughts. 'How deep might I go and still have enough air to return? This water is so clear I see far below. Does that mean the seabed is further than my eyes tell me? Above me the boat hovers like a dark bird whilst I drift in a cavern that has no bounds. Oh, there is such peace here. Down I go and my time is measured in heartbeats. Already I feel the pressure on my chest but – but there, I see plants growing on the bottom. It cannot be far. Not so far. Not now.'

Some plants were broad-leaved, spreading low over the sand; others waved tendril-like in weak currents. None looked like the plant described by Ziusudra, none like the fragment shown by his wife. Tension on the cord eased as he reached the sea floor, the impact of the stone causing sand to billow up and obscure his vision. Feeling the need to ascend, he looked desperately about as the water cleared. He swam awkwardly, the rock dragging to raise up plumes of sand in his wake.

'Where, where, where! I have so little time! So little time!'

Then he saw it. Not far away, where the sand dipped, there grew a single plant. Gilgamesh tugged the cord, released the rock and swam forward, unwinding the cloth from his arm as he went. 'This must be what I seek. It has to be!'

408

He held out the strip, curled it about the prickled plant then wrenched hard. For alarming moments it resisted then suddenly pulled free, trailing thin roots from the sand. But his need for air was pressing as he began to kick his legs and rise. He must reach the surface quickly though the boat appeared very distant and the plant, suspended in his loop of cloth, slowed his ascent. Bubbles quivered by. Drums thundered in his ears. Gilgamesh kicked harder, no longer free in this novel domain but struggling now to escape encroaching death. Toward flashing sunlight he went but his need for air was desperate and the drag of the plant demanded he release his grip. Sound, bubbles, colour raged all about. There gloated with vengeance Huwawa, there snorted in triumph Gugalanna - then the voice of Enkidu ringing as a war cry, 'On, brother! On!'

Roaring assailed him, light blazed wild confusion then blue sky opened wide above. He was gulping air to reclaim a life that had almost been wrested from him. 'Ah!' he gasped hoarsely, 'This day is not to be my last!'

He had surfaced some way from the boat and so began swimming toward it. Secured by the cloth, swirling about in the water by his side, the plant several times brushed against him to sting with harsh, needle thorns. He slowed so as to keep it at arm's length but at last he was at the boat and holding the plant out for Urshanabi to take from his grasp.

'Are there many of 'em down there?' asked the boatman as Gilgamesh, shedding sapphire drops, heaved himself up without Urshanabi's help. Safe

409

aboard, he shook wet hair from his eyes and turned to face the welcoming heat of the sun whilst Urshanabi hooked the cloth and its contents up against the mast. 'I saw only that one,' he answered, 'but I won't be going down for a second look.'

'Hm,' muttered Urshanabi, 'whoever 'eard of a king divin' for weeds anyway?'

Gilgamesh overheard him while pulling on the new tunic and answered, 'Oh, diving for weeds is a long established royal sport in the land of Sumer, friend Urshanabi. You should come and see.'

The plant swung dark and dripping in a warm breeze and Urshanabi said, 'What did old Ziusudra tell you – break off the spines and throw 'em away? That was it, wasn't it?'

'Something of the sort,' answered Gilgamesh, pushing back his hair then fitting on the headband. 'And that we can do once the thing is dried out.'

They were in open water, the big sail crowding in a lively breeze, the waves buffeting as sea spray hissed by. In the stern stood Gilgamesh, a hand shading his eyes, just able to make out the now deserted jetty where had stood ancient Ziusudra, the ancient wife whose name had never been spoken and the boy who in manhood must inherit the island realm from those too wearied by their lives to carry on. Urshanabi secured the yardarm then turned an eye to Gilgamesh. 'It's the last time I'll sail to the island – you know that, don't you?'

'I know it. They wish for no more visitors.'

'You're the cause of that,' he grumbled, running fingers up and down his beard. 'I could 'ave carried on as I was if you 'adn't stuck yer nose

410

in. They paid me well. Yes, ten years - maybe more, then I'd 'ave quit and started a farm.'

'Maybe they did pay you well,' responded Gilgamesh, eyeing the copper banded pine chest that lay ahead of the mast, 'but I suspect you've gained generous compensation - greater by far than you'd have made over the next ten years sailing back and forth to that island and risking the Waters of Death. You'll also have more say in the use of your boat than you had before. You have a good sail so you can go wherever you please and no longer need those abominations you called a crew. I think, my disgruntled friend, you're a lucky fellow but unwilling to admit it.'

'Lucky is it, your 'ighness?' responded Urshanabi, lifting his leather flask to take a gulp, only to find it empty. 'Could be - unless the pirates 'ave us. They won't much care what you're king of when they cut our throats and there are a good few of the buggers about where we're 'eaded. The Stone Ones scared 'em off in the past, see.'

'Aye, well,' responded Gilgamesh, watching him turn his attention to one of the smaller pitchers from which the flask would soon be refilled, 'no pirate will enter this vessel while I'm on board and I'm sure you would give a good account of yourself.' As he spoke, he noticed in the bow an object part hidden by matting that had not been there on the outward journey. 'And I see,' he continued, 'that during our brief stay on the island you have also acquired a new and better axe. Now we're in open water, who'll man the tiller first?'

***

411

The weather remained fair through those passing days. There was consolation, too, in the food and beer given them for the voyage. Gilgamesh, however, derived little solace from the acerbic conversation of his companion though Urshanabi, in spite of occasional gulps from the flask, tended his boat with the same care an overland trader of fine goods might reserve for his best camels or asses.

The sea offered a certain fascination now Gilgamesh had become used to it, though after the fourth day he found himself preoccupied once more with thoughts of his wasted journey. 'Were it not for the demands and diversions of the boat I think I might languish in despair. This man whose company I am obliged to suffer will never know the service he has rendered and will never admit to that accruing from me.'

'Tell me more about this Uruk of yours and the cities of Sumer,' Urshanabi asked at one point whilst sitting at the tiller. Gilgamesh wondered why he now expressed such interest when having shown little enough before. But as he described the great temples, the markets and the people, Urshanabi looked hard at him with one eye or the other, now and then muttering, 'Hm, not for me.'

'You ask me what you do simply so you can reject with words the sights you have never witnessed,' responded Gilgamesh. 'You could sail upriver if you wanted. The boats of Ur trade with foreign places more than any other town because she lies in the south of Sumer and is closer to the sea. Her quay would be easy enough for you to reach and you now have the means to buy things you'd never find in your own part of the world.'

'Don't expect I'll bother,' replied Urshanabi, scratching his thick beard then spitting dismissively over the side of the boat. 'Too many people. Too much noise. Anyway, there's the language. I wouldn't understand a word of it – no, not a word.'

'But it's my language and the language of Ziusudra. You speak it perfectly well.'

'Oh, no, majesty,' objected Urshanabi, 'the gods gave 'im *my* tongue and you must 'ave picked it up somewhere else. I've no language but my own.'

Gilgamesh did not reply but pondered on the matter. 'Apart from my own, I speak no language other than that of the Semite peoples north of Uruk - and then with no great skill. Yet the creatures guarding the mountains of Mashu and the woman at the tavern, I conversed with as easily as I do with this ill-mannered oaf. How is that, brother Enkidu? You could do it because the gods gave you such understanding. Why should it be passed on to me, for it surely has been?'

His thoughts were interrupted when Urshanabi called, 'Your turn to steer the boat, great king – if you've no prior engagements, that is.'

'How would you deal with this man, brother Enkidu?' he asked himself, settling into the stern. 'I think you would draw him along and jest at his expense, though I doubt you'd find him of like spirit. I'm tempted to heave him overboard and tow him along at the end of a rope but I fear at present his company is of greater value to me than mine is

413

to him. Ah, well, I'll let memories of your patience and forbearance guide me.'

Another day and a fresher wind herded ragged clouds across the sky. Salt spray hissed across, the sea thumped, the boat rolled alarmingly. Urshanabi had both himself and Gilgamesh lower the yardarm and shorten sail. 'It's been fair enough 'til now,' he declared, lashing the tiller in place, 'but it'll soon pass and we're still on course! I notice you're not so put out by it as you were first time around.'

'These boisterous seas find you in your element, friend Urshanabi, but how can you know our direction? You've not used the iron spindle that always points the same way and we've seen no land!'

'The sun's passage and the flight of the birds,' he replied as the boat shuddered, 'just as people do on land! We'll 'ave sight of the coast tomorrow though there'll still be two day's sailing ahead of us!'

'Then do I take it we'll have reached Sumer?' asked Gilgamesh.

'We'll be as close as I'm willin' to take us and when you're out of my boat I've more days sailin' ahead of me. I'll not be content until I'm in sight of my own shore.'

'Oh, so you'll be contented at last and I won't be there to witness it! Such a pity.'

Clutching the side of the boat, Urshanabi took a draught from his flask, belched loudly and replied, 'No, 'ighness you won't - and that *is* a pity I must say!'

On the following day land appeared on the horizon, hazy and indistinct, but it was soon evident that Urshanabi was not headed toward it. The winds had eased during the night, the sky was clear and the morning sun intensely hot. As the day wore on into afternoon, the land resolved itself into a featureless coastline backed by brown hills that showed no sign of habitation. White water could be seen close to the shores and Urshanabi gestured toward this, muttering, 'Dangerous rocks.'

Night-time left the hills vague against the stars and brightest of all shone the light of Inanna. Gilgamesh sat by the mast, having long since relaxed his vow not to gaze at her light. 'Is the Queen of Heaven hostile or benign?' he whispered into cool night air. 'No, I think you are quite indifferent. You brought suffering to my kingdom and as much grief to me as ever a man knew – and now I dare say you occupy yourself with other diversions.'

A half-moon shimmered above the sea. With the gentle lapping of water, the whisper of the sail and creak of the rigging, he was soon asleep.

There was laughter. Her laughter. 'Shamkhat,' he whispered, looking about in the darkness. 'Shamkhat, are you there?'

More laughter, then, 'Come along, now. Come with me. Let me show you the temples and the town then we'll take wine together.'

There were her eyes, large in the night. She was watching. Waiting.

'But I know the temples and the town. I am Gilgamesh. Why talk to me as if I'm a stranger?'

'The Gilgamesh I knew is gone forever,' she answered, backing into darkness. 'You are what you are and never before were.'

415

'No, don't leave! Speak to me! I am Gilgamesh! I *am* Gilgamesh!'

Several times he called her name but there was only the echo of her voice.

He awoke to pre-dawn light, to the sound of the sail flapping and the sight of Urshanabi swinging the yardarm about. 'While you're jabberin' away in yer sleep about that woman of yours,' announced the boatman, 'there's another vessel passing. Look - between us and the shore.'

Gilgamesh raised himself, confused over the dream. 'Woman?' he murmured. 'Yes, she was there. I was talking to her - to Shamkhat!' There was ample light for him to observe the boat and see the land to their right was much nearer than on the previous day. 'She's a large vessel,' he observed. 'A cargo ship out from the town of Ur and on her way to the spice lands. She'll stay close to the shore for most of her voyage.'

'So,' leered Urshanabi, 'the men of Sumer fear the open sea more than they do the pirates who lie waitin' in the coves hereabouts.'

'They don't venture far out because they believe there is nothing beyond the sea. And their vessels are not built for rough water.'

'Probably just as well,' came the mumbled reply as Urshanabi raised his flask.

In the distance to their left another coastline had already fallen behind. Gilgamesh looked about and asked, 'How long now - and where will we set foot on land?'

'Early tomorrow if the wind stays good - and we'll pull in when I care to go no further. I've sailed into this gulf before. I know there's marshland

416

ahead and desert either side of us. The heat and the flies are not to my likin' and I've no wish to encounter anyone 'ereabouts, as you already know.'

The following morning, small, barren islands were in evidence with several fishing boats dotted about the water. To their left, broken by bays and inlets, the land rose gently to where a scattering of ruined dwellings could be seen. When the sun was past its height, the land appeared continuous and Urshanabi said, 'There's a village with a small jetty over there but no royal deputation. Maybe everyone saw sense and quit the place.'

'Yes, it looks deserted. Perhaps high tides or flooding have driven them away.'

'D'you know where you are, yet?' asked the boatman.

'From the direction those fishing boats sail,' answered Gilgamesh, 'I'd say we're to the west of the great river. If so I'll be three or four days journey on foot from the fields of Uruk.'

'And there you fancy you'll be king again. Is that it?'

'You still doubt I ever was in spite of the weapons I carry, but if the people will forgive my having abandoned them, perhaps I will be king again.'

'Does it matter what I believe?' responded Urshanabi. 'Anyway, those weapons could be stolen for all I know. Still, I'll remember you each time I trip over what's left of the Stone Ones. That'll be enough.'

'And I'll remember you whenever I encounter an ill-mannered boor and perhaps have him flogged all the harder. Still, we've worked together well

417

enough so I expect you'll not begrudge my taking enough food and water to carry me through at least part of my journey, and you'll have your piece of the plant I recovered.'

'I'll begrudge you neither food nor water, royal one,' he answered, bringing the tiller over, 'but I'll not give more of my time than it takes to get you ashore while I still have the tide.'

***

It was a forlorn shore onto which Gilgamesh stepped. With sword at his belt was also fixed the strange plant, reduced in size by the removal of its spines and by the portion he had left with Urshanabi. Over his shoulder hung his water flask and leather bag containing food. The small cluster of dried mud and reed huts appeared to have been deserted for some time. He turned to see the boat going about and watched it head in full sail for open water.

'Goodbye my ill-humoured friend,' he murmured. 'Against my better judgement it may be but I wish you safe journey in those dangerous waters.'

Urshanabi never once glanced back.

'As you wish,' breathed Gilgamesh, setting on his way. 'You at least should return with some advantage to the home you had. And what will be my lot, brother Enkidu? Is your spirit still with me? Did Utu in his kingdom note the offerings I made or hear the prayers I spoke or did they fall as seed on arid ground? I'm sure you'd forgive me for wondering.'

CHAPTER 11
THE FINAL CHALLENGE

But for the comfort provided by the white tunic, he would have found the heat oppressive after the fresh breezes of the sea. It was a gift for which he was to become ever more grateful in the hot and humid land through which he was obliged to pass. He walked on, seeing how, to his right, the scoured flatlands of the estuary were becoming greener. In the hazed distance he was able to make out the reed huts of the marsh people for whom the city dwellers of Sumer had little time. He was aware, too, of the busy marsh birds whose call drifted on heat-shimmering air. Until this day he had never ventured into their territory, had never considered their existence or marvelled at their sheer variety. Yet they now seemed to him unaccountably familiar. 'I'll not be far off course if I skirt the marshes,' he breathed, 'and in time I should meet a shepherd or a traveller.'

He was to encounter no one that day but strode on alone through the afternoon. With the sun low to his left he observed the land becoming rougher with stunted bushes and hardy grasses much in evidence. Far away to his right must begin the territory of Ur. Also would be the great river on which, further to the north, stood Uruk. 'Soon I must look for a place to rest. Soon I'll need fresh water to replenish my flask. Ah, I see a group of trees where the land dips to a shallow valley ahead. Perhaps there is water. I'll reach it before the sun is gone.'

419

Gilgamesh found himself crossing a broad depression though for a time the trees were lost from sight by a low rise, which at last he crested. 'Yes, there are creatures gathered there. I see birds amongst the reeds. I see there's water so that's where I'll make my camp for the night.'

At his approach gazelles retreated from the pool. The birds rose up to vanish in an evening sky. The pool, dark and deserted when he reached it, lay close to a long, irregular outcrop of rocks, sections of which lay tumbled about close to the water. 'I'll make my camp on the other side. Those rocks may harbour scorpions. I've no wish to end up one of their victims.'

Gilgamesh laid his weapons by a bush then hung his flask and pouch of food from its meagre branches. The plant from beneath the sea he placed by the pool with its stem in the water in hope of reviving the withered leaves. 'I'll have your leaves ground to a paste then added to beer. Then I'll take you to the temple and let the old priest who showed me the tablets have first taste, if he's still alive. If you can ease the burden of age for him then surely I'll present no challenge. For now I'll taste again the waters of Sumer then I'll gather enough reeds for my pillow.'

The pool was flat as a bronze mirror as he knelt above it. The water reflected placid clouds that hung white against the dimming vault of an evening sky. He leaned closer to the water until his own reflection appeared. 'Brother Enkidu!' he exclaimed. 'You look at me from the pool. Your spirit keeps me company even now. Will you speak?'

The image remained silent and only moved as he moved. 'I delude myself into thinking I see my dead brother's face. That's because I'm tired and my mind wanders. I have travelled far but tomorrow I must hurry on until I skirt the fields of Larsa, and then –. And then -!'

Sleep took him as the first stars appeared. Inanna's light hung as a pale jewel high above the horizon.

Close to the pool, amid the shadows of the rocks, moved a darker shadow spawned by the night. It made no sound other than a long hiss like the escape of air from a sealed tomb. It moved away from the rocks to glide silently along the ground. By its strange senses it knew the warmth of the man. It knew what he was, but cared only that he did not wake up. Closer moved the shadow, passing by the one who slept, weaving a cunning path to the edge of the pool where the precious plant lay. For a moment the intruder lay still. The man was becoming restless. He was murmuring with the voice of his dreams. As the dark form once more slithered on his voice became louder.

'Where am I? What is this desolation that was once a city? Is it Uruk I see? Yes! Yes, it is once proud Uruk reduced to utter ruin. I walk about barefoot and in rags, wanting no one to look at me. Why? What disaster could have befallen the city I once knew?'

'Oh, no disaster,' rolled back and forth their hollow laugh. 'No disaster at all!'

'What – who mocks me? Who is there? The day is clear but I see no one!'

'It is no disaster, Gilgamesh. Only time. The truth of an immortality that could never be yours.'

'Immortality, you say! I see only clay and dust where once stood a great city – where once people went to and fro in temple and market. The temple is a pitiful mound, the walls destroyed. If this is Uruk then her soul has long since fled, her foundations laid open as the gaping jaws of a skull. Why, even the river has deserted her. The gods themselves have departed and devils of another faith have taken hold! And what is this? A beast has entered. It sits amidst the ruins. Ah! - people spill from its belly like maggots from a corpse. I cannot remain - the sight of such desolation will destroy me. Wait! Someone calls my name from where my brother's grave lay. Hers is a voice from years beyond imagining. I do not understand. I must go from here! I must go!'

The stars were beginning to retreat from a brightening sky when he awoke, limbs aching. On clambering up he saw the plant was gone. Something lay close by on the ground and in the early morning gloom he knelt to pick it up, turning the soft, translucent object slowly in his hands. 'This is the skin of a serpent. It has robbed me while I slept. It has shed its years and gone.' He let the skin drop, adding bitterly, 'What little I had to show for my journey that damnable creature has taken.'

Filling his leather flask then bathing in cool water, he saw clouds high above gilded by the yet unrisen sun. Overhead circled the birds of morning, anxious for the man to leave. Gazelles passed in the distance, silhouetted against a brightening horizon. Daylight was gaining the land as he sat to take out his food. The dates and cheese were still good, as were the fruits, but the bread had mouldered. He threw it in amongst the rocks, calling, 'There, take that as well and choke on it!'

Gathering up his weapons, he glanced one last time at the shrivelled skin then turned his face to the morning star. 'And need I ask whose hand is set against me? If so I'll not surrender to self-pity. I'll not give her that satisfaction. I am Gilgamesh. I will go on through this day and the next. Through all the days and nights, d'you hear! I am Gilgamesh! I will go on!'

***

During that last day he turned eastward, striding across tracks left by the nomads and their herds heading north. They would not pass too close to the city as no one could be quite sure where the pastures of temple and landowner ended and no-man's land began. The boundary stones were not always where they ought to be. To move a boundary stone incurred the death penalty but rarely was anyone sure who had done it. Lion, wolf or jackal might take their toll in the wild but where the city reached out the beasts ran a poor second to the tax collector.

The sun was at its highest when, the water in his flask low, his food meagre, he spotted the small oasis. He headed toward it with a keen eye for any creature that might loiter long enough for him to strike down with his spear. 'I see nothing other than birds. It's a small water hole but nonetheless welcome. I'll refresh myself there but I won't stay long.'

Gilgamesh laid aside spear, axe and sword and sat down to rest, part shaded from the fierce heat of the sun by a bush. Insects skimmed low over the pool and among gently swaying reeds. He watched the play of light on water, the glint of dragonfly wings. 'There is such peace, such tranquillity,' he sighed. 'Time seems no longer a burden. Perhaps a benign spirit dwells here.'

He had sat at ease for some time before recognition dawned. 'But – but surely this is the very spot where I came upon my brother after he'd fled the city to find solitude. Yes - this is where we planned our enterprise. This *is* where we talked of the Cedar Forest and Huwawa – and of Shamkhat, to whom he was so devoted. Now thoughts of her fill my mind as though I am heir to that devotion. I hear her voice in the breeze. I feel her hand on my cheek. I desire her now as Enkidu once did. How can this be?' He looked up at the sky to see birds passing overhead, then he closed his eyes. 'It's so strange,' he breathed. 'I feel I've returned in my brother's footsteps. It's as if some great, unseen circle wrought by the gods of time closes – as if I consummate the journey through a life he never completed. When we talked together I recall one of us saying that there is meaning here beyond our grasp. Was it he or – or was it I who said it? Ah, the pool bids me stay and rest as it did Enkidu, but I cannot. At least I know before the sun goes down I will reach Uruk. And then – yes, what then?'

***

The sun was still high when he entered a greener land. He had expected to encounter flocks, shepherds or passing traders but noted only the occasional scurrying rabbit or wild dog.

'How odd the land seems. The city is not far away yet I've encountered neither man nor beast. I'll walk on until I reach the barley fields. I'll find a peasant - someone who will not recognise me. I'll question them about the affairs of the city.'

He continued through the heat of the afternoon until the barley fields came into view. The sun was low and threw his shadow ahead as he looked about. At the first of the main irrigation ditches he stopped. Ahead lay Uruk.

The city stood bathed in late sunlight beyond the date palms, her defensive wall glowing white, the recessed facades of the temples rising above. The sight should have beckoned him on but Gilgamesh halted with a frown. 'What has happened here? Where are the people who tend the fields? It's as if they've fled yet I see smoke from the forges and kilns drifting above the city. The crops are untended. In places they are trodden down - and there's a foulness in the air that speaks of death. I'll go on but I must avoid exposed ground. I'll make my way through the standing barley until I reach the river where I can observe closer. Wait - something moves where the barley lies crushed.'

What he glimpsed was quivering, glistening, black.'

He stepped forward, spear at the ready. Five paces on and a ghastly sight confronted him. There were three of them, each a pallid corpse clothed in a writhing cocoon of flies that bustled in and out of gaping mouths and bird-picked eye sockets and clustered within the open wounds of severed throats. 'By the gods their blood is long dried, they are part eaten by dogs yet they remain unburied! Who has done this? What has befallen Uruk? Wait – someone is watching me from where the barley stands thick.'

With spear raised, he strode forward calling, 'Show yourself! Come on out or my spear will find you!'

'Don't harm us!' came a boy's cry. 'Don't kill us! Please don't!'

From amid the stalks a face appeared, distress and confusion written large across it.

'Come out and speak to me!' called Gilgamesh. 'That's all I ask! I'll not harm you!'

Two of them crawled into the open and rose to their feet - a small boy and a man, each with fear shining bright in his eyes. Both were begrimed, both manifestly ill-nourished, the former with inflamed eyes and a disarrayed mop of hair, the latter a man of much greater years than Gilgamesh though almost as tall. Gilgamesh regarded their wretched clothes of mired wool, their limbs fouled with mud of the ditches, and observed that the man's right arm was withered and could be of little use. His eyes, blue and intense, stared warily from a gaunt, all but toothless face framed by matted black hair and soiled beard.

'Who are you?' asked Gilgamesh. 'What has happened here?'

'Are you a stranger, sir?' croaked the man with a question of his own. 'Are you not from Uruk or Kish?'

'I am a traveller but I know Uruk well. Why are the fields untended? Why are the crops trodden down? Why are the dead laying over there unburied and who are they?'

'They drove us from our fields!' blurted the boy. 'They killed my father and my brothers!'

'It's the men of Kish did this, sir,' said the other. 'They came two days ago. They rode their chariots through our crops an' ordered the men and women to clear off. Any who stayed behind were hunted down an' slain. They rounded up our oxen our sheep an' our cattle; that's why the fields are empty. Me and the boy 'id ourselves in the ditches to avoid bein' seen.'

'The men of Kish,' breathed Gilgamesh. 'And what has happened within Uruk – can you tell me that?'

'We don't know, sir,' answered the man. 'We labour in the fields. We enter Uruk only as needs be or when there's a festival – but I believe the city is taken. One of the dead back there is this boy's father, the other two 'is older brothers. We wanted to bury them but we've no implements to dig their graves with. The men of Kish took everythin' of use and our bare 'ands are not enough. We dare not return to our 'omes even if they're still standin'. We've no food, sir. We've only foul water from the ditches to drink.'

Gilgamesh studied them calmly yet within him welled flames of anger. He had to go on for behind him lay only emptiness and greater despair.

'You must take what little food and water I have,' he said at last, unfastening the leather pouch and offering it, with his water flask, to the man. 'Tell me - what d'you think of Kish and of what has happened here.'

'What think I?' growled the man as he reached out a trembling hand to accept. 'I think them worse than rabid dogs for what they've done to us.'

'Then are you willing to help Uruk?'

'Help Uruk, sir? We've not even the means to 'elp ourselves. I don't know who can 'elp Uruk unless it be the gods above and there's no sign of that. If you ask me, the gods 'ave looked the other way these past months. A while back we were stricken with the drought – then the king disappeared - and now this!' He gestured toward the boy. 'Look at 'im, sir – what's he got left? There's precious little I can offer 'im, let alone 'elp Uruk.'

'But you *can* help,' said Gilgamesh. 'If you do not, you will most likely starve or be killed.'

'How, sir?' asked the man. 'You carry the arms of a nobleman in spite of the plainness of yer tunic. We've a small flint knife between us an' that's it.'

'What I will ask of you might achieve nothing,' answered Gilgamesh, 'but still I'll ask for all our sakes and for the sake of Uruk.'

'I'll listen, sir' replied the man. 'There's no 'arm in that.'

Gilgamesh held out his hand to show the bronze ring on his finger. 'I want you to take this ring into the city and to the temple of Inanna. It's a simple task, my friend, but a most important one.'

The man glanced down at his own ragged attire, shook his head and raised his good hand. 'Me, sir? Me take the ring of a nobleman into the city? Look at me. They'd seize me as a thief if I was seen, sir - seize me and flog me as a thief! I dare not do that.'

'They might if you appeared as you are at present,' replied Gilgamesh, 'but if you wash the

428

dirt from yourself and put on my tunic and headband, you'll attract little attention. You could place the ring on a finger of your lesser arm and clutch your hand to conceal it.'

'Well, sir, I never 'eard the likes of it,' the man responded, 'and carry *that* ring? He looked down at the boy, who continued to stare, now in awe, at Gilgamesh.

'We'll go a short way in the direction of Larsa,' continued Gilgamesh, 'then we'll join the river. There it should be safer. There you can bathe and afterwards exchange your clothes for mine.'

Exchange?' grated the man. 'You mean, sir, you'd exchange your good tunic for - for this?'

'If it serves my purpose,' replied Gilgamesh, 'and provided you wash it as well in the river as I intend you should wash yourself.'

It occurred only briefly to Gilgamesh that not so long ago he would have avoided all contact not only with such a man but with anything he had touched. Now he felt only pity.

'An' what's to become of 'im?' the man asked, placing a hand on the boy's shoulder.

'I'll take care of the boy until you return,' answered Gilgamesh. 'So let's get moving now. The day is late and we've little time.'

They set off through the fields, keeping low as they followed the line of a disused irrigation ditch. Once south of the city, they turned toward the river, soon emerging through clusters of date palms and onto the bank. 'I see no one close by,' said Gilgamesh as they stepped down to the water.'

'There are men with spears!' exclaimed the boy.

429

Gilgamesh, too, had seen them on the far side of the river. 'They're heading to the city,' he reassured the pair. 'They'll not concern themselves with us.'

From where they stood he was able to make out the fat-bellied transports moored at the quay. They bore the pennants of Kish and so he concluded they must have carried at least a part of Agga's army and supplies to Uruk.

The sun was low in the sky when the man, having washed as best as he was able in river water, presented himself to Gilgamesh. The boy, meanwhile, had swirled and squeezed out his companion's ragged tunic several times, before offering it up with a reticent, 'There, sir, it's all I can do.'

Gilgamesh laid his weapons aside – concealed as best he was able by a wide bush. He took the old man's garment then helped him pull on the new tunic, saying, 'It fits you well enough, my friend. Now put the ring on your finger.'

The man stared at Gilgamesh, now attired in his own dripping clothes. 'Sir I don't know your name, nor you mine. At first I thought you were a warrior because of the weapons you carried but now, even dressed as you are in my rags, I think you're a man of authority, a man of great importance, and that's why I do as you ask. Still, sir, will you not tell me your name and your purpose?'

'Not now, my friend; we have too little time. Go back along the river and get into the city before darkness via the floating bridge; quickly or you may find the gates barred. Make your way to the temple of Inanna. Look only ahead as you go but do not hurry. Ascend the steps to the upper precinct as if you are familiar, as if you go there often, but do not let anyone see the ring. Find a priest of Inanna. I take it you know what they look like?'

'I do, sir. I've seen 'em at the ceremonies.'

'Good - then ask to be taken to the house of scribes. Do not demand. Do not raise your voice. Only speak as I speak now. If he wants to know why, tell him a boy of yours trains there whose name is Shannu. Remember – Shannu. Tell them you have a message for him then wait for as long as you must. Be patient and humble in your manner. Avoid staring at other people or they may begin to notice you.'

'I'll do all you ask, sir. And then?'

'When the boy comes out,' continued Gilgamesh, 'confirm his name then take him aside. Tell him you are sent by a stranger who wishes not to be seen, then give him the ring. He will recognise it, that I do know. Tell him to meet me here as soon as he is able. See, on the opposite shore there are small boats. He must take one of them and row across; that way he is less likely to be seen. I know he'll find a way. Do not remain with him but leave the city by the bridge. If by then the gates are closed, tell the keeper you are owner of a boat with supplies for the men of Kish and maybe they will allow you through the postern. I'll have this boy of yours wait at the other side of the bridge – until morning if they prevent you leaving tonight. Do you understand all I have said, friend? Will you faithfully and in haste do all I have asked?'

'I'll do it, sir, so I will, but how am I to return your fine tunic?'

'The tunic is yours to keep. You'll find it serves you as could no other. Go now.'

The man departed, passing through the date palms then vanishing from sight. Gilgamesh and the boy sat down on the bank to watch the water flow tranquil in mellow light. That same light cast shadows across the wall of Uruk; a wall that should have kept her enemies at bay but now, he realised to his shame and anger, must encompass them within its circuit.

***

Gilgamesh waited alone, spear in hand, axe over his shoulder and sword at his belt. A shadow amongst shadows. On calm air drifted the sounds of night. The hoot of an owl. The gruff call of a fox. From the city a distant barking of dogs.

Somewhere in the darkness the sound of lapping water was followed by a dull thump. But the moon was low and starlight not enough to reveal the source of the sounds. Splashing. This time closer and at last he made out a vague form. Darker than the dark water, an elusive shape moved close to the river bank. The sound of oars being drawn in reached his ear, then a low call, 'Lord Gilgamesh.'

He recognised the voice and replied, 'I am here.'

Treading cautiously along the bank he could make out a figure emerging from the small boat. He would have stepped forward to help had he not seen close behind Shannu the vague outline of a second person.

'Who is with you?' asked Gilgamesh.

'It's me,' came her voice as Shannu dragged the boat aground.

432

'Shamkhat, you – you should not have come here.'

'Please don't be angry Lord Gilgamesh. I saw that old man hand something to Shannu. I made him tell me what the man's errand was. When I saw what he'd brought, I knew you had returned.'

'You called me lord,' he said, facing them, 'but I am lord of nothing. I left Uruk to seek fulfilment of my desires. I should have known what would happen once our enemies found out but I was blinded by my own conceit.'

'There is no other lord of Uruk, master,' grinned Shannu, handing back the bronze ring.

'Uruk weeps for her king,' said Shamkhat. 'She lies as a lamb before vultures who will soon pick her clean, body and soul.'

'What happened when I left the city?' asked Gilgamesh. 'That I must know.'

'When you left, master,' replied Shannu, 'the people thought little of it for a time, even though your companions walked the streets armed and many of them came and went from the House of Assembly. Envoys arrived from Larsa demanding to see you as they often have. Eventually they learned you were absent and no one could say when you would return. Perhaps, mightiness, it was the Man of Larsa who told the Man of Kish you were gone because not long afterward a delegation from Kish arrived and demanded to speak with you. The elders told them you would soon be back within the city but every few days they came asking until they believed you would not return.'

'When pilgrims came to our shrines,' added Shamkhat, 'we knew there were spies from Kish

433

among them; not just because of their speech but because of the way some of them wandered about the city looking at our gates and our walls.'

'Then, great lord,' continued Shannu, 'the raids on our sheep and cattle began. 'First one and then another to see what the people of Uruk would do. At first your companions set out to drive them away but the raids became worse, with lots more men, and they moved closer to Uruk. Kish and Larsa demanded concessions over land and waterways. They said they would invade if they didn't have their way. Then Kish and Larsa fell out with each other over who should lay claim to what, so the Man of Larsa refused to support the King of Kish and does nothing.'

'I asked only about matters in the city,' said Gilgamesh, 'but now you give me an account of our enemy's affairs as well. How can you, a student of the temple school know all this?'

'How, mightiness?' the boy grinned, eyes bright in the darkness. 'I moved about the city as and when it pleased me. Few people take notice of a temple slave. I mingled with priests and traders as if I was about the business of one or the other and I listened out of sight at the House of Assembly. I carried tablets about your palace as if ordered to do so and stood close by when your companions spoke among themselves. I was always there to wait upon the envoys of Kish when they came into the city. I know their tongue well because my father came from the north. I was always on hand when they demanded food and beer. Always I smiled and they trusted me because I told them I also came from the territory of Kish. The silver they gave me for my service I wagered on your returning to Uruk. Some wealthier citizens thought it no gamble at all and accepted high odds against it.'

'And what of the merchants of Aratta?' Gilgamesh asked. 'Did they become involved?'

'No, Lord, when matters became difficult they stayed aside to wait and see what was to happen. Agga's men were ordered not to harm them because he wants to take over the trade with their town.'

'Young Shannu,' smiled Gilgamesh, placing a hand on the boy's shoulder, 'you could be one of the greatest rogues in Sumer but I wager no grown man has served Uruk better. And what of my mother – is she safe? And my companions, and the elders – how did they account for themselves when Kish threatened Uruk?'

'Lady Ninsun is safe, I know that,' put in Shamkhat. 'I was with her today. She always believed you would return.'

The boy lowered his head before giving his answer. 'Your elders, lordship - they argued about what to do late into the night. Some thought they should choose a leader from amongst your companions to head the people in resisting Kish; others said not. Some said Uruk must talk peace with Kish even if it meant them taking some of our land.'

'Do I hear the voice of Kuraka in this?' breathed Gilgamesh.

'Well,' continued Shannu, 'he no longer spoke against Kish when the envoys made their demands, but twice went out of the city to meet with their king. As for your lordship's companions – most of them wanted to take up their arms in defence of

Uruk but could not agree on a plan. A few only said it was no longer their concern as their king had deserted them. They said they would accept the gifts of Agga because they would have a strong ruler and so might continue as they were.'

'Did no one oppose his men at the city gate?' asked Gilgamesh.

'Some did, master. Some of your companions and the younger men of the town gathered weapons but no one could say who was leader and because of that, others would not join them. Sheshkalla the metalworker would have rallied his men and many of the people would have joined them but the elders considered it beneath their dignity to deal with him as a leader. Some of your companions also refused because Sheshkalla is not of noble blood.'

'Not of noble blood!' responded Gilgamesh, angrily. 'By the gods, Sheshkalla is sound as a rock and worth any ten of them. But go on young Shannu, finish your account.'

'When the army of Kish appeared at our gates and their captains entered the city, those who still tried to rally the people were rounded up. They were later flayed alive in the market square by order of Agga and no one dared speak out for them. Their screams carried throughout the city. Their skins he ordered nailed to the walls about the Nippur gate. Their families were sent to Kish as slaves.'

'His anger casts a terrible shadow,' said Shamkhat.

'Those elders who Agga learned had spoken against him,' continued Shannu, 'were forced to stand before the House of Assembly with their tongues cut out and hung about their necks by a cord. The few amongst them who could work were sent to the brick kilns of Kish. Those who could not, his men put to death with much sport outside the city wall as he looked on. Their bodies were thrown into the river but their heads are displayed on poles about the palace square.'

'The soldiers of Kish treat our people worse than dogs,' said Shamkhat. 'They steal and drag away and use the women as they please. Shannu hid me safely in a secret vault below the temple when they came searching. An old priest said it was one you had discovered. Both brought me food and drink. The day after tomorrow the Man of Kish will return from his camp north of the city. Shannu heard them say he will enter Uruk in great ceremony and claim it as his vassal. He will go up to the shrine of Inanna and will be proclaimed Lord of Uruk by his own priests. He will demand homage from the elders, priests and all the people of Uruk. His priests and his officials are preparing for this.'

'His men already keep guard at the city gates and in the public places,' added Shannu.

'The day after tomorrow,' breathed Gilgamesh. 'And in victory I spared him.'

'Our priests say Agga's men will seize the images from our temples,' continued Shamkhat. 'Once in Kish they will place them at the shrine of their god, Zababa, to show all the people of Sumer how Uruk was defeated. They will search every corner of the temple for hidden valuables and they will find where I am hiding.'

'Already, master,' said Shannu, 'they have taken chests and furnishings from your palace. Items of great value they have presented to Enlil's shrine at Nippur as gifts of war. The soldiers of Kish may yet burn your palace to the ground and destroy the city wall. I've heard some of them say that's what they'll do.'

Gilgamesh was silent for a time then said, 'Only a fool would claim our city is not lost. But a fool is what I've been all along.' He peered over the river to where lights glowed above the temple precinct, then turned to face Shamkhat and Shannu with hands raised before them. 'But I tell you this now; while my heart beats, the dog of Kish will *not* have Uruk! I swear before you both and let the gods of heaven and earth hear me! No - he will *not* have Uruk!'

'Master,' declared Shannu, 'there are many who wait for a chance. There are many who have arms hidden and ready. Sheshkalla and his men are chief among them but he fears he, his metalworkers and their families will be forced out of Uruk into the service of Kish. He forges bronze blades and makes arrowheads from the star that fell out of the sky. All of these he keeps hidden above the forges.'

'What are we to do?' asked Shamkhat.

I have searched my soul as we talked,' replied Gilgamesh, eyeing the boy. 'Shannu, take this ring again and listen to what I tell you. If what I have in mind gains success, I swear upon my brother's memory you shall never regret the courage and steadfastness you have shown. I swear also that you will never again call another man your master. Many of those I thought loyal are not fit to wash your feet. First you must return this lady safely to the temple and then -.'

'No!' interrupted Shamkhat, 'I'll not go back now. There's more I have to say to you.'

Gilgamesh hesitated. 'Very well, wait here. I'll talk with Shannu by the boat then help him out into the river.'

She heard none of their conversation because Gilgamesh kept his voice low. When he returned to her side they stood hand in hand to hear the splash of oars and watch the boat vanish into obscurity.

'Shannu knows well enough who can be trusted. He will take my ring and inform those of my trusted companions, and Sheshkalla, but none of our priests because Agga's own will be inside the temple, and none of the elders for reasons we both know. Before sunrise the boy will return here to take us across the river to where the small boats lie and will also confirm who he's seen. He will bring the garment of a minor priest for me, you he will return by the back alleys he knows well to the safety of my mother's house. After sunrise when there are people going about their business, I will enter Uruk as a humble priest and I will visit all those who the boy has contacted. This will allow us a day and a night to prepare for Agga's arrival.

'May the gods go with Shannu,' whispered Shamkhat.

'I think he might persuade them even if they cared not to,' answered Gilgamesh. 'But you shouldn't have risked coming here. Everywhere there could be danger, even in the night.'

'But you didn't insist on me returning, Lord Gilgamesh.'

No, I did not. There have been times of late when I've not known what was real and what was not real – and sometimes I hardly cared. Now I have spoken to you both – now I realise the plight of our city and its people – I see what I must do, whatever the outcome.'

'I have wanted so much for you to return,' she whispered. 'After you left the city our elders consulted the soothsayers. Some predicted a great king was to die within one year but could not or would not say more.'

'Yes, even kings die sooner or later - that I know well enough.' He slipped an arm about her waist, pulling her closer. 'But you - you shone in my thoughts often, even before I reached the Great Water, though I'd always regarded you as my brother's consort. My envy of that lay buried deep by my love and my respect for him. Now that envy has awoken and will not rest. If I'm your lord then you are my lady. That is dearly how I would have it.'

Shamkhat raised up on her toes and pressed warm lips to his, saying, 'Dear Gilgamesh. Even now you don't understand. Even now, though I began to see it long before Enkidu was gone, as did Ninsun. The knowledge was hers even before it was truly mine, perhaps from the very beginning. We talked of it often during the months you were away.'

'Understand?' he sighed, holding her tighter. 'What do I not understand?'

'Why, Aruru created Enkidu in the same fashion as yourself but the clay that was lost in your making was in him complete. He was a Gilgamesh that might have been. Within him was a compassion for others you carried in little measure, just as he had not the urge to conquer - that was always your strength and the strength of Uruk. As you both lived, as you set out and faced dangers together – even then you each had become a reflection of the other. Those were words you yourself used after his death, though I'm not sure it was what the gods intended. When he died, his spirit remained wandering in search of its true home. That home it found in those wild places when you needed the strength he also possessed. There his spirit joined with yours. Now I see both men shine as one bright star in our time of darkness. His touch is in your hand. I hear the tenderness of his voice when you speak. Enkidu was never truly born and never truly died. Now do you understand?'

'Understand,' he sighed. 'I've not known of late what I understand. I wonder if we are vessels – shells within shells, each one concealing yet another beneath. Who knows what hides within – a paragon of goodness, a ruthless conqueror or a blackened, malignant gnome. Maybe it's all of them.'

'Don't say that,' she whispered, placing her arms about his neck. 'No, not when I see within you the humanity of my Enkidu and the greatness of my Gilgamesh.'

'Well,' whispered Gilgamesh, 'if the spirit of Enkidu is now mine and you still desire it, then I consider myself more fortunate than any man alive in spite of our circumstances and in spite of this wretched tunic I was obliged to put on. But still I am Gilgamesh and Gilgamesh will fight for Uruk until his last breath.'

'All of Uruk desires it though few think it can ever happen,' she said, pushing back his hair and splaying fingers across his cheek. 'But - if victory was yours -.'

'If victory was mine,' he answered, holding her close, 'it would be a tainted cup if you were not to share it as my lady.'

'And I'd not wish to see you drink from it if you were not my lord,' she breathed as they sat together by the river.

***

Under a brightening sky the temple drum rolled three times across the city in ominous summons. As people began to gather in subdued conversation outside Eanna's wall, other sounds caught their attention. From the ceremonial gate of the wide street opposite that led from the quay, small drums rattled, drawing closer and louder. From beneath this gate streamed a column of soldiers in helmets of polished bronze, cloaks of black swaying about their leather kilts, swords and spears at the ready. People were forced roughly aside as this substantial company deployed itself about the periphery of the great square and close to the gateway of the temple precinct, some of them finding their way to the rooftops of nearby buildings where they stood in menacing silhouette against the sky.

Next appeared twenty more armed men, evidently the vanguard of a procession because they were attired in more ornate helmets and patterned cloaks, as appropriate for ceremony as for combat. They marched as one toward the precinct gate, clearing a path through the people who fell back before verbal abuse or the threat of sword and spear. These men would position themselves at close intervals on the lower stairs so as to secure the way to the temple of Inanna above.

Close in their wake followed a pair of heralds in gilded, deep red tunics, two plain-kilted drummers and a group of ten or more shaven-headed priests in plain woollen robes – some of these latter responsible for the clashing cymbals and braying rams' horns. The crowd fell silent, faces turning to see what followed behind the priests.

From beneath the deep shadows of the gate emerged an extravagantly wrought, gauze-curtained sedan chair of gilded cedar inlaid with lapis lazuli and light-shimmering gemstones. This was supported on a pair of ornately carved cedar poles that boasted gilded lion's head finials. The weight of this regal conveyance was borne by four tall and resolute nobles of Kish, two at the front and two at the back, resplendent in long robes of white and gold. Within its plush interior was seated Agga, King of Kish. To enhance the security of his elevated person and his disdainful bearers strode Agga's stern-faced bodyguard, six at either side. Their engraved bronze helmets glinted beneath swaying red plumes, the overlapping scales of bronze covering their leather tunics gleamed also. Each man gripped a short but deadly spear, intended for stabbing at close quarters, as well as a small, round shield of bronze-banded wood with pointed metal boss. At the stout but finely decorated belt of each hung a short sword with ornately gilded hilt. A small column of regular soldiers followed at the rear, each of grim expression, each man ready to deal with anyone rash enough to approach their precious charge.

Through a brooding crowd the sedan was conducted in solemn, measured step, gently, ominously swaying. Its occupant cared not at all that the people of Uruk were unable to see him. Few in Kish, certainly no common man, would dare look into the face of Agga on pain of death.

'At least he cannot make the people cheer,' said the first priest, gazing down over the low wall of the upper precinct.

Behind them Inanna's temple glowed in morning sunlight. Armed guards had already taken up position by the main doors. There they awaited the climactic event when the all-conquering Lord of Kish would be conveyed in solemn ceremony up the staircase. There he would emerge in splendour from his carriage and enter the temple to declare himself high priest of Uruk's greatest shrine.

'It's a sight I never thought to witness,' groaned the second priest. 'Not in my worst dreams did I see the dog of Kish anywhere near our city, let alone our temple.'

'There should have been an heir to the throne ready and waiting to deal with this,' added the portly third priest, reaching into his bowl of dried figs.

'Gilgamesh had no heirs,' responded the first priest.

'Oh, really,' added the second, 'well at least none he ever cared to recognise.'

'Look at that,' remarked the third priest, gesturing with his bowl. 'Those soldiers are gone from the rooftops. Now they've placed archers there instead. What's happening?'

All three stared across the precinct to observe, spaced about its wall, men dressed in similar fashion to those they had replaced; each with quiver laid at his feet and powerful composite bow resting upright in his hand.

'Why have they done that, I wonder,' remarked the second priest.

'There must have been a change of plan,' responded the first.

'All the easier to pick off troublemakers; that'll be the reason,' concluded the second.

'It looks to me,' munched the third priest, 'as if a good many of our citizens are keeping away. The crowds may have grown but we've had the square and the precinct busier than this often enough.'

'All the citizens of Uruk were commanded to attend,' said the first, raising a hand to shade his eyes. 'Men, women, young and old, sick and healthy. Those who disobey Agga will surely suffer. The man is cold-hearted and vengeful. He'll spare no one who dares contravene his will - including those of his own family so we hear. And do I imagine things or are his guards proliferating up here? There's a bunch of them idling about at the far side of our temple and there are more waiting inside.'

They could be the men sent down from the precinct wall,' offered the second priest.

'The name of Gilgamesh ought to be cursed,' declared the third. 'If we'd had a proper king -.'

'It's what the gods have decreed,' cut in the second priest, 'and to that we must acquiesce.'

'I suppose we must,' agreed the first, 'even though we of all people – we who serve at Inanna's temple, are excluded from our own holiest shrine.'

'I for one am not sorry since I'd not care to be involved,' munched the third. 'I cannot imagine any of this bodes well for the likes of us once Agga's on the throne of Uruk. No, I cannot.'

The heralds' drummers ceased, giving way to raucous horn and shattering cymbal from the eager priests of Kish. Having passed through the precinct gateway, and now reaching the steps leading to the upper level surrounding the temple proper, the royal procession commenced a stately ascent. The two men supporting Agga's sedan in front stooped low whilst those at the rear raised their arms high in order to maintain their sovereign charge level during his grand progress. The rearmost soldiers remained where they were to keep townspeople clear of the stairway.

Scampering ahead to the top of the steps, the two heralds of Kish passed between impassive guards at the portal and stopped before the great doors. Behind them the clamour of ram's horn and bronze cymbal stopped abruptly to leave only brief echoes. The heralds, grasping wooden staffs of office capped with gilded bronze, struck the doors in measured deliberation to demand entry in the name of Agga, their intention being to see that all had been maintained within the shrine as had been ordered earlier. Three times the timbers echoed a resonant boom then they stepped back to wait in an abject silence that had settled over the entire precinct.

Bronze grated in stone sockets. Timbers creaked. The doors rumbled slowly inward, opening sufficiently for the first and then the second herald to pass through.

A vision of glittering opulence, the royal entourage continued its ascent. At halfway point one of Agga's priests detached himself and hurried ahead to the top of the steps from where he strode purposefully with anger-darkened face toward the three priests of Inanna. 'I do not see the chorus assembled to sing in his majesty's honour!' he barked in the accent of Kish. 'Where are those commanded to do so?'

'We know of no such command,' replied the second priest.'

'We were not required to officiate,' added the first, 'therefore we have no responsibility in the conduct of your affairs.'

'None at all,' mumbled the third.'

'Then get yourselves clear of the steps,' sneered the priest of Kish, 'or prepare to do homage face down on the floor when his majesty alights.'

'Damned insolence,' muttered the first priest as they shuffled back from the spot they had occupied. 'You'd think they -.' But his voice was drowned by the discord of horns and cymbals that began again as the priests of Kish arrived at the top of the stairs prior to stepping onto the temple platform. 'I suppose that confounded noise is to disguise the fact that they've bungled the chorus,' remarked the second priest.

'I imagine their damnable king won't be too pleased,' added the first.

447

Swaying behind the priests of Kish, the royal conveyance rose up in baleful glory – higher until it was clear of the steps and poised to approach the portal of Uruk's holy of holies. The common people below maintained a dour silence.

The three priests of Inanna continued to observe from a more discreet vantage point. One of them, glancing over the parapet, noticed a number of men and women making their casual way through the crowd, each with a basket of fruit poised upon their head. They appeared to show little interest in selling their produce but merely stood about to witness the spectacle with the rest of the onlookers. 'I see the fruit sellers are out in force,' muttered the second priest.

'A curse on them for wanting to do business on this of all days,' added the first.

At that moment the king of Kish's sedan and its twelve attendant guards came to a halt. The four nobles set their royal burden down with practised care. As the great doors opened further, the priests of Kish ceased playing their instruments and entered the temple as official procedure demanded. The priests of Uruk knew as well as did the priests of Kish, that at this point the chorus of praise should have been in full spate. But still there was no one to sing it.

'Stand further away, holy ones!' called one of the guards who, positioned from the outset at the temple doors, gestured at them with his spear.

'He didn't speak with the accent of Kish,' said the second priest as they shuffled back toward the corner of the building.

'No he did not,' replied the first priest, angrily, 'it seems many of our own citizens have gone into the service of the enemy these last few days. May Agga's silver poison them if that is so.'

'Shameful!' declared the third, clutching his bowl and looking behind in case some unseen obstacle should cause him to stumble.

'It will serve us well to keep our voices down,' added the second priest, glancing about.

They watched the four nobles flutter moth-like about the sedan. Saw one of their number hurry to the side with a gilded parchment parasol raised high whilst another stood ready to ease their precious lord from shaded comfort into hot, sultry daylight. The twelve spearmen who had been Agga's bodyguard hurried back past the sedan to position themselves at intervals on the upper section of the stairs, which they could easily defend if others managed to push by the soldiers further down.

The sedan chair quivered. The gauze curtain twitched.

'It is forbidden for all except those closest to look him in the face,' hissed the second priest. 'Should we not lower our eyes? They say he has offenders blinded or executed.'

'I will *not* lower my eyes,' responded the first. 'We are priests of Inanna and this is *our* temple. Gilgamesh never required that of us, nor of anybody - and wayward as he may have been, he was a better prospect by far than this contemptible dog and his grovelling minions. Kish always claimed kingship over Sumer but this man is not fit to clear out the latrine ditches.'

'By the gods they might hear us,' whimpered the third priest, eyes darting this way and that.

The gauze curtain shifted aside, helped by one of the nobles who reached out an arm in readiness to assist. A hand appeared from behind the curtain. A bejewelled hand possessed of long, well-manicured fingers - a pale spider quivering at the portal of its lair. The nobleman reached inside and took the arm, supporting it as the figure, clutching lavish robes, emerged into the shadow of the parasol to place an elegant, gem encrusted, crimson-slippered foot onto the flagstones.

A slender man of average height, Agga appeared older than his true years. His head jutted forward to give the appearance of one constantly peering about. His eyes, pale and unblinking, gazed from beneath heavy-browed, tinted lids. The eagle nose and waxen cheeks were framed by thick-textured black hair, which, like the abundant beard, hung plaited and entwined with gold and silver wire. About his head sat a band of braided gold, encrusted with lapis-lazuli and coiled tendrils of silver. Devoid of expression, he stepped away from the sedan to face the temple doors, ignoring altogether the remaining two nobles who had fallen to their knees with heads bowed.

From their vantage point, the three priests observed his tunic of rich maroon and the pectoral of embossed gold and silver. They noted, too, the wide elaborately decorated belt and jewel-studded scabbard from which protruded the inlaid ivory hilt of a long, curved dagger. Sunlight glowed upon the pale saffron robe, fringed with red and held at his neck by an ornate golden clasp in the form of an

450

open-jawed lion. To their disgust they observed, grasped in Agga's left hand, a short staff bearing the golden emblem of the warrior god, Zababa, guardian deity of Kish. This was said to be a son of Enlil but was recognised by few beyond the confines of Agga's own city. It was considered by many an abomination.

For the first time they heard Agga speak. His voice was measured, unemotional and grated like that of one burdened by twice his years and more. This was nevertheless a voice of harsh authority - a voice that seldom needed to be raised for always there would be others close by to hear and obey. 'We were given to understand a chorus would be present to greet us yet there is none. It is the custom in this as well as every city, is it not?'

Without raising his head, one of the nobles responded, 'We will seek out those guilty of such neglect and present their names, Majesty - be assured of it.'

The other nobles eyed each other in the hope that, by some unknown means, a satisfactory answer might manifest itself before the ceremony was ended.

'Very well,' continued Agga, 'inform those within the temple that we are arrived and the doors may be fully opened. We shall not be pleased to wait long.'

Hardly had the words left his lips when the two kneeling nobles sprang up and hurried to the half-opened temple doors where they stepped inside. Agga and his two remaining attendants stood as a motionless tableau.

The doors began to move once more, grating fully inward to reveal only the impenetrable gloom of the atrium. Three figures, robed and hooded in gowns of dark linen, emerged together from the shadows. The outer two halted at the portal, close to the guards while the third and tallest continued forward, his head lowered. In his hands he cradled a small, plain casket of copper-banded pine. Halting before a cold-eyed Agga, he fell down upon one knee to place the casket at the glorious King of Kish's bejewelled feet. He then rose up to stand before Agga, arms loosely folded, head still bowed, his face still obscured by the cowl.

'What is the purpose of this?' demanded Agga with thinly disguised impatience. 'What does it contain that needs delay our entry into the temple? And why on this day ordained by the gods do the priests of Uruk choose to cover their heads?'

'The casket is empty, mighty king,' replied the figure in a whisper meant only for Agga, 'and we cover our heads out of sorrow for the dead - and for those yet to die.'

Agga's eyes narrowed. He glanced briefly at the guards on either side of the doors who remained stiff and impassive. Slowly, his right hand shifted across to rest above the hilt of the dagger.

'Then,' he grated angrily, raising the staff, 'if the casket serves no purpose, remove it and conduct us to the shrine of Lady Inanna. We grow impatient.'

'Ah, but no casket could be of greater use to your majesty,' breathed the figure.

'To us?' hissed Agga, eyes widening, fingers about to close upon the knife. 'And what, yes what, is the worth to us of an empty box?'

'Why great king,' answered the figure, calmly, 'this humble casket is soon to hold your ashes.'

Agga grasped the hilt but barely had he begun to draw the blade from its sheath when sunlight flashed on bright metal and the hood slipped from the raven-haired head of the man facing him.

'You!' cried Agga. 'You cursed devil!'

The precious dagger never left its precious scabbard for in that brief moment the sword blade of Gilgamesh, the blade wrought by Sheshkalla, struck and pierced him to the hilt. It was for Agga a moment that budded from the stream of time. A moment when the King of Kish gazed about a slowly turning world of utter silence. The men-at-arms might have been idols fashioned in clay, the city a stark white mirage in the morning sun. Only the figure before him lived. And it grew. It grew and spread as a thundercloud across his vision until it extinguished the light of day. His staff clattered at his feet. Agga reeled back, mouth wide as the sword was wrenched from his body, his mortal cry stifled by the life-blood choked up with his last breath to blurt from his lips and befoul his beard and regal finery.

As he sprawled quivering to the ground the guards on the upper staircase shouted, scrambling on with swords drawn. Less than half would reach the top. A whiplash hiss and arrows sped from the temple roof, iron points piercing helmet and bronze scale to revel in the soft flesh beneath. The two guards at the temple doors, joined by others from within and from close by, ended the lives of Agga's company with brutal swiftness. Those who had reached the upper precinct from the stairs and the two remaining nobles were cut down as they cowered by the temple wall. Rivulets of their blood pooled over hard stone to mingle glinting with that of their fallen lord.

Agga's men on the lower stairs gazed up in confusion, for the moment unable to act.

The temple guards moved quickly to join Gilgamesh as he stepped over Agga's wide-staring, grotesquely grinning corpse and those of his men who in their zeal had hurried to share his fate. At the head of the stairs Gilgamesh placed a foot against the fancy, gilded and bejewelled contrivance that had delivered the King of Kish to the threshold of Uruk's temple. He heaved it over to roll crashing down the steps where it splintered asunder, its glorious form in shattered ruination before startled eyes. He next placed his foot against the body of Agga, heaving this over and over until it tumbled, drizzling blood, down the stairs to land sprawling in full, ghastly view before his own men.

He let slip the gore stained robe that had concealed his warrior's tunic, held the reddened sword high in one hand, Agga's crown in the other whilst his voice rolled over the precinct, 'I, Gilgamesh have returned! I am with you once more! The Man of Kish is dead! Rise up, citizens of Uruk and strike off the shackles laid upon us by the enemy!'

With that he flung Agga's crown through the open doors of the temple.

Confusion lifted from the minds of the people in the square but it lifted even quicker from their enemies who already had sword or spear at hand. Those citizens of Uruk bearing baskets had let their burdens down to spill over the ground and now called for others nearby to seize not fruit from the orchards but the keen daggers and short swords of bronze that had lain hidden beneath.

The soldiers of Kish rallied to the calls of their captains but not all the captains were of like mind. Those close to or on the stairway urged their men upward to storm the temple of Inanna and slay Gilgamesh whilst the far greater number in the square prepared to do battle and crush the men of Uruk who they could see were quickly arming. Some of the enemy's number, isolated from the main corps at the far side of the square, were cut down then trampled underfoot. Further orders went unheard as the people began to chant in wild enthusiasm, 'Gil-ga-mesh! Gil-ga-mesh! Gil-ga-mesh!

But the soldier of Kish, united with his corps, employed his arms to greater effect than the stallholder, potter and merchant of Uruk who was less well prepared and too poorly organised for combat. The several hundred strong main body of the enemy in the square, outraged by the death of their king, set about to cut down any who stood in the way, young or old, armed or defenceless. They were determined to hold the city until reinforcements could be summoned from Agga's main camp close outside the Southern Gate. This they proceeded to do by means of their drummer's rapid beat whilst several of their number had fallen already, struck by arrows from above. More voices arose to drown those of the wounded and dying. Cries to press on in the name of Kish and Zababa, cries of defiance in the name of Uruk and Gilgamesh.

Gilgamesh swooped down the temple stairs as an avenging eagle, his citizen soldiers close behind, falling upon the foe, blade flashing to drive them reeling in bloody confusion. Lower down the stairs the enemy still pushed on, determined to advance, though some of their number also had fallen to the lethal sting of the archer's shot. In the crush above them, the width of the staircase prevented no few from employing their weapons. Some fell back and, eyeing the befouled, rag-doll body of their king, attempted to cut a path through unarmed and disorganised citizens in the precinct and join the bulk of their men. Those higher up, slipping in the blood of slaughtered comrades, saw destruction loom and threw aside their weapons, some begging Gilgamesh to grant them mercy before they received in full measure what they had intended to inflict upon others.

In the turmoil of the precinct those fifty or more of the enemy saw Gilgamesh and his men about to descend upon them with the fury of a raging storm. Though greater in number they fled in disorder to the gate, intent upon joining their comrades in the market square. But in their desire to push through the bottleneck created by the gate they were harassed by townsman at the flank and by the archers on wall and rooftop.

The main body of Agga's men were fighting well, gaining ground in places, but witnessing the plight of their comrades in the precinct they began to split up. Most battled on with no thought of retreat but growing numbers fought their way in groups toward the wide street by which they had entered the square, uncertain over whether or not their call for reinforcements would be answered.

More drumming sounded above the clamour from the direction of that same street. Those soldiers heading there, knowing this to signal the approach of reinforcements, turned about. Some began to cheer whilst all fought with renewed vigour to drive back the citizens who confronted them but were themselves hardly aware of what was happening. The drumming grew louder, fiercer, and into the market square were streaming hundreds more soldiers fresh from Agga's camp.

With their arrival Uruk's men were sorely pressed and it looked certain the men of Kish would be strong enough to pursue the battle to their full advantage. Soon the men of Uruk were reeling back. The clamour and screams of the stricken rose into morning heat, consuming the city until her very walls seemed to cry out in despair.

In the temple precinct, those of Agga's remaining soldiers still able to fight took their chance, cried aloud and charged forward, thinking good fortune was again theirs. But the lethal blades of Gilgamesh and his men were to be the arbiters and for the men of Kish, this reckless foray was their last. When those able to escape the precinct fled out into the square, the gate at last was clear.

Gilgamesh and his men pushed through. They were now in the square and fighting their way toward the enemy reinforcements when yet more drumming rose above the turmoil – a rapid, metallic rhythm harsher than anything that had gone before. It issued this time from a point to the far right of the square. From a narrow street advanced a motley band of armed men, few of soldierly aspect. None of them boasted tunic or bronze helmet but they needed no insignia because at their head, with great hammer at the ready, strode bearded Sheshkalla, broad of chest and firm of jaw, the dark anger of his countenance enough to drive the sun from the sky. Close about him were gathered his men, large and small, young and old, the firm of body and the lame, all stained with the soot of the forges, all with an eye to set about the men of Kish with bloody violence. More citizens, also armed by the forges, swelled his number. It was Sheshkalla who struck first, striding ahead to smash down two of the enemy at once with a mighty swing of his hammer. His men tumbled into the fray with a grim zeal that dismayed utterly those unfortunate enough to confront them.

From another street closer to the precinct yet more men emerged. These were attired in the manner of Uruk's warriors – the youthful companions of Gilgamesh, or those of their number who had remained loyal and managed to survive the wrath of Agga. Bronze helmets and scale armour gleaming, they were eager for a battle too long denied them. The commotion hardly abated as the citizens scrambled aside to allow both parties through before joining one or the other band. As they advanced in grim resolution a howling deadly flock sped over their heads toward the enemy, unleashed by Uruk's archers now established along the precinct wall. Against those arrows the men of Kish found their small shields of little use.

Wild shouts upwelled once more from the citizens – once more the name of Gilgamesh.

The priests on the temple platform above watched him lead his band of men on, watched him scythe his way into the blood-spattered square with his comrades battling eagerly at his side.

'Uruk will be ours again!' shouted the first priest. 'Of that I have no doubt!'

'It will! It will!' cried the second, whilst the third priest, transfixed by the spectacle below, frantically stuffed his mouth with food.

As Gilgamesh and his men pushed ahead, a noble, a captain and hero of Kish in scale armour dashed out from the chaos, shield and sword raised, with a cry of, 'Die! Die now!'

This was a burly, hard-eyed man Gilgamesh knew well. He was brother of the man who had slashed the King of Uruk's thigh before paying with his own life during Agga's first attempt to conquer the city. He had negotiated surrender terms on Agga's behalf after that first conflict but had sworn revenge for the death of his brother at the hand of Gilgamesh. Just in time Gilgamesh saw him. The man's blade hissed in deadly arc, deflected with little margin to spare by the sword of its intended victim. More agile through his lack of armour or shield, Gilgamesh spun about to strike his adversary's shield with such a blow it was flung splintering from his grasp. Others backed away as each crouched, as each circled the other with an eye for the vital, lethal chance, levelled blades twitching in anticipation. Gilgamesh parried, caused his adversary to jump back then appeared to relax. Taunting the man with a smile he called, 'Ah, my friend – you dance as well as our temple girls! Fit employment for you there, I think!'

With a curse, the soldier sprang at him, sword raised high, his judgement marred by seething anger. Gilgamesh leapt aside to avoid the intended fatal stroke then swung his own blade down with such force it split the man's helmet, cleaving his skull to the ear. He fell without a cry, his helmet spinning aside. Those men of Uruk seeing his brains exposed were charged with greater courage – those of Kish with bone-chilling dread.

Many on both sides fell bleeding in the dust but in the confusion, those of the enemy freshly arrived from outside the city wall, not knowing their king was slain, still pushed hard to advance. They mingled with men who saw flight as the sole alternative to death - men who in their turn spread a contagion of fear and panic through their comrades. A sound of rushing wind brought another hail of death from archers repositioned on rooftops closer to the scene of battle.

Those of the enemy massed close to the edge of the square, unable to use their weapons, suffered additional assault when the women and young boys of the town appeared on the rooftops above them. From there were hurled down all manner of weighty objects from bricks and jars to bronze ornaments, with most claiming a strike.

A prey to the arrows, the soldiers of Kish were also grievously beset also at one flank by Sheshkalla's resolute company and at the other by an unstoppable Gilgamesh, now joined by his well-practised companions and vengeful men of the town once more themselves warriors. To the would-be conquerors, now outnumbered in arms, Uruk was becoming a pen of beasts awaiting slaughter. They shifted back en-masse, still many hundreds strong to find the narrow streets blocked and defended and the temple of Inanna an objective which, even had they taken it, would have gained them nothing.

The men of Kish fought on in desperation behind their shields, determined now to reach the Southern Gate and the quay where their boats waited. But the road to the quay was barred by the metalworkers with, striding before them, Sheshkalla, sword at his belt and bronze hammer swinging to smash the bones or drive back in panic any number of men rash enough to attempt a breakout.

In the tumult of violence, in the thrusting of spear and sword, in the hiss of the arrow, death arose from the swirling dust of the square to grin down at the men of Kish. Some threw aside their weapons and dropped to the ground, resigned to their fate. Others continued the fight, falling to blade or arrow, or until exhaustion overcame them. A few turned their swords against themselves rather than face the displeasure of a king who they imagined was still alive and watching.

In their thirst for revenge the men of Uruk saw not others like themselves but cowering, rabid dogs whose fate was already settled. For the soldiers of Kish, their remaining time would have been measured in heartbeats had not the rattle of a herald's drum sounded above the din of battle. The melee faltered. Heads switched about. Then across the square came the voice of Gilgamesh, loud and clear. 'Hold! Stay your weapons! Hold, I tell you!'

His men parted as he strode to a low brick wall where, with sword held high, he stepped up so both citizen and enemy could see him. The cries of wounded and dying broke the silence as he called aloud, 'There has been enough killing! The Man of Kish is dead! His army is defeated!'

'They must die, too!' shouted one of the crowd. 'Cut 'em down here and now we say!' Shouts of agreement sprang from amidst the citizens and spread wide as they brandished their weapons.

'I say, no!' declared Gilgamesh. 'No! Do we want the stench of blood to stalk our city as do the dogs of night? Was Uruk raised in greatness to become a charnel house? If they will lay aside their weapons then we must spare them! We will show the people of Kish, we will show all of Sumer that Uruk is mighty enough to grant life as well as take it – even to her bitterest enemy! Did you not love my brother - the brother whose death so grieved me that I abandoned our city? Did he not grant life and hope to those we, those I regarded with scorn? I say we follow his example! I say we spare these men of Kish whose lives we hold in our hands, even though they were led here to destroy us! We should let them take up their dead and return to their families. It is a gift you, the people of Uruk, have the power to offer. Think on it – that is what I ask of you.' He turned to see those of Agga's men still bearing weapons, throw them clattering to the ground.

'And we say do not spare them, Lord Gilgamesh!' came a voice. 'We say in the name of

462

the people they must all pay with their lives for what they have done.'

From among the crowd appeared a small group of men attired in white caps and long gowns. At their head stood one who Gilgamesh knew well; a tall, slightly stooping figure with braided beard who offered the customary homage of clasped hands and modest bow.

'Ah, Kuraka the elder!' responded Gilgamesh. 'You seem able enough now to give your tongue freedom, though I hear it remained as a serpent asleep in its lair when others of the council lost theirs in speaking out in defence of Uruk. You see fit to use it now the enemy is done for and you are no longer in danger.'

The elder looked around at his companions. None of them spoke.

'I merely reflect the mood of the people and of our council,' offered Kuraka. His companions glanced uneasily at one another. Two glanced nervously aside as people hearing his words began to jeer. A gruff voice added, 'His tongue would be busy around the Man of Kish's arse all right if our king hadn't come back!' Sheshkalla stood with a leer on his face, gore-spattered bronze hammer resting on his shoulder, his dusty kilt streaked with the blood and sweat of combat.

Laughter ensued but Gilgamesh levelled his sword at Kuraka and declared, 'I ask the forgiveness of my people for having left them to face our enemies, but you – you should have counselled them. You as chief amongst the elders should have brought together my companions. You should have consulted with the leading men of the guilds, especially our worthy Sheshkalla. He enjoys few of your many privileges but was all the while ready with his good men to stand firm for Uruk. To you they might have listened but you did nothing other than make concessions and so persuade Kish of Uruk's weakness. Were it not for my own sins I might find yours a charge impossible to bear. You will gather your possessions and leave the city before sunrise tomorrow. You will take yourself into the mountains and to Aratta and there you will stay! Go from my sight before anger takes a hold on me for by the gods this blade of mine is not yet sated!'

Kuraka and his companions needed no persuading but hurried in consternation through a crowd whose hostile mood served to quicken their retreat. Gilgamesh sheathed his sword and once more addressed the people. 'I turned my back on Uruk and because of that you have suffered. Yet on my journey I found truth and understanding. If you will take me back I'll not desert our city again as long as I live. And know this - know that I have a consort and will have an heir to follow in my wake. Look now,' he continued with sweeping gesture. 'Look about at our temples and our city wall. They stand mighty as before but we will make Uruk greater than ever she was. I will endeavour to safeguard all, rich and poor alike, for I have learned how precious life is and how easily it might be taken from us. Let us renew and build upon the glory of Uruk! Let us bury our dead and begin today!'

'Gilgamesh!' they cried. 'Gilgamesh! Gilgamesh!'

The men of Kish also took up the chant because they had come to realise the King of Uruk was their master, too, and would be a lesser burden on their lives than the one so recently departed.

'Gilgamesh!' the people chanted until it seemed as if they would never stop.

***

The sky was darkening as they looked across the city from the roof of the palace. In the square below, Agga's pyre still smouldered but most who had gathered to watch the man who would have been master of Uruk consumed by flames had departed. Small groups still passed back and forth from the shadowed streets, some family members carrying their dead, others for reasons only they knew. Smoke carried up with chanting voices from the temples, where sacrifice was being made for the redemption of the city. The ceremonies would continue for days ahead. Armed men from Uruk would enter Kish at first light the next day and seize all that had been removed from their own city and temple. The gods of Uruk would be returning home. The gods of Kish, set up in the sanctuary of Inanna, would be removed and destroyed.

***

'It seems a lifetime since I stood on this spot,' said Gilgamesh. 'There were times when I thought I might never see Uruk again. Yes, many times.'

'That I understand,' she replied, 'but Ninsun never doubted you would return.'

'All the world passed before me on that journey. It is a world beyond imagining and I wondered then as I do now, if there can ever be an end to it.'

'For most of us the world is Sumer. That is enough.'

'For many it is Uruk,' he replied, slipping an arm about her. 'Yet I had a vision one night as I slept in the desert. I came upon our city to find it laid waste and in utter ruin. There were voices telling me why I saw what I saw but still, I ask how that could be.'

'Might it have been a vision of Uruk's fate if you did not return?' asked Shamkhat, looking into his eyes.

'Oh, I can't say but I doubt even the malice of Agga could have brought about such desolation.'

'And what of Kish now her power is broken?'

'Yes,' he smiled, 'what of Kish, and what of those in Uruk who encouraged our enemy by their reticence or their treachery? The Gilgamesh of old would have dealt with them more harshly than this Gilgamesh feels inclined to do. Yet I must act - a king must rule in deed as well as in name. Tomorrow I'll send an envoy with my companions to Kish to enter upon a new treaty. The family of Agga I will banish to Aratta. They'll have good company since Kuraka and his bedfellows will be there to offer consolation.'

'Won't they see Aratta as a haven for conspiracy?' she asked.

'I doubt it. Agents of Uruk reside there and it is not in their king's interest to aid our enemies. And don't forget the traders from Aratta still present within our own walls. No, those I banish will have their time cut out in finding the comforts they took for granted here. Aratta is a harsher and colder place than Uruk or Kish. As for those of my companions who thought to betray Uruk – I cannot forgive them. Even the compassion of Enkidu could not embrace the magnitude of their crimes. They were men of privilege - men who enjoyed the fruits of this city yet would have left those fruits to rot whilst they accepted the baubles of Kish. It's not just I who hold them in contempt but all the people of Uruk. The judges and elders of the city will determine their fate but I'll make no public spectacle of it and there will be no work for the torturer's hand.'

'I am grieved by all the suffering and death,' she sighed, slipping her arm in turn about him. 'What is it for? What do we - what does anyone gain in the end?'

'It's the way we have always been and probably always will be,' he replied. 'But there's much to be done here – that is now my objective – and we have our lives to live. I will have recorded for those who come after us all that I saw and did in this world. I'll tell of Enkidu's coming to Uruk, our journey to the Cedar Mountain, of Huwawa and the Bull of Heaven. I'll tell of Enkidu's death and my journey to discover the immortal man.'

'And will you tell of Kish and her taking up arms against Uruk a second time?'

'No,' he answered, 'that is to my shame and I do not wish it to be remembered. But let's not dwell further on misfortune. Let us see what has been recovered from Kish or was left untouched within my palace. I fancy my bed – our bed, will be there if nothing else, and it's time we took ourselves to it.'

As they passed through the arch to descend from the roof, a breeze whispered at her cheek. Shamkhat turned to glance back at the sky where

Inanna's star hung like a jewel above the city. It shone in her eyes. It enchanted. It entered her soul even as she turned to follow him. It grew brighter within her as they trod the dark stairway and Shamkhat smiled.

THE END

Author's Afterword

I must thank Lynda Buxton for her care and attention in checking through to find my numerous typographical and grammatical errors.

MAIN REFERENCES

Bienkowski and Millard
DICTIONARY of the ANCIENT NEAR EAST
British Museum Press. 2000

Stephen Bertman
ANCIENT MESOPOTAMIA
Facts on File. 2003

Sonia Cole
THE NEOLITHIC REVOLUTION
British Museum. 1959

Arthur Cotterell
ILLUSTRATED   ENCYCLOPEDIA   OF
MYTHS AND LEGENDS
Marshall Editions. 1989

Andrew George
THE EPIC OF GILGAMESH
Penguin Press. 1999

Samuel Noah Kramer
HISTORY BEGINS AT SUMER
University of Pennsylvania Press. 1981 revised edition

Gwendolyn Leick
MESOPOTAMIA - THE INVENTION OF THE CITY
Penguin Press. 2001

Michael Roaf
CULTURAL ATLAS OF MESOPOTAMIA
Equinox. 1990

Bruce D. Smith
THE EMERGENCE OF AGRICULTURE
Scientific American Library. 1995

Various Authors
EVERYDAY LIFE THROUGH THE AGES
Readers Digest. 1992

Various Authors
THE EPIC OF MAN
Time-Life Books. 1962

Various Authors
THE HUMAN PAST
Thames and Hudson. 2005.

Other information located on various university websites via internet.